HARBINGER OF NIGHTMARES

MICHELLE ROSSA

Michelle Rossa

Copyright © 2025 by Michelle Rossa
Cover design by Michelle Rossa
Paperback ISBN: 9798218698379

1

To those who have suffered hard battles in silence, and need a reason to keep going.

Michelle Rossa

CONTENT WARNING

The material in this novel is for mature audiences only, and is not suitable for minors. Themes in this novel may be triggering, and should be read at your discretion. Themes of which include dissociation, depression, torture/physical abuse, death, and explicit sexual content.

Themes in this book include hearing voices that are outside of your own. This is a work of fiction, and should be treated as such.

Michelle Rossa

CHAPTER 1

Reimus

A torrential downpour pelts itself against my skin, my wings fanned out wide beside me as I glide my way through the overcast sky. I narrow my gaze far below and watch as the people of Vulir scurry themselves back indoors. Shop business owners who elected to open their windows to allow the fresh spring air in now hurry to pull them shut as rain threatens to soak their floorboards. A miniscule fear that will be entirely short lived once the rain subsides, and the sky clears once again.

A burden that is one of the simplest of things someone from this village ever needs to concern themselves with. A result of my loyal diligence that I will never cease maintaining, so my people only need to be encumbered with the trivial things in life and never the horrors that could threaten their safety.

A constant ease that settles deeply within my bones. Even if I failed to provide that same safety for the ones who meant most to me.

The memory flashes like a big-screen projector within the walls of my mind, highlighting the day my world ceased to exist entirely.

As if my feet are still planted in that rickety room, an overwhelming smell of iron wafts towards my nose. The potency of it exacerbated from my heightened senses, enough to cause me to stop dead in my tracks as the contents of my stomach threatened to purge itself up my throat. But as my eyes train upon that soft, porcelain face, everything that roils within me solidifies and freezes in place.

I rush to her side, my legs making the conscious decision to move themselves for me. My mind bottoms out as my heart splinters right down the middle as I stare upon her face. Her crimson splattered cheeks ice cold as I trace my fingers along her skin, the temperature similar to the rage and initial denial that blankets my skin.

I brush a dark strand of her long hair aside, my fingers trembling with the movement. A choked cry creeps up my throat as tears stream from my eyes. "I'm so sorry, mother."

I lower my hands underneath her shoulders, bringing her blood soaked body up to my chest. I cradle her head with a trembling hand, brushing my fingers through her midnight black strands. "I failed you." I whisper to her, pain lancing my voice.

We're here.

Dimitri's voice down the Guardian's channel chokes the memory from my mind as we approach the shield. I store the memory away for another time to punish myself with as we both bank down through the treeline.

My gaze sets on Charon as we both land at the shield, my gaze landing on the girl unconscious on the ground next to his feet. My head lifts to him as I say down the channel. Who is she?

"Her name is Melinoë. She's traveled here from Elzwin." *He says, nodding to her.* "I heard her yelling for entry in, and once I opened the shield for her she was unconscious."

I watch as a sleek black steed stands next to her, his back towards her as he eyes all of us. I tilt my head as I study the horse, curiosity piquing my interest at the lack of fear he shows around us. The sight unusual though impressive considering both mine and Dimitri's size is about triple to his. I watch as he lowers his head and sniffs at the girl, nudging her gently with his muzzle.

Do we know what she wants? What her motives are? *Dimitri says down the channel.*

"Her intentions are pure, that much I know." *Charon glances at the girl again, this time his gaze staying cemented on her for a long moment. As if something about her registers in his mind.*

Do you know her? *I ask down the channel.*

Charon hesitates before lifting his gaze to us. His features showing no indication of what he's thinking. "No. Not yet at least."

Dimitri suddenly shifts from his drago form, the rain now pelting down on his short brown hair. "We could keep her at The Sanctuary, but we have nowhere to house him." He says gesturing to the horse.

I lower my gaze back down to the girl—Melinoë. I inch myself closer to her, the horse still not spooked by my large size. I note the mud-drenched clothing, particularly at the knees and shins as if she'd been crawling her way through it. Her long, dark disheveled hair splayed along her face, against cheeks that have begun to sunken in. My chest grows heavy as I wonder what this woman has endured just to get here. I lower my nose down to her, sniffing when I smell it.

Blood.

As my back stiffens at the smell that threatens to jog my memories once more, I'm greeted with the scent of vanilla and rose, as well as a faint note of lavender. The aroma of her scent travels itself inside of me, cocooning itself along the barriers of my skin. Something that feels familiar, yet foreign all the same.

I look up at the steed who has his sights on me. Like darkened voids that penetrate my gaze, watching intently. Waiting for me to make what could be a reckless decision. But one that intrigues me enough that I can't not make it nonetheless.

She stays at the Guardian's Palace. *I say down the channel.*

Dimitri whips his gaze to me, scrunching his brows. "Are you mad?"

A chuckle travels itself down the channel. More like…curious. *I lift my gaze back up to him.* Walk the horse back to the pasture. I'll carry her.

Dimitri watches me for a long moment before nodding his head. He makes his way over to the horse, tentatively approaching him as he raises his hands. "Please be friendly." *He draws out slowly.*

The horse huffs at him as he closes the distance to Dimitri, nudging his hand gently. He stands there patiently until Dimitri turns around and brings a hand up to his bridle. And as Dimitri begins walking, the steed follows him without breaking away from him.

I look back to Melinoë as I lower my arms down, my claws gently curling themselves underneath her as I scoop her up. Her mouth parts open ever so slightly as I bring her body up to my chest. The rain suddenly ceases its downpour upon her face as my body now acts as an umbrella for her. I secure her snugly against my chest as I leap up into the sky, breaking my way through the treeline until I'm high above.

I spread my wings out wide once more as I glide us across the sky.

At the slight movement in my grasp I catch myself glancing down to see her nudge her head against me. Her eyes peek open by just a fraction as the deepest, most vibrant shade of green I've ever seen before graces me with its stark beauty. A shade of green that not even the most well-watered grass could compete with, like twin pools of shining emeralds.

She seals her eyes shut once more as her body settles against me. I continue gazing at her exhausted face for a moment longer before lifting my gaze ahead as I fly us to her new temporary home. My grip around her tightening ever so slightly in an unconscious movement.

"Reimus."

Dimitri's voice interrupts the fog I've subjected myself to in order to escape for a moment of reprieve. A moment that seemed trivial at the time but altered my life completely for the better. A sigh leaves me as I force myself back to the present. A place that, for the first time in a while, I dread being in.

The condensation that trickles down my fingertips is the only indication to remind myself that I was holding a glass of whiskey in my hand. I lift the glass to my lips, tipping it back as the amber liquid travels down my throat. I lower the glass back to the fireplace mantel before turning around.

Dimitri approaches me, a calloused hand raising to rest along my shoulder. His stern, golden brown gaze meets mine. "I'm here, man." He gives my shoulder a squeeze, a gesture given by a friend who is more like a brother to me. "I haven't gotten the chance to know Melinoë very well, but we're in this together. Whatever needs to be done to bring her home, it'll be done."

I nod my head vaguely, going to open my mouth when an energy charges beside us. Dimitri lowers his hand, stepping to my side as we watch a portal open up before us in the living room.

We watch as not only The Queen of The Underworld—Melinoë's mother Persephone, walks through the portal, but also who joins her at her side.

His gaze immediately comes to mine, piercing into mine with both a guilt and a rage that is palpable enough to feel. His midnight-black hair swept away from his face, his jaw set and clenched.

I stand there as The King of The Underworld, Hades himself, steps towards us. Making his first arrival to the land of the living in eons.

CHAPTER 2

"When."

The words escape from Persephone immediately without any dictation of a question, and moreover as a command. Her emerald eyes track over me, her stare alone pinning me in place by the intensity of the rage that boils beneath her gaze.

I glance over to Hades, him not having spoken a word yet. But his silence does not fool me. I know beneath that calm exterior there is a war raging both in the recesses of his mind, and inside of his chest. I fixate my gaze back onto Melinoë's mother. "About an hour ago."

She loosens a ragged breath as her gaze hardens on me. The energy charges around us, ramping up in intensity until Hades steps to her side and rests a steady hand on her trembling one. Though the energy does not falter even in the slightest.

"There was a woman who went with her. Whom I suspect to have been a part of—" I hesitate as my own rage and guilt builds within me. I clench my jaw, starting again. "She has not been seen since she left with Melinoë this morning for the Sephyra Forest."

Hades watches me, his gaze hardening. "Who?"

"Her name is Semele. We brought her in only a few weeks ago under the guise that she was running from an abusive partner. But clearly that was all a lie."

"Clearly." Persephone seethes through her teeth, her emerald eyes that are entirely identical to her daughter's blazing brightly.

A frown pulls at my lips as I internally blame myself for Melinoë's capture. Not having wanted to be this dictator of a boyfriend who tells her what she can and cannot do, knowing that that's the last thing Melinoë needed from me. Knowing she had already dealt with that from Zeus growing up, she needed someone to show her that she's worthy of being her own person and making her own decisions.

But a part of me wonders if I was too lenient in the process of trying to give the woman I love free will. Was I supposed to tell her no when she told me she was going to the forest? Was I supposed to damn the freedom that I know she so desperately needed when she was younger, even if she would've fought against me? To keep her safe even if it meant taking a part of her free will away?

A part of me wants to blame myself that I wasn't those things, just this once so I could've prevented this. But deep down, I know I would never be that for her. I would never be the kind of man who tells her what to do against her own will just to appease my own restlessness concerning her safety. Because I know that's not what she would've wanted from me no matter the circumstance.

"What do you know about Semele?" Hades asks, pulling me back from my thoughts.

"She *claimed* she's from Lothario. Said it was a village outside of Olympia."

Persephone tilts her head, assessing as she shakes her head. "Lothario is a real village."

I fix my gaze on her.

"It's a village that's been around as long as Olympia has been. So if she's mortal, why would you suspect she'd be working with Zeus?"

"Because she is not a mortal."

Persephone watches me before her eyes widen. She looks over to her husband, meeting his gaze.

I tentatively step towards them. "But if she's a goddess, wouldn't you both know her?"

Hades looks towards me, shaking his head. "In any other case, yes. But Semele is not someone we've ever heard of before. You're positive she's immortal?"

I sigh, bringing my thumb and index finger to the bridge of my nose. Gently pinching the skin there. "I don't know." I lower my hand back to my side, frustrated. "But it seems pretty fucking strange that she goes into the forest with Melinoë, never to be seen again."

"I say we just go in there and find out for ourselves." Dimitri says beside me, a cool rage pilling his energy.

"We can't."

We all turn to Hecate as she glides through the opening of a portal, her infamous amethyst robe billowing behind her as she approaches us. The portal closing behind her.

Persephone and Hades turn towards her, the former clenching her fists at her sides. "Like Fates we're not going in there and getting Melinoë—"

"We can't," Hecate begins again, her honey-hued gaze boring into Persephone with a gentle look. "Because there is something we need to discuss first."

Hades turns his gaze from his wife to Hecate. "Discuss what?"

Hecate looks towards me, an understanding on her face as she sighs. "Melinoë came to me weeks ago asking for me to put a protection spell on her mind. Specifically from Zeus."

We all stand there in silence as Hecate continues.

"It was meant to be a *precaution*, she said in case anything ever happened." She works on a swallow as she locks her gaze onto Persephone. "But even though she said nothing of it, I knew she wasn't telling me something."

My eyes widen as my mind drudges up the past week of Melinoë waking up in a cold sweat beside me, having assured me that they were just bad dreams. Though I saw the terror written all over her face. I knew they were more than just average bad dreams.

"She knew." I mutter breathlessly.

"What?" Persephone asks.

I shake my head slowly. "For the last week or so she'd been waking up in a terror, claiming they were just dreams but…" I lift my gaze up to Hecate, my heart straining that the love of my life didn't tell me that they were actually visions. "She was having visions this whole time."

"What were these dreams?"

"I have no idea. I asked her if she had wanted to talk about it, but she always said they were nothing." A burst of sadness stinging my heart that she hadn't felt comfortable to tell me. Knowing it has nothing to do with me, but because of how she's been conditioned to do everything on her own. How those trauma responses still play a part in her everyday life. "I figured when she was ready to, that she would open up about them."

Persephone shakes her head, grief straining her face. "Why wouldn't she tell any of us?"

Before I can say it, Hades speaks it for me instead. "She thought she was sparing us the worry."

"But if Zeus does use compulsion against her, won't he know it right away then?" Dimitri asks, glancing over at me with sorrow on his face for having to even ask.

"That's if she doesn't follow through with the façade."

"What façade?" Dimitri asks.

My gaze lifts to Hades, and I watch as understanding pools there before tension brackets the creases in his face. "Meaning she must go along with whatever Zeus asks of her."

Persephone raises her hand up to her mouth to stifle the noise that creeps out of her throat.

The shadows around Hades billow out from him as he squares his shoulders. "Meaning that until we free her, if Zeus asks her to cause mass destruction, she will have no choice but to follow through. Whatever he asks of her," He pauses, exhaling a breath as he glances at me. The truth of what he's saying sucker punching me in the stomach. "It must be done."

I watch as Persephone pulls her trembling hand away from her mouth, having no doubt that she knows better than anyone the type of cruelty that Zeus can enact on another. My stomach churns violently at the thought.

"So what do we do?" Dimitri asks beside me. I feel him glance at me but I keep my gaze trained forward on The King of The Underworld. Trying to keep everything together inside of me when all I yearn to do right now is break down.

"Zeus likely is expecting a reaction. At the very least, he's expecting a visit from Persephone and I. If we don't and instead lie low, he'll become suspicious and think something is up." Hades says as the shadows licking at his legs coil around him like a second skin. He glances at his wife, giving her a silent exchange before training his gaze forward again. "Which could jeopardize Melinoë maintaining her façade until we're able to execute her freedom."

"So what's the plan?" I ask, curling my fists inward before releasing them again. If Zeus places even just one hand on Melinoë's head I will see to it that he has the most sufferable death one could imagine. I don't give a fuck if he's King of Gods or not. I will defy any laws by The Fates if it means ensuring my queen makes it safely home.

I feel the energy intensify in the room, flicking my gaze to Persephone's face as a cruel and wicked smirk curves up her lips. And in a voice colder than death itself, she responds all too calmly. "We give him what he's expecting."

19

CHAPTER 3

Melinoë

A fine trickle of sweat beads down my forehead as the warm, stale air surrounding me clings to my skin. With no windows to give it an escape, no cracks in the walls to allow it to slither out and free itself from the dimly-lit cell.

The two of us trapped with nowhere to go.

My back leaned up against the jagged wall, my gaze remained fixated straight ahead. Staring blankly at the identical stone wall across from me with only the weak flicker of a flame from a lit torch jutting out from the wall to accompany me. My eyes blink slowly as my stomach growls wildly, hunger clawing at my insides.

I can't remember the last time I ate, but if I had to guess, I won't be eating anytime soon.

As I sink further down the wall, I feel the rough stones scrape against my arms. The only sting of pain I've allowed myself to feel since facing Zeus in the throne room hours ago.

Sinking further into the depths of my mind, further down into a place that I've called home for many years. A fortress created long ago to protect myself from the dangers outside of myself, a hollow void to reprieve myself from the turmoil above the surface.

I close my eyes as I travel further down into that space of nothingness that I've once grown to be familiar with. A space where I can hide and retract myself until I am safe in my surroundings once again.

My stomach growls again, trying to ignore it as I numb myself from the hunger growing within.

"Sheesh, I can hear that from over here."

I open my eyes, turning my head towards my left as I'm met with the darkness on the other side of the iron bars. I peer through that nothingness, huffing to myself when I turn my head forward again. "I must *really* be starving if I'm hallucinating now." I mumble beneath my breath.

A laugh echoes around the stone chamber, skittering along my skin as my head snaps in that direction again. "You'd probably wish I were one if you met me." That voice speaks again. A feminine voice I realize.

I lift my back, separating myself from the stone wall as I crawl as close to the gate as I can get. The chains connected to the wall tugging on the shackles around my wrists and ankles as I reach within a foot of the iron bars. I plop myself onto the cool cemented ground, sighing as I bring a hand up to the bar. My gaze flicks up the grooves that make the cell door. "Who are you?"

She chuckles as I begin to hear a quick, sharp clicking noise. As if tapping her nails onto the cement surface beneath our feet. "That depends on who you ask."

My brows knit together before I try to inch my face closer to the bars. Noticing the outline of a set of stairs towards the far wall in front of me. "What'd you do to get put down here?"

That tapping noise continues, piercing the silence deafening around us. "Be exactly who I was meant to be."

The screech of a door scraping across the cement ground from the top of the stairs draws my attention, the tapping of that woman stifling with it. I squint against the bright light filtering down into the dungeons as I peer my gaze up to see who is behind the footsteps that make their way down into the darkness.

I separate myself from the bars, inching backwards until I'm flush up against the wall again. The sound of those footsteps draw closer until a familiar woman stands before my cell door.

I roll my eyes as I look straight ahead, that internal numbness beckoning me to keep my composure so I don't threaten the façade I'm trying desperately to maintain.

Such as—oh, I don't know. Strangling her again?. "Come to pay me a visit?" I ask dryly as I look over at her.

Semele chuckles lazily as she brings a hand to the iron bars, her hand wrapping around it. "You're wanted in the throne room."

In a monotone voice, I say, "Great."

I hear her dangle a set of keys before inserting one into the lock, the gears making a brief click before Semele pushes the cell door open. I force myself to remain seated there instead of throwing myself at her like I *really* want to do.

"Do you know who I am?" She asks as she kneels down in front of me. A question meant to test me. To gauge whether Zeus' compulsion to erase my memories truly worked or not.

I force my face to remain neutral, keeping my breathing under control and my body relaxed so as to not give away that Zeus' erasing of my memory failed. "No, but I'm guessing you're going to tell me." I keep my gaze trained on her, to portray that I'm unaffected by her presence.
That I'm unaware that she's the one who helped Zeus kidnap me in the first place.

She stares at me for a moment longer before she steps further into the cell, grabbing me by my arm and dragging me up onto my feet. She grabs my face, keeping my gaze on her as her nails dig into my chin. Her sapphire eyes hardening onto me as her gaze flicks over my face. "Do you know why you're here?"

I keep my gaze steady as I force my brows to knit together, shaking my head. "No. But it'd be pretty sweet if I were at least given better living conditions. Unless I really did something to deserve staying in a dirty dungeon." I fight the smirk that wants to crawl up my lips and keep my body relaxed. Letting a hint of confusion intentionally slip through my tone.

She watches me for a few more moments before releasing her hold on my chin. She chuckles beneath her breath before she steps back from me. "I'm afraid this is what His Majesty has requested for you. So any *displeasures* with your living conditions will need to be taken up with him."

It takes everything in me to not laugh at her use of the title given to a man who—

I quickly pull myself back, unwilling to allow myself to feel any kind of emotion. Knowing it's the only way I'll be able to maintain the illusion that I need Zeus to believe. Knowing that any bouts of emotion can sway my pulse to thrum just a hair faster, could cause the subtlest hardness in my jaw to surface, displaying the rage within.

I sink myself far, far below to that state of numbness, and allow that void of nothingness to swallow me whole once again.

I faintly hear Semele unlocking my chains before pulling me by my shoulder. Halting, she gives me a shake. "No longer interested in talking, huh?"

I stand there, completely mute as I stare straight ahead.

She huffs out a noise before her hand on my shoulder guides me out of the cell, a feeling I can hardly feel the lower I sink into that pit of nothingness. "Suit yourself."

I keep my gaze trained forward as Semele guides me out of the darkness, all the way up those stairs until we enter the brightly lit throne room.

CHAPTER 4

My bare feet shuffle along the pearl white ground, the sunlight through the floor to ceiling arches glittering the gold flakes hidden within the polished floor. I lift my gaze up to the large columns on each side of the throne room, beside large ivory tapestries to accompany each pillar. Each tapestry with a gold thunderbolt embroidered in the middle of a wreath of ivy leaves, detailings of bronze filigree trimmed around all four sides.

Semele and I approach the steps to the dais, lifting my gaze up to Zeus sitting atop of the throne situated at the center. I stare blankly at him as my gaze lifts to the gold crown that rests on top of his light blonde hair. The crown fashioned with sharp points that protrude upwards with rich blue jewels. A golden laurel wreath woven into the base of the crown.

His back remains leaned up against the chair as his arms lay themselves lazily over the armrest. His relaxed composure insinuates that I'm of no threat, even though he watches me closely, intently.

Semele climbs the gold flecked steps with me until we reach the top of the dais. As I stand before him, Semele drops her hold on my wrists, the sound of the chains clanking as my arms lower in front of me.

I watch as Zeus looks over my face once before waving his hand at Semele. "You're free to leave."

I watch from my peripheral as Semele bows gently at her waist before excusing herself altogether. I hear the sound of her light footsteps make their way back down the steps until she's exited the room entirely. Leaving me alone with Zeus.

I stand there, blinking once at him as I deafen out any anger, any disgust for his treatment towards me. I stand there and—for the safety of everyone I love, I'm forced to become what I'd been for him once before.

Silent.

I feel his power rise to the surface, the faint tickle of electricity brushing along my arms as it slithers up to my face. A subtle zap stinging my cheek, causing me to jerk my face away.

I feel his power latch onto me as he speaks. "Do you know how you got here?" His voice carrying the energy of compulsion.

I feel his power trying to slither itself into my mind, and before it can venture any further, I give him the only thing that would prove to him that his attempt would've worked. "No, Your Majesty."

I feel his power draw back as he chuckles deeply, the use of that title like vinegar against my tongue. A bitterness that is immediately washed away as I stand before him, keeping my composure.

"Well, I'm going to explain everything you need to know."

I nod in response. "Understood, Your Majesty."

He stands up from the chair as he walks slowly around me. "As my daughter, you carry an essence of me within you. A power that many could only dream of attaining, though it is currently unclear how strong that power lies within you." He steps around until he stands before me, tilting his head down at me. "But you also carry something that does not belong to me."

As Zeus stares down at me I focus on my breathing. And when I feel his energy surge between us again, I keep those mental shields intact.

He leans forward as those bright golden eyes churn brightly. "Do you know who your mother is?"

I stand there, numbing myself to any memory of my mother. Numbing myself to any laugh I've shared with her, any hug that she ever wrapped around me. I blink at him slowly as that compulsion of him reaches out for me, waiting a few moments before I shake my head. "I—I can't seem to recall." I scrunch my brows together, painting a quizzical look on my face.

He stands there watching me, assessing for any micromovements that might give away that I'm lying. Any movement or tell-tale sign that would tell him that his erasing of my memory hadn't worked. But if there is one thing I've learned by being related to a man who speaks with his fists and his need for control, it's that I can distance myself entirely from my body when I direly need to.

He watches me for a few more moments before I feel his energy slip away like a heavy, wool blanket falling off of me. He nods slowly before he grabs the chains around my wrists. "Come." He says as he yanks me down the dais with him.

We walk down to the center of the throne room, halting as he loosens his grip on my chains. With his back turned towards me, he walks a few feet in front of me, creating distance between us. At the lazy wave of his hand, the chains around my wrist and ankles vanish like smoke dissipating from my skin. I lift my hands up to my chest, turning them before rubbing the indentation marks left behind. I look up at him to find that he's now turned around, facing me.

"You will become a great asset to me, Melinoë. With the duality of your powers, you can become a feared weapon to anyone who attacks Olympia."

"What do you mean? I—I don't have any powers. At least...not that I can recall." I lift my hands up to my face, examining them before lowering them again. "But if this is my home, and I can protect my people, I'd like to learn."

A smug smirk creeps up his face as he nods slowly. "Yes, you will be a fierce protector. Not only of Olympia but of me as well." I feel his power reach out again, latching onto me. "You and I are a team, Melinoë."

The numbness within stifles the immediate disgust that threatens to course through my body.

He is nothing to you. Agreeing with him does not change that.

I force a faint grin up my face as I nod. "I'm grateful to be able to learn from you, father." I force myself to bow slightly at the waist, just to add in an extra boost to sate his obscenely large ego.

His gaze pierces mine. "Good. Now we're going to see how strong that essence inside of you is." He takes a step back as his energy charges around the room.

I immediately find it challenging to breathe at the potency of it, causing my numbness to falter for a fraction of a moment before I reinforce it again.

"I'm going to force that power out of you." He says before I feel his energy latch onto me again. His eyes burn brightly as the red-hot zaps of his power torch my skin. "Use it."

His method, his approach, is nothing like what Hades did for me. Hades forced that power out of me—yes, but never did it in a way to *actually* hurt me. He goaded me through it, but deep down I knew he wasn't trying to hurt me.

I knew he was able to see when enough was enough. But with Zeus, I know in my bones he won't care about limits. As he isn't wanting to pull my power out to help me, but to help himself.

Zeus' lightning strikes, causing my skin to feel like it's on fire. A horrible torture that is anything far from helpful.

I fall to my knees as my hand grips at my chest, maintaining that mental barrier from him with everything I've got. "It—hurts." I manage to seethe out.

"It doesn't have to hurt." His voice coming from every direction, a manifestation of his compulsion.

I force myself to look up at him, and shakily get myself back onto my feet. I take ragged deep breaths in and out, trying to stifle the sharp pain he's exuding over my body. Until finally, I give him what he wants.

My hands thrust up towards him as shadows spew out of my fingertips, aiming to wrap themselves around his arms before his own eather throws up a shield, preventing me from reaching further.

His eather polarly opposite from mine. Thick, golden tendrils that spark like tiny balls of lightning. The shield starts at the ground and builds up until it hovers above him, impenetrable from my shadows.

I pull them back as I step back, forcing myself to fall on my ass.

The shield in front of Zeus slowly disintegrates before his power retracts back into him. He steps forward as he places his hands behind his back. "Not bad, but not impressive either." He looks down at me, nodding his head with anything but compassion in his gaze. "Stand up. You never want an opponent to get you down."

I stand myself up again, nodding my silent agreement. I look down at my arms, noticing tiny welts on my skin from where Zeus' power attacked me. I take a hand, gently rubbing at the skin there before I flinch my hand away.

"That will happen." He says blandly before he turns his head to the side, looking away from me. "All a part of our training, daughter. You will become stronger in time."

Yet no amount of numbness could ever dull the fact that this is not about training me, it's about punishing me.

"Amalthea." Zeus rings out. A short moment later a woman in white robes comes hurrying out, her face lowered to the ground even after she approaches us.

She bows low at the waist, placing her lithe hands in her lap as she stands straight again. "Yes, Your Majesty?" Her voice is sweet, lovely even. And she sounds way too nice to be serving a man so cruel and violent.

I fix my gaze back over to him as he nods at me again. "Give her a salve for the welts. I can't practice with her if she'll be too preoccupied with them."

"Right away, Your Majesty." She says before hurrying off back to where she came from, which I realize is from a hidden door leading to Fates knows where.

She comes back a few moments later carrying a tiny metal tin container, her head remaining lowered to the ground with each step she makes towards me.

When she approaches me, she only looks up briefly before lowering her gaze again. And in that brief moment, I catch a glance of stark blue eyes. The kind that threatens to remind me of someone else's momentarily before I shove it down, down, down.

"This may sting a bit. But it will help." Amalthea says quietly before she opens the tin up, revealing a slimy paste the color of cantaloupe. She dips her finger into it before smearing it over the welts.

"Let me know when you're finished." Zeus drawls before he makes his way back towards the dais, presumably to seat himself back onto the throne.

I lower my gaze to Amalthea, the cool salve bringing an immediate relief to the tender skin there. "Thank you." I whisper to her.

She stops rubbing the salve momentarily as if stunned by my words before continuing again.

Once she's rubbed the salve in completely, she closes the tin container up. "There. All better—"

Her words are cut off on a strangled choke, immediately drawing my gaze up to find her actually looking up at me with her eyes nearly bulging out of their sockets. Her mouth gaping open as she struggles for breath, dropping the tin container on the ground as she claws at her neck even though nothing is there.

A moment later, I watch the life drain from her face as Amalthea's body goes limp, collapsing to the floor. My gaze only remains on her for a short moment when I feel the energy pulsate in front of me. I raise my gaze up, and my heart sinks to the pit of my stomach when a woman emerges out of the invisibility she's cloaked herself in, materializing right in front of me.

Not just any woman, but my mother.

With a cruel smile on her face as invisible shadows reveal themselves, I watch as the midnight black eather slowly retracts themselves back into her. Her eyes lock with mine, and it takes everything inside of me to keep it all together.

Because that fire in her eyes, that anger scorching beneath that emerald gaze, she stands before me more as The Queen of The Underworld now then I've ever seen her.

Her gaze quickly latches onto Zeus who makes his way towards us, and I watch as the towers around us begin to tremble with the force of her power, her wrath. "Sorry for the mess, Zeus. Though I can't imagine she was ever that important to you anyway." Her smile deepened into something fearsome, wicked. Her voice steady and calm.

A dangerous combination.

Zeus chuckles as he walks casually towards us, his stride slow and intentional. As if he has all the time in the world and didn't just watch one of his people get murdered. As if my mother doesn't stand before us now. "I fear your anger is misplaced, Persephone."

The energy charges the room around us as those same shadows ripple next to my mother, creating an opening of darkness until Hades himself emerges out of it. With his hands placed behind his back, and violence brewing beneath that calm exterior.

He stands next to my mother, lifting his hard gaze to Zeus. "Careful, Zeus. You've only been shown a fraction of what my wife is capable of. But at the rate you're going, I fear you'll find yourself at the full extent of her anger sooner than later."

"Ah, I was wondering when you'd make your appearance Hades." Zeus says. "A rarity considering you're only allowed out of your realm when called to council." Zeus tilts his head as he stands before us now.

Hades stands there donned in an all black suit, his gaze locked onto Zeus. I lower my gaze briefly to his hands behind his back, his fists clenching into themselves. As if to keep the rage within at bay. I watch as his fists loosen before turning his gaze over to me. An uncompromising look to his features as he says, "Some things are worth damning the agreement for."

CHAPTER 5

I watch as my mother and Hades keep their gazes latched onto Zeus, no longer even glancing in my direction.

Do they know about what Hecate did for me? Has she been able to tell them yet? How will they know that I have to pretend not to know them? Where is—

"Amalthea is only one of many handmaids I have in the palace. So please, forgive me if I am not terribly perplexed by her death." Zeus approaches us, a grin curving his lips.

"Does that same carelessness apply to all of your people?" Persephone says sweetly, tauntingly. "Would you share the same lack of remorse?"

"I'm willing to find out."

Behind Hades a tall man appears, no longer masked by a cloud of invisibility. At the sight of him it takes every strength of my being to not weep in relief to be in his presence again.

Reimus.

He stalks forward in his casual stride with Dimitri flanking him. I watch as he glances over at me, staring at me for a brief moment before locking his sights on Zeus.

Reimus stands next to Hades, a smirk curving up his full lips as those blue and silver eyes lock onto Zeus. My pulse threatens to palpitate at the sight of him here, showing up for me but I force it all away. I keep my face blank, showing no emotional reaction whatsoever. As I feel the stare of Zeus not on Reimus, but on me. Watching me to see how I react to seeing the love of my life standing before me.

His stare bores into the side of my face like a suffocating brand, waiting for my cover to slip up. Waiting to see recognition flare in my gaze. Though to some miracle, my face remains unchanged, unmoved through every will of my being preventing it from slipping. After a few long, agonizing moments, I feel the potency of his stare slip away as a laugh slips out of his mouth. "What a brave man you are. Reimus, is it?"

A low huff gets trapped in Reimus' throat, a calm rage settling over him. "And what of yours? Coward, perhaps?"

I hear Dimitri stifle a chuckle in his throat as I reel myself back from the situation entirely, hiding into myself.

"I think King would do just fine." Zeus purrs, unaffected by his insult.

"Well surely that title is only reserved for rulers who actually protect the people he watches over." His face finally turns over to me, and I watch for a split moment as something like relief washes over his face. Whether it's because I'm still alive, or that I'm in one piece, I can't be sure. But when his gaze lowers to the welts on my arms, I watch that relief quickly change into a cold ire.

Hade notices where Reimus' gaze has fallen, and steps forward before Reimus can say anything more. Before he can unleash that anger that palpitates beneath his stare. "I think we can agree why we're all here today, Zeus. And that what will follow, if Melinoë is not freed, is completely preventable."

"Very well, then. Melinoë," Zeus turns his gaze over to me, waving me over. "Come."

I pick up my feet which suddenly feel like boulders weighing down my limbs that have nothing to do with the shackles at my ankles. I approach his side as I bow slightly at the waist, lowering my head. "Yes, Your Majesty?"

I keep my gaze on Zeus because if I turn towards Reimus and see the ire in his eyes that I know is swelling there, I don't know how well I'll be able to maintain this façade. Especially not after hearing what he says next.

"You son of a bitch—" I hear Dimitri pushing Reimus back from advancing further on Zeus, drowning everything out to keep myself from feeling any emotion about it. Feeling a spark of embarrassment at how I addressed Zeus in front of them, but hoping they understand I wouldn't dare unless it were necessary. But as I faintly hear Dimitri talking Reimus down, I'm suddenly caught by the faint touch of a familiar poke at my mental barrier. This time, it's not Zeus trying to pry into my mind.

It's Hades.

I keep my gaze on Zeus as I feel Hades watching me, feeling his power quietly trying to pry into my mind. So for the first time since I've been here, I allow just a crack to open up for him. Allowing him access into my thoughts and my memories.

I feel him dig through the recesses of my mind like someone shuffling through a rack of records, feeling him peek at the memories since I've been here. Of Zeus erasing my memories, but unaware that I've had Hecate place a protection spell on my mind against his compulsion. I allow him to see into the fake obedience I'm displaying, and that he will kill everyone in Elzwin, everyone I love if I don't comply.

I allow him to see the numbness I'm shielding myself behind, the nothingness I have to put on because otherwise I will crumble right in front of him.

And I won't give him that satisfaction.

I feel Hades begin to pull out of my mind, slipping himself out of that crack I've split open for him before quickly closing it again. But before he slips completely free from my mind, I hear his faint words echo around my head.

We will get you out of here, Melinoë. But remember for now, he cannot break you. You are stronger than him.

"Melinoë—" My mother starts as she steps towards me. That anger quickly turned into sorrow. "Come."

I look at her, catching a glance over to Hades as understanding paints his face. I look over to Zeus, forcing a confused look on my face as I shake my head. "I—I don't know you people." I then do the one thing I would never do in a million years.

I step closer to Zeus, and further away from my mother.

Zeus chuckles as he rests a hand on my shoulder. "I think she'd like to remain here. Isn't that right, Melinoë?"

I look up at him, nodding. "Yes, father."

I can feel my mother blanch with hot anger as she steps forward. The columns in the throne room begin to rattle with the wrath of her fury, the tremors surfacing from the pearl white and gold flecked floor vibrating along my feet. "What did you do to—"

In the next moment, my mother is swallowed up by a portal that Hades materializes, a will of his own power that happens in the blink of an eye. Stifling the throne room around us entirely as Hades, my mother, Dimitri, and Reimus portal back to where they came from. My real home.

Leaving me here with Zeus, all alone.

CHAPTER 6

Reimus

My feet slam against my living room floor, stumbling forward as Dimitri bumps into me. As I regain my balance I look up, whipping my gaze around to Hades. My stern gaze glancing up at the portal he willed and watching it close behind him before lowering my gaze back to him. "Why'd you do that?" I seethe as I clench my fists, angling my body fully towards him. I advance forward in a blind fury. "I needed more time—"

Dimitri steps in front of me, keeping me back before I decide to do something completely irrational. Like, punch the fuck out of a literal god—The King of The Underworld at that.

Hades' gaze latches onto me. "We had to leave."

I feel Persephone look over to her husband, a sorrow evident in her face as she stands next to him. I watch as she reaches for his hand, stifling the tension in his fists as his fingers curl tightly into his palms. A tension that shows he's anything but pleased that we had to leave Melinoë, a reaction that even through all of this, coils a tiny string of warmth inside my chest.

A warmth that reminds me that Melinoë may not be loved or respected by her own father, but that she is cared for by a man who is not blood-related to her, who would damn an agreement made between three gods eons ago if it meant ensuring her safety. An agreement where he is to stay in The Underworld while Zeus rules over Olympia, and Poseidon the seas.

He unclenches his fist, looking over at her before gently grasping her hand into his. I watch as his shoulders relax as he loosens a long breath, gently squeezing Persephone's hand.

A gentle act I would give anything to do for Melinoë right now.

Hades turns his gaze back to Dimitri and I. "I reached into Melinoë's mind, and I found exactly what I thought I would."

Suddenly I hear Hecate hurrying down the hallway, turning into the living room and approaching us. The charge of energy from Hades' portal must've alerted her to our return home from Olympia. "What happened?"

Hades sighs before he continues. "Zeus compelled her to erase her memories. All she is supposed to know, and is being fed to, is that Zeus is her father, and that he wants to make her an *ally*."

I watch as Persephone squeezes her husband's hand, both to comfort him, and to ease the worrying tension building within her.

Hades turns his gaze to Hecate, narrowing his chin. "The protection spell you placed around Melinoë's mind worked, though."

I feel a sharp overwhelming relief wash over the room around us, as if everyone in here was hanging onto Hades' words. Hoping, waiting for some tiny sliver of good news. For any indication that the protection spell had worked.

And it did. Thank fuck it did.

"She has to still play along, so in order to keep her façade intact, she's resorting to distancing herself from her emotions." Hades pauses for a moment, lifting his gaze to mine. "Numbing herself."

My heart sinks to the bottom of my stomach at his words, devastated that the love of my life has to put herself through so much just to survive being in her own father's vicinity, even if temporarily.

We will all come up with a plan to free her. I won't rest until we do.

"But she was hanging on by a thread in there by our appearance. It was too much for her, I could feel her control on her emotions wavering. That's why I pulled us out when I did."

"But does she know? Does she know that we won't stop until we bring her home?" My words ending on a roughness as I step towards Hades, uncaring at the level of desperation in my voice.

He nods slowly. "She knows. Deep down, she does. But if we're going to execute an escape plan then we have to do it without jeopardizing the mask she's maintaining currently. Because Zeus told her prior to thinking he wiped her memories, that if she didn't comply that he'd kill everyone in Elzwin. And everyone she loves, including you." Hades' gaze cemented on mine.

I blink at his words before stepping away and approach the calmly roaring fireplace, resting a hand on the mantel. I lower my gaze, trying to dull the rage that's burning within me. Melinoë would do absolutely anything for the people she loved, and I'm normally grateful for that selflessness about her. But I can't help but to feel ashamed that she's willing to put herself through so much mental anguish, being in his presence, just because she loves me.

We were supposed to handle this *together.* Whatever Zeus threw our way, for freeing her sister Makaria from her own imprisonment, we were supposed to tackle it all *together*. Not apart.

The palm of my hand curls underneath the lip of the mantle, my fist gripping the intricate wood carvings. My anger begins to overwhelm me as I feel a heaving sensation pushing against my insides, threatening to involuntarily shift me into my drago form. I breathe in deeply, exhaling slowly as I reel it in.

I suddenly feel Hecate step up to my side, her hand lowering on top of mine. Her skin cool against the sudden warmth enveloping my hand, warming that raging fire within. She must feel it as well because she quickly lifts her hand from mine, slowly lowering it back to her side. "He's right." Hecate says, tilting her head as I look over at her. "We need to execute her freedom without blowing her cover."

"That's the only reason why she addressed him with his formal title." Persephone says, drawing my gaze over to her. Disgust rippled on her face. "Melinoë would *never* address him as such unless she was really trying to persuade him that his efforts in erasing her memory worked." She sighs as she shakes her head. "As much as it angers me too, I know she's faking it. All of it." Her gaze gently bores into mine.

Even if Melinoë is faking all of it, what will this do to her mental state? When we do free her, how will this affect her long-term? Will she resent and hate herself for having to suck up to him just to play along?

I feel my skin warm from the inside out, forcing myself to lower my hand from the mantle and step away. Needing to alleviate myself from shifting involuntarily and being around the fire seems to not be helping.

Because my greatest fear is not that she won't be strong enough to endure everything Zeus will throw her way. The cruel remarks, the imprisonment he's imposing on her. No, what I'm worried about is that he will break her spirit so badly that just as I started to finally see a spark light up in Melinoë, he will take it all away from her.

And *that* is what I cannot accept to be the outcome from all of this.

"Okay. So we plan." I say, turning to face everyone again. I take one last breath in, slowly releasing the worry and the building inferno within as I exhale. I can allow myself to be worried in the privacy of my company at another time. Right now, I need to be focused. "I want to know what Zeus' security measures are, the ins and outs of Olympia. Who his allies are, and his enemies." I fixate my gaze on Hades, knowing that if I looked in a mirror I'd find the same determination on his face to match my own. "I want to know it all."

He nods before a moment later, a crinkle of light ruptures through the space between us. I watch as that fissure of light expands, forming the outline of a rectangle as it hovers in front of us. I watch as muted colors ranging from beige, pewter, cobalt, ivory, and forest green fill in the center. With details of landscapes, buildings and mountains etched into sections of the map.

I feel Dimitri and Hecate close in behind me, their heads leaning down slightly with mine to observe the map of Olympia before us.

Hades steps closer to the map, Persephone following suit as he lifts his gaze to me. "Let's begin then."

CHAPTER 7

Melinoë

Semele leads me lower down the stairwell, back down into the darkness below. Zeus having materialized the shackles around my wrists and ankles once again, fastened as snugly around my skin as the anxiousness threatening to burrow deeply within my chest.

Eleven. Twelve. Thirteen.

I count in my head as we near the bottom of the steps, the warmth that was beneath my feet as we stood in the throne room cooling only a few degrees with each step down into the dungeons. The stale, warm air greeting me once again as we land at the bottom of the steps.

Twenty. Twenty steps down.

"How did it feel?"

I blink slowly, facing straight ahead as Semele leads me back to my cell. "How did what feel?" I ask plainly.

"Seeing them." She asks, curiosity in her tone. I feel the brush of her long imperial blue skirt brush up against my leg, a material that would feel smooth like velvet against my skin had it not been for my leggings intercepting.

Which are filthy by now from sitting on the dirty ground. Yet, no one seems keen on having me change into some clean clothes anytime soon.

I shrug my shoulders, knowing her gaze is fully concentrated on me. "It felt like nothing." I say absentmindedly. I turn my gaze over to her, scrunching my brows. "Am I supposed to know them?"

Her sapphire gaze studies me before facing forward again. "No, I suppose not."

We approach my cell as she opens the gate, guiding us inside and over to the side wall. She hooks my chains back up to the wall, and steps back as I seat myself down onto the ground.

I press my back up against the stone wall, leaning my head back as I stare straight ahead. With nothing to say, nothing to do but wait.

"You're not going to ask why you're down here and not in a guest chamber above?" She asks. Her voice threatening to grate itself along my skin with annoyance before I quickly shove it down.

I shrug my shoulders again. "I presume His Majesty has a good enough reason for my living conditions, so I will not question it."

Semele huffs out a strangled laugh as she steps out of the cell, locking it. "Every King has secrets, and every King has their own mannerisms. And he has…much of both."

"Nice." I say listlessly as I lay my hands on top of my lap.

I hear Semele tap a nail against the iron bar idly. "I'm going to tell you a story."

I shrug again. "Great."

Her tapping stops as she begins slowly walking back and forth beside the bars, her low heels clicking against the cement with each move. "Once upon a time, there was a boy. Who had no idea the cruelty that life could bestow onto someone, but would one day soon understand the multitude of it."

"I'm assuming we're talking about Zeus?" I ask.

Semele only huffs out a soft noise before continuing. "The boy had everything he could ever need, more than most could ever pray to have. At birth, he already had more riches than most men can make in their entire lifetimes. He had honor, and he already had a fated destiny forged for himself in this life. But some did not see him as a beacon of great power. Some saw him as a terrible threat because of the bloodline he belonged to."

I listen as she slows her pace, pausing for a moment. "One day, a group of individuals sought a means to end him. They decided that this boy cannot grow any older, as the power inherited through his bloodline could overthrow most gods. So one day, as the boy was playing with his toys, they dismembered him. Tore his infant body limb from limb, and killed him."

I finally pull my gaze from straight ahead and look at Semele. "He was just a baby?" My heart hollows out inside of my chest at that knowledge. Realizing that this may not be a story about Zeus after all. But then who is this boy and why does she want to tell me this story—

"Yes. He was only a baby."

I shake my head as I narrow my gaze. Still highly untrusting of Semele after deceiving me and helping Zeus to bring me here, but wanting to hear the rest of the story nonetheless. "How could someone hurt an innocent baby?" My grief for the child rises within me, threatening to overwhelm me with the grief for seeing the worry on Reimus' face today. Seeing the immense displeasure of the welts that were on my arms. Looking down at my arms now to see that they're no longer there, but the sting of Zeus' lightning threatens to remind me of the pain that they inflicted. I take a sharp inhale in, exhaling it.

Keep it together, Melinoë. We can break down later when no one is around.

"Some were outraged at the way he was brought into this life, and pitied the child. But most were wholly threatened by the power the child would bring. But little would they know that their attempt failed."

I turn my body towards Semele, the chains around my wrists clanking as I lower them in front of me. Leaning the side of my body up against the wall as I face her completely.

"They burned every last bit of flesh, rendering him completely disposed of. Except they left only one piece of him left: his heart."

I shake my head, knitting my brows together. "Why wouldn't they have burned that?"

Semele faintly shrugs her shoulders. "Nobody knows. But what they failed to realize is that the boy's father was desperate to carry out his legacy, a prophecy that only he knew about and would stop at nothing to execute. So he took his son's heart, and brought it to his mistress. And she ate it."

A grimace shoots up onto my face as I nearly gag. "Ew, what the fuck? She *ate* it?" I shake my head quickly. "That's fucking disgusting."

A chuckle escapes from Semele's lips as she shakes her head. "It is pretty grotesque, but many immortals back then participated in similar pleasures. Drinking blood to name one." She raises her eyebrows, smirking briefly before smoothing her lips out. "It was also heard of for gods to turn mortals immortal, but it was quickly seen as an abomination and became frowned upon. But the man's mistress was mortal, and knew that if he did what he needed to do to bring his son back, he would have to do the one thing that The Fates would seek balance for. But he didn't care about the repercussions. So he turned his mistress into a goddess."

"I...didn't even think you could do that." I say, wondering if the process is painful or at the very least enjoyable. But I could never imagine making that decision lightly. So I can't help but think that this woman had wanted to become immortal well before she was sleeping with this man.

"It's possible but—again, greatly frowned upon. But in this case, it was necessary in order for her to carry out his new son to term. Otherwise as a mortal, her chances of dying due to all of that power and essence coursing through her from his seed would ultimately kill her before the child was even born."

"So…she ate the heart, and had sex with him so that he could have another child?"

"Not just any child, but the same son reincarnated. Who would now be known today as The Twice Born. A son made of entirely new flesh and features, but bearing not one but two souls within him."

Holy shit. I was thinking that he just wanted to make another child but to reincarnate the same exact boy just into another body? How is that—

Is that even allowed? Considering the souls who die end up in The Underworld, and the only two—other than The Fates, who are allowed to reincarnate a soul had no part in this, I can't imagine this was done *ethically*. Do Hades and my mother know about this? What do they think—

"I'm assuming from your silence and staring off into nothingness that you're perplexed by this."

I lift my gaze up from the ground, my eyes widened as I work on a swallow. "How can that even be possible? And the mistress—she must've really loved him to do that for him? So, is the boy alive and well today then?"

Semele looks at me for a moment before nodding her head, removing her hand from the bars and lowering it back to her side. She clasps her hands together in front of her. "The boy is alive and well today." She says matter-of-factly as she steps back from the gate. "I think that's enough story time for today."

She turns away from the cell and begins walking towards the stairs leading up to the throne room. "Dinner, some clean clothes and a bath will be brought down in a few hours." She stops her stride, halting as she turns her head to the side. "I'd advise you to utilize both when it does arrive." She sniffs at the air before turning her head around and continuing up the staircase.

I lower my nose to my shirt, sniffing as I smell the ting of sweat. An inconvenient side effect of having anxiety and being kidnapped to your abusive father's palace to say the least.

I straighten my back up against the wall again, hiking my knees up to my chest as I look around the cell. To my right I see a toilet mounted to the stone wall with a tiny sink next to it, yet no tub accompanies me in the cell. No windows, no lights other than the torch jutted from the wall. Casting a weak orange glow onto the wall beside it, the toilet and sink hidden in a cast of darkness as the light from the flames barely reaches them.

As I lean my head up against the wall, I close my eyes and sink deeply into the numbness deep within me. Opening itself up to me like a funnel coaxing me down into its safe abyss. The story of the boy who died and was reborn again preoccupies my mind, distracting me from drowning in the misery of being kept in my father's dungeon.

CHAPTER 8

Reimus

"This here is Lothario." Hades begins, pointing to a village on the south-eastern border of Olympia. "Majority of the population that resides here are mortals, though it's not uncommon to find immortals roaming around here."

"Why would they have any interest in being in a mortal village?" Dimitri asks from beside me, overlooking the map before us.

"Because immortal beings can become bored over time, depending on how long they've been around for." Persephone begins, glancing up at Dimitri and myself. "There are also a many number of gods who find delight in having...*intimate* interactions with the women who reside there. Lothario, though it resides on the border of Olympia, is not a very wealthy village. The people there make do and live decently, but their conditions are nowhere near wealthy, such as those who reside in Olympia. So for them, it's a great honor for a god willing to pay special interest in them, even if just for a night."

"And I assume with that intimate exchange, there are some gods who use that to their benefit." I say, repugnance in my tone.

Persephone nods. "You'd assume correctly. Some gods are already married, but again, that boredom and lack of moral compass doesn't fare the same as a mortal's would. They usually offer their mistresses wealth to keep their affair a secret, and agree because the thought of having an extra abundance of wealth to care for their families is enough to say yes when they don't see enough of it in Lothario. And since the gods know about the lack of resources and wealth in Lothario, they know most won't say no. It's an unfortunate cycle of manipulation that has been going on for eons."

"Why hasn't anyone intervened to do something about it? Why hasn't anyone made an effort to stop this abuse of power dynamics?" I curl my fist inward, feeling the beds of my fingertips glide across the palm of my hand. Saddened that these women have been living with these unfair living conditions with no other option.

Where are the men in this village that are outraged by their women being treated this way? The men that claim to be protectors but turn a blind eye to the abuse being enacted on their mothers, their sisters, their daughters.

I loosen a long sigh as I uncurl my fist, splaying my hand open before relaxing at my side.

"Because the only one who can do anything about it finds nothing wrong with it. That it's still all *consensual* between both parties." Hades says with a disapproving edge to his tone. "I have expressed my disgust with it to The Fates many times, but am always denied any intervention as I do not hold power over that realm."

My gaze hardens on the map hovering before me, on the palace that Melinoë is being held prisoner in. "And as long as Zeus is King of Olympia, he will never change their conditions." I clench my jaw, unwilling to think about what torture Melinoë is facing right at this moment. I nod my head to a section of land to the west of Olympia, detailed with raised edges shaded with blotches of grey and dark green. "What's this?"

"Those are the Casalas Mountains." Hades says before enlarging that section of the map, showing the mountain range more clearly. "These mountains have been here long before Zeus decided to build Olympia here. Aside from The Aegean Sea over here," He points to a channel of water running along the entire east border of Olympia, moving south along Lothario and expanding to the right of the map. "The sea that is ruled by Poseidon."

At the name of those mountains a shred of familiarity sparks within me, having no idea when I might have heard that name before but feeling oddly called to it nonetheless.

"When Zeus proclaimed this as his land," Hades says, gesturing to the entirety of the map aside from the sea that Poseidon rules over. "It was rumored that there were people that lived in these mountains, and were wholly outraged by his invasion, regardless of his title."

"So what happened? Did they fight back?" Dimitri asks beside me.

"They did." Hecate says, breaking her silence. I look over at her as her gaze remains on the map. "Their leader was rumored to be a powerful seer, who predicted that someone would come to conquer their land for their own some day. So they always remained alert, and prepared." She looks up to meet my gaze. "When Zeus infiltrated their home, they fought with everything that they had. Even knowing that most would go down fighting in the end. But even though Zeus won, they still held onto hope. Because they knew their land would one day be avenged, one way or another."

"Where did they go then?" I ask curiously.

Hecate shrugs her shoulders. "No one knows. It's been rumored that they all died off, it's also been rumored that some have retreated to Lothario. Laying low until the right moment to act again."

I shake my head, a small burst of anger pulsing through me momentarily. "No one should ever have to be forced out of their home."

Hecate nods slowly. "I would agree."

"Therefore his allies keep a close eye on the Casalas Mountains." Hades says, pulling my gaze back to him again. "And there's one in particular who keeps watch of what goes on in those mountains and surrounding it."

"Who?"

"Artemis." Hades sighs after he says her name. "The Goddess of The Hunt. She has been a loyal ally to Zeus for thousands of years."

"But we think this is because she is either being manipulated into being loyal to him, or she has her own ulterior motive for staying close to his side." Persephone interjects carefully.

"What would make you suspect that?" I ask, tilting my head.

"Because everything that Artemis stands for is opposite from who Zeus is at his core. She's a fierce protector of the wilderness, the wild animals that inhabit it, mortals, and young children—girls to be exact. All things that Zeus could give a damn about." Persephone rolls her eyes. "So why would she be so loyal to someone who is polarly opposite from who she is…it never added up."

"She has a twin brother, Apollo, who is also loyal to Zeus." Hades adds. "He has similar attributes to Artemis, and is a god to many things. Music, poetry, archery, prophecy." He lowers his gaze briefly down to the map. "They are both fair gods, but are entirely loyal to Zeus."

I nod, letting everything we've discussed so far sink in. "What about enemies?"

I watch as Persephone lifts her gaze back to mine, a brightness shining in her gaze. "Besides myself and Hades—"

"And myself." Hecate adds quickly.

Persephone glances over at her, nodding as a faint grin curves one side of her lips. "And Hecate," She turns her gaze back to me. "The only other enemy that was vocal about his dislike for Zeus' behavior was Cronus. Before Zeus executed him hundreds of years ago."

"Why did he kill him?"

"That will have to be a story for another time, as the details to that whole...*situation* are long and complex." Hades adds, sighing with a beat of frustration. Stifling talking about it any further. "But there is one more person that has quite a particularly *challenging* relationship with Zeus. Her name is Hera."

"Hera is a very vengeful and wrathful goddess." Persephone begins. "She bows to no one, and is not a merciful goddess. Zeus saw this about her and is why he forced her to be his bride."

"Wait, Hera is his *wife*?" I blurt out.

Imagine your own wife hating you. Dimitri says down the Guardian's Channel. For the first time since Melinoë was taken from us, I have to stifle the weak chuckle that bubbles up my throat.

Hades nods his head. "Hera, aside from being The Goddess of Marriage and Childbirth, is also The Queen of Gods."

CHAPTER 9

The energy around us charges suddenly as I look up at Persephone. Her gaze suddenly a palpable, aimless cold rage. My gaze lifts to the empty whiskey glass on the mantel as it trembles from the force of her power, teetering closer to the edge.

I watch as Hades rests a steady hand over hers, stifling the sudden charge of power as Persephone fixes her gaze on her husband. I watch her chest sink as she exhales, finding comfort in Hades' touch before her gaze lands on me again. The glass on the mantel ceases its movement.

My curiosity almost outweighs my common sense to ask if she has a personal vendetta against Hera due to her quick display of anger towards her, but something tells me very quickly at that moment that it's best I just keep my mouth shut and mind my business on the matter.

"Zeus is a very unfaithful god—" Hades begins, pausing as he mentally collects himself. The reminder of Zeus taking advantage of his wife written in anger all over his face before forcing it away, even if just for the moment.

He begins again. "Throughout their marriage, Zeus has dabbled in various romantic affairs. Hera is not oblivious to it, and she has enacted revenge on his mistresses many times."

"Why hasn't she divorced him then?" I ask.

"Because it would contradict her role as The Goddess of Marriage. Her embodiment of that title essentially contradicts her being able to ever divorce. Not only that, but Zeus holds the ultimate power. He would never give Hera the option to divorce him. So instead, she takes her rage out on his mistresses. And because Zeus cares for no one but himself, he finds her wrath not to be terrifying but to be entertaining."

My brows knit together as I shake my head. "What a sick fucking bastard."

Hecate makes a low humming noise. "Sick indeed." She mutters beneath her breath.

"Okay we know who his allies are—or at least some of them. We know his own wife hates him, the layout of Olympia. Great. But now the real question is how are we enacting our plan on getting Melinoë out of there?" I ask.

"I think the better question is, if we're to get Zeus away from the palace, and away from Melinoë long enough to get to her, what is the only thing that would drag Zeus out?" Dimitri asks.

"That is the golden question." Hades says, bringing his hand up to his face. His index finger and thumb gently pinching the bridge of his nose before lowering his hand down again.

"Well, threatening the people of Lothario won't be enough." I say, feeling sorry for the innocents that have to deal with such a cruel King. "And when we do figure out how to, do any of us even know where Melinoë is being held?"

"Zeus has a prisoner's holding dungeon below the throne room. It's where he'd keep anyone he was questioning, or just out of spite for their betrayal." Persephone says, a sternness etched into her face. "It'd be too much of a risk for him to keep Melinoë in a bedchamber above, even if he's convinced that he succeeded in erasing her memories. He's far too paranoid of a god to not think his strategy through."

I knew he wasn't keeping Melinoë in comfortable conditions. I tried to almost ignore that fact entirely so it would keep me from spiraling even more into a pit of shame. But hearing it confirmed from her mother now locks in that pit in my stomach that's been hardening since she was taken from me. I shake my head slowly. "It just doesn't make sense." I say aloud, quietly.

The map finally vanishes as Persephone steps towards me, a strong scent of lavender wafting towards me. A scent I've smelt on Melinoë before, just a faint trace of it beneath the rose and vanilla.

She places her hand gently on my arm, pulling my gaze up from the floor. She tilts her head to the side as she sighs, sorrow evident on her face. "If I have learned anything from Zeus, it is that he enacts terrible things that never make sense." I watch her gaze narrow briefly.

"Zeus has never expressed care for Melinoë. Why would he be so interested in having Melinoë close to him?" I curl my fist in, watching her gaze dip to my arm as tension hardens my skin.

Persephone lowers her hand slowly as she keeps her gaze trained on me. "I have asked myself that question for years. But I agree with you, there is some deeper reason why Zeus is insistent on keeping my children from me." She nearly chokes on that last word but remains standing tall in her marigold dress. The color brings out the sharpness in her emerald eyes, contrasting against her long black hair. "And we will find out why."

I nod my head as I suddenly feel an energy stir itself in the room. An energy far more subtle than what I felt from Persephone earlier, like a calm, light presence hovering several feet behind me. I see it on Persephone's face that I'm not the only one who feels it as she steps away from me, stepping closer to the presence.

I turn around to see a man standing near the fireplace. A man of the physical world no longer, and now a spirit of the afterlife. His body a silhouette of the form he once took when he was alive, his features still mostly intact though blurred around the edges. And as I look at him, this knowingness of exactly who stands before me floods me.

"Eiran." Persephone says before I can, the word as light and breathless from her lips as my feet feel on the ground right now.

Eiran nods his head as he looks amongst us all. He steps closer to us and fixes his gaze on me, grinning faintly. *"It's good to finally meet you, Reimus."*

His words echo through my mind and around the room at the same time. A sensation that only occurs when someone from the dead is speaking. My desperation causes me to step closer to him. "Have you been able to see her? Is she doing okay?" My voice teetered on the edge of pleading.

Eiran's lips turn downward into a frown as he shakes his head. *"Zeus has immensely powerful wards put into place that keep my kind from interfering at the palace. So I cannot reach her."*

I run my hand over my face, through my hair to hopefully stifle the building frustration. Or desperation. They both feel the same at the moment.

"But I do know how to entice Zeus enough to get him away from the palace. Long enough to give Hecate her way in to extract Melinoë from the dungeons."

"Wait, why Hecate?" I ask. I look over to her, not meaning to sound offensive. In which she gives me a gesture as if to say none taken. "I had assumed I'd be the one going in to extract Melinoë."

"Because Zeus is expecting that, and won't leave the palace if he thinks you're hanging around. He must believe that you are in Lothario, with Persephone and Hades, for him to come willingly. And it must be with an offering enticing enough for him to leave the palace." Eiran's gaze shifts over to Persephone, landing on her and remaining there.

I hear Persephone suck in a sharp breath before shaking her head curtly. "Absolutely not. I will *not* put Makaria in the middle of all of this. She stays out of it." The Queen of The Underworld seethes.

"What is the only thing that Zeus has a strange obsession over?" Eiran asks softly to Persephone.

She clenches her teeth as she shutters and exhales. She shakes her head. "There has to be another way."

Hades steps up next to his wife, looking towards her with empathy on his face. "Persephone is right." He turns his gaze back towards us. "We don't involve Makaria in this. She's still recovering from the compulsion spell Zeus placed on her. Getting familiar with her new life."

Eiran sighs as discontent etches on his ghost of a face. *"I'm afraid this is the only way."*

"Then I want in."

I whip my head around to see Makaria standing there with some tall man with wings spanned wide beside him, a quiet fury on her face as she stalks forward. The portal behind them closes as the man inches towards us behind her.

Hades looks over to him. "Thanatos? What are you doing here—"

"I made him portal me." Makaria seethes as she stalks up to her mother. When she approaches her she fists her hands down at her sides. "Why didn't you tell me that he took Melinoë?" Leaning her head in towards her mother.

Persephone's worry enhances on her face as she goes to grab Makaria's hands when she jerks them away. Persephone sighs as she places her hands in front of her lap. "We were just made aware of this. I promise I had every intention of coming to discuss it with you upon our arrival back home."

Makaria stands there staring at her mother for a long time. The rage, the anguish, all of it brewing just beneath the surface. Mingled with it I see the exhaustion on her face, both physically and mentally. My heart lunges for her, wondering how she must be coping with all of this.

Now to only find out her sister has been kidnapped.

A few long moments later, her shoulders lessen the tension and she uncrosses her arms. Lowering them to her sides. I watch as the hard glare in her face slowly melts into a sorrowful frown. "Did he take her because of what she did for me?" Her voice cracking beneath her words.

"Sweetheart, no. He did not." Persephone reassures her as she finally brings her daughter in for a hug. "This is in no way your fault."

I watch Hades' gaze fixate on the man—Thanatos again. His stare stern, as if he's planning on having a chat with Thanatos the moment they leave here.

Makaria pulls away from her mother, her hands clasped around Persephone's shoulders as she says in a clear and steady voice. "I am helping with this whether you agree to it or not."

Persephone watches her daughter, a mix of pride for her fearlessness to help her sister, and also her anguish of her children being caught in the middle of such a tumultuous situation.

When Persephone doesn't answer, Makaria lowers her hands and steps back. "I will do this, mother. With or without you."

Persephone looks over to Hades, a silent exchange happening between the both of them before she fixes her gaze back onto Eiran. Standing quietly. "You're absolutely positive this is the only way it will work?"

Eiran nods his head. *"There are many fates I cannot reveal truths about, but this one I can reveal. It will work."*

"And Makaria will be kept safe." Persephone steps closer to Eiran as her power ripples the air around us. "As Queen of The Underworld, I am requesting your oath that I have your *word*. Regardless of The Fates' laws, Makaria will not be taken nor harmed in this plan." Her voice carrying an ember of raw power.

Eiran stands there without a lick of doubt in his expression. *"You have my word, Queen of The Underworld."*

She stares at him a moment longer before stifling the power altogether. She faces Makaria again, the tension in her shoulders not easing when she exhales. She gazes at her daughter for a moment before forcing a ghost of a smile on her face. "Then it's settled."

CHAPTER 10

Melinoë

Hours later I hear the door at the top of the steps slide open, scraping against the cement ground as it closes shut. The sound of heavy footsteps follows in its wake.

Footsteps that do not sound like Semele's.

My skin pricks the hairs on my arms to stand up as a gut-wrenching anxiousness settles in my stomach. I lift my back away from the stone wall, jolting myself onto my feet as the footsteps draw closer to me. The chains around my wrists and ankles clanking in the silence around me.

I hope it's not Zeus coming down here to fetch me for another round of practicing wielding my powers again. I imagined I'd at least get a little reprieve from having to be near him until the morning at the very least. I really do not want to have to play pretend again today.

I just want to take a break.

The booted footsteps walk closer to the cage as I peer my gaze through the bars to see who's coming towards me.

A few moments later a man dressed in black breeches and an ivory tunic approaches my cell door.

He inserts the key into the lock, turning it until the lock clicks. He opens the gate and steps inside, the simmering fire from the torch on the wall above dimly lighting his warm porcelain face. He steps forward as I retreat backwards, pressing myself back into the wall.

He glances up at me, huffing. "Relax, I'm just bringing you food," He sniffs at the air, a grimace scrunching his face. "And a bath."

He holds out his hand as a tray materializes on top of his palm, my breath hitching when a large metal bucket materializes to my right. I swing my gaze over to the bucket, watching as hot water begins to fill its way up to the top, apparently an attribute to his own power that he wields. A sigh silently escapes me as I examine the size of it, big enough to allow me to seat myself but nowhere near large enough for me to move around once inside.

I look back over to the man, watching him kneel down until he drops the tray of food on the ground. The metal tray clanks against the cement as the fixings of a sandwich scatter from the impact. Wanting to roll my eyes at the rudeness of his delivery but my stomach growls at the sight of the food on that tray, betraying any intention of denying what this man has brought me.

I continue to stand there, looking up at him as he makes his way to stand with his back to the cell door, stumbling slightly as he does. I watch as he places his hands in front of him, clasping them together as he lets out a long exhale.

"First time walking, huh?" I mutter under my breath as I go to lean down over the tray. Piling the turkey and swiss cheese sandwich back together.

He glares down at me as I finally catch a glance at his face. A pair of what look like hazel eyes lower themselves as he knits his thick brows at me, annoyance creasing itself onto his soft, round face. I glance over his brown hair as it falls just above his shoulders, wavy strands kissing the tip of his jaw.

He scoffs at me, a particular smell wafting over to me as he turns his gaze over to the far wall. "At least I don't smell like I haven't bathed in days." He mumbles out.

"Because smelling like a pint of alcohol is any better." I retort back, bringing the sandwich up to my mouth as I take a bite. As the cheese and turkey reaches my tongue I moan softly to myself as I close my eyes, uncaring of any masks I'm supposed to portray right now as I devour the sandwich.

"Hurry up so I can get back to my festivities." He says, his booted foot toeing a pebble across the floor.

I finish eating my sandwich before moving onto the grapes, which some have scattered onto the ground. "Festivities that involve you drinking yourself into an oblivion?" I say as I pick one up, wiping it on my leggings before plopping it into my mouth. I take each one into my mouth greedily, clearing every last one from my plate.

He tilts his head slightly, a smug grin curving his lips. "Anything's better than being locked down here."

I push the tray away from me, shoving it towards him as I look up at him, stifling the rage brewing beneath.

Who is this guy? Well, one thing I know for sure is that he's no mortal. And if he has access to the dungeons, then I can only presume he's close to Zeus.

Which means he's already on my shit list.

I watch his hand unclasp from the other, waving lazily at the air before the tray vanishes from the ground. He steps away from the iron bars as he steps towards me. I retreat backwards until he stops.

He sighs. "I have to unlock your chains if you're going to use that thing." He nods over to the bucket of hot water.

I look over to it, then down at myself before meeting his gaze again. "And you think you're going to get a free show out of it by *watching*?" My shoulders tense as I cross my arms over my chest. "I think the fuck not." I snarl.

His brows slam together as he grimaces, jerking his head back. The repulsion on his face was convincing enough that he did *not* plan on watching me bathe. "I'm not going to *watch* you pervert." He lifts a different key out of his pocket. "My back will be turned from the other side of the cell."

Still, I do not know who this man is and have no interest in having any new company. "I am *not* bathing with you in the same vicinity as me." I seethe once more, my feet planting themselves firmly into the hard ground.

He lets out a long exhale as he rolls his eyes, dangling the key in front of him. "Considering I have to place those back on you the moment you finish," He says, nodding down to the chains. "You don't get that option. Either you utilize the bath, or you don't."

I loosen an aggravated sigh, my gaze darting over to the bucket as I watch the heat rising from the water. Heat I would love nothing more than to feel right now if I am not to feel anything at all while I'm here. A short, momentary reprieve to feel something, if anything at all.

I look back over to him, letting out a sharp huff. "Fine." I say before lifting my arms out for him. "But if you peek over at me I will claw those eyes from their sockets."

He steps towards me. "Trust me, I have no intention of doing so." He grabs my wrist as he lowers the key into the lock, hesitating before unlocking it as his gaze lifts up to mine. I notice then, up close, that his eyes are different from the average hazel eyes. Nowhere near similar to Nora's, with shades of honey-brown and green apparent. His have a lighter color to them, as if some shade of blue mixed with…green? A unique set of eyes to say the least—

"But if you try to harm me once I take these off, you can say goodbye to the generosity of me bringing you a bath or food at all. Clear?"

I roll my eyes. "Fine." I force out.

He turns the key, unlocking the chains before slipping my wrists free from them. I watch as the chains fall to the ground before he kneels down to unlock the ones as my ankles. After my ankles have been freed, he stands himself up again and locks eyes with me. "You have fifteen minutes to wash up."

He goes to exit out of the cell when I call after him. "So I'm expected to wear the same dirty clothes I had on?" Making sure to choose my words carefully. Initially wanting to say *the clothes I came here in*, but knowing it would've implied I knew I was kidnapped and brought here. Ruining everything I've worked to keep hidden thus far.

I watch him lock the gate before turning his back to me. A moment later a folded up pair of clean clothing appears on the ground next to the bucket. I glance at it for a long moment before jerking my gaze back over to him. Watching him, hesitating making my way over to the bucket.

After a long moment, he sighs. "You now have thirteen minutes."

I rub both of my wrists before I decide to make my way over to the bucket. I lean over it, assessing the water before lowering a hand inside. The immediate warmth sends a dizzying relief over my body. Momentarily threatening to bring every emotion I've had to deny myself to feel up to the surface. I clamp it all down, stifling it as I begin lifting my dirty clothing off of me.

I keep my back facing him as I turn my head around my shoulder, making sure he's exactly where he's supposed to be. With his back turned towards me.

I quickly step inside of the bucket and lower myself down until the water reaches my shoulders. I exhale a long breath as the warmth immediately envelopes me. Soothing my tired skin, and my tired mind.

I cup water into my hands, splashing it onto my face before moving onto my hair. When I realize I don't have anything to wash myself with, I grip the edges of the bucket. Leaning down to look around the outside of it until I see a small bar of soap on the bottom.

"Ten minutes now."

I lean down, grabbing it as I firmly press my fingers around the rose-scented, pink bar of soap. Wishing it was his neck I was gripping instead.

I begin washing my hair quickly, doing what I can for the time being before moving onto my arms and legs, and then the rest of my body. I drop the soap onto the ground before rinsing the last bit of soap off, squeezing any excess water out of my hair before turning my head around over my shoulder.

Noticing his back is still turned towards me.

"I'm stepping out now. Just so you know to keep that gaze exactly where it's at right now."

He sighs as he leans the back of his head against the bars. "Just hurry up."

I turn my head back around to the pile of clean clothing laid out there, along with a clean towel. I quickly step out of the bucket, grabbing the towel and quickly wrapping it around my body. Dripping water from my hair and body begins to dampen the ground around me.

I wipe the towel over my body before grabbing the clean article of clothing left out for me. A long, floor length white linen gown. Something I'd most definitely never wear.

I pull it over me, smoothing it out as I fix the straps on my shoulders. I use the towel to then pat dry my damp hair, gently wringing the excess water from the ends.

"Are you dressed now?" He asks.

"Yes." I state plainly.

A moment later he turns around, pulling out the key from his pocket, and turning it into the lock again before stepping inside. "Another tray will be brought down for breakfast."

"What time is it?" I ask, finding myself wanting to know. Wanting to know exactly how long I've been here for. Knowing it hasn't been long, though it still feels like it when you have nothing surrounding you but darkness.

"A little after six o'clock."

Seven hours. I've been here for only seven hours and I feel like I've spent three days locked down here already. I tamper the sudden anxiousness that begins to rise within me, electing to remain silent and nod my head instead.

The man steps towards me, grabbing the chains from the ground before he nods at my hands still holding the towel to my hair. "Wrists."

I slowly lower the towel from my hair, dropping it to the ground before hesitatingly holding my wrists out for him so he can place my temporary shackles back on me.

He clasps the heavy chains onto my wrists, clasping them closed before dropping my wrists in front of me.

Is this what my days will be like from now on? My days filled with appeasing Zeus' ego for the betterment of my survival here, with my nights filled with lonely, quiet baths and just enough food to get me by?

No longer filled with the warmth, the closeness of Reimus to fill my quiet days with the ferocity of his love and generosity. Something I miss terribly.

The man lowers down to my ankles, fixing the chains back on before standing up again. He looks at me once, and for a moment I wonder what he's going to say.

Not particularly interested in anything he has to say, and still not open to having company from anyone who is closely tied to Zeus—which I presume he is. But somehow still hoping it'll be anything but the punishment of silence that I'm being forced to endure while down here. A torture of silence I've felt all my life and had finally found freedom from.

Just to be sucked right back into it again.

Except the man only turns around, exiting out of the cell before locking it once more.

I watch as he begins his trek back up the stairs as I retreat to sitting myself up against the wall, hiking my knees up to my chest as I lean my head up against the stone wall.

My damp hair trails itself over my shoulders, given no brush to detangle the snarls out. Left with only the option to let it air dry as memories of Reimus brushing my hair for me resurface. Memories of me sitting at my vanity as I watch him from the mirror before me, gently weaving my brush through my hair. One of the many simplest of intimacies shared between us, moments I hold dearly to my heart.

Tears begin to prick my eyes as I hear that door at the top of the steps open up, allowing in a single strip of light from the palace above. I turn towards it, the semblance of it an irony to how it felt to meet Reimus. A light that I never knew how badly I needed, shining life onto all of the darkest parts of a world I was sure I would never find solace in again.

Tears begin to stream down my face as I watch that strip of light thin out, until fully burning out as the door closes. Suffocating me into the darkness once more.

CHAPTER 11

Reimus

The next morning I find myself laying in bed long after I've awoken. Dreading wanting to do much of anything other than sulk in the fact that today was the first day I'd woken up to Melinoë not laying beside me.

I lay on my side facing the empty space beside me, my gaze on the pillow that has laid beneath her head for months now. My hand reaches out, tracing over the dark charcoal pillowcase, a shade to closely match that of her long hair.

I bring my hand back down to the space beside me, slipping it beneath the silk sheets. Met with the painful reminder of her absence.

I feel the sunlight warming my bare back as it creeps in from the balcony doors behind me. Allowing the warmth to guide my eyes closed as I drift off to an imaginary place.

Where Melinoë is laying right beside me, tucked into my arms.

But my thoughts are quickly interrupted by the sound of our front door swinging open, the faint sound of chatter between two people before the front door closes.

"I *understand that*," Dimitri begins, my enhanced hearing from my drago abilities picking up his whispered words to another. "But nothing will make him feel better until Melinoë is back."

"I'm not saying it'll cure *everything*," A familiar voice seethes at him. "But he needs to see that people have his back right now. He needs support. Both of them do." Nora says as I hear them both make their way up the palace stairs. I hear something crinkling as they make their way up, unable to pin what exactly it is.

I hear their footsteps drawing closer to my room, her feet walking more hurriedly then Dimitri's. Until a moment later I hear someone knocking on my door. "Reimus, are you naked?"

I furrow my brows together as I elect not to answer, hoping they will go away if I remain silent.

"Well, I'm coming in so be decent." She yells before opening my door and barging in.

I lift my head up from my pillow, briefly glancing at Nora and Dimitri before narrowing my gaze down to what she's holding in her hands.

A basket full of snacks and baked goods. I sniff, and smell an array of nuts, fresh fruit, baked vanilla muffins, cheese, crackers, salami, and some kind of baked croissant.

"Dimitri says you're not really eating so I come bearing gifts." Nora says as she approaches the bed, seating herself on the edge of it. She sets the basket onto the bed beside her as she hesitates. "Wait, seriously. You're not naked under there right?" She points to the sheets draped over my waist.

I huff out a lazy chuckle as I seat myself up onto the bed, shaking my head. "I can assure you I'm not naked under here."

She lets out a relieved exhale. "Good. That would've been quite disturbing."

Dimitri moves closer into the room, standing beside Nora with a slight frown. "I told her to wait until later to bring it but she insisted right away." He says.

"It's okay." I glance down at the basket before meeting Nora's hazel eyes. "Thank you. It's very kind."

She nods, keeping her gaze on me as a frown slowly pulls at her lips. Silence follows for a long moment before she says, "Dimitri told me what happened." Her voice lowered a notch, quieter.

I say nothing at first as I go to grab the care basket that Nora—and I assume some of the other girls at The Sanctuary, have put together for me. My heart through the recent turmoil warms briefly at the gesture.

"What is the plan?" She asks.

I twist the plastic surrounding the basket off, opening it up and grabbing a muffin from inside. Not having eaten since yesterday morning before Melinoë left the house to venture into the Sephyra Forest with Semele.

A traitor who took advantage of Melinoë's kindness, pretending to have come to Vulir because she was running from a toxic, abusive relationship.

All lies from her mouth.

I wonder if Semele is even her real name or not. "The plan is to bring something to Olympia that Zeus can't resist stepping out of the palace for."

Nora tilts her head. "Bring what?" She demands. Her eyes grow wide as she leans back, quickly understanding as I give her a look. "No. He'll kidnap her too."

"That's…kind of the point." I say, before taking a bite of the muffin.

"Makaria will go to Lothario, where word will spread that she's just outside of Olympia. Zeus will hear of it and take the bait, because he has this weird obsession with controlling his children and wanting them under his wing. He'll need to go see for himself." Dimitri begins, explaining for me while I eat for the first time in twenty-four hours. "When he finds Makaria there, his first instinct will be to capture her. But that's where Hades, Persephone and Reimus will come in. They'll be there with her, proving to be more of a distraction."

"And what about you?" Nora asks, looking up at Dimitri.

"I'll be waiting at the ready in the Casalas Mountains. Where Hecate will meet me with Melinoë." He says calmly and confidently.

"And then what?" She turns her gaze back onto me. "How will you know once Hecate gets Melinoë out of Zeus' palace?"

I tap the side of my forehead with my free hand. "In here." I take the last bite of the muffins before grabbing a pack of salted almonds.

"Right. The Guardian's Channel." Her gaze adverts to me grabbing the almonds, a sliver of a satisfied grin curving one half of her lips as I toss one into my mouth. "Okay, so when is it happening?" That determination overrides her grin.

I meet her gaze. "We don't know yet." I admit after swallowing my food. At the sight of Nora's brows scrunching together, I explain. "Makaria hasn't even come into her powers yet. All of this—who she is, it's still all very new for her. And Persephone and Hades agreed that we wouldn't make our move until Makaria could at least learn to portal."

"Well, how long did it take Melinoë to learn how to portal?" She asks.

"Not long. A few days maybe. But that doesn't guarantee Makaria will learn as quickly as her sister." I shove another almond into my mouth, feeling the sting of hunger begin to ease and feeling entirely grateful for Nora right now.

Feeling grateful that when we bring Melinoë home, that she'll have a solid friend to lean on for support. In any way she'll need it.

Nora lets out a soft sigh, nodding her head. She glances up at Dimitri and I. "So…what will you both do until then? Just wait?"

I shove the last few almonds into my mouth, chewing as I place the empty bag into the basket. I swallow them down as desolation weighs down on me, along with the festering restlessness that's beginning to consume me from the inside out. "Unfortunately, that's all we can do at the moment." I look down at the basket before me, gazing aimlessly as thoughts of how I'm going to preoccupy my time flood my mind.

How am I expected to just sit around and wait for Makaria to learn to portal? I can't just sit around and do nothing while the love of my life suffers.

Frustration pricks my skin as Eiran's words come through again. Grateful for his help in all of this, but aggravated that he assured us that this is the best course of action to free Melinoë.

Because if I did what I *really* want to do right now, which is to burn everything Zeus rules over to the ground and break Melinoë out now, I know deep in my bones that that's not the best course of action.

No matter how badly I want it to be, I know I'd be jeopardizing her safety in the process.

Nora reaches out for my hand, pulling my gaze up to hers as she gently holds it. "She's coming home." She assures me. "This will all have only just been a nightmare then."

I almost laugh at Nora's use of the word, the irony of it is that when Melinoë came into my life she eased the nightmares that kept me awake at night. Nightmares that played over and over again, reminding me of the day I was too late getting back to that safe house, costing me the greatest loss I'd ever felt.

So last night, I was once again reacquainted with the horrors of my past through my sleep. Reminded with the same dreams to torture me with their mocking reminder of my failure.

A failure that I will not make with Melinoë.

I nod my head at Nora, giving her a forced close-lipped grin. "She'll be home soon." Repeating her words back to her.

Knowing that she's right, because I won't rest until Melinoë is back home with me. No matter what it takes.

Yet the worry of what state of mind Melinoë will be in when I do finally bring her home haunts my thoughts.

CHAPTER 12

The cool wind lightly glides against my still damp hair, the warmth of summer seeming to have passed us by overnight as the cool fall weather now takes its place.

I glide the brush over Gizelle's back, hoping my time out here with my horse can pave a moment of reprieve from my own thoughts threatening to subdue me in place. Every now and then she presses her nose into my abdomen, and each time it curves a half grin up my lips.

Her way of telling me she's here for me.

I hear the whinny of another horse knowing it's not Arion—Dimitri's horse. This whinny sounds far too pained to be Arion.

I turn my head around to see Alastor walking towards me, the whites of his eyes visible as he looks at me. He whinnies again, stomping on the ground with an all-black hoof as he stands before me.

I lower the brush from Gizelle, turning towards him. I hold my other hand out for him, allowing him to sniff me before petting his mane. I watch as worry and sorrow fills his eyes, a steed that originally belongs to Hades we came to find out. A steed of his own that he sent to the mortal world to watch over Melinoë during some of her darkest times.

I run my hand along his mane as I speak to the steed who I can see has become protective of her. As protective as I have become for her as well. "I know. I miss her terribly, too."

He leans into my touch before turning his head towards Gizelle. He sniffs at her before raising his head to nuzzle himself along her neck.

I chuckle to myself as I drop the grooming brush into her grooming bucket. "Don't tell me you're jealous now, Alastor."

He continues nuzzling on Gizelle, fixing his body to stand closer to her. I pick the grooming bucket up, giving Gizelle and Alastor one last pet before I put the bucket back into the barn. Giving them their little moment together.

Awe, my horse has a boyfriend.

I chuckle again to myself as I make my way back to the palace, crossing over the large open terrain. I look up towards the far end of it, remembering what Melinoë once told me.

"You have all this land out here, but nothing to show for it. No foliage, no flowers, it's so...bare."

"And I'm assuming you have an idea of what you'd plant out here? I'd asked her.

I still remember everything she mentioned, as if I was saving it for a mental checklist inside of my head, even though at that moment I swore I had no interest outside of being a good host to a woman I didn't know. But little did I know I was making a mental note for a future time.

She'd started naming off the kind of flowers she'd plant here. Lavender, hyacinth, asphodel, as well as ferns and shrubs along the exterior walls. That she'd place a little deck area for her to sit and read in near the terrain entrance. She had no idea that I was gazing at her, starstruck at the way her emerald eyes had lit up when she named all of the ways that she'd redesign this outdoor terrain. Even the smaller details on adding bird feeders and a little fountain for the birds to bathe in.

And when she finally turned her gaze towards me, she nearly rooted me in place with the force of her gaze. The way it did, and still does, penetrate into the very core of my existence.

I remember stumbling like an idiot trying to think of anything to excuse my staring at her. But I knew at that moment, even though I denied it initially.

I knew I had found the love of my life.

As I enter the palace I make my way down the hall and over to the kitchen. I step through the dining room, hearing a soft rustling around from someone behind the swinging door.

I step into the kitchen, noticing Aven rummaging through the fridge. At the sound of me walking in, he turns around and brings a hand up to his mouth as he gasps. "My Lord," He begins as he hurries over to me, resting a hand on my arm. "Dimitri told me the news. I am so sorry to hear about our soon-to-be Lady." A frown pulls at his lips.

I immediately thought to myself *who did Dimitri all tell?* Knowing that it's no irony that Dimitri slept here for the first time in a while last night, knowing it was because he wanted to keep me company even if it was a few rooms away. Realizing that when I didn't show up for dinner last night, Dimitri must've filled Aven in on what's going on. Rightfully so, since Aven is not just my cook, but also a trusted friend.

I nod. "Thank you, Aven. All will be right again soon."

Aven nods his head curtly. "That it will be." He lowers his hand as he places his hands behind his back. "I was going to make a roast tonight. Dimitri tells me the lovely Nora will be joining us. Shall I expect to see you at the dining room table or would you prefer me to bring a plate to your room?"

His gesture claws at my heart as I shake my head. "I'll be down for dinner tonight." I force a shy grin.

He nods, grinning. "Happy to hear it, My Lord." He turns around as he begins rummaging around in the fridge again.

I make my way over to the kitchen sink, washing off my hands from grooming Gizelle. I dry them off on a paper towel, tossing it into the garbage before exiting the kitchen again.

I walk down to the front entrance, opening the door and stepping outside when Dimitri says something down The Guardian's channel.

The girls have questions. I haven't shared anything, thinking you would want to do the explaining when you're ready to.

After Nora left this morning Dimitri set out to do his security sweep, telling him I'd be out there after I showered and groomed Gizelle. Knowing that he's at The Sanctuary now and that it was only a matter of time before the women had questions for us.

Questions that I have no issue answering, but ones I had wanted to wait to address until I knew exactly what to tell them. How to address everything so the women at The Sanctuary could not only understand the totality of the situation effectively, but could also still remain to feel safe in their homes.

Homes that I've worked extremely hard for to ensure that the people of Vulir can find comfort and solace in.

I'm on my way. I will hold a meeting once I arrive.

I feel Dimitri give me a nudge down the channel, letting me know he's received my response.

I step a few feet away from The Guardian's Palace before shifting into my drago form, shooting up into the sky. Aven's words cycling themselves through my head.

Our soon-to-be-Lady.

A weight settles itself on top of my chest at the reminder that I had planned to ask Melinoë to marry me, that black velvet box now residing in the top drawer of our dresser. A ring that I had bought shortly after I met Melinoë, remembering how fucking crazy I felt because I had barely known her at the time.

But something in the pit of my soul told me that this was it.

She was the one, and there would be absolutely no one else after her. Because there is no one on this earth meant more for me than her.

As I fly over to The Sanctuary I try to stifle the hollow pressure caving in on me, but like the impact that Melinoë has had on me, it doesn't go away. And instead, swallows me whole.

CHAPTER 13

Melinoë

Semele holds me by the chains linked to the shackles at my wrists. The glow of the palace above becomes clearer and clearer the higher we descend up the steps from the dungeon.

We reach the top of the stairs, the light blinding my eyes as we walk through the doorway onto the palace floor. Semele shutting the door behind us.

She looks at my face, glaring at me with those luminous sapphire eyes. Praying my cheeks aren't puffy from the tears I shed silently in my cell all night.

She turns her gaze straight ahead, yanking my chains as I jerk forward. We turn the corner and the throne at the top of the dais comes into view.

With Zeus sitting on top of it.

He stares down at me, his gaze lowering to the dress I changed into after my bath yesterday. He huffs to himself as we descend the dais towards him. "Interesting dress." He says, lifting his gaze to Semele. A sternness etches itself into those golden-brown eyes momentarily.

She says nothing as she pulls my chains up, guiding me up the steps until we stand right before him. Either she doesn't see the intense disapproval in his gaze, or she doesn't care as she says, "Here she is. Can I leave now?"

I hear the bite of annoyance in her tone, and almost become confused by it. Just yesterday she was submissive, almost honored to be in his presence.

But today, it seems like that has all slipped from her demeanor as I watch the way she stares at him.

He chuckles as he waves a hand at her. "You're free to go, Semele. For now."

She lowers her head, a weak gesture at a bow before letting go of my chains and turning on her heels, walking away from the dais.

Zeus lifts his gaze up to me, assessing me as I wield my composure and emotionless face intact. "Good morning, Your Majesty." The lie flowing out of my lips like thick molasses. Smooth, yet hard to swallow. I bow slightly at the waist.

A grin curves his lips, his silver-blonde hair glinting against the bright sun shining through the tall arches to his right. "Are you ready for our next practice session today?"

I nod my head, keeping my hands folded in front of my lap. "Yes." I say quietly.

A sudden strike of electricity snaps at my leg, causing me to collapse to the floor in anguish as it remains latched onto me.

I look down at the thread latched onto my ankle, like a brand of fire-hot electricity burning my skin. I scream out in pain.

"Yes, what?" He demands, anger lancing his tone.

My breathing becomes ragged as I look up at him. "Yes, Your Majesty. My—" My words end on a harsh cry as the thread tightens around my leg, feeling like the blood flow to my feet is being suffocated. The heat spiderwebs itself up my leg. "My apologies, Your Majesty." I managed to force out.

He stares down at me for a long moment before releasing the tether altogether. My hand lowering to where the thread was attached to me, rubbing the angry burn mark that it left behind as warmth scorches my palm.

"You will do well to respect your King, Melinoë. You're lucky that was far kinder than what I would've given another who was not blood related to me."

Far kinder? I could barely take breath into my lungs from the fierceness of the pain you fucking—

Focus, Melinoë.

I hear that thought slither its way through my mind as I take another shuddering breath in, releasing as I look up to Zeus again. Nodding my head. "It will never happen again, Your Majesty. I fear I might have misplaced my manners as I am still a little tired from a long slumber."

Lies, ofcourse. I barely slept for two hours.

He stands up from the dais, lifting his hand as his power lifts me from the ground until I'm standing back up on my feet again. My legs slightly wobbly. "Let's just begin." He says disinterestedly.

The power propelling me to step down the dais guides me to walk beside him, focusing to not allow it to alarm me that his power can do such a thing.

Alarmed at what else his power can propel another to do.

We reach the palace floor when I feel his power lift from me, dissipating entirely as I lower my hands back down in front of my lap. In the next moment, I feel a cool breeze kiss my wrists and ankles as the chains around them vanish. "We're going to try and bring what power you possess to the surface again today." He says before he turns around to face me. Standing a few feet away from me.

My gaze tracks over his face, nodding absentmindedly. "I'm eager to demonstrate, Your Majesty. But I fear I do not recall what it is that I possess. What if I disappoint you again, Your Majesty?"

He tilts his head, pondering before he makes a low noise in his throat. "Maybe that's where I went wrong. I should've allowed you to at least remember that."

Suddenly I feel his power surrounding me, trying to latch itself onto my mind but I block it out. I feel the compulsion of his words, the energy that surrounds them magnifies in the air around us before he speaks.

"You will remember what you already know of your powers, and how to wield them."

His words rush me as the compulsion works to fix his error in erasing my memories. I pretend to let the energy take over me, bulging my eyes slightly until his power slowly slips away from me. I wait a few moments, blinking before lifting my gaze to his.

He stands there, watching me intently.

I blink once more before forcing my face to smooth out. Understanding blanching my face.

"Are you ready now, Melinoë?" He asks.

I nod at him, though a large part of me on the inside is unsure how much of my powers I should expose. Knowing that he won't stop pushing me to wield them until he feels it's to his satisfaction, but not wanting to reveal too much at the same time.

I decide at that moment that since I've only brushed the surface of what I'm capable of thus far with Hades, that he won't get a taste of what I truly am capable of as I do not even know the answer to that myself yet.

So, I give him what I know. "Yes, Your Majesty."

"Good. Now let's begin."

At the very moment that he shoots out a ray of blinding gold light towards me is the moment I thrust my hands up, blocking those electrifying threads from latching onto me with my shadows.

Those black tendrils of smoke spring out as if having been dying to be wielded to the surface, fisting themselves onto his threads of eather and pushing them away from me. I remain in control, holding onto my focus as I begin visualizing armor to wrap itself around my arms, then my chest, and finally down to my legs.

Protecting myself from any blasts of his lightning from branding my skin.

I quickly lift my gaze up to him to see a grin forming his lips, a distraction long enough to keep me from seeing his threads of light pushing back against my shadows.

My shadows begin snapping off, unable to handle the magnitude of his force. I take a ragged exhale out before I hone my gaze in on those threads.

Visualizing that my shadows suffocate the light out of them, just as he has tried to do the same for me.

I imagine them corroding the very life from his power, swallowing it whole like the pride I have been swallowing deep inside me to keep from blowing my cover. An agony that burns itself from the inside out.

In the next moment, I thrust my hands out again as my shadows spring out at him once more. And this time, they do exactly what I envisioned them to do.

I watch as my shadows slither along the lightning he uses to try and subdue me, but my shadows work quicker. They shrink the light from them completely before closing themselves in on him. Reaching closer and closer to his arms until I watch the light trickle out from his fingertips, a brief splash of surprise washing over his face right before my shadows latch onto his hands, clamping on.

I feel my energy latch onto him as a surge of electricity surges over my fingertips, and up my arms. It slams into me like red-hot agony, causing me to retract my shadows entirely and fall back onto my ass.

I take a few deep breaths in and out, calming myself until the after-shock of the electricity evades my body entirely.

"Now that was actually impressive."

I lift my gaze up, noticing him staring down at me with a grin on his face. A funny feeling slithers its way through my chest at his words, making my chest feel like it's caving inwards on itself. Words that I've never heard from my father ever in my life before.

Never having heard words of encouragement, never hearing words at all from him unless it was to tell me to make dinner for the night. Or to make sure Makaria gets ready for bed. Or to stop asking about my dead mother when I was just a little girl with questions.

That feeling quickly slithers its way out of me as I really look up at Zeus, and realize that he doesn't actually find what I did impressive because I wielded it myself.

He only sees me as a weapon to be wielded for his gain. Always for his gain, and never for any other reason.

That harsh slap brings me so quickly back to reality I almost pity myself for having even noticed anything at all. I mask my emotions, standing myself back up onto my feet as I smooth my hands over my linen dress.

Looking up at him I force the widest, fakest smile I've ever given. "Thank you, Your Majesty."

"Zeus, I am going into the village. I have some business to attend—"

A woman halts a few feet in front of me, having come from the throne hall entrance. Her gaze immediately locks onto me, her eyes tracking over me like an insect that needs to be squashed. She steps closer to us, staring at me.

"That is fine, Hera. I have some things I need to take care of as well." He says.

She—Hera, continues staring at me, advancing closer to me until she stands before me. Her rich brown eyes tracking me like a vulture beneath defined brows. Rich, curly brown hair falls down to her chest as she dons a bright gold dress, matching the golden crown atop of her—

Holy shit, this must be—

"Melinoë," Zeus draws out before I look over to him. "This is Hera, Queen of Gods."

I take a sharp breath in, my eyes widening as I jerk my gaze back to Hera. The haunting, stark features in her face cause me to stumble internally like a buffoon before I remember my part in all of this.

I quickly bow at the waist. "Pleasure to meet you, Your Majesty." I say, standing up straight again. I look back up to see her gaze has not left me, and to be honest, I don't think she's blinked even once.

Like a hauntingly beautiful painting that just watches you no matter where you stand in the room. Poised, and elegant in their demeanor with a cold and razor-sharp gaze.

I watch as a hint of disgust seeps into her gaze before finally turning away from me altogether. As if she can't stand to look at me any longer.

She faces Zeus, groaning. "Why is *she* here?"

Wait—she knows who I am? Does that mean she knows who Makaria is, too? And about my mother, and what Zeus did to her? Surely if she's The Queen of Gods, that means she's—

Awareness slithers itself down my neck as a chill snakes itself down my back.

She's Zeus's *wife*.

"She is here as a courtesy. To become my ally." He says as he steps towards Hera.

She huffs at him. "Interesting." Yet the bite of her tone tells me she's anything but. "I shall return later." She turns on her heels and makes her exit out of the throne room. Her golden gown lightly kissing the ground as it trails behind her.

I don't know why I'm so surprised. I knew that once I found out the truth about my lineage—about my mother and Zeus, that it was possible for him to be married. Or at the very least have a Consort being he's The King of Olympia and all. But somehow, I still found myself wholly unprepared to come face-to-face with her.

And strangely, rather than being perplexed by how she stared at me, a spark of satisfaction blooms. Because judging by her tone towards him, and the obvious lack of enthusiasm she held to be in his presence, that not even she shares the kind of love and respect that he demands from others. And if that doesn't scream you reap what you sow, then I don't know what does.

CHAPTER 14

"I want to try something else now."

I peel my gaze away from the throne room entrance, forcing it back onto Zeus. I watch as he folds his hands behind his back, squaring his shoulders. "Instead of wielding your shadows to defend yourself, I want you to try and use them to build a wall."

I hear the faintest echo of disdain at his use of the word shadows. His repulsion for my difference in power from his mimicking the brand of disgust weighing on me the more I have to play pretend in front of him.

"Yes, Your Majesty. I can certainly try." I respond, nodding.

I bring my power to the surface, droning out every emotion, every hint of a feeling and focus in on that darkness. That darkness that has threatened to swallow me whole many, many times before. Unknowing that the longer I denied it, the longer I was denying a vital part of myself all along.

Knowing it wasn't trying to harm me, but protect me.

I let that knowledge be the focal point as I focus on bringing a barrier between myself and Zeus. I close my eyes, breathing in deeply before exhaling slowly. I concentrate on how the shadows feel inside of my body, and how they feel when they're trying to protect me. As I continue breathing evenly, a reminder of Hades' words slither through me.

Your shadows are there to protect you, Melinoë. Use them.

I visualize a fortress being placed in front of me, holding my hands out as I feel the energy of my will course from my fingertips. I keep my eyes closed, continuing to visualize that wall until the sunlight beaming against my eyelids from the open arches slowly dims. That dimness of light begins to rise against my eyelids until that darkness covers me entirely.

I open my eyes to see a wall of shadows barricading me from Zeus before me, droning out every lick of light shining from the wall behind it.

My gaze roams over the thick swirls of shadows as they bind themselves together, tightening together as impenetrable knots and locking themselves in place. My gaze lifts to the very top as it hovers a few feet above me, tall enough to hover a few inches above Zeus himself.

"Good. Now let's test it." He says behind the wall, his voice faintly mumbled behind the thickness of the wall I've created.

In the next moment I feel the sharp zap of electricity against my shield, the power ricocheting itself onto me. I keep my feet firm against the polished ground, focusing on keeping my shield up through the sharp bite of pain. I breathe raggedly through my nose as I maintain every will of power I have left in me to keep my shield up.

I feel that zap of power again, watching as a brief spark of light pierces into my shield. I watch as it latches onto my barrier, suctioning itself there until it slowly starts to slither its way down from the top.

My hands tremble in front of me as I fight against Zeus' charge of lightning, chanting to myself internally. Chanting to that dark reservoir of power within.

I am stronger than him.

I am *stronger than him.*

We *are stronger than him.*

Suddenly my hands steady themselves as I feel the bite of his power lessen over my body, over my shield.

I jerk my gaze back up, my eyes widening as I watch my shadows begin to fight against his hold, pulsating outwardly as they halt his power from lowering down my shield any further. I watch as a new layer of my shadows slither over his eather attached to my barricade, slowly swallowing it whole until that light bleeds into that darkness, before suffocating that light out completely.

Along with the burst of pain that lingered from it.

I feel the charge of Zeus' energy dissipate entirely, followed by a long moment of silence. And for just a split moment, I watch as that charge of lightning that my shadows snuffed out from him glitters at me through my barrier. It is then that I realize my shadows not only snuffed out his charge of power.

They *absorbed* it.

"That's enough." Zeus rings out, his voice echoing around the throne room.

I retract my power back into myself, watching that barrier I built up slowly dismantle itself down. Until I'm standing before Zeus once more, his gaze hard and piercing onto mine.

A chill skitters itself down my back as the shadows crawl back to me, licking the pearl white floor like thick wisps of smoke. As the last of my shadows dissipate, Zeus takes a step towards me.

His gaze tracks over me, a familiar sternness tensing the skin beneath his eyes. Further creasing that disapproving gaze. I stand there for what feels like a painfully long time as he assesses me.

Did he not think I could actually build a fortress against him? Or did he not think my power could actually absorb his?

The latter having me feeling all sorts of perplexed as I didn't know that was even possible. I've never had that happen before, but then again I've never—

"Bethesda." The sharpness of his tone breaks me away from my thoughts. His gaze remains on me as my attention becomes drawn to the sound of a door opening from my right.

I watch as a woman enters the throne room from a door—the same one that the other handmaid ventured from the other day. I watch as she walks towards us, keeping her head down as her hands fold themselves in front of her all white robes.

She approaches us, bowing at the waist. "Yes, Your Majesty?" Her long lashes lowered above an array of freckles over the bridge of her nose. Her short strawberry blonde hair fanning forward as she keeps her gaze on the ground.

"Take Melinoë back downstairs."

"Right away, Your Majesty." She nods her head before lifting her gaze up to me tentatively. Her striking hazel eyes numb me momentarily as the familiarity of them reminds me of a friend back home. A friendship that I was just beginning to form, a bond that I was allowing myself to get close to after years of thinking I was destined to be alone and misunderstood by others.

I deny myself permission to reminisce longer on Nora as Bethesda gently reaches for my hand. She stops as a brief charge of energy lifts in the air around us, stifling quickly after the chains around my wrists and ankles appear once more.

She reaches for my hand again, her skin soft against mine as she ushers us away.

I jerk my gaze around as I look at Zeus, trying to find some semblance of a clue as to what made his mood change just now. From pretending to be cordial, to slipping that mask away as the disdain for me glitters on his face once again.

I stare at him a moment longer, turning around when the impassivity on his face does not change. I look ahead at the door to the dungeon below, remembering that Zeus takes pride in having complete control over anyone and everything.

Including Makaria and myself.

I take that thought and drill it into my mind, submerging it with the emotionless interior that I've been fighting to uphold. I let the coldness of it drench itself inside every crevice, every ruinous thought, and I allow myself to bask in it.

I straighten my back, squaring my shoulders as the comfort of a certain knowing takes over. I walk with my head held high, my gaze remained forward and my hands held together casually in front of me as Bethesda walks me to that door.

Knowing that Zeus' change in behavior can only mean that I revealed something to him that he did not expect, something that could defy and dismantle his grasp for control, even if only slightly. Whether it was that I was actually able to build a wall to protect myself against him, or that I was able to alchemize and absorb his power into my fortress for my own gain.

Either way, I store that information deep into my psyche for a later time. And when Bethesda finally opens the door to my cell below, this time I have to fight the grin that threatens to curve up my lips.

CHAPTER 15

Reimus

I land in front of The Sanctuary, shifting just before my feet can touch the ground. I smooth a hand over my arm as my palm glides over the black long-sleeved shirt I've willed over myself. I go to shove that same hand in my pocket as the other reaches to open the entrance door. My hand stilling momentarily at the emptiness in my pocket.

An emptiness that was occupied just days ago with a small black, velvet box. Safeguarding the ring I was going to present to Melinoë when I asked her to marry me.

That hole inside of my chest splinters open once again, cleaving my insides to feel raw and exposed at the reminder of Zeus' interference with what would have been a memorable, special moment.

That gut-wrenching sorrow quickly transitions into a burning hot anger, causing the collar around my neck to suddenly become too tight against my skin.

I take a deep breath in, exhaling it out for myself to agonize over later as right now I need to put on a steady and brave face for my people. For the women who reside here.

I reach for the door handle, grasping it as the brisk coldness on the metal handle faintly sizzles beneath my touch.

I jerk my hand away, lifting my palm up to inspect it. I cradle it with my other hand, feeling the noticeable change in temperature seep out of my fingers. I press my thumb over the center, tracing the heat lingering there before it swiftly dulls itself back to a normal body temperature.

Are you coming?

Dimitri's voice travels down the channel. *Yes, coming in now.*

I tentatively reach for the door handle again, pulling it open slowly. My gaze lowered to my hand as I wait to see if it'll happen again, but the coldness against the palm of my hand remains idle beneath my touch this time.

I pull it open, stepping inside The Sanctuary as a gentle rush of warmth greets me. I walk through the main entrance to a set of stairs at the far wall leading me upstairs where everyone is waiting for me.

And as I make my way up the steps, I put on a brave and strong face for my people. Even when strong is the furthest of what I feel in the absence of Melinoë.

I stand before everyone gathered around me, seated in a circular fashion as Dimitri stands to my right. "Thank you all for meeting with me. I know there are many questions you all have, and I am here to address them and explain to the best of my ability. As you all deserve that right."

I watch Nora's gaze remain on me, a slight nod of her head and a ghost of a grin flattening her lips before she glances over at Dimitri.

"Where is Melinoë? Semele?" Thalia rings out. Her two sisters—Euphrosyne and Aglaea, seated on either side of her as they stare up at me in both wonder and perplexity.

"Many of you know that Melinoë is immortal, but I am aware not many of you know the nature of where her divinity lies. And what her lineage entails." My gaze looks over the women before me, their gazes wholly on me as some of them turn to each other and whisper amongst themselves. Confusion hissing quietly in their words. "Many of you know of the incident that occurred months ago in the village, where Melinoë assisted a dying man over to the afterlife." I pause as some of them nod their understanding. "This gift of hers stems from her being The Goddess of Ghosts, a Guardian of Souls. Amongst other things."

"What other things?" Euphrosyne asks.

I keep my gaze on her, bracing myself for whatever initial reaction they will have at my response. But giving them the truth anyhow because they deserve to know. "She is also The Goddess of Nightmares."

I watch as some of the women turn towards each other again, whispering to one another as shock ripples on some of their faces.

"Is she…dangerous? How could we have not known her true nature?" Carina says, her honey-hued eyes wide and alert as she gazes at me. Her attention momentarily fixates on her daughter seated on her lap when she begins to softly cry. Elise tries leaning down to pick up the small toy doll she dropped, becoming frustrated at Carina's arm holding her up and inhibiting her from reaching it.

Carina leans down, grabbing the doll and handing it to Elise. Her crying stifles the moment her favorite toy rests in her small hands again. A warmth spirals in my chest as I watch her hug the doll close to her chest, a wide smile curving up her rich, almond skin. Her mother leans her face down, pressing a soft kiss between her daughter's braided pigtails before lifting her gaze back up to me.

"Does this mean she took Semele?" Another woman chimes out. I watch as Leia looks over at Carina, her sun-kissed hand reaching out to grab hers as worry creeps over her body. Her shoulders tensing and locking up.

"Melinoë did not take Semele. Semele lied to us on the true nature of who she was, and kidnapped Melinoë."

A few gasps sound in the seats of the women before me.

"Melinoë wanted to tell you all who she really was at the right moment. She did not want you all to fear her, as all she only ever wanted was to be accepted." Emotion clogs the pit of my stomach and throat as I exhale a quiet breath. "And you all gave her that. You all made her feel more welcomed than she ever has felt before. But she was afraid that you would not be so accepting of her if you all knew the title she bore. As she did not want to be solely known for her divinity, but for who she was outside of it."

I watch as the women turn their glances to one another as that worry in some of their expressions smooths over. The tension in some of their shoulders slowly loosening.

Their silence stretches on until Euphrosyne stands up from her seat. "I believe you." She says softly, looking down at her sisters before lifting her gaze back up to me. "And I trust your judgement and your word, as you have never led us wrong before."

I watch as Thalia and Aglaea stand up with their sister, nodding their heads as Aglaea speaks. "I have only just begun to get to know Melinoë, but I find that I am a good judge of character."

"But she's a goddess of *nightmares*. How do we even know what that entails?" Lucille speaks out, standing up from her seat as she glares at Aglaea.

Aglaea turns around, looking at Lucille in a stern, yet graceful stance. "We don't. But do you have no trust in our Guardian's?" She glances over at me, tilting her hand up in mine and Dimitri's direction. "Do you have no trust in the men who ensure our safety each and every day?"

Lucille's fists ball slightly inward. "Not if his judgement is clouded by his *feelings* for her." She seethes as she glances over at me.

The one thing I was afraid of begins to unfold on Lucille's face. Her worry, her fear of a woman who would go to great lengths to protect the people of Vulir. People that she barely knows, but is still willing to risk her life for.

A stern gaze lands on Lucille as I straighten my back. The force of my words carries a gentle, yet sharp edge to them. "Melinoë is protecting the people here in Vulir at the expense of her safety. At the expense of her well-being to keep *you* alive. So if there is anything about her character that you should believe, it is that she would risk her own life to protect people that barely know her. Including those who doubt her intentions."

Silence fills the room around us as Lucille stares at me, everyone else sharing similar widened gazes by my statement. By the subtle bite of my words.

It is not often that I assert myself in such a way, but when it comes to defending Melinoë, I will not shrink from the force of my loyalty to her. I will let them drown in the seriousness of my words before I ever back down from giving Melinoë the credit she deserves.

Because under no circumstance will I allow slander, nor mistrust for a woman who has done nothing to deserve it.

She stares at me a moment longer before she slowly nods her head. "You're right. I am sorry for my outburst. I'm just—" She sighs as she looks around at some of the women seated next to her. "Some of us are just worried. If one of our own kidnapped Melinoë, someone who is as powerful as you make her to be, then what does that mean for us?"

I take a step forward, understanding sweeping over me as I narrow my gaze. "I understand your worries." My gaze roams over each of the women before me. "Semele kidnapping Melinoë was out of convenience and intentionally orchestrated. It was her motive for coming here all along."

My fingers press against each other behind my back, stifling the unrest that I feel deep in my bones at Melinoë's absence. I loosen a breath as I continue. "I never want any of you to feel unsafe here as this is your home just as much as it is mine. But it is also my duty to be honest with you all, and to give you some semblance of peace knowing the truth of what is happening."

Lucille briefly glances at Dimitri, blinking once before training her cerulean gaze back onto me. Lucille—a woman who came here years ago as she fled from her captor. She had no destination, no idea where to turn to for refuge. She'd only known that when the man she had been sold to through an underground sex trafficking ring, who had repeatedly beaten and raped her, made the mistake of leaving the ambien medication he'd used for Lucille out instead of locking it back up, that she found her one chance at escaping. That as soon as he passed out from the one too many ambien she crushed up in his dinner, that she'd have her only shot at freedom.

I'll never forget the way her hands trembled before me when first meeting her at the shield. The way her shoulders shook so violently I had almost worried she'd been having a seizure.

The way her cries deafened the Sephyra Forest around us. I knew the signs as I looked upon her, of a woman who had been so severely abused and was both substantially relieved to be free, yet also still suffocating greatly internally from the treatment she endured. I'll never forget the one thing she managed to stutter out after first looking upon me. After gently introducing myself, opting to keep a safe distance for fear of frightening her even more. For fear of sending the wrong message of the type of man I am.

She'd taken a long, long look at me as she trembled. Until her shoulders began to finally relax to some degree, her gaze shifting periodically to Charon who stood beside me. She'd looked at me and all she said was, *"I followed them."* Her hand trembled as she pointed upward into the night sky, at the formation of a cluster of stars that shine brightly over, and guide one directly to Vulir.

She'd looked at me through red-rimmed eyes and said, *"I—I ran as fast as I could. I didn't know where to go. But I looked up,"* She stifled a choked cry as tears streamed down her eyes. Her dark brown matted hair doing little to hide the bruises on her cheeks. *"Something told me to follow them. So I did."*

A cluster of stars known through generations of those who have lived in Vulir. A nameless constellation that was always known to point to home. But as the name Melinoë mentioned to me resurfaces in my mind, I begin to wonder if the constellation was always meant to also point to a place of change for those in need of it.

A village where one can not only find peace, but also rebirth. Just as The Phoenix symbolizes.

Lucille nods her head as she seats herself back down, pulling my attention back from my thoughts and regrounding myself in the present.

"We do appreciate knowing the truth," Nora says from her seat, fixing my gaze on her. "And we still stand with Melinoë. Regardless of what her title bears." She stands up from her seat, turning her head around to look at everyone else before landing her hazel gaze on Lucille.

Lucille nods her head as she continues standing, folding her hands in front of her lap. Calm, and steady now after years of trembling anytime she stood in the presence of a man. Her calmness is a show of trust that has taken a very long time for me to build with her, and something that I will never take for granted. "We trust you. Therefore, we trust Melinoë as one of our own." She says as she looks over to her right, then her left.

Then, as one by one, each woman stands up from their seat.

Some with children hugging onto their hips as they hold them up, or nuzzling their small heads against their mothers' calves. Children who have ventured with their mothers to start over in a place where they can finally live safely, and have the childhood that they rightfully deserve.

As I look upon the thirty uniting faces standing before me, I wish more than ever that Melinoë were here to see this. To see and believe that she is not fighting this battle alone.

CHAPTER 16

After checking in with the women at the shelter to make sure they had everything they needed, I made my exit and headed down the cobblestone road to the shop at the corner of the street.

I glance up at the black letters etched into the violet hanging sign. A faint gust of wind rushes over me, causing the sign protruded above the entrance door to gently swing backwards.

I grab the bronzed handle, pulling the door open as I step inside The Raven's Claw. Immediately greeted with strong scents of rosemary and cypress.

The bells hanging from the door handle jangle together as I step inside, clinking together once more as I close the door behind me. My attention is drawn to the smoke emanating off of a lit incense stick on a nearby shelf, surrounded by crystals ranging from onyx black to moonstone white.

"I was wondering when you were going to pay me a visit." I hear the soft padding of low-heeled boots as Hecate emerges from her back room, meeting my gaze.

A soft chuckle escapes me as I move further into her shop. "I'm afraid that you will be seeing much more of me since all I have right now is time." A sadness pulls at my words as I lower my gaze to her robe resting on her shoulders.

An amethyst robe that I cannot recall ever seeing her without.

She steps forward as I bring my gaze back up to meet hers. Her mauve painted lips force a close-lipped grin, her chest sinking as a sigh softly escapes her. "Well, I will never turn down the company." Her grin curving deeper onto her face before smoothing out again. "But I'm afraid that I do not have what you came here looking for."

"That obvious?" I ask, picking up a glass jar full of some kind of red liquid. I turn it over, noticing the words *come to me* labeled on a vintage sticker. Tiny specs of herbs float around in the oil as I swirl the mixture around.

Hecate approaches me, grabbing the jar from my hands. "No touching my spelled oils when your energy is off." She sets the jar back down onto the wooden table, setting it next to an array of similar ones as a beat of silence passes us. "I have no news on the progress of Makaria's training."

Disappointment plunges deep in my gut, but then I remember that it's only been one day. And the hollowness I feel inside has nothing to do with how fast Makaria can learn her gifts, and at the very least how to portal.

But has everything to do with my growing restlessness at Melinoë's absence.

I nod my head. "I understand. I do not mean to be a bother, I just—"

"Miss her?" Hecate cuts in.

I sigh, nodding. Gods, do I ever miss her. As if a piece of myself has been ripped right out from me, now left completely exposed until she's back home where she belongs with me.

She tilts her head to the side as she rests a hand on my shoulder. "I know this isn't easy, dear. For either of you." She lowers her hand as she steps away. "Come. I want to show you something."

I follow Hecate into the back of her store, walking through an open doorway with hanging beads leading to her back room.

I step inside as my gaze fixates on an active spell she's working on, set on her work station at the far back table. Pillars of black candles stationed atop symbols drawn onto the table's surface, with flames igniting far higher than a candle not powered by magic would.

"What is this for?" I ask as I step closer but still keeping a healthy distance back. If there's one thing I know about Hecate, she doesn't like people poking and interfering with her spellwork.

That's a sure fire way to get put on Hecate's shit list.

She steps towards her work station, gazing down at the flames growing to life. Flickering at her presence, then stilling when she lifts her hand up as if silencing their movement. "I cannot see inside Zeus' palace. His wards are far too powerful for me to do any scrying, to see what's going on inside."

My gaze lifts to her face, stilling in place as understanding beckons me. "But you've still been trying to."

She looks over at me, her golden gaze piercing mine as she nods. "If I cannot see inside, then I am trying my hardest to at least send protection her way. But I've—" She looks back down at the spell before her, hesitating. "Even with my power and my skill, I've still come up unsuccessful. But that doesn't mean I won't keep trying."

My chest caves into itself at Hecate's effort to try and keep Melinoë safe, even at a distance. Her efforts at guiding Melinoë even before she made her venture to Vulir. My thoughts fall onto the talisman that Hecate spelled for her months ago. "When I saw her, she wasn't wearing her necklace."

Hecate looks up at me, a frown pulling down on her face. "I know."

I tilt my head. "How?"

The flames from one of the black candles shoot up, going erratic until Hecate waves a hand over it. Willing the flame to simmer once more. "When I spelled her necklace to protect her, I didn't just design it to protect her from the physical world. But also the astral."

She walks over to a neighboring table, reaching for a small wooden box. "Since I was the one who spelled it, I could always locate it—locate *her* if needed."

I watch as she lifts the top, lowering her fingers inside until she pulls out Melinoë's obsidian necklace. Dangling it between her thumb and index finger.

I walk towards it, my gaze wholly on a talisman that Melinoë has not been without ever since Hecate crafted it for her. Emotion threatens to clog my throat as I stare at it.

"I did a locator spell on it, and went to retrieve it." She lowers the necklace into the palm of my hand. The energy charging me momentarily before subsiding. "It was buried beneath the soil in the Sephyra Forest. Assumingly the exact spot where Zeus abducted her from."

I cradle the pristine black crystal in my hand, curling my fingers inward as I briefly close my eyes. The image of Melinoë wearing this before she left our bedroom, to go and check in on Sage with Semele.

"Though it had a feminine scent on it not belonging to Melinoë." She says tentatively. "So I believe it was Semele who tried to dispose of it."

I open my eyes, looking at Hecate. "If Semele is immortal, then why just bury it? Why not use magic—or rather her powers to shatter it?"

Hecate shrugs her shoulders. "I pondered over the same question. Though she knew it was spelled for protection, otherwise she wouldn't have known to take it off of Melinoë's neck. Perhaps she did not know that I could locate it"

I look down at my hand again, opening my palm and inspecting it. Not a lick of a scratch or dent on it.

I lower my hand down to my pants, placing the necklace into my pocket. Where it will safely stay until I am able to give it back to Melinoë. "Perhaps."

I hear the faint sound of bells jingling from the front of the store. Hecate lifts her head as the sound of footsteps slowly walk along the hardwood floors. "Looks like company time will have to be cut short, dear."

She lowers her head down towards her work station, mumbling a few words to herself until the flames on her working dim to an almost nothingness, before everything on her work station vanishes.

My head jerks back, peering my gaze sidelong. "Where'd it go?"

She looks up at me, a brief chuckle escaping her lips as her gaze drifts off to someplace else. As if being reminded of a different time.

She loosens a breath, patting my shoulder with a hand decorated with gold rings. "It's still there. Just invisible to anyone but myself now." She winks before she lowers her hand, stepping away to make her way to the front of the store.

It would be an understatement if I said I wasn't in awe at everything that Hecate is skilled at doing. It seems like just yesterday I thought she was a skilled witch, who also happened to be a trusted ally and friend to me.

But ever since the day that Melinoë found out her mother was alive, I found out that Hecate was a goddess all this time—The Goddess of Witchcraft and The Crossroads, at that. Wondering why she never expressed it before, and always kept it hidden.

"Hey, Hecate." I say, turning away from the table to face her.

She turns around, meeting my gaze.

"Why did you keep it a secret?"

She tilts her head, confusion slightly rippling on her expression as her brows knit together.

"All this time I was under the impression you were mortal. But you're a goddess who chooses to stick around Vulir. Why?"

A grin curves up her lips, a lazy shrug of her shoulders as she says, "You never asked." She huffs out a soft laugh, continuing after she exhales. "But because I want to be more than just my divinity. Someone who helps the mortals that reside here. Guides them." The side of her mouth kicks up, pulling her grin up that side of her face. "I guess much like how Melinoë wants to be known for more than just the title she bears."

Hecate turns on her heels and exits her back room, leaving me to stand there and process her words for a brief moment.

My hand lowers to my pants, smoothing my hand over the hard surface of the crystal hidden underneath. A faint pulse of energy charges my hand before quickly simmering, the second reaction now to my hand touching it. The sensation not feeling threatening or discomforting in the slightest.

Oddly enough, even though it is not a talisman spelled for me, the energy feels as if it's *excited* at my presence, at my touch. As if being ignited for a brief moment from my touch, greeting me before dulling itself into a slumber once more.

An energy that washes over me and reminds me of how it feels to be near the person it belongs to.

Home.

CHAPTER 17

Melinoë

Hours tick by as I cement myself in the same spot I've been in since Bethesda put me back in my prison cell.

Lying out on the cool ground, my hands folded on top of my stomach as my gaze blankly fixates on the vaulted ceiling above.

I watch as the flames from the burning torch cast themselves closer to the center of the arch, the light dimly illuminating the stone interior. My gaze follows the orange glow as it creeps over each divot and crevice, sinking into the distraction as it numbs me from the inside out.

I follow those dancing shadows, breathing in and out slowly as I wander to a place far away from here.

The coolness on my back slowly melts into warmth, the dense cemented ground molding itself into lush, short grass as I sink into it. The suffocating, dreary ceiling above breaks open and expands into endless swatches of warm magenta. The smell of mold disappearing as a gentle breeze carries a whiff of the asphodel flowers nearby over my nose.

"Is it always like this?"

I look over to my sister laying in the grass next to me, her gaze fixated on the sky above. A calmness blanketing her face as a soft grin curves up her lips. Yet as I watch the vigilance in her gaze roaming over every inch of the sky, the slight tremor in her hand above her stomach, I see my sister fighting to keep herself together as she's drowning in pain on the inside.

I give her a half grin as I shrug my shoulders. "Pretty much."

Makaria turns to look at me then, catching my gaze before forcing a grin herself. "I expected The Underworld to be more…gloomy. But this," She turns her head back to look up at the sky, loosening a breath. "I could get used to this."

I chuckle as I lean myself up onto my elbows, my hair falling over my bare shoulders. My gaze narrows to a ladybug crawling on my beige tank top, lifting my hand as I lower a finger to it. "Trust me, I shared similar expectations and was just as pleasantly surprised." I watch as the ladybug crawls onto my index finger, making his way down until he expands his wings and flies away. My gaze remained in the direction he flew towards. "The weather is also always pleasant here. No winters, though it does tend to get hot here some days."

My sister lifts herself up onto her elbows before stretching up into a seated position. She fans a hand over her mouth as she yawns. "Well then I guess I will be finding myself here when it is winter up there." Nodding upwards, insinuating the upper world.

I huff out a laugh that gets trapped inside my mouth. "I'd probably do the same if it weren't for Reimus."

A wide grin curves my lips, thinking of the home I've forged with Reimus in Vulir. The friends I've begun to make, the routine I've begun to form for myself. The warmth festering inside of me for a life I'm genuinely happy about living, matching the warmth surrounding me from the weather in The Underworld today.

A rightness that I've never known before, that has always been lacking up until now. And now that my sister is finally back home, safe from Zeus' compulsion, everything is exactly how it should be.

Even though I know my sister is not back to herself yet. Though I brought her back from the memory loss, I know that there's a large part of her that didn't come back with her. A part of her that experiences joy at the little things, that lights up from the birds chirping and watching flowers bloom in the springtime. An innocence that believes in fairytales and love at first sight.

A woman who views life through a lens of light and optimism, now dulled by the trenches of pain that our father left her to be blinded with.

"I'm really happy for you, Melinoë."

I look over at my sister, a genuineness to the smile on her face right now.

"You have done enough, been through enough in this lifetime. You deserve to be *happy*."

Emotion clogs my throat as I grin deeply at my not-so-little-anymore sister. "Thank you." I lift myself into a seated position, crossing my legs. "You deserve to be happy, too."

The genuineness in her smile fades as she nods her head, lowering her gaze to a tiny stalk of grass. "I know." She says quietly as she brushes it with her thumb. She moves her hand away as she lifts her gaze back up to me, exhaling. "I'll get there."

I reach my hand out for hers, cupping it into mine as I give it a gentle squeeze. "You will."

I grin at her as her fingers wrap around mine. The slight tremor in her hand slowly fading as her hand rests calmly inside of mine.

"Get up."

At the interruption of Semele's voice I'm jolted back to the present. Back into the dimly lit prison cell, void of any light aside from the torch on the wall. Where I lay on the stiff hard ground with chains fastened to my wrists and ankles.

No longer able to hide myself away in a memory of my sister and I laying in the Asphodel Meadows. A memory where my life was beginning to feel simple, feel ordinary for the first time.

Only to be drudged back to reality.

I lean my head over to the side towards the cell door, the sound of keys jingling harshly against the silence around us as she lowers it into the lock. "Why?" I ask plainly, numbly.

Semele turns the key, unlocking the cell door before she steps inside. It's only then that I notice something bulging out of the pocket of her royal blue robe. She lowers her hand inside, pulling out an apple, a chunk of bread, and a water bottle. She extends her arm, holding it out for me. "Unless you plan to starve and dehydrate yourself. In which case, I can't control."

I look at the thick slice of bread and the apple, apparent that Zeus is also punishing me now by barely feeding me. I stare at it for a moment, exhaling softly the disdain that tries to push through the numbed barrier I've set in place.

Though by now, I shouldn't be surprised. He's neglected and abused me in other ways before.

I lean my back off the wall, standing up onto my feet before stepping towards Semele. I watch her posture, her body language. Vigilant and steady, but undefensive. I almost tilt my head and ask *no longer afraid I'm going to try to choke you out?* But I quickly remember that was before Zeus erased my memories.

Well—attempted to.

I lift my hand up, holding my palm up as I look up at Semele. "Thank you." I say plainly.

She watches me as she places the apple, bread and water into my hands, nodding once before she lowers her hands to her side.

I take the food and move myself back over to the wall, seating myself down as I immediately open the water bottle, taking a few long sips. Closing the cap back on before bringing the bread up to my lips. I take a bite, noticing the dryness of it as I chew and swallow it. Willing myself to be grateful for anything at all.

"I heard that you met Hera today."

I take another bite of the bread, finishing it off. "She didn't appear to like me very much."

Semele forces a sharp laugh as she leans against the iron bars. "Hera does not like anyone." She retorts as she crosses her arms over her chest. "And she definitely does not like *outsiders*."

I notice the emphasis that she makes on that last word, making a mental note of it. "Well then that's probably why I'm down here and not up there." I feel the ripeness of the apple, fully expected to have been given a too-ripe one. I take a bite, the sweet and tart flavor welcoming.

"You're not down here just because of her. She's, in fact, the furthest reason why you're down here."

I swallow what's in my mouth before nodding, taking another bite as I remain silent. Fixing my gaze on a random spot on the wall ahead of me.

"You're not going to ask me to tell you why you're down here in the first place?" She queries as she leans away from the cell bars.

I shrug my shoulders lazily, numbly. "It doesn't matter." I say beneath my breath.

Semele stands there silently, the brand of her gaze on the side of my face for a long moment until she steps out of the cell and closes the gate in front of her. "Someone will collect what's left tomorrow."

She turns around to walk back up the steps as I set the apple in my lap, taking another sip of water. I down the rest of what's left before setting the empty plastic bottle to the side.

After I finish my apple, I toss the core to the side before I lay myself down onto my side. Curling my hands beneath my head, and my legs up to my chest as I wander off to another place for the rest of the night.

CHAPTER 18

Reimus

I twirl my fork into slices of roasted carrots, far from enticed to eat anything on my plate but knowing I need to.

Melinoë would want me to.

But I can't help but feel overly preoccupied with the cruelty that Zeus can inflict on others, and how I can't imagine he's gracing Melinoë with the courtesy of a full meal. I would be a fool to think that he'd be that giving.

My fingers pinch the fork as those thoughts try to plague me. Wondering if she's even given the decency of food at all. Or the dignity of a bath—

"Reimus." Dimitri says gently, breaking my ruminating thoughts.

I look over at him, his gaze lowering to the fork in my hand. I look down, noticing I've been gripping it so hard that the metal has started to bend. I loosen my grip, exhaling a breath. "Sorry." I say as I fork some carrots and bring them to my mouth.

"You don't need to apologize." Nora says, seated next to Dimitri on my right side. I watch as she brings her glass of wine to her lips, taking a sip before setting it down again. "We're here for you."

I glance over at her, forcing a shy grin as I witness the concern and empathy forged on her face. "I know." I say before going back to picking through my carrots.

"The women at The Sanctuary talked after you left today." Nora says as she forks a piece of roast in her gravy, dipping it. "They want to help, want to learn to better protect themselves as mortals. I suggested maybe Hecate would be willing to teach them a bit of protection magic." She lifts her fork to her mouth. "Teach them how to shield themselves."

I fork a piece of roast into my mouth, chewing slowly as I ponder Nora's words. It does not surprise me that the women, after learning what happened with Melinoë, would feel a bit on edge with their safety. I know that the only way I can ease their apprehension is to continue protecting my people to the best of my abilities. Though a part of me feels guilty for willingly allowing Semele into Vulir, into our home without having some intuitive indication that she would've plotted kidnapping Melinoë the whole time.

The question then begs how she would've been able to get through the shield? It's energy, it's magic powered by Hades and intended to keep everyone out who has ill intentions for the people within. But if she had intentions for taking Melinoë, that her story for why she was seeking refuge was bullshit, then how did the shield not pick that up?

Better yet, how did Charon not pick that up? Being an entity that can see through people's souls. See their intentions the moment he lays his gaze on them.

I reach for my whiskey, loosening a breath as I null the wandering thoughts away. "I can talk with Hecate, see if she'd be willing to hold classes at her shop." I take a sip before setting the glass down. "I'm sure given the circumstances she'd be happy to."

I fork another helping of roast into my mouth, chewing as I glance over to the seat to my left. The hollowness lingering in the pit of my stomach expanding at the emptiness of it. The seat that Melinoë sat in when everything was right, and was just as it was supposed to be.

My gaze narrows as memories of watching her eating dinner there surface in my mind, or watching her face light up when she laughed. The absence of her presence a heavy weight on my soul.

I set my fork down, scooting my chair out as I grab my glass of whiskey.

"You barely ate." Nora says softly.

I step out of my chair, glancing down at my half-eaten plate. "I ate enough." I lift my gaze to Nora then Dimitri, forcing a weak, close-lipped grin. "Enjoy your night."

I step away from the table, making my exit out of the dining room as I walk the winding hallway up to Melinoë and I's bedchamber.

My feet heavy with each step, as if guided by some force separate from myself as my mind lulls itself into an anxious oblivion. My fingers pinching into the glass in my hand as my breathing begins to ramp up.

The dimming glow of the sunset reflecting through the hallway windows beats on the side of my face. Its presence the only thing I feel outside of the nerves inflating and taking up every space inside of me.

I make my way to the staircase, ascending up them until I reach the landing. Making my way down the hallway until I reach our bedroom, shutting the door behind me.

I rest my back against the door, my chest feeling tight and constricted.

Breathe, Reimus.

I try to slow down my breathing when the hand holding my whiskey trembles slightly, threatening to drop it entirely. I walk over to the fireplace mantel, setting it down as I prop both hands onto the lip of the wood. My thumbs gripping under the edge as I inhale and exhale slowly.

She will come home to me.

I will bring her home.

I force those words to ingrain themselves into my mind, trying desperately to replace the ones that tell me that I failed her entirely, at the possibility that she won't come home to me at all.

That I not only failed my duty to protect my people, but also to protect her. A duty I swore I'd never fail again after failing my mother and family many years ago.

I take another long inhale in, exhaling slowly when my gaze looks over to the nightstand and what lays on top of it. I stare at it for a long moment, knowing I've had no desire to write as of late. That the words I've been pouring into that black journal of mine have been full of words of yearning and admiration, fueled by the presence of my entire existence to inspire me. Yet all I can feel right now is shame and a deep loneliness.

A pain that needs to be expunged one way or another.

I step away from the mantel, going to grab my journal and pen and seat myself on the lounge chair beside the simmering fire. I flip open the journal until I land on a blank page, staring at the empty lines before me. Waiting for me to fill them, use them to pour my thoughts onto.

It takes me only moments until those words flow out of me, and my pen glides across that parchment paper with ease.

I am not a man of pride, but of indignation for my past,
For the core of my being suffocates from the crimson spilled from my mother's bravery to defend in my absence.

My inability to spare her last breath from slipping from her lungs. A moment that changed me in the most erroneously strong, and most incurable way possible.

A sorrow so infinite that I never granted myself closeness like that again, believing I would never be deserving. Allowing the agony of my mistake to haunt me, signing myself blindly away to the numbness that eroded within.

But then, just as I became deluded with the false prospects of my life, I see a glimpse of green. A shade so radiant that it would put even the most magnetizing siren to shame. Reaching itself far into the depths of my soul, quickly opening and crumbling the fortress I've hid myself behind.

Rushing me in place as they siphon every ounce of numbness from my body, jolting me awake from a slumber I fell deeply into. Those twin spheres of rich emerald melting the hardness from the inside out, releasing my gripping restraint on that softness I've shamed within.

She looks at me and everything I thought I knew vanishes. Every cold ache in my body mollifies, every horrid reminder of my past eases.

As I stare at the face of a divine blessing who owes me no kindness, no generosity of being in her presence. But the face of a woman who tells me how much I have saved her, yet has no idea the level of sureness to my purpose, and silence to my mind she brings to me.

By being by my side, by merely existing.

Though now her absence challenges those thoughts once again, as my duty to protect those I love is highlighted once more. An unfair reminder of what I could not do before, happening all over again.

I feel lost without her. I feel empty. But there is a drive that roars within me that won't allow me to harden this time.

That won't allow me to succumb to that numbness. As there is a violent determination that surrounds me, an itch that cannot be scratched until she is with me again.

As she will be safe with me again, even if it is my dying vow.

I close my journal, setting it back down on the nightstand with my pen atop of it. I lift my gaze over to the balcony doors, noticing the moonlight beginning to seep through as the day turns to night.

I stand up from the chair, approaching the double doors as I pull one open. Stepping out onto the balcony and into the cool night air.

I reach the balcony railing, looking out ahead to the village of Vulir. Counting the lights shining from people's homes, from some of the shops still open. My mind feeling a bit more at ease after unleashing everything onto paper, but still feeling restless nonetheless.

I sigh as I brush a hand over my hair, pushing it back from my face before lowering my hand back down to the cool railing again. I know that there is nothing I can do at this point, not until Makaria has learned to at least portal with her mother and Hades. So I'm left to just wait, and I cannot stand it.

If Zeus did not have such strong protective measures in place at his palace, I would've stormed Olympia by now. But after Hades telling me it would be a bloodbath, and one not in my favor, I hated to admit that he was right. That as Eiran had stated, it's essential we free Melinoë with Makaria acting as bait. That our plans to free her will turn unsuccessful if we act irrationally and impulsively.

My gaze lands on the grass below me, on the open landscape of our palace. I lift it over to the pasture far ahead, noticing Alastor grazing near Gizelle. Arion standing off to the side but still within distance to them.

I huff to myself. Arion is probably just as stubborn as his owner is. Not wanting to admit that he might actually like Alastor, but being hard-headed by keeping his distance anyway. Kind of like how Dimitri won't just admit to Nora that he has feelings for her.

A grin curves up my lips as I remember my own stubbornness when I wouldn't admit the same to Melinoë.

At the thought of her again, I look down to the landscape below. Tilting my head as my gaze roams around it, pondering over the abundance of ideas floating inside of my head. After a few long moments, a smirk curves up one side of my lips. The ideas in my head giving me the perfect remedy of how I can best spend my time while we wait.

CHAPTER 19

Melinoë

I spend the entire next day rotting down here, with no interference from Semele or Bethesda to come and grab me for more *training lessons* with Zeus. No tray of breakfast, no bucket of hot water to bathe myself in.

It's not until far later in the day that I wake up from dozing off to notice the apple core and empty water bottle are gone, replaced by a fresh water bottle and a bitten-into ham and cheese sandwich.

I see that we've evolved to me being given already eaten food now.

Nice.

I lift myself up from the ground, peering into the darkness that reaches up the steps and to the door. Seeing that whoever brought this down didn't care to stick around.

I reach over and grab the sandwich and water, devouring both before setting the empty plastic bottle near the cell door. I stand up from the ground, walking the short distance to the toilet nearby. My chains stretch just far enough for me to reach it.

At least they aren't making me piss in a bucket. Makes me wonder if they didn't want anybody having to come down here and change it out every now and then. Maybe not just for me but for anyone they've ever kept down here.

I utilize the toilet before flushing, washing my hands with the small bar of ivory soap after under a rusted sink mounted into the stone wall. Not even allowing myself to consider who else has used this same bar of soap.

I make my way back over to the familiar spot I've been rotting in for days now, seating myself back down onto the hard ground. I lean my head back up against the wall when I hear a repetitive clicking noise from a cell nearby.

I sigh to myself, closing my eyes as I try to ignore it and force myself back to sleep.

What else am I supposed to do at this point?

"They won't come back ya know."

I open my eyes, blinking at that familiar feminine voice. I turn my head to the side, looking out into the darkness but finding nothing. "I figured as much."

She laughs as that tapping noise continues. Like a shard of glass tapping against the stone floor. "That should delight you. They only bring those up to train when they feel they can be controlled." That tapping noise idly continues, filling the silence with her words. "Very few do they leave to deteriorate down here."

I turn onto my side, facing the cell door. "Who else is down here?"

"Just us. For now." She says, her husky tone insinuating the grin behind her words.

"Why are you down here?"

"I already told you. I am down here because of who I am."

I lift my hands up, lowering my gaze to them as I try to wield my powers to the surface. Something I've tried many times now since I've been down here, but are suffocated from the magic placed on them. Binding my abilities and keeping them stifled.

"Save your strength. It will go to waste down here." The tapping on the ground turns into a quick swipe across the ground. Similar to that of the tip of a sword scraping across stone.

The noise skitters a chill down my back. Does this woman have a knife with her in her cell? How are they letting her keep that?

I lower my hands back down to my lap, knitting my brows together. "How did you know? That I was trying just now to—"

"You ask a lot of questions for someone who invokes terror onto others."

My spine stiffens as my hands go numb, knowing I'm supposed to be pretending here. I shake my head. "I don't know what you're talking about."

She laughs, a sound that both invokes a sense of humor and a defiance. "You think that I cannot feel your divinity? That I cannot *smell* who you really are? Or the tears I hear you softly crying to yourself at night." She huffs out into the nothingness between us, that tapping noise beginning again.

"Anyone who was really under Zeus' compulsion would not be so sad."

I still in place as I peer down into the darkness again, making sure nobody is coming from the door at the top of the landing. I hesitate, thinking how to respond back. "Why haven't you said anything to them then? Why not use that knowledge to sell me out for your freedom?"

"Because of what I am, they will never free me." She says, that tapping noise stilling.

"What are you?" I ask tentatively.

She hesitates for a moment. "I am what I was designed to be. A carrier of bloodshed, of violence."

My eyes widened at her response. "Are…are you mortal?"

She huffs out as a hum vibrates the space between us, pausing for a moment. "Not particularly." I hear something ruffle in the darkness upon her response. The sound of the air fanning briefly before suddenly stilling.

I decide to ask a different question and let the vagueness of who—or what she is, go for the moment. "Did Zeus try to compel you?"

"Yes. Many, many years ago. I did not pretend that it worked, though. The moment he released the shackles on me in the throne room, wondering if it had worked, I only grinned in his face before taking out his guards. One by one until their bodies were severed around the throne room."

"Shit." I say aloud, both horrified and also fascinated.

"He realized the error of his mistake very quickly, that my kind is impervious to mind control. So he put me down here, and that was nearly twenty years ago."

"They don't bring food down here for you at all? No baths?" The sound of sadness eludes itself into my tone, realizing this is the first time I allowed myself to even feel a lick of it since being here.

"My kind do not feel hunger the same way you do. As it is not a hunger for food that we need to satiate, but for bloodshed. Though we can live very, very long without the urge to satisfy it."

"Wow. That's—"

"Terrifying?" She coos.

I huff out a strangled chuckle. "Yeah. Though I guess I cannot talk, seeing as who I am." I look down at my hands again, wishing that I were able to produce a lick of my shadows to the surface. Or even inflict the mind terrors onto others. Instead, I'm completely stifled.

Not only that, but I can't connect with anyone on the other side either. Assumingly because of some grand protections that Zeus has over his palace, I haven't been able to see Eiran. I haven't been able to connect to my astral body at all.

If I could, I would've traveled to see Reimus immediately. Even if he weren't able to see or hear me, it would be the first thing I'd do.

"I would not worry, Goddess of Nightmares, as I feel you have only just begun to tap into your divinity. And those gifts of yours is actually why you're down here and not up there." I hear a final tap before it stills completely. "It is why he no longer sends for you to train with him. He fears he will not be able to control you. So if there is anything you take comfort in, let it be that."

I go to open my mouth when I hear her shuffling across the floor, a quickness that a mortal could definitely not enact.

"Someone's here." She says quietly before going mute altogether.

After a few seconds I hear someone opening up the door at the top of the stairs, pushing it open before descending the twenty steps. I listen to the footsteps, how heavy or light they feel against the ground to gauge who it might be. And when I hear the heaviness to those steps, I buck up and sit straight up against the wall until they approach my cell door.

I look up to see the same man who came here the other night. Who gave me a tray of food and manifested a bucket of hot water into my cell for me to bathe in.

He looks down at me before averting his gaze to the empty water bottle near the door. He jerks his head up at me, knitting his brows together. "Who brought you this?"

My gaze roams over his face, the glossiness to his eyes and the disheveledness of his hair. I shrug my shoulders as I shake my head. "I don't know."

He groans to himself as he unlocks the gate, lowering down to grab the empty water bottle before standing up straight again. "Whatever. Get up, he wants you upstairs."

I try to keep my face neutral as I stand up slowly from the wall. "To train?"

A smug grin works its way on his lips as he approaches me, wholly unafraid of me and realizing why when I smell the liquor on his breath. "Not quite."

Nerves begin to plague me before I will myself back into a fake submission. Willing myself to appear emotionless and distant. Remembering that until I figure out an escape plan, until they come to ensure my freedom out of here, I am keeping them all safe by keeping quiet.

Remembering the threat that Zeus promised if I retaliated.

The man grabs the chains on my wrists, realizing he's already disconnected me from the wall. "Let's go." He says as he tugs me forward.

I feel myself begin to slip that control I have over my emotions, wondering if Zeus is not bringing me up there to train, then what for?

I will myself to keep my breathing steady as he yanks me out of my cell, my bare feet shuffling along the ground as we approach the steps.

I look over to my side nonchalantly, looking at the cells lined up next to mine. Trying to see if I can peer into them and find the woman—or creature that I've been talking to, or if I'm just going crazy and it's been my imagination this entire time.

When all I can see is darkness, I train my gaze forward as we climb the steps to the top.

And as we near the top of the steps, I hear the faint echo of that tapping noise again. Just twice, and just enough to drag my attention back below as the sunlight from above begins to wash over me.

A quick, but powerful reminder at what the woman said prior to the man retrieving me.

At the terrors that I can invoke out of these chains, and how I will seize the opportunity to as soon as I'm granted that moment.

CHAPTER 20

The door closes behind me as he tugs on my chains forward, bringing me deeper into the throne room when I realize we are not alone.

Drenched in the brightness of the sun shining in, I see Zeus seated on his throne at the top of the dais. A tall, bronzed man with a face of steel flanking his rear.

The man guides me to the top of the dais as Zeus keeps his gaze on me, watching and assessing. I force myself to remain emotionless, even when Zeus nudges his head over to the side. "In there."

I shift my gaze to the direction he's referring to, landing on a large iron cage. It takes everything in me to keep my eyes from not bulging out of their sockets with alarm as the man yanks me forward, guiding me into the cage before slamming it shut and locking it.

I stand there, replaced with a different cage from the one below, and clasp my hands together to keep them from trembling. Both with rage and violent anxiousness.

At the same cage that plagued me in my nightmares, the restless nights leading up to this. I stifle a shutter as I pull myself back, sinking into that numb reservoir within myself.

"Am I free to go now? I was in the middle of something." The man who brought me up here says to Zeus. His tone, even though clouded by the intoxication, rings of a slight annoyance that one can't miss.

Zeus sighs, waving his hand at him. "Yes, Dionysus. Leave us to get back to your regular routine of drinking yourself into an oblivion."

"There's nothing else to do. Besides, drinking isn't the only way I spend my time." He winks at Zeus before descending the dais.

I nearly barf right there at his reference, easy to see he must be just as vile as Zeus.

"What is your plan, Your Majesty?"

My gaze lifts to the man flanking Zeus's rear. I glance over his sun-kissed skin, over the toned muscles rippling over his arms and back. The top of his chest visible over the golden robe, his muscles just as defined and chiseled as someone would expect an immortal to be.

I glance over to the pristine golden bow and quiver strapped to his back, the fletchings encased in pure gold glinting off of the sunlight beaming into the throne room.

"The plan is to hold council." Zeus says as he looks over to me, his grin anything but welcoming. "But I thought it would be wise to finally show the people of Lothario our new *ally*."

"I hardly think the people will see her as such when she's placed in a cage." The man with the bow and arrow says, keeping his gaze trained forward.

Zeus chuckles as he waves a hand, opening the double doors to the throne room as people begin to start moving in. "Rid your worries, Apollo. They will see her place in all of this just fine."

In other words, he means to show off me being a weak goddess in front of his people. A way for him to not only see if I'm truly compliant or not, but also as a way to show his people the control he has over others.

To instill fear into them that he cannot ever be challenged.

I keep myself from clenching my jaw, knowing that his gaze has moved to me. Gauging my response and would be able to see the tick in my jaw had I not forced myself to keep my jaw and body relaxed.

I keep my gaze straight ahead as I try not to think about the cage around me, about the public humiliation that he's enacting on me right now. I forget about the chains around my wrists and ankles, and how badly I want to let myself cry at the disgrace of it all.

Knowing that I have not had a bath since the day before, knowing that my unkemptness in my tangled hair also displays a level of weakness to the people moving closer into the throne room.

I keep my body still as I look over to Zeus, desperate to get his gaze off of me so I say, "Honored to be able to join you for council, Your Majesty." I bend at the waist, bowing before standing up right again.

Zeus huffs out a quiet noise before turning his gaze back onto his people.

And as they all file in, all of their gazes shoot to me. Though none of them dare say a word. None of them yell out the outrage for keeping a woman prisoner in a cell, set out on a sadistic, public display.

No one says a single word and I watch as they all quickly avert their gazes, as Zeus begins council.

⌒

Thirty minutes into council and I finally lowered myself to the ground, my back leaned up against the cage bars as I sat myself down. Waiting for as long as I could until the soles of my feet ached too greatly from standing on the metal platform.

Fully expecting Zeus to order me to remain standing once I moved to the ground, but he didn't even look my way. I was surprised by this initially, expecting him to see it as a display of disrespect and would direct too many gazes my way.

Until I realized that his silence at my needing to sit down was more from satisfaction than anything. Realizing that me needing to sit down only further shows my level of weakness to the people before us, further boosting his power-hungry ego.

That understanding would've normally halted me from seating myself altogether, choosing to stand up despite my feet hurting and my back aching. Choosing to defy him in any way that I could without outright doing it, without being vocal about it.

But none of that matters as the façade I've been masquerading is plaguing my body and mind in ways that I cannot shake. So if this shows him I'm weak, then so be it.

I can't begin to care right now. Not without breaking down.

I watch as an older man comes to the bottom of the dais, his dark brown hair turning grey in some sections. I watch as he keeps his gaze focused on Zeus, evident that he's forcing himself not to stray his gaze away to what lies in the cage next to him.

He bows at the waist, his hands folded in front of his beige pants. "Your Majesty," He begins, slowly standing himself up straight again. "I wish to bring a concern to your attention." His voice calm aside from the slight tremble lingering in his words. His head bowed just slightly, as if fearing how Zeus will react to his plea.

Zeus narrows his gaze onto the man. "State your concern, Thomas." He says plainly. No hint of concern or empathy present in his tone, only the sound of boredom and disinterest.

Thomas nervously nods his head as he lifts his gaze back up to Zeus. He unfolds his hands, bringing them up closer to his chest and placing them in a praying position. "Your Majesty, our crops are dying. We haven't had rain in weeks and could risk losing much of our source of food." He says tentatively, pausing before resuming again. "My hope, Your Majesty, is that you could allow for a day of rain to be bestowed upon Lothario and Olympia? I—"

"If you water them regularly then they will be fine, Thomas. This does not sound like a concern that has any direct reflection of my duty as your King." Zeus cuts in, his index finger tapping along the armrest of his golden seat. His golden laurel wreath crown with spikes sticking upwards fixed on the top of his head, above his bright blonde hair.

I watch as Thomas fidgets with his fingers, a nervousness ensuing in his energy. "My apologies, Your Majesty. I meant no offense to your position of power or to come off as someone challenging it." He moves his hands up, his palms facing towards Zeus for a moment before lowering them back down to his sides. He takes a step forward, the strap around his ankle of his sandals frayed and tearing at the seams.

I observe his clothing in greater detail. Beige linen pants suitable for the warm weather, but the trim at his ankles stained a darker hue. As if after time and time again of wearing them in the fields, they began to stain no matter how many times he washed them.

As if he could not afford to buy himself a new pair.

The cream colored, short-sleeved shirt doing little to hide the thinning of his skin beneath. A sadness pulls at my heart, at the bravery of him to come forward to The King of Olympia, to express his concerns and be treated with such little regard.

"I only wished to bring it to your attention since you have the ability to grant a change in the weather." I watch him work on a swallow. "I know your fondness for summer heat, Your Majesty. But if you would be so gracious as to allow for one day of rain, it would help tremendously as we wouldn't have to worry about the great possibility of losing some of our food sources. Most of us own acres of land, and it proves to be nearly impossible to water them ourselves—"

"I've heard enough." Zeus rings out, his voice carrying throughout the throne room as everyone goes still. Even Thomas, whose lips close shut and his eyes go wide-eyed.

Zeus's chest sinks as he sighs, tilting his head as he looks down at Thomas. "I hear and understand your complaints, Thomas. But it appears others are managing just fine without the rain. So I'd advise you to reconsider how you grow your crops, and come up with a different solution."

Fury threatens to send me into a blind rage as I sit there and am forced to push it all down. I force myself to maintain my breathing as I watch the hope in Thomas' face burn out, a lick of his own fury gracing his face before he too, shoves it all down. After a long moment, he nods his head. "Yes, Your Majesty. I will do my due diligence to figure something out. Thank you for hearing my plea." He turns slowly on his heels and walks back into the crowd of people standing, his shoulders slumped forward in defeat.

My gaze roams over a few other faces, mostly men who share the same defeat on their faces before smoothing their expressions into neutrality. My heart sinks lower in my chest for Thomas as, regardless of being turned down on a very reasonable concern, he was still the only brave one to come forward and take a stand at the crops dying.

And his courage for that alone, should be commemorated rather than dismissed. And if it weren't for my tight grasp on my emotions right now, that alone would send me into a blind outrage.

My gaze turns once more to Thomas and we lock gazes, finding he finally lifted his gaze to the woman in the cage. We stare at one another for a brief moment before he looks away, training his gaze forward again.

"Does anyone have anything else to share before we end council for today?" Zeus asks the small crowd of people standing before him. I'd say roughly fifty townspeople who mostly just came to be in attendance, while only a few of them came forward to speak to Zeus.

The few others prior to Thomas coming forward to mainly present offerings of their gratitude to Zeus. Presenting him things such as knit robes, home-made beer, and wine. I wanted to barf each time they came, wondering why anyone in their right mind would give an offering to a ruler who loudly doesn't give a shit about his people.

"At your silence I will take that as council has concluded. You may all be excused." Zeus says, nodding to the people of Lothario.

I watch as at the lazy flick of his wrist, the throne room entrance doors slowly push forward. Those double doors slowly swing open as people begin to file out of the room.

I sit there, watching each person, each family shuffle out of the throne room until it's just Zeus, Apollo and I left.

"Bethesda." Zeus rings out. A short moment later Bethesda comes hurrying out of the door in the wall, gaze lowered to the ground until she approaches the dais.

She lowers into a low bow. "Yes, Your Majesty?"

"Please take Melinoë back down to the dungeons." He says as he begins to stand up from his seat.

I watch as Bethesda nods her head before turning to face me, approaching the cage. I realized at that moment that when Hades slid into my mind, telling me that they would be back for me, I believed him. I trust that him, my mother, and Reimus will all come back for me.

But if I'm going to aid in my freedom, I need to play smarter and figure out what I'm working with here. How the palace is laid out, who all lives here. And I realize my opening to do that is standing just before me.

"Your Majesty," I begin as I turn to face Zeus.

He stands up from his seat, turning around to face me.

"If it would be no trouble at all, I'd like to pay my respects for staying at the palace, and show my gratitude for being here. I could help with any cleaning, and duties that need to be done around the palace." I glance over to Bethesda. "It would be a great honor to make you proud, father."

Those words tasting like hot acid on my tongue, but knowing I need to milk my fake respect for him if I'm really going to be convincing.

Bethesda halts herself from going to open the cage, nervously waiting for Zeus' response.

He stares at me for a long moment, his brows knitting together momentarily. Alarm bells ring on the inside that I just blew my cover somehow. But instead, a smug grin curves up his lips as he nods to Bethesda. "Show Melinoë to the kitchen. We made quite a mess this morning at breakfast," He turns his full gaze now to Bethesda. "You two will work there today. Refrain from showing her anywhere else at this time."

Bethesda turns around, facing Zeus as she nods. "Of course, Your Majesty." She turns around, going to unlock the cage and standing there waiting for me to approach when she does.

"Thank you, father. I won't let you down." I say before approaching the cage door, allowing Bethesda to grab my hand and escort me out.

"You will do well not to." Zeus says before descending the dais, not turning his gaze once towards me.

I reel in the disgust for myself for sucking up to him, keeping it from overwhelming me.

It's all fake.

It's all fake. Remember, this is all for your survival.

I glance over to Apollo who I find is already looking at me. His thick brows rest above stern, wide set brown eyes. A golden halo wrapped around the iris of each, giving them a vibrant glow. His short brown hair cropped close to his head, the thick curly strands resting at the top of his forehead.

His gaze pierces into mine, watching me momentarily until turning his gaze forward before he stalks down the dais.

His shoulders tucked back as he strides fluidly down the steps while Bethesda gently tugs on the chains at my wrists.

I turn my gaze to her. She forces a faint grin before guiding us down the dais, towing me by the chains on my wrists.

Hating myself for seeming so weak to Zeus, but thankful that I was able to fakely persuade him enough to let me venture to someplace other than the throne room.

To begin scoping out my surroundings, and to figure out how the hell I can get myself out of here.

CHAPTER 21

I walk with Bethesda out of the throne room, towards an open arch behind the dais. My gaze lifts to stone white pillars mounted into each side with shining gold molding trimmed at the tops and bottoms. We walk beneath the tall stone architecture, the ground transferring from polished marble to linoleum.

My gaze roams over the gleaming ivory walls, pillars molded along the walls every few feet. Flecks of gold glinting from the sunlight beaming through floor to ceiling arches. Ferns billowing out of large, golden vases. Reminding me briefly of the ferns that grew in our backyard from our home in Elzwin.

Bethesda takes me down the long hallway until we reach another large, open doorway. Unable to help my mouth from hanging open when we step into the kitchen.

A room large enough to fit one hundred people, roughly about the size of your average ballroom. The left and right side of the room mimicked the other, each with a large stainless steel fridge and two sets of double wall ovens, separated by an obscenely large island in the middle.

My gaze travels down the cream white counters, stretching all the way down to the ends of the room with slate blue countertops. The golden chandeliers above reflect off of the glossy counters.

"This is the kitchen." Bethesda says, her voice hardly above a whisper as she guides me deeper into the kitchen.

As we pass the wrap around kitchen island my gaze tracks over the finished plates of food scattered about. Leftover bits of scrambled eggs, bacon and crusts of bread left behind. I look over it all and feel my stomach growl softly as I stare at everything that was left behind. Looking at the mess that these people left behind and how little regard they have for cleaning up after themselves.

At that thought my mind surfaces on meeting Reimus, and how he would offer to clean up my plates for me when I was finished eating. How he still does that simple, kind gesture that I initially was repulsed by, that I initially hated out of my own fear of allowing someone in.

A fear that was conditioned by learning that doing everything on my own was the only way to survive. To keep myself safe. Because trusting others to be there for me was something foreign to me at that time in my life, and something that I was not yet comfortable exploring.

But now, I can't imagine what my life would've looked like had I not taken that leap. After seeing time and time again, the love and care Reimus had shown for me. Strong enough to bring those mental guards down, and never for one second giving me a reason to regret my decision to. Because I trust Reimus with my life, and know that he will not rest until I am back home with him, that I can believe that I will be freed from this temporary prison.

Even in moments when that flicker of hope seems to nearly snuff out.

Bethesda takes me to a large pantry door, letting go of my chains as she opens it. "This pantry is for us." She looks at me, lifting a lithe hand and gently waving me over.

I step closer to her, looking inside to see an abundance of cleaning supplies stored within. Everything from mopping buckets, brooms, cleaning solutions, garbage bags, you name it. Everything neatly stored inside on porcelain white shelves and a tiled floor.

"That over there," She turns around, pointing to another identical pantry on the other side of the room behind us. "That is the food pantry." She turns around, piercing her gaze onto me as she rests her hand on my shoulder. "We do not go in there." She narrows her chin slightly as her tone hovers over a charge of earnestness.

I nod my head. "Understood."

Bethesda lets go of my shoulder as she nods to venture into the pantry. I take a step forward, finding my gaze shifting over to the food pantry. Sighing internally before shifting my gaze back on Bethesda.

We step inside and she shows me the solutions she uses to clean the kitchen each day, after each meal. Shortly after she's pouring a generous amount of purple floor cleaner into an empty mop bucket before wheeling it out of the closet. "Go fill this up at one of the sinks. I'll start by clearing the dirty dishes."

I push the mop bucket out, finding a stainless steel sink nearby, one out of the other four in here. I lift the yellow bucket up into the basin, turning the faucet on as hot water pours inside.

I turn around, watching Bethesda begin clearing away the plates and dishes on the kitchen island. "Do you live here? In the palace?"

Bethesda doesn't meet my gaze and continues cleaning up. "Yes. His Majesty graces me with a room here at the expense of my tending to and keeping the palace clean. Just as the other handmaids do."

"How many of you are there?"

I watch as she clenches her jaw, sorrow splashing across her face before taking a plate to a pull-out metal waste bin from a lower cabinet. She begins quickly scraping the leftover food into the garbage. "There are three of us now." She places the plate into the neighboring sink.

I immediately think about Amalthea and wonder if she knew her well. Though I don't particularly blame my mother for reacting the way that she did, I still can't imagine that it hurt any less for Bethesda to hear that one of her own was murdered.

I wonder what my mother is thinking right now. Does she suspect that Zeus is treating me as badly as he is? And Makaria—

She has to know what is happening by now. She would've been curious and asked mother about my whereabouts. Sorrow caves my chest inward as I think about the kinds of feelings she must be experiencing about all of this—

"Melinoë, are you alright?"

I snap out of my spiral of emotions, stifling them down as I exhale slowly. I shake my head, turning around to see the water has filled up halfway already. "Yes." I turn the water off, picking the bucket up and putting it back into the container holder. "My apologies, Bethesda. I'm just…sorry for Amalthea is all." I lift my gaze up to hers.

She stares at me, something akin to angst washing over her gaze before she nods her head. "She was a great woman." She forces herself back to the kitchen island as she collects more dishes.

I push the bucket over to the side of the kitchen, making my way around the island to help clean up the remaining dishes. I go to grab the two last remaining plates, bringing them over to the porcelain sink.

Holding the plates in one hand I go to reach for the faucet with the other, the chains at my wrists tugging roughly on my skin before I halt. Looking down, realizing that just for a split moment I forgot about them entirely.

As if becoming something familiar.

Before panic can ensue internally, I feel Bethesda's hand rest along my arm. I lift my gaze up to hers, seeing understanding blossom in her gaze as she nods at the plates in my hand. "I can take care of this if you want to sweep." She gently pries the dishes out of my hand.

I nod my head, stepping away from the sink altogether as I walk back over to the handmaid's pantry, grabbing a broom from within. I start from one section of the kitchen, glancing down at my wrists once more before beginning to sweep. Working from one end of the kitchen to the other, as I keep my emotions at bay. Something that I never thought I would force myself to do again, but needing to at this moment in order to keep my sanity at bay.

To keep me from breaking entirely.

I look down at myself, then at Bethesda, as we clean the kitchen together in silence. The roaring reminder that tries to violently show me what a disgrace this is to not only myself, but also to the growth I've made thus far. Going from promising myself to never step foot inside that mental prison again, to willingly taking myself there anyhow.

It's not real.

The façade is not real. It's all fake.

I clench my jaw as I turn my back towards Bethesda, willing myself to keep the tears at bay as the thoughts ruminate within the walls of my mind. Keeping that inferno of betrayal and pain from pouring out of me, when it deserves to be freely expressed.

Reminding me of a time in my life where numbing my emotions and forcing myself to remain mute was a very real reality for me. A part of my life I never, ever wanted to relive again.

This is just temporary. This is not our life now, Melinoë.

I repeat those words to myself over and over again as I place the broom back into the closet as Bethesda finishes wiping down the counters. No playful words expressed with one another, no ambiance of joy at all. Nothing to remind me of the exuberance of life like the one I've forged with Reimus back home. Just two servants doing work for a man who is not even remotely close to deserving of it.

As I continue to repeat those words in my head over, and over, and over again. To remind myself that I just need to survive a little while longer, and then I'll never need to ever again.

This is temporary.

It's all temporary.

CHAPTER 22

Reimus

I wipe the back of my hand across my forehead. The weather is fairly pleasant today, but after hours of intensive labor it's no surprise I've broken out into a sweat.

I lift myself from the ground, standing up as I observe what I've accomplished so far. Feeling like I've hardly made a dent, knowing I still have a ways to go. But none of the labor I have ahead of myself matters when the love I have for Melinoë makes it all worth it.

I would do absolutely anything in this world to see her smile. To see her whole and happy.

I wipe my hands along my dirt covered pants, wiping the excess off when I feel someone standing behind me. At the subtle whiff of lavender I know who I'll turn around to see standing before me.

I nod my head at her. "Good evening, Queen Persephone."

She snorts as she waves a hand. "Please, you may address me as Persephone."

I nod once more as I force a grin. "Understood."

She narrows her gaze to the ground beside her feet, a flat layer of paver sand covering what used to be grass. "I believe these kinds of projects are best done in spring, don't you think?" Her gaze roams over the curve of the freshly dug out section, narrowing and curving away from the palace.

A low huff escapes me as I grab the shovel and spade set next to a large pile of dug out grass. "Seems like the best way I can make use of my time presently." I walk both tools to the entrance of the palace, setting them up against the exterior wall.

"It appears so." She says, slowly following me. "I wish I could bring you good news on Makaria's training, but I regretfully cannot."

I turn around to face her, keeping the defeat from showing on my face as best as I can. "Then may I ask what brings you to see me today?"

She folds her hands in front of her lap, her pale violet nails several shades lighter than her tunic. "I came to check on you. See how you've been doing these past few days." Her bright emerald eyes roam over my face.

I study her for a moment as I roll my cream-colored sleeves up, blotches of deep brown now stained into the cotton fabric. I only have myself to blame for wearing a light-colored shirt while doing yard work. "Did you come to see how I was doing, or to check and make sure I wasn't planning anything reckless?"

She blinks once. "Both."

I hear Gizelle whinny from down by the pastures, guiding my gaze over to see her looking in my direction. Her attention quickly becomes distracted, her moon white tail swishing to the side when she hears Alastor walking towards her. "I know the consequences I could impose upon Melinoë if I were to avenge her freedom on my own accord." I turn my gaze back over to Persephone. "Though that desire itches violently within me, I assure you I will stick with the plan we've set."

Persephone nods her head, taking a step forward. "I know this cannot be easy, Reimus."

A broken laugh jolts itself through my lips as I shake my head. "Nothing about this is easy." I sigh heavily as I wipe my hands over my shirt, uncaring now how dirty it is. A ruined shirt is the least of my concerns at the moment. "There is also no guarantee when Makaria will be ready—and, I cannot hold that against her. But the longer that Melinoë stays locked prisoner in there—" I turn my gaze away, looking out towards my terrain as I shake my head. "There's no telling the kind of mental damage she's forced to endure there." I turn my gaze back to Persephone, meeting those emerald eyes that identically mimic her daughter's. "The kind of damage that will follow her long after we've brought her back home."

"I know." Persephone says as she takes another step towards me.

The look on her face reminds me that Melinoë is not the only one who knows first hand the kind of mental turmoil that Zeus can inflict. The reminder of her own trauma with him causing me to release the tension I've unintentionally placed on my jaw. Smoothing my expression out.

"But she will have us all to lean onto. She will most of all have you." She says, narrowing her chin slightly as she approaches me. She gently rests a hand on my arm.

"We both know Melinoë will not be so willing to come forward with what she's endured." The anger that's been brewing within me begins to gently boil once more. "What if she retreats to bottling everything up again? What if he changes her in ways that she cannot come back from—"

The anger stirring within me begins to heighten as I clench my fists at my sides. I feel the warmth of my ire quickly wash over me, like a brand heating my arms and hands.

I watch as Persephone's gaze lowers to my arms, then my hands. Her gaze remains fixed there for a moment before she trails it back up to me, lowering her hand away from my arm. "I have no doubt that Melinoë will be tempted to bottle her feelings up when she's home. I also have no doubt that she will come back changed, as much as I don't want to admit it." A soft exhale causes her chest to sink, a mother's concern etched into her gaze. "But she only needs to see we are here for her. That we—that *you* love her, and will be ready to listen when she's willing to talk."

The warmth that was suddenly radiating in my body cools down to a regular temp, the sudden anger settling with it. I know that everything Persephone is saying is true. Melinoë just needs to see that I am by her side through it all, in any capacity she needs me to be. That she won't face the internal thoughts that taunt her, the pain that tries to deceive the strength and courageousness she's built out of her own ability to survive and keep going.

And once we get the opportunity to, we'll put down Zeus together.

I nod my head. "Thank you for checking on me. I appreciate the kindness."

Persephone gives me a faint smile, clasping her hands together as she nods. "Of course." She trains her gaze away from mine to look down at the ground behind us, at the project I've started. "You know, I could help you with some of this. If you wanted." She steps over to the edge of the paver sand I've put down so far. "Aside from being Queen of The Underworld, I am The Goddess of Spring." She lifts her gaze up to mine again, smirking.

I chuckle as I walk along the edge of the paver sand, my gaze following what I've managed to dig out so far. A twelve-foot section right outside of the palace back door, where grass once was now laid with sand before I start on placing the red brick pavers. My gaze narrows out towards where the paver sand stops at, about eleven feet away from what will now be our patio door.

I lift my gaze up to Persephone's, tilting my head slightly as the side of my lips kick up. "I was planning on planting everything on my own, but realized with all of this land to cover—" I stretch my hand out towards the open landscape that will soon become something far different. "That might take me months. Plus, with winter approaching in a few months I guess I don't have the luxury of time right now."

Persephone tilts her head, shrugging her shoulders. "You could always plant more next year."

"No." I say, shaking my head. "It has to be done before she gets home." I glance over all of the plans that I have for recreating the palace landscape. *Our* home's landscape. Everything that she brought to my attention months ago, that I only wish to bring to life for her now. "I have to be doing something now. Otherwise—" I cut myself off, not needing to explain further.

I hear Gizelle whinny again, lifting my gaze over to the pasture down the far side of the landscape. A warmth blossoming in my heart at the companion she's found in Alastor, along with a sting of anguish over the absence of mine.

"Then let me help."

I turn my attention away from Gizelle and Alastor, looking at Persephone.

"Explain to me the vision you have," She says as she lifts her hand up, her fingers pointed towards the grassy terrain. "And I'll plant anything you need. Besides, my method will be far quicker." She grins

A grin of my own curves up my lips as I nod my head, and explain everything that I have planned for mine and Melinoë's up and coming outdoor oasis.

CHAPTER 23

An hour later after I've taken it upon myself to shower and change my clothes, I shift into my drago form and do an evening security sweep above Vulir.

The setting sun casts itself like a ray of melting gold against my onyx-hued wings. Fanned out wide beside me, with the occasional brush of wind gliding over them as I soar through the open sky. My gaze tracks over every shop, every home, every walkway down below in Vulir. Scanning for any disturbances, anything out of the ordinary. I send word down the Guardian's channel to Dimitri.

All clear. Heading out towards the forest now.

I feel the subtle nudge of his energy push along the channel. No exchange of words spoken, just a silent gesture to let me know he's gotten my message.

I glide along the sky as I reach the edge of Vulir, approaching the shield before meeting the lip of the Sephyra Forest.

I gaze down below, assessing the structure of the forest, surveying for any indications of suspicious activity or wanderers taking residence here. Nothing catches my eye until I see a familiar someone looking up at me, waving me down.

I bank downwards through the treeline, shifting into my mortal form the moment I touch the ground. I take a few steps forward towards the Fae. "Everything alright, Sage?"

He looks at me with those wide voids for eyes, blinking as he huffs at me. "Yes, all is well." He says as a hint of pain still lingers in his words. The pain of losing the female Fae he was close to, the only family that he had. The stains of rich wine from every orifice jogging my memory as well, something that I still don't understand to this day. "I just wanted to tell you to let Melinoë know that she can stop by anytime. Just because I won't leave the forest, doesn't mean that I'm not accepting of company." He kicks up a half grin, the first sign of anything remotely playful lightning up his face for the first time in weeks.

My gaze tracks over him as a frown tugs on my lips. I work on a swallow as I watch the grin on his face slowly fade away as he watches the lack of amusement steal mine. "I will be sure to tell her that when she is safely back home."

Sage watches me, shaking his head slowly. "He came for her, didn't he?" More of a statement of understanding than a question.

I sigh as I nod my head. "Yes."

A look of defeat dances across Sage's face before understanding kicks in. "It is truly unfair what that girl has been through." A moment of silence stretches between us. "All that lies on her shoulders."

I suddenly hear the piercing cry of a hawk flying up above. I watch as he soars through the treeline before stooping downward and landing on a branch. He cocks his head at me, watching us.

I lower my gaze back down to Sage as he turns around and walks deeper into the forest, leaving me standing there as Melinoë's tasliman in my pocket sends me a brief pulse of energy. I rest my hand over my pant pocket, feeling the energy pulse against my hand. A quick spurt as if to greet me, or remind me.

Who knows.

I shift back into my drago form, banking upwards through the trees and continue my security sweep over the Sephyra Forest. Once I've cleared the forest and Vulir as all good, I shift back into my mortal form as I land in the village. I make my way down the cobblestone road until I approach The Raven's Claw.

I push the door open, the bells on the golden handle softly clanking against one another. I look up to see Hecate behind her counter, ringing a customer up and handing their change back. She hands them a small brown paper bag before lifting her gaze to meet theirs. "Enjoy." She says, winking at the woman.

The woman—Stella, nods her head before turning away from the counter. When she meets my gaze she says, "Good evening, Reimus."

"Hello, Stella." I say before approaching the counter.

As Stella walks out of the shop Hecate turns her gaze to me. "Come to pay me another visit?"

"Yes. Though I had something I wanted to discuss with you as well."

Hecate nods. "Of course." She steps around from behind her counter, standing in front of me.

"The women at The Sanctuary know now that Melinoë is...*away*." I work on a swallow, smothering the sting of despair that follows. "Since then they've had some concerns. Something I expected once they were revealed the truth of what occurred. Some wonder what they can do to better protect themselves in the event that they should need to."

She tilts her head slightly, placing her hands behind her back.

"Some of them have expressed a willingness to learn some protection magic, even how to energetically shield themselves, if you'd be willing to teach them."

Hecate looks at me for a long moment before fixing a grin on her face. "I'd be pleased to. I can set some time aside the day after tomorrow in the afternoon"

I nod. "That would be perfect. Thank you, Hecate. For everything."

She nods. "You're welcome, dear. Tell the girls to plan to spend a couple of hours here, so I can make sure everyone leaves here having a clear understanding of my teachings."

"I'm sure they will be fine with that. Would you mind if I joined as well?"

"Certainly not. Everyone should learn a little magic, even those who aren't fully mortal." She grins as she turns to walk towards her back room, stepping through the beads hanging from the top of the doorframe.

I follow behind her as my hand parts those beads aside, slipping inside the room. "I can't say that I am familiar with the inner workings of spell casting."

"There is far more to being a sorceress—or sorcerer, than just casting spells." She chuckles as she turns back around to face me, a hand lifting with her palm facing the ceiling. "For starters, there is shielding."

A second later materials appear on her work table. This time with only a large cast iron bowl and a white pillar candle. The flame high and steady.

"And there's scrying. Which is what I've been doing several times today as you can see." Her hand moves to point towards the table.

"Can I ask what you're scrying for?"

Her chest raises then sinks again as she lets out a sigh. "To better understand Zeus' wards."

I look up at her.

"If I can study the structure of his wards, then I can gain insight and confidence to know exactly what I'm working with when the time comes."

"I thought his wards were impenetrable?"

"Technically, yes. But when you've done magic for as long as I have, you know that there is always a loophole to slipping your way through someone's wards. No matter how powerful they are."

I nod my head. "And what about the astral realm? Are the wards effective there as well?"

She nods her head. "Unfortunately, yes. I attempted to break through them the day you all went to Olympia. I was unable to get past the exterior of Zeus' palace."

The possibility of us not finding that loophole, and therefore having the way in to get Melinoë out surfaces in my mind. I can't imagine Zeus would have made it easy for anyone to get in, especially now that he has Melinoë under his watchful eye. Knowing that not even someone like Eiran can get close to Melinoë makes me sad.

"We will figure it out." Hecate says gently.

I lift my gaze back up to hers, nodding. "I know." I take a step back, shoving my hands in my pant pockets. "I should probably be getting back home. Aven will worry if I'm late for dinner."

Hecate nods her head. "I'll see you the day after tomorrow then."

I nod. "I'll be here."

I turn to make my way out of Hecate's shop, choosing to walk the whole way back to the palace instead of shifting and flying back. The cool gentle wind the only thing I feel aside from the restlessness eating away at me internally.

CHAPTER 24

Melinoë

The next morning I wake up to the sound of the door opening, followed by the heavy footsteps of someone walking down the stairs.

I lift my head from the ground, scooting myself up as tiredness quickly evades me. Having barely slept through the night to begin with anyway.

I lean myself up against the wall, my head turned towards the gate as I wait to see who approaches it. A few long moments later, I see Dionysus standing in front of it. His bloodshot eyes squinting against the gentle roar of the torch above, his hair as much a disheveled mess as the clothes on his back. "Get up." He mumbles.

He opens the door as I tentatively stand up on my feet, keeping my back tucked up against the wall. "What are you doing?"

He turns to close the gate behind him, locking himself in essentially. A moment later, I gasp as that same large bucket appears a few feet beside me. I whip my gaze back to him.

"Yeah, yeah. I know. You're not bathing with me in here, trust me I don't want to be here any more than you do." He waves a hand at me as he tucks the key back into his pocket. "But I'm told you need a bath. So here we are." He waves both of his hands out.

I watch him for a moment, my gaze jolting back over to the bucket as I can hear the water filling inside of it. As if an invisible faucet is hanging over it and pouring hot water into the bucket. I watch as warm steam rises from the metal before I turn my gaze back over.

Dionysus takes another step towards me, causing me to back up further into the wall. Whether it's the fact that I wasn't expecting to see anyone at all today and I'm caught by surprise, or of how he spoke about being in the middle of *something* yesterday that makes me think he isn't very respectful of women.

The type of man I've dealt with before, both in the Sephyra Forest and in the astral realm when that vile bastard tried to have his way with me.

A cold sweat trickles down my back as I step away from the wall, inching myself as far away as possible from him.

Dionysus stops, cementing himself in place as his eyes open themselves up wider. No longer droopy and studying the panic that's eroding all over my body.

He holds his hands up, a sincereness crawling over his face and replacing the hungover haze. "I'm going to just unlock those for you," He says, gesturing to the chains at my risks and my ankles. "I'll step out, lock the door and wait at the top of the stairs until you're done."

"How do I know you can't see me from up there?" I sneer at him.

He blinks, then nods his head. "I can't. But if you'd prefer, I can throw the key over to you after I've locked you in, and I'll wait here where you can see me. Like last time."

My gaze roams over him, studying him. His hands relaxed as they hover above his shoulders. His expression void of any aggression or hostility. After a few moments, I nod my head quickly before stepping closer to him.

He lowers his hands as one calmly pulls the key out of his pocket. "I'm going to unlock these now. Is that okay?"

Confusion settles within me for a moment at the display of genuinity that he's so rarely shown since I've been here. I nod my head.

He lowers the key then to my wrists, unlocking those before moving to my ankles. Once the chains are off, he stands up again and steps back to the door.

He opens it, slipping through it until he's on the other side. He locks the gate, then tosses the key over to me, watching as it lands near the bucket of hot water. "When you're done just toss it back over."

I nod my head.

"Don't get any ideas about escaping either. I promise you'd never make it past me." He turns his back towards me before lowering himself down to the ground, seating himself up against the iron bars.

"I would say in your state that might be a little hard to believe." I lift my hands to my dress, lowering it down my body before quickly settling myself inside the tub. My back facing the wall this time, purposefully to keep a close eye on him.

He chuckles. "Just because I reek of alcohol does not mean I am impaired. I thought you'd understand this of immortals by now."

I grab the soap and begin washing my hair, gently lathering it through the dark strands. I gently weave my fingers through the angry tangles snarled at my ends, freeing them as best as I'm able to. "Why do you drink so much?"

I notice the way he shrugs his shoulders. Lazily, uncaringly. "It has a great way of dulling the noise in here." He lifts an index finger to the side of his head.

I set the soap down, lathering what's in my hands into my scalp. The citrus scent is overpowering, but I'll take it nonetheless. "What could you possibly be trying to drone out when you live the way you do?"

He sits there silent for a long time, not speaking again until I've begun to rinse out my hair. "He has you down here. Why?"

It's probably a great thing that he's facing away from me so he's unable to see the shock roil through me momentarily. The way he talked to Zeus I would've imagined he'd known exactly why I was down here. Or at the very least, would know who I am to Zeus. But either he's baiting me to see if I slip up with my act to pretend like Zeus' compulsion worked on me, or he's genuinely asking. "This is where His Majesty puts me. That is all I know."

A sharp laugh escapes him, followed by a long audible yawn. "Yeah, people do have a funny way of obeying him without any inclination to understand why."

I knit my brows together, confused by his statement. I open my mouth to ask him what he means by that, but instead opt with something else. "Do many of his people do that? Obey blindly?"

"Pretty much."

I rinse the rest of the soap out of my hair, tossing it behind my back as I begin washing my body. Starting with my arms and working down. "And what is your relationship to His Majesty?"

Dionysus doesn't answer for a long time, not until I've finished washing my body and have begun to rinse myself clean. "I'm whatever he needs me to be so I can get what I want."

My brows knit together. "And what is that?" I ask as I rinse the water over my shoulders and under my pits.

He leans his head up against the bars, crossing his legs out in front of him at the ankles. "Just let me know when you're finished."

I stare at the back of his head a little longer before I finish washing and rinsing my body. Whatever he needs him to be? What does that even mean?

I figured that he must've been a close ally to Zeus, especially if he lives here in the palace. But his vagueness now makes all of that seem…uncertain.

I finish rinsing in silence, rinsing my hair once more before going to get up from the bucket. I halt, remembering

I, of course, don't have any clean clothing. When I go to open my mouth to protest not wanting to put my dirty clothes back on, I look over to see a towel and pile of clean clothes laid out for me. A pair of pale gold breeches and a matching tunic.

I grab the towel, standing up from the bucket as I wrap it around myself. I take in the softness of the fabric, the ivory cotton snug like a warm hug around my body. A warmth that is hard to feel here.

I quickly dry myself off, drying off my hair before pulling on the breeches and tunic. "Did you get these clothes from someplace in the palace or just materialize it out of mental will?"

He chuckles. "They were extras that I was told to give to you."

I smooth the tunic over my chest, looking up at him. "From who?"

"Are you done yet?"

I sigh. "Yes, I'm finished. You can turn around now."

He hesitates for a moment before slowly standing himself up from the ground. He turns around, meeting my gaze before nudging towards the floor. "The key."

I kneel down, grabbing it and then tossing it towards him. I watch as he lowers a hand at the exact moment it lands in it.

He turns the key into the lock, opening the door as I move away from the bucket. The door creaks ajar as he steps inside. "Hold your wrists out."

I nod, lifting my hands and doing what he says. As he lowers himself down to grab the key I glance over past him, the rest of the dungeon dark but the faint illumination of the stairs visible.

That's when I make my move.

I dash out of his vicinity, flooring it out of the cell as I race up the steps. Before I can make it to the top to yank the door open, I feel a hand at the back of my head, yanking me down by my hair.

Suddenly I'm tumbling down all twenty steps, no amount of immortality could stifle the cracks of pain I feel every step down.

I land on the bottom as that same hand grabs my hair, yanking my head up as a knee slams itself into my back. I begin to feel like my insides are expanding in a way that's unfamiliar. As if being suffocated from the inside out. And it has nothing to do with the pressure of his knee lodged into my back.

"For someone who speaks so properly of the King you sure were eager to escape."

"Please—" My words cut off as he digs his knee deeper into my spine. I cry out in pain as he yanks my head up further, painfully bending my back deeper.

I took what seemed like my only opportunity of freeing myself from here and I royally fucked up. Because not only did I not succeed, but now the question begs of why I would flee when I have shown to be so subservient to Zeus while I've been here.

"You're lucky it's just a knee to the back."

That suffocating feeling begins to grow, my hand coming to my throat as a drowning sensation overwhelms me. Like liquid pooling in my throat, building until pressure causes my eyes to bulge wide.

Is this part of his gift? His power? That he can suffocate people with—

"I could do so much worse." He says wickedly before yanking me up onto my feet.

That drowning sensation vanishes suddenly, my arms trembling in the after effect of it as he drags me back to the cell. I cough violently, catching my breath as my feet stumble over themselves at the quickness of his pace as he pushes me into the cell.

I almost stumble to the ground but keep myself standing up, quickly turning around towards him. My lips trembling as worry erodes every crevice in my body.

Stilling me in place in frozen fear at what will happen next.

"Please, don't—"

"Save your pity for someone else." Dionysus says as he grabs the chains from the ground before clasping them to my wrists. He snaps them shut, the sharp sound of the iron clicking jolting me in place. He lowers himself down, snapping shut the ones around my ankles.

He stands up, looking me dead in my eyes for a moment. Panic eroding me from the inside out, the first time I've allowed it to actually take shape and surface after days of keeping it shoved down.

And just when I think he's going to say something, he turns around, locking the gate before walking his way up the steps. My arms tremble in front of me as I hear the door open up, a ray of sunlight from above shining down the steps until it reaches the bottom.

My body begins to tremble, subtly until it turns violent as everything rushes to the surface at once.

The door at the top of the landing shuts as my breathing quickens abruptly, the air in my lungs quickly passing in and out of me. I bring my hands up to my mouth, my fingers trembling against my lips as I move over to the wall where the iron mounts connected to my chains are.

I place my palm on the wall, my eyes widening as every emotion crashes over me.

The despair of not being with Reimus. Not having his hand to hold, or his kiss to quell the sea of storms raging inside of me.

The anger of trusting Semele to be a friend to me, to turning around and being manipulated by her from the start.

The cage in the throne room, the public humiliation of standing before his people. Made to look like a weak animal with no way out, no escape from his power—

My rampant breathing turns into full blown hyperventilating as I curl my fingernails into the stone wall, desperate to feel something to ground me. Absolutely anything to dull the overwhelming tightness exploding in my chest.

"Melinoë."

Even at the sound of that familiar, feminine voice, I cannot stop the panic attack from taking over. The trauma of everything that has happened makes its violent appearance. Tears stream to my eyes and I choke at the feeling of wetness gracing my eyes. Something that I've denied myself of doing since I got here. The agony of being a prisoner to a man, to my own father, causing me to cry violently as I hyperventilate harder.

"*Breathe*, Melinoë. Listen to the sound of my voice." She says.

I try to listen, I try to make it lessen but the pain suffocates me. I fall to the ground, the sound of the chains clanking down with me briefly until all that there is left is the sound of my gut wrenching agony. "I—can't." I manage to choke out. I lower my hands to the ground, pressing them into the hard surface as my head lowers. "I—"

"Listen to me, Melinoë—"

"No. I—" I lift my hands from the ground, pressing them against my cheeks as I try to steady my breathing but continue to fail to. "Can't breathe." My crying stifles as panic erodes deeper within me, the breath from my lungs feeling nonexistent.

"Melinoë, sit on your rear. Do it now." She says.

I do what she says and position myself onto my rear, my back pressed up against the stone wall.

"Now bring your knees up to your chest, and lower your head down."

I hike my knees up, my belly hurting from how hard I'm hyperventilating. I lower my head down until my forehead touches my knees.

"Now just listen to the sound of my voice. Can you do that for me? Just listen, and do as I say."

Tears stream down my face once again as I nod into my knees. "Yes."

"Breathe in." She says slowly, taking an audible breath in.

I do as she says, taking a shaky inhale in and quickly blowing it out.

"Try again. Breathe in, Melinoë." She takes another audible breath in.

I try it again, managing to take a slightly deeper, shaky breath in and holding it.

"Now release." She says before audibly exhaling.

I exhale it out of me, feeling my tremors still racking my body but my breathing settling to some degree. She repeats the same thing over, and over, and over again until my breathing has finally regained normalcy.

"Good. That's good work, Melinoë. Just keep breathing. Just like that."

I continue focusing on my breathing, wishing Reimus were here to comfort me right now. Wishing I could feel his arms wrapping around me, snug in his embrace.

I feel my heart crack open as tears stream down my cheeks. "I miss him." I say out loud, pain lancing my words.

She remains silent for a moment before she speaks. "I know." She says softly, quietly.

As I sit there in the darkness, aside from the glow of the torch mounted on the wall above me, I continue my steady breathing. My head feeling light and fuzzy as tears stream down my cheeks.

"Let that pain of what he's done to you not break you, but *mold* you, Melinoë."

I sniffle as I wipe the dampness from beneath my eyes. The puffiness that I know is there if I were to look in a mirror right now. I turn to my side as I lay myself down, my hands coming up to my chest as I hike my knees up with them.

"Let it mold you into a weapon that he'll never be able to tame."

I let her words glide through the haziness of my mind, the worry of what will happen when Dionysus tells Zeus what happened today taking ownership in my mind. Will Zeus know then that his compulsion didn't work and will he retaliate against the people of Elzwin?

Against the people of Vulir? Or worse—

Against Reimus.

That worry clenches itself deep within my stomach as I try to force myself to sleep, but fail in my attempt to do so. As for the rest of the night, I lay there awake. Immobilized by what's to come the next time that door opens again.

CHAPTER 25

Reimus

The sharp tip of a curved dagger parts my flesh in two as the man above me burrows it deep beneath my skin. My hand gripped around his, forcing him off of me before he succeeded in what he's after. Knowing that only few know how to truly end a drago's life.

Severing their heart right from their chest.

The man stumbles backwards as I thrust him off of me, the blade piercing my chest withdrawing out of my skin. A trail of blood runs down in its absence as I jolt up onto my feet, advancing on one of the many soldiers who have come to wreak havoc on our home.

They came in the dead of night, thinking that it would aid them in the element of surprise. But little do they understand you can't outsmart the Draghi in their natural habitat. With senses that pick up scents from miles away, hearing that can pick up on the softest of whispers. Though no amount of surprise would have made any difference for them. For months we've known that they were coming.

We knew to be prepared.

He tries swiping the dagger across my chest, missing as I quickly parry backwards. A smirk crawls up my face as I hone in on the man before me. "An unwise attempt."

Knowing he'd try to swipe at me again, I step to the side and swipe my arm up as I block the blow to my neck. Forcing his arm down I parry with my other hand, hooking it over his wrist as I slam my other arm over his. Disarming the dagger in his hands.

I catch it and thrust it through his neck, his eyes bulging out as his hands come up to try and pry it out when I drive it deeper into his throat. I let go of the blade as I kick him down, his hands still wrapped around the blade as blood pours from his lips. A moment later, his hands fall limp next to his body.

As I rush out of there the scenery around me begins to dissolve. Swatches of evergreen and walnut melt from the memory around me, turning into an abyss of never-ending darkness.

"Remember."

The faint echo of that word bounces in the small space around me, slithering in and out of the darkness as if to taunt me. A word that has plagued my dreams before, goading me to remember the worst day of my life. Whose voice is always by the same woman that this nightmare centers around.

My mother.

"Remember, Reimus. It is time."

"No—" I call out into the nothingness. "Mother, why must I remember that day? Why must you make me remember?"

I bring my hands up to my head as violent screams fill the space around me now. The sound of my people being killed off for being themselves, for being free in a world that tries to control those they cannot tame.

"We must do it, Eileen. It's the only way."

My hands lower from my face as the sound of my father talking to my mother travels towards me. I look up to where his voice originated from, and follow it into oblivion through the darkness.

"You said it yourself. After what he told us, it's what we've been preparing for—"

"I know it is, Callen." My mother seethes at my father. An edge to her voice that she never used towards my father when they were alive.

I try walking closer towards where their voices are coming from, desperate to see a glimpse of them one more time. But all I continue to see ahead of me is bleak darkness.

Suddenly I feel myself propel backwards, back to where I was standing as my feet cement themselves to the ground.

"He will remember." My father says to my mother, a caress to his voice. A gentleness he always had with my mother, a love he had for her that could surmount the thickest of storms. The grandest of upheaval. "The fate will lie in his hands when the time comes."

I try lifting my foot up when suddenly something begins anchoring me down below the ground. Lower and lower until I'm suffocating beneath the surface, a void of nothingness swallowing me whole—

I jolt upright in bed, breathing heavily as sweat beads above my brow. I look around the room as moonlight glows through my balcony doors, casting itself onto my bed. I lean myself up against the headboard as I brush my hair back, trying to shove away the eeriness of the familiar nightmare.

I instinctively look over to my right, knowing I'd see an empty spot next to me but unable to help myself anyway. The midnight black sheets encased over pillows where Melinoë's head would be lying if she were here with me now.

I sigh as I lay myself back onto my side, pulling the pillow close to my face as I inhale deeply.

The scent of her still lingering on the silk material.

I bring the pillow close to my chest, hugging it close to me as I close my eyes and force myself to calm.

Allowing the scent of her to lull me back to sleep.

⁓

I wake up sometime later to the smell of bacon wafting towards my nose. Or rather what my drago senses can pick up from downstairs. After twenty minutes of lying there I decided to finally get up, making my way to the closet to throw on a white shirt and black sweatpants.

I make my way downstairs where the faint trace of voices creep closer towards me.

"I will have as much bacon as I'd like, thank you very much you ass." Nora says presumingly to Dimitri as the scent of him lingers towards me.

"When did I ever say you couldn't have bacon?"

"When you told me I already had seven pieces on my plate." The sound of her taking a bite follows.

My feet pad along the hallway floor as I get closer to the dining room.

"How is that me saying you can't have bacon? That's just me saying *'hey, you already have seven pieces there. Why not make sure you save some for the rest of us'*?"

I make my way to the dining room entrance as I enter the room. "I'm sure there is plenty to go around." I say, smirking at Nora.

She lifts her hand as a wide grin plasters her face. Seated to Dimitri's right, she leans her head closer towards him in a mocking stance. "Thank you." She says enthusiastically as she lowers her hand.

Dimitri lifts both of his hands up as an expression of slight annoyance covers it. He sighs audibly. "You are going to give me a brain aneurysm one of these days, woman."

"Is that even possible? You know, because of what you both are?" Nora asks as she looks up to me now.

I take my seat at the head of the table, an empty plate set out in front of me with a cup of coffee. I look towards the whiskey and decanter glass before me as well, something I'm sure Aven set out for me in case coffee wasn't strong enough for me to start my day. I almost reach for it, but realize it wouldn't be wise to start my day off with booze—even if just an earful, with how I plan to spend my day. So, I settle with the coffee.

For now.

"Given our strength and our ability to heal quickly, it would be pretty rare for us to experience an aneurysm. But it's not impossible." I bring the coffee to my lips as I take a sip, letting the warmth soothe me as my attention begs to look over at Melinoë's empty seat. But there's no use in torturing myself with it when I already know the plainly obvious.

"Interesting." Nora looks over at Dimitri as a grin curves up her lips.

He stares at her as he reaches for his coffee mug. "Don't get any bright ideas, Nora." His voice dipping an octave as he smirks at her.

I watch as Nora's cheeks pinken slightly, having the complete opposite reaction to what Dimitri probably thought it would. I force the chuckle that threatens to escape my lips back down my throat.

She turns her gaze back down to her food as she pushes her fork through her scrambled eggs. She takes a bite, chewing silently this time.

"I spoke with Hecate yesterday." I say as I fill my plate with scrambled eggs, smoked sausage and an English muffin.

She looks up at me. "What did she say?"

I set my plate down, grabbing a fork. "She said she'd be happy to teach you all some protection magic and how to shield." I jab it into my small pile of scrambled eggs, taking a bite.

"That's great. The girls will be happy to hear that."

I nod. "She's agreed to have you all meet her at her shop tomorrow afternoon. She said plan to spend a few hours going over the material. I've agreed to join as well."

"I thought the Draghi already knew how to shield?"

"We do." I set my fork down, picking up the English muffin. "I've still agreed to go anyway. Besides, I don't know much about magic so it may prove to be beneficial for me to learn."

"Oh, I'm excited to learn. I mean yeah, I can heal people, but if I could also perform protection spells? Or learn how to perform other kinds of spells? Oh, I'm in." Nora says.

Aven walks into the dining room and approaches the dining table. "Goodmorning, My Lord." A smile on his face.

I nod towards him. "Goodmorning, Aven. Food is delicious as always."

Aven brings a hand up to his chest, right over his heart. "Oh, you are too kind to me Reimus." A soft laugh escapes his lips as he glances over to the door. "I see we have taken to starting a project out in the yard."

Nora looks over to me. "What project?" Interest evident in her tone.

I look up at her, smirking. "It's a surprise."

Nora gasps as she looks over to Aven. "Aven, you must tell me. I am not fond of surprises as I am nosey."

Aven walks over to her side of the table, leaning over to grab her mug. A rim of dark mocha stained inside the white ceramic where coffee once was. "I know you are terrible with surprises." He leans closer. "So am I."

They chuckle amongst each other as he pours more coffee into her mug.

Nora lifts a hand. "That's perfect. Otherwise I'll be jittery for the rest of the day."

Aven lowers her mug down as well as the pot of coffee back into the middle on the table. "We wouldn't want that now."

"The jitters should be the least of your worries. It's that mouth that won't stop yapping once you've had too much coffee—"

Nora gasps as she swats at Dimitri's arm. "Don't be a rude ass now. Besides, you love it when I yap to you." She wiggles her eyebrows.

Dimitri huffs at her as a grin sneaks up onto his lips. I watch as the both of them continue their morning conversation as we all eat breakfast together.

Eager to get outside and get back to working on my project.

CHAPTER 26

Melinoë

My head jerks upright as I awake from a fitful sleep. The worry of what today will bring has gnawed its way through the tether of sanity I've been desperately trying to cling onto. The agony of waiting to see how Zeus will retaliate against those I love, or even myself, once he learns from Dionysus what happened last night.

I turn my head towards the prison bars, the darkness through them to greet me once again. The nothingness of it begins to feel similarly to how I feel inside the longer I remain trapped in here.

My gaze lowers to the ground, noticing no scraps of food have been left out for me this morning. No fresh bottle of water, nothing.

A nervousness begins to expand within me as the reality of Zeus' knowing becomes apparent. He must know that I tried to escape now, otherwise why wouldn't there be any food for me this morning?

Or is it even morning right now? What if it's still night? I've been down here, submerged in the darkness with no window of light to guide me to what time of the day it is. Only ever given an inclination when I've been brought up to the throne room for training or council.

He's going to keep me down here to starve, and that should bother me more than it does. But I'm presently too overly consumed with what will happen outside of these palace walls.

I hear the opening of the door above the steps and I shoot upright onto my feet. I listen to what kind of footsteps will be coming down those concrete steps. Steps that sound similar to Semele's yet lighter. Almost too quiet for me to focus on.

The light from above filtering down here tells me I was right initially. It's morning. Before I can think of anything else, the steps stop in front of my cell door.

Bethesda stands in front of the door with a key in her hand. Her soft, tired face glances up at me. Nodding once as she inserts the lock. "It's time for afternoon clean up."

Afternoon? I thought for sure it was morning, knowing that Zeus loves to inflict punishment onto people. Knowing that once he found out about me attempting to flee he would've seized the opportunity to interrogate me immediately.

I look at Bethesda. "Who sent you to retrieve me?"

She looks up at me, almost confused by my question as she unlocks the door. "Why, His Majesty of course."

I blink once at her, confused at why he would be allowing me to walk around the palace. Even if I'm still in handcuffs, even if I'm only allowed to clean the kitchen. Why wouldn't he keep me down here to rot as punishment if not to interrogate me?

I blink again, remaining silent as Bethesda steps inside the cell. Her lithe hand reaches up to grab my chains, unlocking the connecting ones from the wall on both my wrists and ankles. When she stands up right again, she gives me a ghost of a grin as she nods towards the steps. "Come. He'll be upset if we run behind."

I follow Bethesda up the steps and into the throne room. I immediately look up towards the dais, seeing it empty. Seeing the entire throne room empty.

Oh gods, what if he's out there causing havoc on the people of Elzwin? Or Vulir?

A nervous sweat begins to dampen my hands and the back of my neck as Bethesda guides us to the kitchen. As we enter I see similarly what I witnessed yesterday.

A kitchen island with dirty dishes as if just because these people are gods that they suddenly don't know how to clean up after themselves.

She lets go of the iron handcuffs as she glances back at me. "Same as yesterday. You sweep and mop, I'll clean the counters and dishes."

My mind goes blank as I try to focus on Bethesda right in front of me, but cannot seem to pull myself back from the worry of the what ifs. I nod once to her, silent as I walk over to the handmaids pantry to retrieve the broom.

I close the pantry door behind me, beginning at one corner of the kitchen as I sweep my way around the room. After I sweep all the crumbs and debris into a dustpan, dumping it into the garbage, I pull the mop bucket out and begin filling water into it. As I set the bucket back into the holder I hear footsteps approach from down the hall.

Bethesda quickly glances over at me, narrowing her chin. "Follow my lead and she won't punish you for disrespect."

She sets the dishes in her hands back down onto the counter, throwing a glare my way to follow her every move.

She places her hands behind her back, straightening her back and looking straight ahead towards the kitchen door. I go to follow her same gesture when the chains on my wrists prevent me from moving them to my back. I decide to keep them in front of my lap, straightening my back and looking ahead.

Shortly after Hera walks into the kitchen, clad in a beautiful ivory dress. Her hair pinned back as it falls down the middle of her back.

"Good afternoon, Your Majesty." Bethesda says as she bows.

I find myself staring at Bethesda for a long moment, swiftly changing my gaze as I bow as well. "Good afternoon, Your Majesty."

When I raise myself back up my gaze meets Hera's. Her haunting gaze piercing into mine as she glares at me. As if utterly appalled by my being here.

Is she even remotely bothered by the chains around my wrists or my ankles? Is she just as bad as Zeus and completely in favor of the kind of punishments he inflicts?

She stares for a long moment until she approaches the fridge closest to her, pulling out a glass decanter of clear liquid. The sound of another set of footsteps draws my attention towards the door when a man walks in.

Dionysus.

My entire body goes ice cold as I force myself to remain neutral on the outside even though I'm panicking on the inside.

He meets my gaze before glancing over to Hera. "Afternoon, mother."

She hardly looks at him, pouring the liquid into a glass before putting the decanter back into the fridge. "Dionysus." She addresses him curtly before walking off with her glass.

Mother? He's related to the queen? But if that's the case then—

Holy fuck.

My hand spasms open as the understanding that Zeus must be his father takes shape in my mind. The memory of how casually he talked to Zeus the other day makes sense now. But it still doesn't explain why he wouldn't just come out and say that he was related to Zeus?

Does he know that I'm related to Zeus? Does he know about Makaria—

"Melinoë." Bethesda says quietly, her head turned towards me as I realize I've just been staring at Dionysus for the past few moments.

I shake myself out of my stupor, blinking before I turn away entirely and continue to fill up the mop bucket. I try my hardest not to turn around and look over my shoulder at him, to see if I can spot similarities of Zeus or Hera in him.

"I am whatever he needs me to be."

The memory of him saying that resurfaces in my mind as I lower the bucket back into the holder. A strange statement to make in regards to your father but I certainly can't blame him if Zeus treats him even partially similarly as he's treated me or Makaria.

I hear his footsteps walk over to the food pantry, pulling the door open before stepping inside of it as I wheel the bucket near the other pantry. I lower the cotton mophead into the sudsy water, dipping it a couple times before plopping the wet mop onto the floor. My chains clank together as I push the mop along the floor, a subtle yet loud reminder at the prison that I'm still in.

From the corner of my eye I see Dionysus close the pantry door and walk towards me with a granola bar in his hand. He opens the packaging up, taking a bite and I'd be lying if I said I didn't desperately want one myself.

Still not a word said yet about what happened yesterday. Or how he told Zeus and that I'll receive my punishment later. Is that why Hera was glaring at me? Did her son tell her what happened and she's furious?

My thoughts are interrupted when Dionysus walks directly over the section I just mopped, his sandals leaving faint traces of dirt in their wake. "Whoops." He says lazily, unenthusiastically through a mouthful of granola. I watch as a crumb slips from his lips, dropping right next to where his sandal print now is.

I clench my teeth together as the impulse to make a snarky remark pushes against my lips. Taking a long breath in, I try to tame the sudden ire that simmers beneath my skin, remembering that my silence is not because I'm afraid for my safety.

But for the people I love.

"Just because you reek like ass doesn't mean you need to act like one."

My head snaps up as Semele walks through the kitchen, her sapphire eyes alight on Dionysus who makes his way to the fruit bowl at the center of the kitchen island.

He reaches into it, pulling out a red apple as he pulls out a stool and seats himself down. "Nobody cares what you think, Semele." He grumbles.

I watch as her stern gaze hardens on Dionysus momentarily before shifting over to where I'm standing. Her sapphire gaze stays on mine before shifting down to my hands, her jaw clenching for a moment before she looks back over to Dionysus. Her long cinnamon brown hair pulled back into a tight bun, exposing her neck and the brief tick of her jugular vein. "Why is she up here?"

Dionysus shrugs his shoulders as he takes a bite out of the apple, leaning back into the stool. "She offered to help."

"And who gave her the okay?" She tilts her head.

Dionysus doesn't even make eye contact with her. As if he can't be bothered while eating his damn apple. As if she's just a fly on the wall, similar to how I feel every day spent here. "Who do you think?" Boredom evident in his tone.

My gaze roams over to the apple in Dionysus' hand, wishing he knew just how fortunate he is to be able to eat what he wants, when he wants. Knowing that not everyone has that privilege, and as it appears from last time Zeus held council, that if something isn't done about watering the crops, more people will have even less opportunities.

My stomach growls and I thank The Fates that it was quiet enough that only I could hear. I decide to stop torturing myself by staring at the food in his hands and train my gaze back over to Semele. Yet when I look at her I find she's already looking at me.

She stares at me for a moment longer before walking over to the fridge, opening it up and pulling out two bottles of water. She closes the fridge, walking over towards me, careful not to step in the areas I've mopped already.

She holds the water bottle out for me. "Here."

My gaze lowers to the water bottle, staring at it for a moment before leaning the mop up against a counter and reaching for it.

"He'll be pissed if he finds out." Dionysus says from his seat.

"It's just water." She says as she turns around, heading to the fruit bowl as she pulls out an apple.

Dionysus slams his hand over her wrist, stilling her as he looks at her. "She is immortal. She does not *need* to eat. Besides, she tried to escape yesterday and doesn't deserve it."

My eyes bulge out as I feel Bethesda whip her head towards me from the sink, pausing washing a dirty dish before continuing as if he didn't just say that.

Semele keeps her hand planted firmly on the apple, not letting go. "Doesn't mean that immortals don't *want* to eat or find sustenance from it. And I can only assume that you haven't told Zeus yet, otherwise she would still be in the dungeons and not up here." She says as her voice carries a particular calm edge to it.

Dionysus whips his hand off of hers. "I haven't gotten around to it yet."

Semele huffs out a chuckle, picking the apple up and holding it upright in her hand. "You mean you don't plan on telling him. We both know that while he'll be furious with her, he'll be even worse with you."

My brows knit together as I continue mopping the floor, trying not to eavesdrop but considering they're only a few feet away it's hard not to. Not to mention when Semele is saying that Dionysus hasn't told Zeus yet about my attempt. But why?

"Just because he's my father doesn't mean I care what he thinks."

Okay so the question of whether or not Zeus is actually his father has now been answered.

Semele shakes her head slowly at him. "I know you better than you think."

As Semele turns around I watch what I noticed in her voice appear on her face. A hint of sorrow splashing across her expression before she notices me watching her, quickly smoothing it out as she hands me the apple. "Just make sure you toss the core out." She points to where the trash is, hidden in a pull out cupboard.

I take the apple, my gaze roaming over her face before she turns around. Feeling presently perplexed by this act of kindness from her when she's the reason I'm here in the first place. The ire that I've felt for her in aiding Zeus in kidnapping me is still simmering beneath the fortress that I'm keeping over my emotions currently. But as I hold the apple in my hand, I'm conflicted with how to feel about her gesture.

"Thank you." I decide to say, almost cringing at myself for saying it after it slips my lips. But as I bring the apple to my mouth and take a bite, nothing else at the moment matters as I sate my hunger.

Semele makes her exit from the kitchen as I scarf down the apple. As soon as I'm finished I toss the remaining core into the garbage, wiping my hands on my breeches before continuing to mop the floor.

I catch myself looking up once to notice Dionysus looking at me. The expression in his eyes unreadable, but teetering between a lack of curiosity and disdain for what Semele said about him. I watch his jaw clench before he leans back into the chair again, pushing the core against the island, closer to me. "Toss mine too while you're at it."

I glare up at him before setting the mop back into the bucket. Walking closer over to him as the urge to inflict hallucinations onto him surfaces. Wanting him to see his unimaginable fears play out in his mind over and over again.

But instead, I settle with being a good servant and tossing the core out for him. Feeling disturbingly small and dehumanized even long after we've finished cleaning the kitchen.

With Dionysus there to watch and remind me of his power over me, over this situation. And how quickly he could exploit me.

An apple that surely did not fall far from the tree.

CHAPTER 27

Reimus

I open the door to Hecate's shop, those golden bells jingling to announce my arrival as I step inside. Not having wanted to step away from my project that I've succumbed to for the past two days, but having already promised Hecate that I would attend her lesson this afternoon.

I presumed when I stepped inside that I would find a majority of the women at The Sanctuary to have shown up. Having thought that maybe not everyone would be interested in learning magic. But as I step inside now, I find I was wrong in my presumptions.

All thirty of the women that reside at The Sanctuary stand before me, facing Hecate until they all look over at me.

"Thank you for joining us, Reimus." Hecate says, standing where her counter normally would be.

I look around the room and notice that all of her things are gone. Her tables with spell jars and oils placed upon them, shelves where her assortment of crystals were, her enormous amount of jarred herbs. All of it gone and in place now is just a massive, empty store.

I lift my gaze up to Hecate's, and as if she can read the curiosity in my stare, she simply gives me a wink before directing her attention back to the women.

"Today I am going to show you all how to shield your energy from physical, spiritual, and mental attack. From there we'll move on to a basic protection spell, something that you will only need three ingredients for, as I want to start off easy and work you all into the craft."

I stand at the back of the crowd, my gaze roaming over all of the faces here.

My gaze fixates on a porcelain hand lifting into the air.

Hecate nods. "Yes, Euphrosyne?"

Euphrosyne lowers her hand back down. "I am curious—as I believe we all are." She looks towards some of the women standing near her. Some of them exchange nods of agreement. "How will anything you teach us truly protect us from those who are stronger than us? Such as gods or goddesses. I mean…we're just mortals."

A faint grin curves up Hecate's lips as she steps forward. "Even the strongest of gods can be the most weak. Not with their physicality, but in their minds." She taps on the side of her forehead. She lowers her hand as her chest sinks subtly at her exhale. "You do not need immortality to be defined as strong. Each and every one of you holds a reservoir of *true* power, of *true* strength that cannot be duplicated nor stolen. A power that even the most feared gods cannot obtain."

"And what is that?" Thalia speaks out.

Hecate's grin deepens subtly. "The duality, and power, of being a woman."

I watch as some of the women turn to one another, exchanging neutral looks before switching their gazes back onto Hecate.

"Men are weak mentally. They have believed for thousands of years that true power lies in being able to out-dominate women. To dominate over people who blindly pledge their allegiances to them just because they are men. But men who lead not with compassion, but with ego, always fear that the other shoe will drop, and therefore will always have a weak spot that can be used against them."

Hecate glances over to me momentarily, a silent exchange between us before continuing on.

"They fear that someday, someone will challenge their position. So they create more restrictions for others so they are left with less and less stamina to demand otherwise, until the courage to stand against them depletes entirely. And this has worked for a millenium, but we stand before a crossroad now where the wheel of change is beckoning us to listen and take action. And this is where I can help you all today."

She takes another step forward, reaching her hands out to Euphrosyne and holding them gently. After a moment, I watch Euphrosyne gasp and almost jolt backwards if it weren't for Hecate keeping her still.

"Can you feel the energy?"

Euphrosyne's gaze roams wildly over their conjoined hands. She lifts her head up, nodding curtly. "Yes."

Hecate smiles. "Then you can also protect yourself from it."

I watch as something pure happens right before my eyes. I watch as Hecate pulls her hands away, that a pulse of giddiness washes over Euphrosyne. I watch as the energy palpitating around her increases into a state of excitement as she turns and whispers to her sisters on each side of her.

"That was so cool." She whispers. Kicking a half grin up my lips.

I watch as the other women begin to show signs of excitement as well, watching some of these women who have come to Vulir in search of a safer life. Some of them with their sparks having been burned out from the treatment they've faced from humans that don't deserve to be called men.

My heart begins to warm as I watch a sense of determination light up in some of their faces. That against all odds, against everything they've been through, they're willing to stand up one more time. And give fighting for themselves, and for their future, one more try.

"I would like you all to imagine an invisible shield surrounding you. Each one of you when imagining it in your mind will look different then the person standing next to you, and that's completely expected. As each shield should be tailored to how it *feels* and looks to you. So, everyone spread out and let's begin."

The women spread themselves out from one another, standing around Hecate.

"Close your eyes."

I watch as all the women do the same before I close my eyes as well.

"Now visualize a shield starting from the ground and working your way up and over your head, connecting back down to the ground again. Hone in on how it appears to you, how it feels and focus on that."

As a drago you're taught as a youngling how to shield until it becomes a mental habit. Pulling it over day in and day out without needing to think much about it. But once in a while, it's nice to refresh what my shield feels and looks like to me.

Since I was a child I've always envisioned my shield to be a warm orange with tendrils of black coiled around it, connected with barbed wires meant to keep parasitic spirits away from latching onto my energy. To keep psychic and mental attacks from even having an affect on me.

I remember the first time Melinoë tried to use her gift of hallucinations on me. I almost chuckle remembering how fiery she was that first day meeting, how she tried wailing a candelabra over my head.

If I were entirely mortal that would've probably left me a hefty bruise.

I remember being unaffected by her hallucinations mainly because of my ability to shield so easily. I guess I can thank my mother for constantly being on my ass to get shielding perfected when I was young.

"This tool could be the very thing that separates you from life and death, Rei." She'd said, a mother's frustration on her face as I tried to slack off.

"But I'm bored of this. Can we just try again tomorrow, mom?"

She'd sighed audibly, looking at me with her hand on her hip. Her fingers pressed into her hip as she carried her weight on her other leg. A moment later, her lips curved up into a grin as she lowered her hand to my face. Pushing my hair back as her gaze roams over my small face. "How about you try one more time for me, and then we can reconvene tomorrow. Okay?"

I'd nodded my head. "What does reconvene mean?"

My mother's laugh graced my ears as her icy blue eyes gazed upon me. My head nuzzled into her soft hand as her thumb grazed my cheek. "I love you, my sweet boy."

I'd smiled into her palm. "I love you, mommy."

I bring myself back from the pleasant memory as I pull my shield up.

"Good. Everyone is doing a great job. Now try to push that shield outward if you can. As far away from your body as you're able to visualize."

I visualize the shield around me expanding, feeling it grow in size. I breathe in and out of my nose steadily, feeling the energy of my shield strong around me.

"Open your eyes."

I open my eyes and witness from my keen drago senses a thick shield surrounding each and everyone of us, powered by the intent of everyone in this room. Knowing that although they may not be able to see it with their mortal eyes, but hoping they understand just how powerful they all are.

Even as mortals.

"Can you all feel the difference between shielding and not?" Hecate asks.

They all nod their heads as some of them even verbally agree that they can feel the difference.

"My head even feels more clear. Like there's less noise." Carina says with wonder in her eyes.

Hecate nods. "There are many benefits to shielding, but you cannot just do it once and then be done with it. I want you all to practice doing it each and everyday, until it becomes second nature for you. Now," Hecate waves her hand as a small table appears in front of her. Some of the women gasp and whisper their intrigue amongst one another. "I will demonstrate for you all, and then answer any questions you all have. First we will start with our three ingredients. A black candle, hyssop, and some cloves of garlic."

She begins demonstrating how to arrange the working, with the herbs and garlic spread around the candle. I watch as the women watch with soft eagerness and curiosity, finding myself even curious as I'm not one to perform witchcraft.

Even though I have an entire room in my palace now that Hecate has dedicated to for such things.

I watch as my own curiosity sparks as Hecate explains how to perform the spell, along with the proper intentions to have—as intention is everything, as she puts it. I watch as an energy begins to change in the air around me as women stand together and initially being afraid of what to expect, but are now curious.

And when a community full of powerful women become curious rather than afraid, then absolutely anything is possible.

CHAPTER 28

As I enter the Guardian's Palace, I make my way over to the kitchen to help myself to some lunch.

Upon entering the kitchen I see Aven pulling out a stainless steel pot, setting it onto the counter before looking up at me with a grin on his face. "Good afternoon, My Lord. I'm heading into the village to retrieve some ingredients for dinner tonight. Is there anything you need while I'm there?"

I shake my head. "Nothing that comes to mind. Thank you, Aven."

He bows his head. "Of course, my Lord." His hands wrap around behind him as he goes to take his apron off. "I shall be back within the hour. Dinner will be ready in three." He walks over to the wall closest to the pantry and hangs the apron on a brass hook mounted on the wall.

"Sounds good." I respond as I approach the stainless steel fridge, pulling one side of it open.

Ever since I took Aven in as my chef, he's always addressed me as Lord, even when I assured him the title was unnecessary. Though he insisted that I be addressed by that, as he said it was to show his gratitude for taking him in and giving him another chance at feeling fulfilled when he had been so lost in grief after his mother's death.

For a long time I wasn't sure what drew me to offering him the job. I'm more than capable of cooking my own meals, a chef isn't mandatory to have here in the palace by any means. But I think what drew me to offering the position to him anyway was when I saw the pain of losing someone he loved very much dull his naturally exuberant nature, and it reminded me of my own pain I was suffocated by at that time. Still grieving my mother, and feeling as if something were missing from my life that I couldn't grasp onto. I drowned in that confusion for a long time until I met Melinoë, then it became crystal clear what exactly I was missing.

She was the answer all along. That aside from being Guardian of Vulir, I was meant to find Melinoë and share every inch of my life with her. A deep knowingness that I've never, ever felt before.

I pull out small containers of sliced turkey breast and provolone cheese, setting them onto the counter before grabbing a loaf of sourdough bread from the pantry. I prepare myself a sandwich onto a plate, putting everything away before seating myself at the kitchen island.

After I finish eating I set the plate into the sink before heading upstairs. I head into our bedroom and slip my shoes off, setting them next to the closet door before plopping myself onto the chaise lounge near the fireplace.

A soft exhale leaves me as I lean my head back, crossing my legs at the ankles when I feel the necklace in my pants pocket send a burst of energy.

My hand lowers beneath my pocket, pulling out Melinoë's talisman and dangling it in front of me. The gentle roar of the fire casts a faint orange glow against the black obsidian crystal. I set the talisman into my palm, assessing it.

"Either I'm hallucinating, or you keep sending me these bursts of energy."

The talisman sends another charge of energy, causing the hairs on my arm to stand up.

"Okay. Definitely not hallucinating."

I hold it there for a long moment, waiting to see if it will do it again. I should probably ask Hecate why it does that, and if it's supposed to have some kind of meaning.

For whatever reason—maybe to feel close to her, I clasp the talisman around my neck and lay it flat on my chest. As my hands slip away I feel a quiet buzzing sensation briefly before it settles entirely. An idle charge of energy I can feel even if gentle.

I reach over to the nightstand beside me, grabbing my leather journal and setting it on my lap. I slip the pen out from the nightstand drawer, opening up to a blank page. Wanting to channel my sadness onto paper, knowing I should but coming up empty as I try to find the inspiration for words. I sit there for a while, staring at the paper and know nothing I write in here will truly fill this bleakness in my heart until Melinoë is in my vicinity again.

So, I lift the pen and begin writing what I feel at this moment.

I need to know what kind of state you're in,
If the will to stay strong is becoming too heavy on your mind.
Let me leverage the deafening silence around me,
For the pain and mental turmoil you're facing.
I'll release it from your possession and carry it for you.
I'll do anything other than be in the absence of you.
I am lost without you.
Please come home to me.
Come home to me, Melinoë.

I close the journal, setting it back down on the nightstand along with the pen. I lean my head back, the heat from the fire warming the soles of my feet. I feel my eyelids becoming heavy suddenly as tiredness swoops over me. Knowing I haven't been sleeping well lately, knowing that I won't rest easy until she's with me again.

But as I close my eyes, the thought of letting myself fall asleep to an afternoon nap sounds like something that I could immensely benefit from. And as a heavy exhaustion plagues me, I fall deep into sleep.

⁓

I groggily open my eyes, the utter darkness of the room telling me I've been asleep far longer than I anticipated. I wipe my eyes, going to push myself off of the chaise lounge when I halt.

I push my fingers firmly against the ground and swing my eyes open when I feel not the plush fabric of my chair beneath my fingertips, but of hard cement.

I look down at myself and my eyes widen at the intangible form I'm in, recognizing it immediately for what it is.

I'm in my astral body.

I stare down at myself for a long moment before I hear the sound of chains clanking against one another from close by, followed by two sets of footsteps.

I whip my head upright as I see I'm sitting inside of a cell, with nothing but stone walls to surround me aside from a toilet and small sink mounted into the wall next to me. I hear those footsteps and chains coming closer and look up at the iron bars in front of me, peering my gaze out before I stand myself up.

"Tomorrow I will be completing chores on my own, as His Majesty has requested you for the afternoon."

I move closer to the cell door, wondering who the feminine voice is that's speaking—

From the soft glow of the torch above me, I watch as a woman in a white linen dress approaches the cell door. And in tow next to her is Melinoë.

Fury immediately swarms me as my gaze fixates on the iron handcuffs around her ankles and wrists, but what infuriates me more is the look imprinted on the love of my life's face.

"Do you know what for?" Melinoë asks with the hint of dread in her voice. The hint of something she should never have to feel again.

Fear.

"His Majesty did not say." The woman says before opening up the cell door—

The fucking *prison* that they've been holding Melinoë in, I realize.

I go to charge forward when the talisman heats up on my chest. My gaze jerks down to see it faintly light up, pulsating a beat of energy before simmering once more.

"That's okay. Thank you, Bethesda." Melinoë says quietly, jerking my gaze back up to her.

I watch as she and Bethesda move into the cell, Melinoë going to stand near an adjacent wall with thick chain connectors attached. I step closer to them as I watch Bethesda move to that wall, finding myself holding my breath every second that passes as Bethesda hooks Melinoë's chains up to that wall.

Eliminating her from both escaping, and moving freely within the prison cell.

Bethesda nods her head before exiting out of the cell, closing it and locking it before walking away. When I go to follow after her, to find out where she's heading off to and where Zeus is in the palace, the talisman heats up on my chest again.

And an instinctive feeling tells me to step out of my fury, and look at what's right in front of me.

I look at Melinoë and watch as she lowers herself to the ground, leaning her back up against the stone wall. I inch closer towards her, afraid to breathe too heavy or make any sudden movements that would wake me from this dream—

No, not a dream. Astral traveling.

I look at her long hair, noticing the tangles throughout. Her face—

Her sweet face which looks like it's gained ten years of life onto it. I fall down to my knees as I stare at her, my heart sinking to the bottom of my stomach with me. "Melinoë." I say through a choked whisper.

She doesn't move an inch, and continues staring straight ahead into the nothingness with the face of someone who is hanging on by a thread.

Tears prick my eyes as I lower down to my hands and knees, crawling on the ground until I'm kneeling at her side. I go to reach my trembling hand out, setting it tentatively over her hand resting on her belly. A tear slips down my cheek as I witness the horrors of what this place—what Zeus has done to her already. "Melinoë." I repeat a little louder.

She remains unaffected, unmoved by my pleas. Wondering why as Guardian of Souls, a goddess who can walk between realms, cannot hear me as I kneel right beside her.

I go to grip her hand when I remember that I am not a physical body and my subtle body cannot produce a grip strong enough to guide her attention. I look down at the chains around her, noticing something peculiar.

I notice the faint glow of light wrapped around her wrists and ankles, my gaze following the light as it travels up the chains connected to the wall. And I realize in that moment why she cannot hear or see me.

These chains are bound by magic to keep her abilities stifled and mute.

I look back up at her again, lifting my hand and trailing the back of my fingers along her cheek. Wishing I could wipe away the dirt and filth blotched onto her skin there. Wishing she could feel my warmth and know that I am here with her now.

"I am here, Melinoë. In this lifetime, and every other."

She goes to close her eyes when they suddenly snap open.

I stop myself from going to move the hair out of her face, an instinct that I know won't matter while I'm in the astral realm but a habit nonetheless. I watch as her gaze moves over to where I'm kneeling and my stomach feels like it's bottoming out. "Melinoë? Can you see me?" Franticness seeping into my tone.

Her gaze wildly roams over where I am, her brows knitting together as she leans away from the wall. Her face now only inches away from mine as confusion and shock paint her expression.

I go to rest my hand on hers again, attempting to squeeze it. "I'm here. I need you to know I'm here. Please, I'll do anything for you to feel I'm—"

She gasps as her gaze shoots down to her hand, in the vicinity where mine rests on top. Her gaze wildly roaming over it before she takes a shuddering breath in. Her chest rising and crashing swiftly before she covers her mouth with her other hand. Her fingers tremble against her lips as tears begin to stream down her face.

My cheeks dampen as tears stream down them, raising both of my hands up to her face as I cradle her in my hands. Her eyes widen as she glances from side to side, her chest rising.

"I love you, Melinoë. I know you can't hear me, but fucking Fates I'm relieved you can at least feel me." I say through trembling words. I wipe my face on my shoulder before fixing my gaze on her again. "We're going to get you out of here. Just hold on a little longer. Please."

Suddenly I feel the talisman vibrate against my chest, my astral body being slowly pulled back from Melinoë. "No! Not yet, I need more time—"

I keep my gaze on Melinoë the entire time that gravity pulls me away from her. Until I'm dropped back into our bedroom, and flung back into my physical body.

CHAPTER 29

I sit up from the chair, looking over to my balcony door and noticing the sun just beginning to set. Telling me it's sometime after five.

I bring my thumb up to my eye, wiping the dampness that's gathered there. My wild gaze lowered to the talisman around my neck, knowing there's only one person I can go to who can give me a semblance of clarity as to what just happened.

I rush to my feet, going over to the closet and slipping my shoes on before hurrying out of the bedroom. I rush down the stairs when Dimitri meets me at the top landing, holding a hand out against my chest as his brows knit together. "What's wrong, Rei?"

I shake my head as I move past him. "I'll explain later. I need to go see Hecate but I'll return as soon as I'm able."

Without waiting for his response I fly down the stairs, landing at the bottom and pushing the front door open and sprint to Hecate's shop.

As my arms pump at my sides all I can think about is how it felt to see Melinoë in that state, how life had begun to drain from her face. The only comfort during that interaction was when she could feel my energy against her, bringing just a hint of a spark of life back into her complexion.

But not enough, and not to mention—how was I able to get past Zeus' wards?

And how did I get myself into the astral realm? Sure, being a drago it makes it easier for me to be able to, but I wasn't *trying* to is the problem.

I make it to Hecate's shop and rush inside, halting as I enter her shop and try to catch my breath.

Standing in front of a table of spell jars, her golden gaze tracks over me before quickly approaching me. Her amethyst robe billowed behind her. "What is it?"

"I saw her—" I say, my breathing labored as I try to slow it down. I work on a swallow as I find the words again. "Just now, I saw her in the astral realm. In the *dungeons* they're keeping her."

Anger swarms to life inside of my body as I feel extreme warmth pulsate along my arms and hands.

"How?" She demands as she closes the distance between us, but my building fury can't comprehend it behind the wrath that threatens to send me overboard.

They have her chained up like a fucking animal, in a cell that may as well have no source of light at all for how pitiful that flame from that torch was smoldering. I open and close my fists, clenching my teeth as I go to step away from Hecate when she stops me.

"Reimus, I need you to breathe and calm yourself. Listen to the sound of my voice."

The blind fury takes over my mind until the sound of her sharp gasp instantly draws me out of it.

The fog from my vision clears as I look at her gaze fixated on her hand, the other cradling it tightly. I lower my gaze to find a mark now placed upon her palm, similar to that of a mark left by a hot brand.

I lean my head forward as my brows knit together. "What just happened?" I slowly lift my hand up, assessing it as shame comes to life. Remembering that one day when I felt the heat from my hand sizzle the door handle to The Sanctuary. I labeled it as a fluke, or from the heat of my skin just reacting strangely to the brisk coldness of the bronzed handle. But now I…I just burned Hecate.

Why is this happening?

She looks up at me, shaking her head as new skin begins to materialize over the burn. Manifested by the will of her magic, of being a goddess. "I went to grab your hand to try to calm you, but your skin was as hot as lava. I—" Her gaze lowers to Melinoë's talisman around my neck. She stares at it for a long moment, and then her eyes widen. "Impossible." She whispers. She slowly lifts her gaze up from the talisman back up to meet my gaze.

"Hecate, I swear I didn't mean to. I've never done something like—"

"Come." She says swiftly as she steps around me to flip the sign on her door to show closed to the street, locking her door before making her way to her back room.

I follow behind her, dipping between the beads and follow her further when she waves me over to her work station.

"Tell me everything that happened." She says as she begins setting her station up, starting with putting a large white pillar candle in the middle.

"I was writing in my journal, thinking about Melinoë and fell asleep afterwards. I woke up in my astral body, somehow managing to make it past Zeus' wards and end up in Melinoë's cell. She couldn't see me or hear me, but I was able to get her to feel my energy. But I swear, Hecate, it was because of this." I say, holding the talisman away from my chest. "I don't know how to explain it, but I put it on to feel closer to her. And it's like it guided me to see her. I felt it heat up against me, even light up."

Hecate looks over at me, slowly nodding her head before approaching me. "That can't be possible, Reimus. I spelled that talisman for Melinoë, and *her* alone." She lowers her gaze to the talisman for a long moment before lifting her gaze back up to me again. "Whether it recognizes you as Melinoë's significant other or not, it should not hold any magical attachment to you. Therefore, you should not have been able to get past Zeus' protective wards—*I* cannot even get past them, Reimus." Hecate sternly declares.

"I know you spelled it for her, but I'm telling you. It was as if it...I don't know." I run my hand through my hair, pushing it back.

Hecate nods to it. "You are absolutely sure you felt it heat up against you? You saw it light up while you were in the astral realm?"

I nod curtly. "I swear it."

Hecate briefly lowers her gaze back to the talisman before holding her hand out, palm facing up. "Take it off."

I wrap my hand around my neck, unclasping the talisman and laying it inside Hecate's palm. She closes her fist around it, closing her eyes as she begins to mumble quietly to herself. She takes a few steps to the right, standing in front of her work station as she chants quietly to herself. A moment later the wick on the candle lights up, the flame dancing erratically.

She opens her hand once more, lowering it away from the talisman as it hovers in front of her. She opens her eyes as the necklace turns slightly to the side, watching as Hecate does whatever it is she's doing.

I wait in silence and allow Hecate to work, and after a few minutes she shakes her head slowly. "It is as I originally spelled it. The talisman is to protect and guide Melinoë in all realms, both living and dead. To be magically bonded to that soul of which it protects, and only to that soul—"

I watch as Hecate's eyes widen, complete and utter silence stretching between us until she finally turns towards me. "I must test something, if you don't mind."

I nod my head.

She holds her palm out again, the talisman dropping down into her palm. She turns fully towards me, closing the distance between us as she holds her other hand up to me.

She meets my gaze briefly before lowering her hand to my chest, a surge of energy coursing through me.

I almost bow backwards at the intensity of it but remain standing there, silent as I allow Hecate to work.

She closes her eyes as she keeps her hand placed firmly on my chest, her other hand closed around the talisman. She quietly chants to herself for a few minutes until her hand lifts off of me and she steps back, opening her eyes.

She blinks at me once, then twice. Her voice lowers a notch, hardly above a whisper as she says, "I spelled it to protect one soul. I just never foresaw this occurring."

"What is it?" I ask impatiently, eagerly.

She straightens her back as she raises her chin. "The talisman protects one soul, but what I failed to understand at the time is that Melinoë's soul is split in half."

I tilt my head to the side. "What do you mean her soul is split into two?"

A faint grin begins to slowly curve up her lips as she stares at me. "It means that the reason why the talisman protects you, and has the same attachment to you as it does to Melinoë, is because you are twin souls, Reimus."

My eyes widen as I try to process what Hecate is saying. I stand there befuddled for a heartbeat before responding, "What?"

Her grin deepens before she waves her hand over the burning candle, dimming the flame to an almost nothingness. "Twin souls. A rarity that only occurs when there is a fated purpose to the pairing's union. A thread of fate that cannot be tampered with, nor altered in any capacity, as it is a divine union intricately woven by The Fates themselves."

She reaches her hand out, handing me back the talisman. I cradle it in the palm of my hand as my mind reels with this term of twin souls. Not something I've ever heard of before, but something that feels…strangely familiar nonetheless.

I remember the first day I met Melinoë, the girl who was passed out at the shield when Charon called me over to investigate. I remember looking at her, feeling sorry for her and though she was a stranger, I wanted to comfort her. To give her clean clothes, to give her a warm bed to rest in as she looked exhausted. I remember feeling utterly intrigued by her, and even surprised by my reckless decision to invite her to stay at the palace. I always thought it was just because I knew at that moment, that there was something about her that drew me to her. That I had met the love of my life, no matter how crazy or absurd that sounds. But now—

It…makes sense.

I lower the talisman into my pants pocket, slowly lifting my gaze back up to meet Hecate's. "If twin souls are supposed to have some divine purpose, then what is ours supposed to be?"

Hecate shakes her head gently. "I don't know. I may be able to find out, but it is not usually possible to see what the Moirai's intentions are. Most destinies are purposefully kept hidden."

"The Moirai?" I ask.

"The three sisters who control and oversee one's destiny. What you know today to be The Fates." Hecate pauses as she steps away from her work station, her golden gaze churning brightly. "Klotho, she who spins the thread of fate. Lakhesis, she who measures it. And Atropos, the goddess who cuts it short. All three of them are otherwise known as The Fates of destiny for both mortals and immortals. As each human and immortal is born, the three of them create the thread that tells of their life from beginning to end. But sometimes, a thread is split into two. With each half—each soul, having its own lessons to face separately before they can be reunited again with their other half."

I go to open my mouth when the words fail me to deliver what I'm feeling.

A soul split into two. Two individuals fated for one another. I..

"When it is time for these two souls to meet together in this lifetime, they will feel an unmistakable familiarity with one another, even if they initially resist it. And while they will have accomplished one aspect of their destiny by coming into union with each other, it doesn't stop there as there is usually an ulterior purpose to The Fates bringing these two souls together."

I stand there immobilized as if I had just been frozen in place, wrapping my mind around everything that has just transpired in the past few minutes. I blink once, then twice. Working on a swallow before finally finding the words to speak. "So, Melinoë and I are one *shared* soul?"

Hecate nods her head. "That is correct."

I slowly nod my head, processing. "But we've both had different experiences. She grew up with a father who showed disdain for her. I grew up with parents who loved me, and showed me compassion and kindness. If we were twin souls, wouldn't we have had similar paths leading up to now?"

"It doesn't always work that way. Sometimes each soul is destined to have different paths, to experience different situations and master those lessons separately. Then as the two come into union with each other, they both have different skills to share with the other. Sometimes to give the other what they lacked, and vice versa."

Hecate's words make sense. When I first met Melinoë, she resisted the hell out of me—and for good reason. When she was manipulated to believe that her mother died, Zeus only ever gave Makaria attention and made it very clear of his detest for Melinoë. To have to accept that as your childhood environment really shapes and molds you into being defensive for others' intentions, and I saw that through her right away. Knowing it would take time for me to gain her trust, but I was willing to wait however long it took because there was something about her that kept magnetizing me to her.

And when she found out that it was all a lie, that her mother was alive and Zeus was actually The King of Gods, she went through the grief of not being able to grasp what is reality and what isn't. And then again, when she freed Makaria from the compulsion spell Zeus placed on her. All of that would make any person go utterly mad, and I instinctively knew that I just needed to be there for Melinoë during every part of those difficult times. As my mother and father showed so effortlessly to me growing up, therefore giving me the tools to be able to enact that same gentleness with Melinoë.

I guess I haven't thought about what Melinoë has taught me. I always told myself that she opened up my heart, showing me that it was okay to put love into another person again after losing my parents. That being hardened to life would only get me so far, and when Melinoë came into my life, it was like everything clicked into place. That I was almost starved for her attention, craving the closeness of her presence instead of the urge to push love away.

But something tells me that there's more that Melinoë will teach me about myself as time progresses.

"How does this explain why I was still able to get past Zeus' wards? I thought those were impenetrable?"

"They are," Hecate says, nodding as a grin forms on her lips again. "But you both are one soul split into two. So when I spelled that talisman to protect one soul, it did what it was asked. With a slight loophole."

"So this means I can get past his protective barriers in the physical world too then?" If that's the case I'll go break Melinoë out right now. I won't make her wait another day.

"Not necessarily. See, Zeus is not a psychopomp. He cannot see the dead like Melinoë or myself can. You are only able to see spirits because of the Draghi blood that runs through your veins. So Zeus' wards in the astral will be powerful, but not as strong as the ones in the physical. Those will be immensely challenging to get past—and I'm still working to dissect them to find loopholes myself." She waves a hand towards her work station before clasping them in front of her. "But there may be one person we can ask."

"Who?"

She huffs out a soft chuckle. "Who do you think?"

As I think about who she's referring to, I think back to why we had to specifically wait until Makaria was tapped into her power—or at the very least, able to portal before we broke Melinoë out. That's when his name pops up into my mind.

I nod as I sigh a relief of understanding. "Eiran."

CHAPTER 30

Melinoë

My hands rest over my navel, unmoving as I wait to see if the energy that radiated over them will surprise me with its appearance again.

I occasionally find myself squeezing my palms inward, hoping to mimic the burst of energy but all I get is the press of my nails embedding into my skin. I know they've begun to feed me far less than when I first arrived, but I know what I felt.

I know whose energy it belonged to.

It reminded me of how Eiran felt when he would visit me, before I was able to see his spirit body. Like a calm blanket emitted all over my body. His way of letting me know that he was around, and that I was not alone.

But this time, it felt different.

Initially I felt the familiar burst of energy that my talisman used to emit to me, but coupled with it was the familiar feeling of one person in particular. Paired with his familiar scent of patchouli and citrus.

Reimus.

My gaze fixates straight ahead as it focuses on a random section on the stone wall, my mind reeling with what just occurred thirty minutes ago. How was he able to astral travel to me? I look down at the chains around my wrists, knowing that because they're spelled by magic, realizing that's why I couldn't see him. But the question of how he got past Zeus' protective wards still stands.

But as the thoughts and questions of the *how* churn in my mind, so does the realization of one answer I can confidently say.

That Reimus came for me. Somehow, someway. And maybe not in the way he or I would've wanted.

But he came nonetheless.

I hear the door open up at the top of the stairs, this time not even flinching with the worry if it's Dionysus. Or if it's someone bringing me up to see Zeus, to be punished for trying to escape.

That is if Dionysus even tells him. Which again, why wouldn't he say anything?

Regardless, I sit there unmoved because as I still have little drive to do much of anything right now, I know that feeling Reimus' energy was all it took to quell the storm within.

It was enough to give me just a tiny sliver of peace of mind that he's still out there, and won't rest until I'm home again. A truth that I know deep within my bones.

I hear footsteps making their way closer to me. The soft slide of sandals, the light-footed step.

Semele approaches my cell door, feeling her gaze on the side of my face for a moment before I hear the thud of keys on the cement ground. *Inside* of the cell.

I look over at the key she tossed through the bars, scrunching my brows as I look up at her.

"Use them to unlock yourself from the wall mounts."

I blink at her once before rushing to grab the key, standing up on my two feet before stalling. Tilting my head at her. "For what?"

She nods over to the side of the room. "Because you need a bath. Badly, if I'm honest."

I look over in the direction she nodded at, finding a large bucket similar to the one Dionysus materialized here before. I notice this time that beside a small pile of folded up clothes, there is also a hair brush and a hair tie. The hair brush is such a small gesture, but I haven't brushed my hair once since I've been here. A small decency for a woman to be able to have that I haven't been afforded down here.

I work on a swallow as I hold back tears from surfacing, clenching my jaw briefly before nodding curtly.

I look back over at Semele who turns her back towards me, leaning against the bars as she folds her arms over her chest. "You have thirty minutes and then I need to be elsewhere."

I lower to the ground, reaching for the key and not wasting a moment on getting them off. After unlocking my handcuffs, I watch as the chains clink to the ground before removing the ones at my ankles. I bring the key with me over to the large metal bucket, rubbing my wrists before setting the key down onto the ground. I look down at the hot water sizzling and don't even care at this point about checking to make sure she's not looking. I don't care at all as I remove my clothing, and lower myself right in.

I sigh contentedly as I submerge myself into the hot water, letting it soothe my skin for a moment before getting right to washing up. Knowing that working the tangles out from my hair is going to take me some time.

"I apologize for Dionysus' behavior the other day. Unfortunately, he takes after his father in the asshole department."

I continue lathering the soap over my body as I glance up at the back of her head. "I'd probably be an asshole too if my mother looked at me the way she glares at him."

Semele huffs out a quiet noise. "Hera gives him the cold shoulder for reasons that shouldn't belong to him. But nonetheless, she does."

I rub the ivory bar of soap over my arms before rinsing the soap off. "He deserves better."

Semele goes rigid against the bars. "You're sympathizing with him? After how he treated you?"

I lather the soap into my hair, making sure I get my roots and my ends as clean as I can. "I'm not excusing his ugly behavior, but it doesn't mean I can't understand the impact a parent plays on their child." I drop the soap onto the ground before rinsing my hair. "Given what I know so far, I'd say he's suffering internally and projecting that pain onto others. Using drinking as a coping mechanism to dull his problems away." I squeeze the excess water out from my hair.

"I greatly dislike him, but I still hope he can work through his shit and see the error in his ways before it's too late."

Semele remains silent for a long moment before shaking her head slowly, the tenseness in her back and shoulders easing. "I'll be damned." She says quietly.

After I wash my body and rinse off, I grab the towel on top of the pile of clothes and stand up from the bucket, wrapping it around my body as I step out. I dry my body off before discarding the towel, dropping it on the floor before pulling the clean tunic over my head. "What happened to the mistress?"

Semele leans her head back into the bars. "Come again?"

"The mistress from that creepy story you told me," I smooth the alabaster tunic over my chest before pulling back on the underwear I came here wearing. Knowing that's definitely not sanitary but having no choice. "You told me she was turned into a goddess, to bear that man's child. What happened to her? Are they still together?" I pull the beige breeches over before grabbing the brush. "I'm dressed now, by the way."

Semele tentatively turns around, unwrapping her arms from over her chest. "The mistress still has a relationship with him solely for the child's sake, but they no longer have an intimate relationship if that's what you're wondering."

I start at my ends and gently run the brush through them, seething at the snarls I brush through. "Well that kind of sucks."

Semele tilts her head at me, slightly knitting her brows together.

"She was human. But she must've loved him enough to agree to let him turn her into a goddess, just to bear a child for him." I grimace at a huge tangle that I brush through. "But then they didn't even work out in the end? That's…I actually feel bad for her."

Semele lowers her gaze to the brush in my hand momentarily before meeting my gaze again. She nods her head slowly. "Well, then you'll be pleased to know that she made peace with it. Though being a mother has made her do things that she never thought she'd do, it has made her better for it."

I work my way up my hair until I'm half way up, my arm starting to get sore from weaving the brush through my hair. "How do you know though? Did you know her?"

She stands there, fixing a faint grin on her face. Hardly noticeable through the dark-lit dungeon. "I know her very well, actually." She nods to the key on the ground next to my feet. "Time is up."

I stop brushing my hair as I lower to the ground, picking up the key and walking over to the chains. I drop the brush on the ground, hooking the cuffs back on around my wrists and ankles. Once I show Semele that they're secured in place, I toss the key back to her. Reaching just outside of the cell door.

She leans down to grab it, sliding it in her breeches pocket. Before she turns away, she reaches for something in her cardigan pocket, pulling it out.

She holds in her hand half of a sandwich wrapped in saran wrap. She lowers to the ground, lightly tossing it over to me before pulling a water out of her other cardigan pocket. Rolling it over to me.

The water bottle stops as it bumps up against my foot. I lift my gaze back up to Semele. Wanting to ask her why the kindness? Why go the extra mile to let me finally use a hairbrush after my bath? Why do all of this when you aided in getting me kidnapped in the first place?

But none of those things are questions I can ask her, as my cover in faking Zeus' success at compelling me to forget everything would instantly be compromised. So instead, I have to force myself to remain silent. Forcing myself to nod. "Thank you."

I lower down to grab the sandwich and water, seating myself down on the ground. Knowing I still haven't brushed the top half of my hair yet but food and water feel just a little more important right now.

I unwrap the saran wrap and take a bite of the sandwich, sighing as the cheese and ham reaches my tastebuds. Cold, but food nonetheless.

"Zeus has requested to see you tomorrow. Bethesda will be retrieving you sometime in the early afternoon." Semele turns around to begin walking away when she turns her head to the side. "I would suggest that you be on your best behavior." She continues walking away from the cell.

I finish eating my sandwich before opening the bottle of water. I take a few long gulps before capping the bottle, setting it down. My attention gets drawn to the disappearance of the bucket and towel, along with the dirty clothes I had on. I look over to my side and expect to see the hair brush gone as well.

But find that it still rests beside me.

I stare at it for a moment before picking it up, wondering why she didn't take this as well. Another kind gesture that begs the question of whose side is Semele really on?

I take the brush, weaving it through the rest of my hair and wonder anxiously what Zeus wants to see me about for the rest of the night.

CHAPTER 31

Reimus

I stand at the center of the one room in my palace that I don't utilize, having been here already when I bought the palace and first moved in. I had thought about turning it into something else, but as I stand here now with Hecate before me, I begin to think that fate truly has a funny way of making irony seem wholly intentional.

No fancy sigils drawn into the floor, no herbs to use with casting a spell. Nothing at all other than the flames from the torches jutted from the walls above, and a single candle lit aflame on the floor between us.

She gives me an intentional nod. "All you need to do is call out to him."

As soon as Hecate and I decided to try getting in touch with Eiran to ask him some questions, she closed up her shop for the night and met me back here once she was ready.

"He will answer."

I take a deep breath in and out, centering into myself. The talisman still hung around my neck, not wanting to take it off after learning what I did just an hour ago.

That Melinoë is not just the love of my life, but the literal other half of my soul.

I keep my gaze on Hecate as I begin. "Eiran." I say aloud.

We both wait there for a long moment, my gaze glancing around the room before landing on Hecate again. She gives me a nod to try again. "Eiran, I need to speak with you. I need your help." I say aloud, raising my voice just a little louder.

I stand there waiting for something, anything to happen. For a long moment there's nothing but utter silence between us until I feel it.

I lift my gaze to Hecate's right, to the subtle body standing next to her and give him a shy grin. "Thank you for coming."

Eiran nods his head as he takes a step away from Hecate, moving to stand next to both of us. "I heard your call."

Hecate turns to Eiran, giving him a grin. "Good to see you again." She goes to clasp her hands in front of her. "I understand that there are certain things you are unable to reveal to us, as it would be a dishonor to The Laws of The Fates. But what can you tell me about Melinoë and Reimus being twin souls?"

Eiran keeps his gaze on Hecate before glancing over at me. "As far as what their journey is in this existence, and the purpose they are to fulfill together, I'm afraid I cannot tell you anything."

"So it's true? We truly are twin souls?" I ask.

Eiran nods. "Yes. That is correct." He lowers his gaze to the talisman, nodding towards it. *"That is why that also protects you."*

I raise my hand up to it, holding it before lowering it again. "If this protects me, then why can't I go and retrieve Melinoë now? Why insist we must stick to Makaria being involved? That the only way to successfully retrieve her is if we all go?"

"Because you may be able to slip past Zeus' wards with that while in the astral realm, but you will not in the physical." Eiran says.

A feeling of defeat blows over as he confirms what I was hoping wasn't the case. That I wouldn't have to wait and potentially put Makaria in danger—even though Eiran insists that she will remain safe, and go to retrieve Melinoë now. Not wanting to wait another day.

"The way to retrieve Melinoë from Zeus' confinement must be followed in the way that we discussed the day she was kidnapped. It is a part of the thread of fate you both share." Eiran reiterates.

"Did you know?"

Eiran stares at me for a long moment, understanding what I mean. Understanding that as a spirit, he can now see the events of one's life.

His body remains still as he gives a short nod, a frown pulling down on his lips. "I did."

I clench my fists together as I almost step forward to advance on him, but remember he's no longer living. And no amount of slapping him will do any harm to him whatsoever.

"Fate is not something that a living mind can conceptualize. Fate is never all good, nor all bad. It is made up of both parts, and no one—not even myself, can alter it. But if I could, I would have picked a much easier way for Melinoë to have stepped into her power."

I shake my head. "She already *has* stepped into her power. She's learned to portal. Learned what her shadows can do for her. How was any of *this* necessary—" I refrain myself from continuing, and possibly saying something that will only begin to make that rage simmering within me stir up again.

"That reservoir of power has barely been tapped into. Neither you or her have seen the totality of what that power is capable of."

I lift my gaze back up to Eiran. "What are you talking about?"

Eiran takes a step closer to me, remaining silent for a long moment.

"You cannot say." Hecate confirms.

Eiran nods his head in confirmation. "You will see soon enough. What I can say is that it won't be long now until you're able to move in. Makaria struggles presently, but she is getting close. But you must stick to the original plan." He pierces his gaze onto mine. "Nobody moves in until all are ready."

I stare at him, frustrated by his vagueness and also by not hearing what I wanted to hear. But nonetheless, though I don't know him well at all, Melinoë trusts him. I can see the care lingering in his gaze for her, ghost or not. So I have to trust what he's saying.

"Thank you, Eiran. We do appreciate what you've been able to divulge." Hecate says, giving him a grin.

Eiran looks over at her, smiling. "You're welcome, Goddess of Witchcraft."

He turns back around, looking at me. "Can I trust that you will follow through on the original plan?"

A long, deep sigh escapes me as I nod my head curtly. "I'll stick with the plan." I groan.

"Good." He takes a few steps back from us. "I'll be in touch soon."

In the next moment he vanishes from us entirely, the candle flame burning out with his absence. Until it's just me and Hecate, and the ruminating thoughts of exactly how long until we're able to execute our plan in saving Melinoë.

Finding his reassurance of it being soon the only thing I can fixate on for the remainder of the night.

CHAPTER 32

Melinoë

I force myself to keep my emotions and my anxiousness in check as I watch Bethesda slide the lock into the keyhole, turning it over. I focus on taking deep breaths in and out as I will myself to remain steady. To remain unafraid for what's waiting for me in the throne room today.

Bethesda closes the door behind herself before coming to unlock the chains connected to my hand and ankle cuffs. She looks up at me, forcing a grin before gently grabbing the chain between my wrists and urging me forward.

We exit out of the cell and begin our trek up the twenty steps. No words exchanged from the mystery woman since the day she calmed me down from my panic attack. Having remained so quiet in her cell that there were moments I wondered if she was even there at all.

We reach the top step as Bethesda pushes the door open, my eyes squinting at the blinding sunlight pooling into the throne room from the windows at the far wall. I blink a few times, adjusting to the brightness before my gaze lands on who stands at the center of the throne room.

My gaze fixates on Zeus before landing on Apollo standing next to him. His golden, sun-kissed skin glistening from the sunlight reflecting off of him. His face impassive as he watches me with his arms at his sides.

Bethesda guides me forward until we stand before both of them. "Good morning, Your Majesty." She says as she dips into a low bow in front of Zeus.

His gaze flicks over to Bethesda, giving her a disingenuous smirk before fixing his gaze back onto me. His stern, golden gaze pierces into mine for a moment before I remember the role I play currently.

I dip into a low bow myself, looking towards the ground when I straighten up again. "Good morning, Your Majesty."

I tentatively lift my gaze up to him, watching as a satisfied grin curves his lips. "You are excused, Bethesda." He says plainly.

"Thank you, Your Majesty." She says as she nods her head, turning around and walking away.

I stand before him as I watch his gaze lower to my clothing, different from what I had on the last time I saw him. I watch as a flash of irritation strikes his gaze, a quick yet subtle flex of his hand at his side catching my attention. I watch as tiny sparks of lightning dance at his fingertips, my stomach threatening to bottom out but keeping it together anyhow.

I lift my gaze to see he's staring at my hair now. Having pulled it back into a long braid behind my back after I finished brushing it out yesterday—thanks to Semele loaning me the hair tie and brush. He exhales a heavy sigh as he clenches his jaw, smoothing his facial expression out. "I brought you here today because there is somewhere I must venture to, and I can only find the answers I need if you accompany me."

I force a nod. "Of course, father. Anything I can do to help, I am willing."

"Very well." He says before he waves his wand, dispelling the chains from my wrists and ankles. I look down at myself, lifting my hands as I rub the small indents in my skin. "But first, I need you to show Apollo what we've practiced so far."

I lift my gaze up, glancing from Zeus to Apollo. Those stunning brown eyes amplified from the golden halo that surrounds them. He stares at me, his expression unreadable against his chiseled jaw. I decide at that moment to not ask questions, and to just do what Zeus asks.

The faster I can do this, and go wherever it is we must go, the faster I can get back down into the dungeon. Where oddly enough I feel the safest here.

I take a few steps back from them, lifting my hands and facing my palms up. I take a deep breath in, releasing that breath as I close my eyes. Centering into myself, drowning everything out.

I fall deep into my power, visualizing my shadows to the surface when I feel them discharging from my fingertips, some of them coiling themselves around my wrists before traveling up my arms. The others pooling outwards and slithering down to the ivory polished floor.

I open my eyes as I watch them create a barrier—a shield in front of me, blocking me from Zeus and Apollo. I focus on the intention of protecting myself from them and watch as it builds higher and higher until it's towering above them.

In an instant—with no warning, I feel Zeus' lightning zap at my barrier, attempting to dismantle it. I stumble backwards as he manages to disburse a small portion of my barrier, the attack dimming the shadows there before coiling together and re-patching what he damaged. I regain my footing and straighten my back, keeping my gaze locked on my barrier when in a flash of a moment, I see it.

"There." Zeus says to Apollo. Referencing the tiny burst of light that pulsated through my barrier, happening quicker than the blink of an eye.

The second time it's happened now. The last time Zeus tried attacking my barrier my shadows engulfed his spark of lightning, as if alchemizing it into my barrier. This time my shadows deflected it, so why would they still pulsate if—

"The prophecy spoke nothing of this…" Apollo begins, his words trailing off before he tries to step around my barrier. Walking around it and facing me before my shadows quickly wrap the barrier backwards, blocking him once more.

The prophecy? What is he talking about?

"You may put them down now, Melinoë." Zeus says from behind my shield.

I tentatively extract my shadows back into my fingertips, watching as the barrier melts downward to the floor. Like a thick fog of darkness lowering to the ground before solidifying into an oil-like substance. Licking the polished floor as they creep back towards me before disappearing into my fingertips once more.

Apollo stands there, tilting his head as he assesses me. He begins his steady stride over to me until only a few inches separates us. His gaze roams over me before he shakes his head. "The prophecy is as I told you. I am only given what I am allowed, visions of what is to come without interference with The Laws of The Fates" He turns around to face Zeus, his voice steady and clear. My gaze lands on his defined back muscles, chiseled as if sculpted from stone. "We knew that there would be some uncertainty with what exactly her gifts extended to. I will still take you to Delphi, but my oracle will tell you no different."

A sliver of panic begins to blossom in the pit of my stomach. So is that what Apollo's divinity is? That he can see into the future? And what he said about me—about my gifts. Has Zeus not known this whole time that I would have different powers than him?

I mean, I can't blame him if he's perplexed by that. Considering I'm his daughter and—well, my gifts are wholly opposite from his. I figured that was just because I inherited my gifts from my mother, though I haven't seen much yet of what she's capable of other than what I'd seen her do to Amalthea.

Zeus takes a step towards us as his gaze flicks over to mine, holding my gaze before fixing it back onto Apollo. "You have been my trusted ally for centuries now, Apollo." He says as he lifts his gaze to the top of the dais. He stares at the chair that sits atop it as something akin to determination subtly washes over his expression. "So I trust what you say. But as King of Olympia, I will still cover all of my tracks."

Apollo nods to Zeus. "I'd expect nothing less."

Zeus sighs before he redirects his gaze from the dais and back over to me. He steps closer to me, willing the cuffs back onto my wrists and ankles before he says, "Then we leave now."

Apollo shoots a look over to me before nodding. "Very well."

A portal opens up behind Apollo, my gaze being pulled to it as I see swatches of evergreen and white stone swirl together in the frame. Swirling vines encased in bright gold and orange swirl along the border of his portal, mimicking the golden glow he emanates.

"You will speak only when you are spoken to by the Pythia."

I turn my gaze back onto Zeus, finding that he's glaring down at me. He grabs my wrists and holds the chains in his hands.

"Other than that, you remain silent and wait quietly until we are finished. Understood?"

I feel the tiny zap of his power strike my wrists, grimacing as I try to pull my arms away but he keeps them locked with his grasp. And as the small burst of ire threatens to push through my barrier, I quickly shove it back down and nod. "Yes, Your Majesty. I will behave." The words tasting like venom on my tongue.

He lifts his gaze to the portal, guiding me forward. "Then let's go."

Apollo walks through the portal first, the iridescent glow in the center swallowing him whole as he steps completely through.

With Zeus gripping the chains at my wrists, he walks us both through the portal as my bare feet step out onto lush grass. Reminding me of the lack of shoes I have on my feet, and nearly weeping at the comfort of walking on something that isn't a hard surface.

My gaze roams over the ground as the smell of fresh air wafts towards me, a simple pleasure that I never thought I'd say that I missed. A gentle breeze glides along my arms as I notice the profound lightness to the energy around me, no longer stifled by the cramped enclosure of my cell. Even if just temporarily.

I lift my gaze up to what stands before us. A colonnade of parian marble, doric designed columns with golden trim at the tops and bottom. Structured on a raised limestone podium. The sunny sky above gleams down through the open temple, brightening the cella hidden within as vibrant green vines intertwine themselves up along the wide steps leading up to the entrance. A large, golden statue of a man situated at the front entrance of the architecture. Standing in an upright position with his body angled into a fighting position. His face intricately designed to mimic the man standing right next to me.

My gaze glances to his back where the golden bow and arrow remain before glancing up at his face. A jaw that could cut through glass, a gaze that could penetrate right through someone. I work on a swallow as I take a steady breath in, releasing slowly through my nose.

Apollo keeps his gaze trained forward as he says, "Welcome to The Temple of Apollo."

CHAPTER 33

So in the past ten minutes I've learned a total of four things. That Apollo can see into the future, that he also has his own oracle who can see the future, that he has his own *Temple*, and most importantly—

There's a prophecy that involves me.

Zeus guides us up the steps as Apollo walks a step in front of us, passersby mingling around the temple bowing to him and Zeus before their gazes land on them. They all make glances at me before lowering to my wrists, whispering to one another before moving on with their day.

Some of them stare for a long moment at me, wondering who this girl is and why she's in chains. Knowing that Zeus is enjoying the kind of attention I'm getting.

The kind that displays silently, but loudly to others who still is in charge here.

We reach the top of the steps and enter into the cella. My feet gliding along the limestone as we advance deeper into the Temple. I almost go to open my mouth to ask where exactly we are, but remember what Zeus said.

Already feeling belittled enough in these chains and not wanting to be more embarrassed by the fury of already disrespecting his orders.

We walk towards another statue of Apollo at the center of the room, set to the far back wall. When we near approaching it, a young woman kneeling at the statue halts in the middle of her prayer. She lifts her head from the ground, turning around to see us walking towards her. She gasps, turning to face towards us but remaining in a kneeling position. "Apollo, what a great honor it is to be in your presence." She lifts her head to Zeus, lowering it once more. "As it is to be in yours, Your Majesty."

"You may rise, Jeneane." Apollo says as he stands in front of me. We all stop before her.

Jeneane lifts her head, rising to her feet quickly. She lifts an arm, extending it behind herself at the laurel plant beneath the statue. "I brought it for you. An offering to show my gratitude for all that you do for us here in Delphi."

I look at the many offerings laid beneath the statue's feet. Numerous offerings of wine, barley, laurel plants and wreaths, and even books. I try to hone in on what the title on some of the books are but Zeus urges me forward, his hand still firmly placed on my chains. I nearly stumble forward but steady my stance.

"I am most grateful, Jeneane. Thank you." Apollo says before joining us, positioning himself in front of us again as he leads us to a door behind the statue.

When he approaches it, he turns the knob, showcasing a set of winding stairs leading down below the Temple. He begins walking down them as Zeus and I follow in tow behind him.

Torches jutted from the wall to my right with gleaming steady flames as we walked further and further down the steps. Only when it is several minutes later do we finally reach the bottom.

We walk into a small room with a tripod cauldron situated in the center. The bronzed cauldron nearly the same size as the buckets I've been bathing in for a week now. I look up from it and notice a woman seated on a raised platform behind it, looking downwards with her eyes closed.

Donned in simple robes with colors ranging from muted red to orange. Her black hair swept back into a low bun beneath a red scarf, the ends sweeping down past her breasts.

Apollo walks towards the center of the room, near the cauldron as Zeus and I follow. I watch as the woman takes a casual inhale in before lifting her head. Her eyes still closed as her porcelain face straightened. "I set some time aside for you today, Apollo." She slowly opens her eyes as she looks straight ahead. "I've been expecting you three. Though I'm afraid I will not tell you anything you have not already heard." She says lifting her gaze to Zeus.

Zeus finally lets go of my wrists and I watch as the woman lowers her gaze to me briefly before staring straight ahead again.

"Then you will have no problem repeating it word for word again." Zeus says as he stands before the cauldron. "Just to make sure nothing has been left out."

"In all the years I have served Apollo, he has never proven to be a dishonest God. But with both the blessing and curse bestowed upon you, King of All Gods, I expect nothing less than the demand of accuracy in such things."

From the corner of my eye I watch as Zeus flexes his hand again, wondering what she means at both the blessing and curse at being King of All Gods.

But before I can ponder much longer about it, Apollo nods his head. "Let us begin."

She blinks as she stares straight ahead. "Very well then." She glances at me casually before lifting herself from the raised limestone and standing before the cauldron. She looks over to Apollo, nodding.

He steps closer to her side as she turns to face him. I watch as some kind of smoke begins to fill the cauldron, wafting around inside of it as Apollo lifts his hand and places it above the bridge of the Pythia's nose, at the center of her brow.

She closes her eyes and begins to hum. Quietly at first, but then it becomes louder and more gruntled. Causing the smoke in the cauldron to intensify until it begins to spill out over the edges. She begins chanting and humming for a long time until Apollo steps away, leaving her still standing there with her eyes closed.

She takes a long inhale in and begins to speak in a trance-like state.

"In a land shared with another, a once great King will fall to the death inflicted by one of his own. The new King, in an attempt to prevent repeating the first King's same end,

will seek counsel from The Oracle of Delphi about the fate of his life, from beginning to end. Only to be disappointed that he will be overthrown by his polar opposite, a karmic retribution for his own inflictions. But then, a prophecy is told of three siblings born under The Queen and King of The Underworld, a mother who will herald three beacons of change. Three immortals of immense power. But the new King will interfere with this prophecy in an attempt to claim the children as his own. But for one to exist, they must all exist. So he uses the prophecy for his own gain, disguising himself as her one true love, and impregnates the goddess three separate times.

The first born, who would be later known as the Twice Born after a fear-induced assassination during his infancy. The King in his desperation to make sure the other two can be born, reincarnates him with the flesh of his mistress. A decision made without the King of The Underworld's blessing, a pain the first mother mourns eternally as the boy lives in secret behind the new King. The second born, not to be confused with the Twice Born, prophesied to bring destruction and endings to all the lands from the North to the South. The Guardian of Souls, A Harbinger of Nightmares, made with pure darkness that reflects little to his power, but instead to whom her father was meant to be. Whose soul is shared with the one who heralds fire, who will become the King's greatest threat. And the third born, a peacekeeper between the living and deceased. A Goddess whose lips will bring comfort and blissful death upon those who are in need of it in passing.

It is with all three children that the King will remain undefeated upon his throne of the bones of his father, and the forging of his own secrets.

The Pythia takes a sharp breath in as the smoke from the cauldron dissipates entirely. Her eyes shoot open as she slowly cranes her neck from side to side, a subtle crack sounding from her bones before straightening her neck out. She blinks once, then twice before shifting her gaze up to Zeus. "That is the end of the prophecy."

I continue staring straight ahead at the Pythia, keeping my gaze neutral even as the tumultuous realizations of numerous things try to threaten a reaction out of me.

"You are sure that is everything?" Zeus muses, tilting his head. "There is nothing particular about what her gifts would entail?" He says, insinuating to me.

The Pythia shakes her head. "That is the prophecy I have for you."

Zeus says nothing for a long moment, a beat of annoyance on his face before he looks over at Apollo. "We're done here."

He grabs my chains and pulls me away from the cauldron, my gazing straying to the Oracle of Delphi who stares at me. She watches me as Zeus hauls me away, and before I turn my head around, I notice the slight curve of her lips.

I turn my gaze forward as Zeus drags me up the long, winding steps back up to the cella. Apollo remains a quiet, looming presence behind us as he follows us up.

"It would be especially wise of you not to repeat what you heard today, Melinoë."

I look up at Zeus who has his gaze trained forward as we ascend the stairs. Impressed with my ability to keep my emotions and my utter shock in check right now, especially as I feel the suffocating power of his compulsion reach out for me. Coercing me to fall deeply under it. "My allegiance lies with you, Your Majesty."

He looks down at me.

"I have no intention of dishonoring that loyalty." I say assuredly through a mouthful of lies.

A smirk curves up Zeus' lips before turning his gaze forward again. But as his gaze turns away, I feel the brand of Apollo's at my back. Wondering if he's suddenly watching me to make sure I mean what I say to Zeus, or if since he's able to tell the future, if he's able to see that I won't be in these chains for long. But if that were the case, I can only imagine he would've warned Zeus by now.

If that's the case, then is he only able to see certain parts of the future? Is he obscured from seeing *everything* that happens? Yet instead of pondering over those questions as we continue ascending the steps, all I can focus on is the brand of his stare on my back the entire way up.

CHAPTER 34

As we step through the portal my feet land on the throne room floor, Zeus letting go of my chains finally as the portal closes behind us. The alarming information that I just learned swarming inside of me, bursting from the inside out.

The prophecy spoken of the Twice Born, who would be assassinated in infancy by those who feared him. The same story that Semele told me—

Suddenly a memory flashes behind my eyes. The day I first met Semele and how distraught she was over losing that golden locket, the one with the picture of her son inside that she claimed to have left behind with the man who abused her. I coined that whole thing as just a way for her to gain her trust with me, that it was all a fake sob story to get closer to me. But as that picture blossoms vividly in my mind now, I realize it's the child version of—

Holy fuck. Dionysus isn't Hera's son, he's *Semele's* son.

"Bethesda, take her downstairs." Zeus says, jogging me from my exploding thoughts. Thank The Fates because I was about to lose my control over my cover just now.

Bethesda approaches my side as I look at Zeus, bowing at the waist. "It was a pleasure to accompany you today, Your Majesty."

He says nothing as he turns away from me entirely, walking with Apollo to who knows where.

As Bethesda and I approach the dungeon door, my mind swarms rampantly inside me with all of the missing dots connecting to one another. With the most obvious one being that Dionysus has no idea that Semele is his mother, and that he's also the Twice Born.

Two souls in one body.

I shake my head to myself as a memory surfaces in my mind. "It can't be." I say softly to myself.

"What did you say, dear?" Bethesda says to my left as we descend downwards.

I clear my throat, shaking my head. "Sorry—nothing." I lied.

For the first time since I've been here, I actually quicken my pace. Wanting to reach my cell and be locked inside, with Bethesda out of sight so I can pace back and forth in my cell, putting every tiny piece of all of this together. Putting every detail that hasn't made sense into the bigger *why* of it all.

As soon as we reach my cell I walk over to the wall, Bethesda chaining me back up before she exits the cell. Locking it and giving me a faint nod. "I will retrieve you tomorrow for chores, Melinoë."

I give her a nod. "See you tomorrow, Bethesda."

She turns on her heels and makes her way up the steps, waiting until I've heard the door close behind her to say something.

"Holy fuck." I say out loud, my hands coming up to my face as I push the tiny strands of my hair back from my cheeks. The memory I just tried to hold back resurfacing again now that I'm alone.

"Zeus shapeshifted himself to appear as my husband. That is…how all of my children were conceived."

The words of my mother the day I learned she was alive this entire time float through my mind, never having realized the way she said *all* of my children. Having only ever presumed she was referring to Makaria and myself—

Standing on the edge of the cliff outside of my mothers and Hades' palace, overlooking the souls in The Asphodel Meadows. I catch my mother looking down upon the souls, her gaze honed in on them as if searching for someone. After a few moments I asked her, "Are you looking for someone?"

She'd denied that she was, but if the prophecy is exactly how the Pythia spoke of it, then that means that while Semele is Dionysus' mother by ingesting his first incarnated heart, and carrying him to term for Zeus, then—

My hands come up to my mouth as my heart feels like it's sinking itself down to my feet as shock explodes inside of me.

"The Titans took something invaluable from me. And they will forever pay for their crime."

I sink to the floor with my hand still clamped up to my mouth, shock widening my gaze. The story my mother told me about The Titans taking something from her, the part in the story that Semele told me of a group of individuals killing that baby. Ingesting everything but his heart. That baby is Dionysus reincarnated.

That baby was my *mother's* child. The true first, and eldest sibling of the prophecy the Pythia spoke of. And Dionysus, in a twisted sort of way, is my brother.

I lower my hands from my mouth slowly to my lap, staring at the wall straight ahead as I digest everything internally. Every little detail spoken about the prophecy ramming itself against the inner walls of my mind, demanding me to look at each part and feeling utterly consumed by it all.

Consumed by the fact that Zeus procreated with my mother in an attempt to favor the prophecy for himself. As it originally spoke of us being born from not my mother and Zeus, but from my mother and—

Hades.

I jolt up from the ground, rushing over to the toilet as I hold my hair back to throw up. All of the morbid, disturbing truths. All of it too much to handle as a cold sweat dampens the back of my neck.

I hover over the toilet as I finish vomiting, taking deep breaths in and out before my hand reaches up to flush the toilet. I look over at the small bit of water I have left in my water bottle, making my way over to it and seating myself back down.

"Well that was an unfortunate way to wake up."

I twist the cap off, downing the rest of what's left before twisting the cap back on, tossing it as I look over to the cell door where her voice wafts from. "Sorry." My voice hardly above a whisper.

"Are you alright?" She asks as I hear movement from her cell. The sound of something gliding across the ground and then stopping. As if stretching her legs but sounding like a larger object than a leg.

"Yeah. I'm…alright." I say absentmindedly.

I lean my head up against the stone wall as the prophecy repeats itself in my mind. Remembering each part, word for word. I rummage through and analyze each word spoken over and over again. Always coming up on the same jarring realizations.

Never having even thought twice about why Hades and I shared similar powers, similar shadows. How he was able to see inside of my soul when training me to unleash my shadows, and rid myself of my fears of them. How my shadows had this moment of recognizing him the first time I showed him, and the subtle facial reaction he had when he saw them. I never understood it.

Until now.

Semele told me that the prophecy was only spoken and known by Zeus, which means my mother and Hades could've never known Zeus' true intentions. And it explains why after all of these years, why he wanted to keep Makaria and I close to him. Never wanting us to be far from him and under his watchful eye.

Which means that if he ends up getting his hands on Makaria, and is able to bring her back here, it's over. And he'll have exactly what he wants.

And the baby—since he never died, my mother and Hades never were able to guide him to The Underworld to rest in the afterlife. My mother has known no peace with where his soul has gone, and the whole time he's been hidden away in Zeus' palace in Olympia. Having reincarnated him by Semele ingesting his heart and carrying him to term.

Why would Semele keep it from Dionysus that she's his mother? Why not save her son the agony of thinking that Hera is his mother?

It explains why Hera looks at him the way she does. She knows who and what he is. It's why she looks at us all in glaring ways. Because it's a testament of Zeus' infidelity and lack of faithfulness.

The irony of it almost comical as he demands blind loyalty from his people.

I still don't understand the beginning about the two Kings. So Zeus killed the first King to rule over Olympia? But why would he do that?

And the part about me sharing a soul with the one who heralds fire. It has to be talking about Reimus, and it has to be talking about it in a spiritual sense. That we were fated to meet each other long before either of us were born.

I rub my hands over my face, sighing deeply.

There's no way I can go on while I'm still here, and force a look of impassivity when I see Dionysus now—or Semele.

All I'm going to be thinking about is the exact reason why Semele kidnapped me. Which was to help Zeus fulfill favoring the prophecy for his gain.

I look up at the torch on the wall, blinking as I realize all I have now is time. Time until Reimus and Hades and my mother come to free me from here, whenever that is. I have to believe that they have a plan, and that is why it hasn't been executed yet. But one thing I know for sure that will stick with me, is one fine detail about the prophecy the Pythia spoke of.

That I was prophesied to be Zeus' greatest threat. And somehow, that begins to melt every shred of weakness I've ever felt around him. Every shred of fake loyalty that I've been forced to portray here. As the façade that I'm playing begins to slowly subside as the thoughts of retribution center themselves in my mind. Knowing I need to keep some level of an act intact to keep the people I love safe, but deciding at this moment that there are some authentic parts of myself that I'm ready to let slip a little.

A sinister side of me that I've kept buried for a long time, fearful of what she's capable of. But as a wicked grin curves up my lips, something switches inside of me. And she begs to be let out of her cage.

CHAPTER 35

Reimus

A few days have passed after Hecate and I met with Eiran, and outside of maintaining security sweeps, I've wholly succumbed to spending every waking moment out in the yard.

And if it weren't for the help of Persephone, it would look as if I've just laid a random trail of red brick down, stretching out to the rest of the terrain.

She had offered to save me time and just will everything into place, but I respectfully declined. I want most of what is going into our shared space to be cultivated from my own hands, from putting in the hard work to bring Melinoë's vision to life—with a few tweaks of my own I think she'd enjoy. I want the countless hours, the stretch of days that went into all of this to mimic the love I have for Melinoë. That I'll never cut corners when it comes to her, and everything I do for her, will be with nothing short of my utmost effort.

Though I would be lying if I said I built and placed the water fountain myself. That I owe to Persephone and bringing my vision for how I wanted it to look perfectly to life.

I stare over at it now, smiling to myself. A few birds perched on the lip of the aged limestone tier have already begun to make use of the water as a bath for themselves. Some of them have elected to bathe themselves in the large, fiore pond below. Nonetheless, it makes me feel a warmth of giddiness inside to know that when Melinoë returns home that she will have a peaceful oasis to return home to.

Knowing that it won't change everything that she's gone through while imprisoned there, but hoping it will still become a safe space nonetheless.

My gaze lowers to the plentiful flowers and bushes placed along our new garden pathway, leading all the way out into the next part of the yard I've been hyperfocusing on.

A grab the structure of wood and lay it down next to the other on the large working table I've brought out here, parallel to one another. I turn around and grab another, drilling each end into the tops of the two others, creating one of several post frames. I continue doing this until I have eight sets of frames, each of them laying flat on the grass next to the raised wooden floor frame.

I lower the drill to the grass as I go to carefully raise one post frame up from the ground when I misjudge just how much of this I'll be able to build on my own.

With each post frame measuring over five feet in width, raising over eight feet tall, there's no way I'll be able to drill each of these on my own without the possibility of it falling over mid-way.

I drop the frame, bringing my thumb and index finger to the bridge of my nose. Pinching the skin there before lowering my hand, turning around at the sound of Dimitri approaching me. "I was just about to call for you."

I turn around to see Dimitri stuff his hands in his pockets, his gaze roaming over all the wood and parts I have laid on the ground. He chuckles. "Did you really think you could build this by yourself?"

I roll my eyes, laughing. "I think I was stubborn enough to, yes."

Dimitri nods to the wooden frame before lowering to one side of it, lifting it. "I see Persephone has already started on planting the flowers."

I lower myself to the other end, lifting that side until we both get it standing completely upright. "She has graciously gotten much of it done. There's just a few other areas I want filled in but not until I get this done."

We both shimmy it over, lifting it up onto the raised platform and angling it to line up with the edge of the floor.

"She's going to love it." Dimitri says.

I look up at him, giving him a brief half grin before stepping away to grab the drill.

"I think she'll also love that she'll be within view of Alastor." He says, holding the post frame up as I begin drilling the connector of one end to the platform.

I look over at the pasture not far from us, watching as Alastor and Gizelle watch us. Arion making his way over to stand near them, a soft whinny sounding from him as he sees Dimitri.

I turn my head around, stepping over to Dimitri's side and drilling the bottom of that post down. "That was my intention."

We both continue moving each set of post frames over next to the other, drilling each one down until all eight sets are drilled to the bottom of the octagon floor. Dimitri walks back inside the palace to bring out a ladder, setting it on the raised floor and positioning it close to one post frame. I walk over to the pile of metal roof beams and carry one over, handing it to Dimitri as I climb the ladder halfway up.

"I've noticed Nora has been here at the palace more often as of late." I say as I turn towards Dimtri.

He hands me the metal beam as I carefully raise it up. "We've been spending a little more time together."

"Does this mean you are finally past the 'I've been in love with you but I'm too afraid to say anything, so I'll just continue acting like I'm perfectly okay as just friends' stage?" I smirk at him before drilling the heavy duty screw into the hold fastened in the beam, connecting it to the wood as it stays sturdy in place.

Dimitri huffs out a soft noise as he grabs another metal beam, waiting for me to position the ladder a few feet over to my right. He hesitates for a moment before responding. "Not quite."

As soon as I get back onto the ladder with my drill, he hands the beam to me as a chuckle slips out of me. But the humor from my smile smooths out as I see the inner turmoil lingering on his expression. "What about telling her makes you most afraid?" I lift the beam up, connecting it to the top of the other edge of the post frame. Drilling it sturdy against it. "Or most resistant?"

"I don't know." He grabs another metal beam. "I think I'm just afraid to lose her if she doesn't feel the same way back. Or to at the very least ruin our friendship."

I step down from the ladder, moving it over as we begin to work our way around the octagon-shaped structure. "Well, I think at some point you're going to have to ask yourself if your fear of pursuing further, is going to matter as much to you, when someone else comes along and you miss your chance."

He looks at me, nodding as he hands me the beam. "Yeah, I know."

I lift it up to the next post frame, angling it at the top. "Nora likes you, though you seem to be the only one who can't see that." I drill the beam into the wood, lowering the drill and my gaze back down to him. "But she knows her worth. I know she cares deeply for you, but she won't wait around on you."

He sighs. "I know."

"Life is too unpredictable to not chase after what you love, to say what you mean." I say as I lower myself from the ladder, moving it over a few feet. The irony of that statement plunging itself deep into my chest at how suddenly Melinoë was taken from me, at how close I was to asking her to marry me. How if it weren't for Eiran's reassurance that Melinoë would be freed from Zeus' imprisonment, I would mourn each and every day if I had lost my only chance of marrying the only woman I had ever wanted to give my entire life to.

I climb up the ladder again, looking down at Dimitri. "So don't let your fear do you a disservice by not sharing how you feel. You should tell her."

He lowers himself over to the pile of metal beams, grabbing another and lifting it up to me. A small inkling of determination blossoming in his gaze as he fixes a faint grin. "I think I'll take your advice…when I'm ready."

I grab the beam and lift it up to the top of the wooden frame.

"Do you think you'll try to visit her again?"

My gaze remains on the beam as I drill it into the wood, Dimitri asking what he probably already knows the answer to. "Yes. Without a question."

The talisman still hung around my neck, feeling the quiet hum of it against my skin before dulling once again. As if wanting me to use it to astral travel to Melinoë again, encouraging me to use what it's designed to do.

Protect.

"Maybe it'll allow you to roam elsewhere in Zeus' palace. Since you both are twin souls, it should keep you concealed from everyone in there. The only worry I have is if they'll still be able to *feel* an energetic presence or not."

That thought having already crossed my mind. The day after Hecate and I met with Eiran, I told Dimitri what was revealed to me—about Melinoë and I. He'd taken it exactly how I did: with surprise. There was then a moment afterwards where I saw a glimpse of anger blanch his face. A reaction not only to having his best friend's partner taken from him and witnessing the turmoil it's taken on me, but also due to a primal instinct of being a drago.

The Draghi don't have fated mates—well, I guess except for me being the exception. Though what Melinoë and I are is slightly different. Many of the Draghi prefer to indulge in polyamorous relationships, as they are comfortable in their sexuality and enjoy having more than one partner to share their life with. But there are still many of us that when we find someone we form that inexplicable bond with, we become incredibly territorial over them.

Well, those of us that used to be at least. Since the only Draghi that are now left are Dimitri and I. A truly unfortunate outcome to losing all of our people, our families, in the war many years ago. With the reminder to hang over my head that when it is both of mine and Dimitri's time to part this existence, that we will then become an extinct kind altogether.

I am grateful that I am still alive today, but a part of me mourns a future knowing that at some point, there will be no Draghi left to inhabit it. A once fearless, extraordinary kind that will eventually be wiped from the face of the realms. "It's worth a try. I'll let you know if I succeed or not when I try again tonight."

With the help of Dimitri I continue setting up and drilling the metal beams to the wooden post frames until we finish all eight, meeting back to where we started. He stays to help me connect the roof ring, connecting it and drilling it to each beam before attaching the metal roof support panels. After hours of labor Dimitri continues to assist and help me with it all, even when I tell him I can take it from here if he's got other things to do. When he tells me he's good where he's at, that he's here to help me in whatever way I need it, it's the subtlest reminder of his loyalty to the people he cares for.

In ways that fear could never take from him, no matter how hard it tries to.

CHAPTER 36

Melinoë

I idly run the brush through my hair as I wait for Bethesda to collect me for our kitchen chores. Knowing that she'll be arriving soon, and having nothing better to do but brush my hair over and over again.

At least now it's soft and untangled.

"If you find it in your heart to retrieve me a little snack while you're up there, I would be most appreciative."

I chuckle, looking over at the cell door towards where her voice is coming from. "The *snack* that you require is going to be a little difficult at the moment, considering I'm supposed to be pious and diligent."

"Oh, but you could just so easily collect it from her veins. Just one small vial is all I need." She says.

"I don't pick Bethesda as the giving kind when it comes to freely giving out her blood."

The past few days the woman—or creature, whatever she is, has been more talkative than prior. Learning that her kind survives on the blood of mortals and gods, particularly from a violent death either enacted on their part or from another.

As with any other entity I've come across, with unusual gifts or sustenances, I didn't become afraid of her.

I mean—sure, blood doesn't sound entirely *appetizing*. But it's hardly my place to call that strange or morbid when I can make people terrified through invoking hallucinations.

Her hiss echoes around the stone walls. "All I need is for one of them to come too close to my cage."

I hear a razor sharp object quickly swipe along the ground, piercing my ears as a faint ruffle of something follows. "But they unfortunately know better than to get too close." I hear an audible, frustrated sigh from her. "Courtesy of *His Majesty*." She says, mockingly.

A snort escapes as I chuckle. When I go to open my mouth, she cuts me off.

"Speaking of which." She says, going silent once again as the dungeon door opens as a ray of sunlight beams itself down along the stairs.

I watch as Bethesda walks down, approaching my cell door and unlocking it. "Good afternoon, Melinoë." She says before slipping inside.

I stand myself up from the ground. "Good afternoon, Bethesda."

She comes to unlock the chains from my wrists and ankles before guiding me out of the cell, leading me up the steps where our chores await us.

Having only volunteered so I could get an idea of what I'm working with here and how things are laid out. But it's impossible for me to sneak away without Bethesda keeping a watchful eye on me. I tried to make an excuse yesterday that

I had to use the bathroom and couldn't wait until I made it back downstairs. But it backfired when she took me all the way back down here, waited for me to use the toilet, and then brought me all the way back up here.

My bare feet pad along the polished floor as we make our way into the kitchen, dirty dishes and cups laid out on the kitchen island. These people really have no sense of basic cleanliness.

We both get right to work on cleaning the kitchen, her washing the dishes and I sweeping and mopping the floor. The whole time wondering when the next time Reimus will come to visit me again in the astral realm. Hoping he does soon so I can tell him everything that I learned. Knowing that I have no idea what exactly their plan is to extract me out of here, and unsure if any part of the prophecy that I tell them will sway their tactics or not. Or the most likely outcome being my mother seeking total destruction over Zeus and Olympia after she finds out that her first born is technically still alive.

His soul just now merged with another in a completely new body.

I still can't believe everything that I learned about the prophecy—about Zeus. I knew his intentions for impregnating my mother were ones of a vile nature, but it really became a reality when I heard it firsthand for myself from the Pythia. The truth of who I, as well as Makaria and Dionysus' first form, were supposed to be born under.

It makes me wonder if Hades ever wanted children. I see the love he has for my mother, how fiercely he stands by her.

I can't imagine he didn't want them. It makes me also wonder what kinds of lengths he will go to when he learns that Zeus took what was fated to be his.

And used it for his selfish gain.

I hate Zeus for everything that he is. What he's taken from me, from my family. How he treats the people of Olympia, as if they're a nuisance to him and cannot be bothered with their concerns. He's the cruelest, most pitiful god I've ever—

I begin to feel the rising tide of my emotions pushing against my skin, swelling in my hands against the spelled cuffs that keep my magic at bay. And for once, feeling somewhat grateful for them as I'm not sure what would've happened just now had I lost control and let that reservoir of power erupted.

I take a deep breath in and out, quelling the rising emotions within me. Lowering them deeper into myself for the time being until I have my opportunity to use them freely.

Because when I get my opportunity to use them against Zeus again…I won't hold back.

After mindlessly sweeping the kitchen floor, I go to the cleaning closet to put the broom away when I see something inside of there.

I set the broom up against the wall and look up at the top shelf, at what lays tucked beside a stack of paper towels. A bottle of water, a blueberry muffin, and a few pieces of bacon.

My mouth against my own control begins watering at the food hidden there, knowing that if someone put this up here for them to eat later, they wouldn't have hid it in a cleaning closet. The only two people to come in here at all being Bethesda, myself, and the other handmaids that reside here in the palace.

It definitely wasn't Dionysus that put that up there for me, so it must've been Semele. But why go through the trouble of doing all of this? I know that she's the mistress in the story she told me, the one in the prophecy who bore Zeus' child for him. She must have some love for him to have done all that—

At that reminder I remember a vital part to that story. That the mistress was first a human before she was turned into a goddess.

Semele was once mortal.

"You okay in there?" Bethesda calls out.

"Yes, sorry!" I blurt out. "I was just looking for the cleaning solution. I found it."

I intentionally pull the bucket out from against the wall, making noise to let her know that I don't need her coming in here for help. I push the bucket out of the closet, setting it into the sink and dumping some cleaning solution in. I twist the cap back on, turn on the faucet and let the hot water stream inside. I move back into the closet to put the floor cleaner away when I grab the bacon from the shelf.

I shove it into my mouth, chewing quickly and also savoring the flavor even though it's cold by now. I close my eyes briefly in utter bliss.

I quickly grab the water, opening it up and taking a few large gulps from it before tightening the lid back on. I set it back onto the shelf, grabbing the mop and walking back out.

I walk over to the sink, shutting the water off and lifting the bucket up and out of the sink. I set it back down onto the floor and began mopping.

After I finish I dump the dirty water down the sink, rinsing it out before wheeling it back into the closet. After I wheel it up against the wall I hurry and reach for the muffin, shoving it into my mouth and devouring it. At the sound of the water running from Bethesda still washing dishes, I hurry and grab the water, twisting the cap off and taking a few last big sips before capping it, hiding it up on the shelf again.

I turn around, exiting the closet and making my way over to Bethesda where I help dry the dishes for her until we're finished.

After wiping down the counters, changing out the garbage, and making sure everything is spotless, Bethesda and I exit the kitchen. "Why do you leave the garbage there instead of taking it out?"

She keeps her gaze forward as her hand rests firmly on my handcuffs. "I take it out once I've put you back in the dungeon. Zeus made it very clear for me to do it that way."

"Oh." I say, fixing my gaze forward as it roams over the detailing in the walls. Elegant molding at the creases in the ceiling with vines carved into the wood. I wonder what their dining room and the rest of the palace looks like—

I hear the swift footsteps of someone and my gaze lowers to a woman walking down the hallway towards us. Her gaze fixates on the hallway stretching behind me, assumingly to the rest of the palace. It isn't until we're within close distance to one another that she looks right at me.

I notice instantly a silver bow and quiver of arrows strapped to her sun-kissed back, her figure lean and muscular. Wearing a similar pair of breeches as me, hers a shade of dark brown instead of beige with a hunting knife strapped to her thigh. The sleeveless, forest green tunic fully exposing a silver band fitted around her bicep.

As Bethesda and I keep walking, this woman stares at me as she continues her same powerful stride. I fixate on her eyes, the shade a cool light grey set beneath a dark brow. I notice a thin halo of silver around her iris, a similar characteristic to Apollo's though instead of warm sunlight, hers remind me of spun moonlight.

She keeps her gaze fixed on me for another stretch of a moment before fixing it forward again, walking down the hallway in silence but with a mission nonetheless it seems. I turn my head to see her long brown hair pulled back into a thick braid, traveling down to the middle of her back.

I turn back around, leaning in closer to Bethesda as I whisper, "Who was that?"

We turn the corner as we step out into the throne room. "That is Lady Artemis. Goddess of The Hunt."

Well, her title sure fits her demeanor. That woman had no shortage of weapons strapped to her. "She looks similar to Apollo. Are they related?"

Bethesda nods. "They are twin siblings."

That explains the impeccable similarities then.

I wonder since Apollo is Zeus' most trusted ally if she knows who I am, why I'm here. Knowing that the prophecy now has supposedly only been spoken to Zeus and myself, but wondering if since that's Apollo's sister if she knows because of him.

Bethesda opens the door to the dungeons, leading me down as she guides me back to my cell. After she gets me situated, she nods her head. "See you tomorrow, Melinoë." She exits out of the cell, closing it and locking it before beginning her trek back up the steps.

"See you tomorrow." I say quietly after her, leaning myself back up against the wall as I lower myself down to the ground.

Once I hear the door close at the top of the stairs, I lean my head back and drift off to a place far from here. Into the recesses of my mind until I'm retrieved once again tomorrow.

CHAPTER 37

Reimus

Fine droplets of rain drip off the tips of my onyx wings as I glide high above, passing the edge of the Sephyra Forest. Glancing downwards at Charon at the shield far below before scanning Vulir as I make sure everything is clear.

Forest is clear.

I feel Charon's energy down the Guardian's channel, affirming the same. *All clear at the shield.*

I continue gliding above Vulir, knowing most people have already retired indoors for the night while very few businesses will still remain open for another thirty minutes. One of which being The Raven's Claw. Having always been curious how much business she still gets at seven-thirty.

As I scope out the rest of Vulir, I send my confirmation down the Guardian's channel. *All clear in the village.*

Charon and Dimitri both brush their energy up against the channel, letting me know they've received my statement. And as the Guardian's Palace comes into view, I soar my way home until I make it to the front entrance.

As I bank down I shift right before I can touch the ground, striding fluidly up to the front door. I push it open, the entryway quiet and dimly lit from the sconces on the walls. I close the door behind me, heading to make my way upstairs when I hear Nora and Dimitri's voice filter from the dining room down the hall.

I chuckle to myself as I listen in.

"You're throwing with just your fist. Engage with your entire body." Dimtri says to her, wondering what exactly I'm about to walk into.

Nora groans at him. "I'm trying—"

"No, you're holding back. Here, watch my form."

At that moment I step into the dining room as I see Dimitri where our coffee table would be, having moved it over to the side to teach and demonstrate. "Rotate your hips," He says before showing her how. "Engage your core and push off your feet." Showing Nora by doing just that, leading it all the way through his slow motioned punch through the air.

I watch as Nora nods her head, getting into stance as she tries herself. She does a little *too much* lifting from her feet and catapults herself into Dimitri. She stumbles into him as she tries catching herself but he catches her in his arms. They both laugh as Nora remains close to him for a moment, their laughter subsiding as they both look at one another. Dimitri's hand lowers from her hip as Nora slowly lowers her hands from his chest. Her chest rising suddenly.

Definitely about to ruin whatever moment they're having right now and it was not intentional.

Maybe if I just slip out quietly they won't even notice. But as Dimitri's gaze lifts up to mine, I forget that our heightened senses are no match for the element of surprise.

"Sorry for intruding on…whatever this is." I say, heading over to the credenza cart of liquor. I lift the cap off the whiskey bottle and fill an earful into a glass.

Nora quickly removes herself from Dimitri's embrace, she being the only one who did not hear me approaching. "After Hecate taught us how to shield and do some protective magic, I felt determined to learn how else to protect myself." She moves herself to the couch, plopping herself down. "So I asked him to teach me how to fight. Turns out I need a lot more practice."

Dimitri chuckles as he makes his way to the credenza cart. "You just have to get your form down. Then you'll be kicking ass before you know it." He grabs the bottle of whiskey, holding it up to Nora as he turns around. "Would you like a drink?"

She shakes her head. "But I will if you guys have some wine."

I chuckle. "I cannot remember the last time we were without wine."

"I'll go grab a bottle from the cellar. Sweet or dry?" Dimtri asks her.

She grins. "Sweet."

He nods his head as he turns around to exit out of the living room. I make my way over to the couch, my gaze lowering to the seat as a memory resurfaces. One of when I had Melinoë's legs spread and my face in between them, seated exactly where I belong and doing exactly what I was meant to do.

Worship her.

"What?" Nora asks, her voice interjecting itself as my thoughts begin to roam.

I shake my head, a quick grin fixing on my face. "Nothing." I take my seat and lean back into the leather couch, lifting the glass to my lips as I take a sip of my whiskey. "How has everyone been feeling since Hecate's lesson?"

"The women feel more at ease, more like they can protect themselves and are not so defenseless." She crosses her legs onto the couch. "They've been practicing. They really appreciated Hecate's willingness to teach them."

A soft grin curves my lips, a warmth seeping over my heart as all I ever wanted is for my people to feel safe. "I'm really glad to hear that."

She nods her head, forcing a grin. Her chest sinks as she sighs. "So…have you heard anything yet? How is Makaria faring in her training?"

I shake my head, lowering the glass down to my knee. "Last I spoke with Persephone she said she has been struggling. My assumption is both with trying to tap into her divinity and mentally." I stare at the fireplace straight ahead, the quiet roar of the fire lulling me. "I can't be angry with her at her pace in all of this. She's been through—and has been revealed to, a lot. I just hope that if she cannot talk to her sister, that she has someone else to confide in. That she doesn't have to process everything on her own."

Nora leans her head against the couch cushion. "I'm sure her mother has been helping her in any way she can. Maybe even Hades, as he seemed to have helped Melinoë a lot when she trained with him."

"Yeah, he did." I take another sip of my whiskey.

"Do you think she'll come home different?" Nora asks tentatively.

Her question is one that I've pondered over many times in my head. The ruinous thoughts of how adversely Zeus' treatment towards her will have affected her, and how that will change her long after she's come home. But in the context of how altered Melinoë is when she returns home to me, how impaired mentally she is, none of that would ever impact the consistency of my devotion to her. As none of it would make me love her any less.

None of it would make me look at her any differently because she will never be too flawed, or too damaged for me to properly love her. Twin souls or not, my love for her is irreplaceable regardless of what state she is in.

I look over at her. "If she does, she will have us by her side to comfort her through it."

Nora lifts her hand up, reaching it over towards me to place it on top of mine. "That she will." She says, smiling.

The bond that her and Melinoë have formed in the short time they've known each other is something I don't take lightly. Outside of it being impossible to not love Melinoë and to not feel genuinely safe and accepted in her presence, I know that the people that care for Melinoë show it in a way where it is visible.

But when I think about the way her father—Zeus treats her, it makes me feel a blind rage within. How can you despise your own child? Put them through the trenches of trauma and pain due to your own delinquency of willingness to put anyone above yourself? Not only to her but to Makaria, too. I'll never understand where he gets off in being a—

"Woah." Nora says as she lifts her hand from mine, looking down at it before glancing at my hand.

I sit up straight, looking at her hand as panic begins to implode within me. As I remember what happened with Hecate the other day.

I grab her hand, turning it over to assess her skin, seeing no burn marks present. I look up at Nora as concern bubbles up and pushes against my chest. "Did I hurt you?"

She shakes her head curtly. "No—it's just…your hand. It was *really* warm."

I shake my head slowly as I don't understand what is going on with my body—my hands lately. I've never known to be so warm-bodied that I burn other people. Or am overly warm when other people notice it.

Dimitri walks back into the room with a dark red bottle of moscato wine. He looks over at us, at the way I'm sitting and probably at the way my energy is appearing to him at the moment. "What's wrong?" He asks before approaching us.

"Nothing." Nora says, looking up at him. "His skin was just really warm is all. Are you feeling okay?" She looks back at me, leaning her head a little closer.

I let go of her hand finally, lowering mine back to my lap. "Yeah," I draw out absentmindedly. "I feel fine. I have noticed lately with my hands they get incredibly warm. I—"

I pause, deciding that telling them I burned Hecate the other day would just arise more unnecessary questions at the moment that I don't have the answers to. So instead, I conclude the conversation as I stand up from the couch. "It's nothing. It's probably just some weird fluke with my body temperature." I force a smile as I pat my hand on Dimitri's back. "You both enjoy your night. I'm going to retire for the night."

"Alright, man. If you need anything let me know." Dimitri says as he makes eye contact with me. Giving me a nod but knowing he's assessing me for anything that should raise concern.

I give him a nod back before turning to look back at Nora. "Goodnight."

She lowers her gaze to my hand briefly before giving me a soft grin. "Nighty night."

I exit out of the dining room, making my way over to the kitchen as I rinse my empty glass off, setting it in the dishwasher. I look down at my hand again, pressing a thumb at the center of my palm. Feeling no temperature difference at all beneath my touch. Either out of the fact that I'm too used to my own body temperature, or that the sudden warmth that Nora felt is already gone.

As I make my way upstairs I quickly dull the rambling thoughts of what it could be, deeming it as something that's not important to obsess over at the time. Knowing that if I'm preoccupied with something else, it may only complicate things when I try to astral travel to Melinoë again tonight.

I make it to our bedroom, opening the door and slipping my shoes off inside near the closet door. I lift off my black long-sleeved shirt, tossing it into the laundry hamper before unbuttoning my pants. Tossing them in there as well before throwing on a pair of grey sweatpants.

I run my hands through my hair as the subtle weight of the talisman rests on my chest, lifting it as I bring it closer to my lips.

"I don't know how exactly this works, but I need you to help aid me in reaching Melinoë tonight."

I look down at it as I make my way over to the bed. Not seeing anything spectacular happen such as a pulse of energy, or it lighting up. I lower my hand from the talisman, lifting the covers back as I crawl into bed.

I lean my head against my pillow, sighing as I try to get comfortable in bed. Glancing over to my right at the empty spot next to me.

I train my gaze back up, sinking in my own loneliness without her near me. Knowing that tonight I planned on astral traveling to her again, hoping that it will work like it did last time.

So before I close my eyes for sleep, I whisper one last time to the talisman on my chest. "Take me to my twin soul."

I close my eyes, settling into myself as I let tiredness plague me to sleep. Feeling a brief pulse of energy against my chest, right below where the talisman rests before I do.

CHAPTER 38

I lay with my eyes closed, the hard cement surface beneath me almost causing me to groan in discomfort until I realize—

I'm astral traveling.

My eyes fling open as I look down at my astral body, the talisman secured still around my neck as I've achieved returning back to the same spot before. In the same cell that they're holding her.

I look over, getting onto my hands and knees before standing up. I notice the way that Melinoë's face appears slightly softer this time as her eyes remain closed, leaned up against the stone wall fast asleep.

Her hair...it's been washed and cleaned since the last time I saw her. I look down at the brush near her side, wondering who brought that for her as it wasn't here last time. Realizing that in a palace of enemies that there's at least one person in this place that's actually looking out for her.

Interesting.

I approach her side, kneeling down as I study not the clean clothes she has on now, or the chains that I know are connected at her wrists and ankles, but at the planes of her face as a hint of life has resurfaced back into it. As if the slightest spark of herself has found its way back again.

Something about her looks…different.

I look down at her arm, wondering if my energy will be strong enough to wake her. Not wanting to disturb her while she's asleep, but knowing she'd want me to if I had managed to make my way back to her again.

I lay my hand on hers, squeezing. "Melinoë."

She doesn't stir awake and continues sleeping, her face remaining the same.

I try again. "Melinoë. My love, wake up. Just for a little bit."

I look down at the talisman, seeing it light up. "Help me." I whisper to it.

The talisman begins to pulsate on my chest, feeling that energy course down my shoulders and lower until it reaches my fingertips. I look up at Melinoë, keeping my gaze on her face. Waiting, hoping that it—

Her arm twitches, her head beginning to lull to the side when she opens her eyes. Her tired gaze lowers down to her hand, right where mine rests above and her eyes widen in surprise. "Rei." She says softly.

The sound of my name from her lips melts me from the inside out, wanting to burrow myself into the sound of her voice and live there forever. Relief washes over me as I see those emerald eyes look up, her gaze roaming around in front of her trying to find me. "I still cannot see you." She whispers.

"I know, my love. But I'm right here." I say, sending a burst of energy to her. I only know that it worked when she softly gasps at it, looking down at her hand again.

Her chest sinks as she exhales a ragged breath. "I still can't hear or see you. But I *feel* you, Rei. I feel you here with me."

I send her two bursts of energy. "I'm right here." I say.

"Two," She says before looking up. "Two means yes."

I send her two more.

A smile lights up her face as she nods. "One means no, then. Good." She closes her eyes briefly, sighing as if relieved as well. "Because I need to tell you something." She opens her eyes, leaning her back away from the wall. She works on a swallow as worry begins to ensue within me at the look in her eyes. "I need to tell you something, and I need you to relay everything I tell you back to my mother and Hades. Promise me."

I send her two pulses, trying to squeeze her hand but knowing she won't feel that. Only the energy I send her.

She nods her head. "Good. Now listen to me very carefully."

I kneel beside Melinoë with my hand still above hers as I wait for her to speak again.

"I know the reason for Zeus' control over me and Makaria. I know everything now."

I keep my gaze fixated on her, waiting.

"There was a prophecy spoken to Zeus long, long ago. It told him of three children that would be born to a goddess of duality, that would wield unimaginable power together." She pauses for a moment before continuing. "Except the children were never meant to be Zeus', they were meant to be Hades'. The children being Makaria and myself, and another we've never known about."

My eyes widen in disbelief. "What?" I exclaim, forgetting for a moment she can't hear me. I shake my head. "Zeus is not supposed to be your father then? Melinoë—"

"I'm going to tell you the whole prophecy, word for word, and you must remember it and tell it to my mother and Hades. Do you understand?"

I sit there, blinking at her before giving her two pulses.

She nods. "This is what was spoken."

As I sit there and listen to her speak a prophecy that was told to Zeus—one about not wanting to repeat the first King's fate, so he tried to manipulate his outcome to his advantage, even when he was destined to receive his father's same end. She tells me the entire prophecy as I train every word to memory, listening and trying to dissect each piece of it. The three descendants of a goddess of duality—Queen Persephone. A Goddess of both light and darkness, A Goddess of Spring and The Queen of The Underworld. Children that were fated to be conceived with Hades instead of Zeus.

The description of each descendant, and how Melinoë would become Zeus' greatest weakness. How with all three by his side, he would be undefeated.

She finishes telling me the prophecy, working on a swallow. "The first born," She begins, looking in the vicinity of where I'm kneeling. As if trying to see me even though she cannot. "He was murdered as an infant. Everything of him was torn apart aside from his heart. Zeus fed it to his mistress so that when she carried his next child it would be the same soul born again. So he could make sure he fulfilled the prophecy in its entirety. And he lives today, in this palace."

My eyes widened as a pressure settled itself in my gut, disbelief crowding me. "That's impossible. You cannot reincarnate a soul unless you are Queen or King of The Underworld."

"His name is Dionysus, and he's not only the Twice Born—reborn from Zeus, but Semele is his mother."

No fucking way.

"Semele is the mistress that carried Zeus' child for him. But Dionysus is under the assumption that Hera is his mother. I don't know why Semele has never told him yet, but I plan to try and find out."

I sat there ingesting everything she just told me. That's how Semele knew Zeus then. That's why she offered to join Melinoë that day in the Sephyra Forest, she knew she could help Zeus get what he wanted.

As Zeus thinks that if Melinoë is by his side, that the largest threat against him is under his control. Already in his possession.

"Show me you heard all of that and will remember it."

I lift my gaze back up to hers, nodding as I send her two pulses.

She forces a weak grin. "I know it's a lot, and I know because I can't hear you that I can't actually answer any questions. I don't know much else outside of what I've told you. I have met other gods here though. Apollo and his twin sister Artemis. I don't have anything on them as I haven't spoken to either, but Apollo is a close ally to Zeus. That much I know."

I sigh, wanting to tell her that I love her and hate that I can't. I send her three pulses, trying anyway.

She shakes her head. "I don't understand, what is three for?"

I do it again, slower this time.

Her brows knit together as she tries to understand. Until I will the talisman to emit a warmth to radiate up her arm, Melinoë's eyes softening as a grin curves her lips. "I love you." She says softly.

I send her two pulses. Yes, my love. You got it.

Tears begin to swell in her eyes as she says, "I love you, Rei. In this lifetime, and every other."

As she says those words I wish I could speak, wishing I could tell her what I learned about us. That we're twin souls, and our destiny—our love is even stronger than what we both knew it could amount to. That both of our paths have been divinely orchestrated together, and apart.

She leans her head back against the wall, her eyes suddenly getting heavy with sleep again. "Will you stay with me until I fall asleep?"

Two pulses.

She smiles. "I miss sleeping next to you." A moment of silence stretches between us as her smile fades. "I miss laying in our bed."

"I miss the same. More than anything, Melinoë." I say aloud, fighting the emotion clogging my throat as I move myself next to her.

I seat myself down with my arm touching hers, laying my hand over hers again as I lean in to give her a kiss on her forehead. "Rest, my love. I'm here."

A tear slips down her cheek as she closes her eyes, lifting her left hand up and trying to grasp onto my astral body to her right. "I never knew the impact someone sitting beside me could have. The deep comfort and harmony one person could bring. I always longed for it when I lived in that cabin, when I thought my mother was dead."

I press another kiss to her forehead, wishing it were my actual lips against her skin right now.

"It wasn't until I met you that I found exactly what I had been yearning for. You complete me in all the best ways, Rei."

I smile as I lift my hand, lightly pushing back a loose strand of her hair away from her face. I watch as she giggles, turning towards my hand and my touch before inhaling deeply, releasing slowly.

I watch as her breathing begins to even out, her face relaxing as she falls asleep next to me. And before I know it, I close my eyes next to her. Falling asleep next to her until I wake up, back in my bed—in my physical body once again.

CHAPTER 39

I need to speak with Persephone and Hades as soon as they're able to meet me.

I send the request to Charon down the Guardian's channel, knowing that I can't block Dimitri from hearing it if he's paying attention enough. That he'll most likely ask what's going on, in which I'll tell him. But for right now, Persephone and Hades deserve to hear everything first.

I will spread word to them now. Charons' words traveling down the bond.

The morning sunshine gleams through my balcony door as I throw on a clean shirt. I pull on a pair of black pants, fixing on a pair of shoes before I make my way downstairs. Preparing to give Persephone some very tumultuous information to say the least.

I tousle my hair as I descend the steps, turning the corner and walking past the living room when I notice Dimitri and Nora still passed out on the couch. Dimitri laying with his feet towards the armrest, laying flat on his back with his arm beneath his head while Nora lays sprawled out with her feet facing the other end. Her head just below his, facing the couch as she snores soundly asleep.

A half-grin curves up one side of my face at the sight before I head to the kitchen. Grabbing a glass of water, sipping it as Charon comes through the bond again.

They are coming now.

I set the glass down, hoping to make my way outside before they've arrived. But as soon as I turn around from the sink, I watch as a portal opens up before me. Stepping through it both The Queen and King of The Underworld.

Persephone wears a soft violet gown with half of her hair pulled up into a bun. Her emerald eyes fixating on me as Hades stands by her side.

Donned in an all black suit, his dark hair pulled back and revealing his sharp jaw. "Reimus."

I nod to them both. "Thank you for coming."

"Charon made it seem like it was urgent." Persephone begins. "What is it?"

I glance over to the doorway. "I don't want to wake the others still sleeping, so I'd prefer to take this outdoors if you don't mind."

Persephone watches me, nodding once.

The three of us walk silently outside, out into the terrain currently under remodeling so as to not wake Dimitri or Nora.

We step far enough out away from the palace entrance before I turn to face them. "I have been visiting Melinoë in the astral realm."

Persephone looks at Hades confused, but it is him that speaks. "That should not be possible."

"His wards should be too powerful for you to sneak past." Persephone gently chimes in.

"I know." I pause, wondering where exactly I'm supposed to start as there is so much to unpack here. I lift the talisman from my chest, showing it to them. "This belonged to Melinoë. Hecate spelled it to—"

"Protect her." Hades finishes for me, looking at it. "I remember seeing it on Melinoë and knew Hecate had gifted it to her."

"We thought it was gone. That Zeus would've shattered it. Where did you find it?" Persephone asks.

"Hecate did a locator spell and found it where we think Melinoë was kidnapped in the Sephyra Forest. She gave it to me to hang onto until Melinoë was returned home. I've been wearing it mostly ever since."

Persephone shakes her head. "That doesn't make any sense. Zeus would've felt the power from it. Why would he have just left it?"

"I don't know, but the point I'm trying to make right now is not about the talisman. It's the reason why it connects with me even though Hecate spelled it to protect only Melinoë." I lower my hand from the talisman, looking at both of them. "It has been able to aid me in astral traveling to Melinoë, where they're keeping her in the dungeons, because Melinoë and I share the same soul."

Persephone steps forward from Hades' side as her eyes widen slightly.

"Hecate did some magic to reveal why it was protecting me even when it wasn't spelled to, and we found that it's because Melinoë and I are twin souls."

"I…" Persephone looks over to her husband, shaking her head. "I haven't heard that phrase in a long time."

"Is it not common for two people to be twin souls?" I ask.

Hades shakes his head. "It's extremely rare. Usually The Fates only weave it into a soul's fate if there is a divine orchestration to go along with it. Separating the soul into two people, two paths meant to come together once again."

"What the divine purpose is that The Fates wants either of them to fulfill is the question then." Persephone states.

"I don't know what that is yet for both of us. But as far as Melinoë's, that's why I had Charon request for you to meet me."

Persephone tilts her head as she looks at me.

I take a long inhale in, releasing slowly. Knowing that no matter how I put this, it won't be easy on either of them. That it will quite literally change everything. "Zeus learned of a prophecy long, long ago. Through something called a Pythia, the Oracle of Delphi she's also referred to. She pledges her loyalty to Apollo I was told from Melinoë last night, but she was turned immortal by Zeus long ago as a bargain to give him insight into what his future would hold."

"The Temple where the oracle resides is on Mount Parthanus. It's situated in Delphi, just south of Olympia and Lothario." Persephone says. "She's served Apollo for eons as his oracle, though part of his divinity lies in the gift of prophecy."

I nod my head, carrying on. "Do you know how Zeus took the throne as King?" I ask both of them.

Hades sighs, nodding. "He killed Kronos, his father." He pulls his hands behind his back, squaring his shoulders. "Even when Zeus was young, he was incredibly arrogant. With Kronos the first King of All Gods, Zeus knew that as his son he would one day bear the same title when it was his time. But Zeus became greedy, and highly impatient as he began to see Kronos as an unfit ruler of Olympia."

"Kronos for a long, long time was a benevolent King. He listened to the people, was a very generous ruler. But when he learned of a prophecy that spoke of his children overruling him, he became highly paranoid." Persephone says. "He became less giving to the people of Olympia, and began to seek out ways to keep Zeus and his children at arms length while still having full dominion over them." Persephone looks over at her husband. "Zeus saw the way his father began to decline rapidly due to his own fear and paranoia, and struck when he was vulnerable." She trains her gaze back onto me. "Why do you ask?"

I nod slowly. "Because his same fate was prophesied to him by Apollo's oracle. His reasoning for trying to keep your children close to him as history is trying to repeat itself, through a new prophecy."

Persephone stares at me, knitting her brows together. "What do you mean *new* prophecy?" She steps closer to me as confusion sparks in her gaze.

"I visited Melinoë last night again, and she told me what was said to Zeus. But before I share it, I think you both might want to take a seat." I say gently.

Persephone continues staring at me as worry blanches her gaze. She shakes her head, crossing her arms over her chest. "I'm fine to stand—"

A chair appears behind her, willed from Hades' magic. She turns around to look down at the chair, then to him as her hardened gaze softens. A chair appearing behind him and myself.

He gives her a gentle nod as he seats himself down right next to her.

She looks at me, clenching her jaw as if she's mentally preparing herself for what's to come. Hating that I have to give her such news that her first born is technically alive, and everything else that comes with it.

After she finally seats herself down I do the same, and tell them exactly what Melinoë told me.

I watch as Persephone's face switches from rage to utter shock, her hand coming up to her mouth to stifle the gasp that threatened to slip out. Hades watched me intently as I watched him process everything with mostly a stern gaze. When I reveal the part about Zeus manipulating fate into bearing Persephone's children, his expression flashes from rage to devastation. Though I watch as he keeps himself together not for himself, but for his wife.

After I finish telling the prophecy and everything else Melinoë revealed to me, Persephone stands up from her chair and steps away from us. Her hand still held against her mouth as if she's going to be sick. And honestly, I wouldn't blame her if she did.

I give her the privacy she needs to process, standing several feet away from Hades and I. Her back facing us as I watch it tremble slightly, her posture rigid as she stands there silently for several long moments.

Once she's decided she's ready to, she turns around and rejoins us. Her cheeks slightly reddened from the tears she's released in private. Easy to see now where Melinoë gets her pride from and will of strength from.

Persephone seats herself back down, grabbing Hades' hand as she squeezes it. He turns to look at her, longing in his gaze. "Sorry, I just needed a minute."

He shakes his head as he lays his other hand on top of hers. "You have nothing to feel sorry for." He leans in to give her a kiss on the cheek, the tension in her posture lessening to some degree as he does.

They share a silent moment together before she faces me again. I watch as her chest rises and then falls again. "His name was Zagreus."

I sit there silently, giving her the space to share whatever she feels comfortable to divulge with me. Knowing she does not owe me any explanation.

"He was my first child years before Melinoë was born. Conceived in the same way all three of them were." She pauses, her hand trembling beneath Hades' as his thumb brushes over her skin. She takes a moment, gathering herself before continuing. "Like Melinoë and Makaria, Zeus never allowed me to take him to my home. To The Underworld. So

I, in an effort to see my son, made visits to Zeus' palace often. As it was the only way to see my boy."

A tear slips down her cheek before she quickly brushes it away. "There was a group of primordial gods well before your time that were incredibly loyal to Kronus. Not only were they blindly loyal, they also were not gods that favored change, as they said everything operated perfectly as is. So when Zeus killed Kronus, and took the throne as King of Olympia, they were in an uproar over it."

She glances over at Hades before continuing.

"When they then learned what happened to me, that Zagreus was conceived by Zeus raping me, they felt there was no other choice but to seek justice. They not only saw Zagreus as a threat because of who his father was, presuming he would turn out just as vile as him, but they also deeply pitied how he came into this life. Claiming it was an abomination of life."

I lower my gaze to Hades' hand wrapped around hers, gently squeezing it for reassurance. I lift my gaze back up to hers as she continues.

"One day when I was away, Zagreus was playing with his toys in the playroom. Zeus was in the throne room while a handmaid was supposed to be watching him. But her neck was snapped and she died by the hands of Themis, a member of The Titans. They all gathered around him, and tore him—"

She stops herself from saying anything further, her other hand coming up to her mouth. She takes a moment before continuing, but looks over to Hades to continue for her.

He gives her a nod before looking at me. "Zeus immediately called council, where we learned of what happened. He told us there was nothing left of him, that they dismembered him completely." He takes a breath in before releasing. "We were all able to retrieve each of them to Zeus' throne room, and they were assassinated immediately. As each of them crossed over, Persephone and I judged them together. We ordered them to an eternal life of misery in Tartarus where they relive the same fate they inflicted upon Zagreus, on a constant loop."

I automatically think about what that kind of punishment must be like, to have your limbs torn from your body over and over and over again. With no reprieve other than their bodies growing back together, piece by piece, just to go through the pain of being torn apart again.

Chills run down my spine at the thought of it, and they do not settle as I see the deep well of hatred in Hades' eyes for not only The Titans having taken Persephone's child from her, but for Zeus. For everything he's done, for everything he continues to keep doing. I watch as though he stands calmly next to his wife, I see the looming energy radiating off of him that tells me there are no bounds, no limitations to what he will do to punish Zeus now.

I stand up from my seat, the chairs beneath the three of us vanishing entirely. "Can I ask you something?"

Hades nods his head.

I sigh before I ask, knowing it's probably insensitive but needing to ask it anyhow. "How did you not kill him? After everything—"

I cut myself off from saying the words that we both know hang between us. My gaze fixated on Persephone momentarily before training it back onto Hades.

I watch as years and years of contemplation of such flashes over his gaze. As something else rests there.

Agony.

He takes a breath before he says, "Shortly after Zeus took over the throne is when he, myself, and Poseidon made our pact with The Fates. Granting each of us rulership over our respective realms and lands. We were then made aware by The Fates that in order to keep the balance in all of the realms, that there must always be a divinity to rule over the lands, the dead, and the seas. That disrupting that balance would therefore disrupt the natural order of everything, and would bear consequences for all involved. Which are all things I would've *gladly* damned to kill that motherfucker who thought putting his hands on my wife even the first time—"

A well of imminent power rushes to the air surrounding us, thickening it and causing the oxygen to deplete. He notices the increase in my breathing to take what little oxygen in and releases the charge of his energy.

Hades works on a swallow before he continues. "But I was denied the justice of seeing him in our realm, dead. Where I could have *my* way with him in Tartarus for eternity because The Fates had made one clause to our pact that prevented me from such."

I tilt my head. "Which is what?"

"That myself, Zeus, and Poseidon can only be killed by those who have the same likeness and abilities as us. Making us, essentially, the only gods who cannot be killed by another."

A wave of fury rushes over me that basically what Hades is saying, is that Zeus is incapable of dying. And now in the times that I've seen, and felt, the smoldering ire that lingers below the surface of Hades, that it is not by choice that Zeus remains standing.

Which makes me sick to believe that Zeus knew that raping Persephone would ultimately have no consequences to him because of that fact.

I shake my head slowly, sorrow in my voice. "It's not right." I lift my gaze to Persephone. "There has to be a loophole—"

My eyes widen as I blink at her for a moment, realizing—

"You three can only be killed by one who shares the same blood as you, shares the same powers that you do."

Hades nods his head. "That's correct."

"So…" My voice trails off for a moment until the confirmation in my head sends a full-blown awareness down my back. "That's why he kept them close to him. Your children." I say to Persephone. "He knows that they are the only ones who can kill him. That's why the prophecy said he'd be undefeated then with them by his side. But then why would the prophecy say specifically that Melinoë was his greatest threat?"

Persephone shakes her head. "I don't know. But everything makes sense. All of it." Her gaze narrows for a moment before retraining back on my face. "Which means in his own downfall of taking the throne, he brought forth the only divinities able to put him down."

I watch as Persephone battles with the turmoil of the truths I'd revealed to her. "I cannot believe that Zagreus is alive in a new body. That after all of these years, Zeus *reincarnated* him. That his soul still lives on today." Her words ending on a harsh force.

I nod slowly, remaining silent as she processes it all. That anger beneath swelling and boiling on the surface.

"Though that doesn't appear to be the worst of it." She seethes. "That I was also some breeding pig for Zeus to make sure he doesn't receive the same fate as his father—" She takes deep breaths in and out as that anger builds. "That *my* children were meant to be my husbands? I—"

She begins pacing as the energy around us charges, palpable enough to feel. Like a heavy wool blanket wrapped around me. I watch as the grass beneath us begins to wilt and die, the ground trembling as Persephone's rage unfolds.

And when she looks at me, it's unlike anything I've ever witnessed before. Staring back at me is a cold, blood-curdling terror. "When I get my hands on him," She says calmly, slowly nodding her head. Far too calmly. "He's going to wish his father was still alive to save him."

Gusts of wind pick up violently around us as Hades grabs both of Persephone's arms. "You will have your revenge when it is time. I will make sure of it." Anger simmering beneath his tone. "But he cannot know what we know yet.

He's still under the presumption that Melinoë is under his compulsion."

"He can't do this to her. To *us*." She screams as the wind around us picks up, accumulating at a rapid pace as my hair whips along my forehead. "He needs to see his death *now*."

"He will, but at the right moment. As we now know that it can be done." Hades says to her, trying to calm her.

She stares at him, angry at his words. Knowing that he's right, that retaliating right now would put Melinoë at risk. Also knowing that she is actually not capable of killing Zeus, and I watch as that immense frustration at the fact boils over her.

She turns away from us, and as the wind dies down, out of her mouth comes a gut-wrenching scream. A deep distress excavated from the pits of her soul that could be felt and heard for miles.

In a ripple effect, the earth below us splits open. A tiny crack in the soil begins to spiderweb outward away from us, the ground trembling as it threatens to split further open.

Dimitri comes running outside with Nora. "What's happening?" He yells out, looking around and pulling Nora behind him as he sees Persephone lose control.

"Persephone, if you don't tame that power he will feel it. He will know there's a large reason for your anger." Hades says as he steps to her side. "You must reel it back in, for now."

Persephone's screaming continues on until a few moments later it slowly subsides, the ground ceasing its tremble as the cracks in the ground halt in place. Her body heaves forward as she breathes deeply. Hades steps in front of her as he holds her trembling hands to his chest. His gaze wholly and completely on her, as if she is the center of his entire universe.

"He will pay. For *all* of it. You have my word, my Queen." He reassures her as he softly kisses the tops of her knuckles.

After a few moments of willing herself to calm, the wind dies down as the energy dissipates altogether. I turn around to look at Dimitri, saying down the bond. *Go back inside, I promise I'll explain everything in a bit.*

Dimitri looks at me skeptically for a moment before turning him and Nora around, guiding them both back inside.

I turn back around towards Hades and Persphone, allowing her as much time as she needs to gather herself. Her revenge and anger all immensely justified for what she's been through—what Zeus has, and continues to put them all through.

And I know in my bones that Hades meant what he said. That he will let his wife get the revenge she so rightfully seeks when Zeus' time for his death leads them right into their territory. Right into The Underworld where they, as King and Queen, can judge his sentence how they see fit.

Knowing that they will give him the worst imaginable fate possible. The cruelest, most wicked punishment for the most vile piece of shit who calls himself a King and a man.

I watch as they share a moment together, not speaking but just by being in each other's embrace as Hades guides her breathing to slow down. An act that I've similarly done for Melinoë.

And as I stand there, I realize one truth in all of this that holds my attention.

That Zeus can effectively be killed, and it's by his own children.

CHAPTER 40

Melinoë

I wait all day for Bethesda to come and collect me for our daily chores, but as the day stretches on, she never shows up.

It isn't until hours later that I finally hear the door open at the top of the steps. Though I quickly find that it is not her light footsteps that I hear coming down to collect me.

Dionysus approaches my cell door, unlocking it as he annoyedly waves his hand up. "Get up."

My brows knit together. "Where is Bethesda?"

He steps inside of the cell as he goes to unlock the chains connected to my handcuffs. "She's preoccupied today." He says plainly.

He unlocks the ones connected to my ankle cuffs before standing upright again. He grabs my wrist, pulling on me as we exit out of my cell. "Where are you taking me?" I demand. Trying to keep myself from stumbling at the force of his stride.

"There's a council meeting. Zeus wants you a part of it."

My palms threaten to clam up as I prepare myself for another council meeting locked in a cage, on public display in front of the people of Lothario. My breathing begins to pick up before I remember what Hades told me once before.

You are stronger than him. He cannot break you.

I repeat those words in my mind over and over again, so that once we make it up to the top of the steps I'm able to walk into that throne room steadily with my head held high.

Except as we walk in I find the throne room is empty. Zeus nowhere to be found with no crowd of villagers to surround the open room. "Where is everyone?"

He guides us down the edge of the throne room. "Not that kind of council meeting today."

Dionysus takes us to the back of the throne room, hooking a left and walking away from the awning that leads to the kitchen. We walk behind the dais to the other side of the room until we approach a large door. Dionysus pushes it open and we step inside.

My gaze lowers to the polished marble floor. At the center is a golden sphere with intricate detailing inside of it, a ring of navy blue shapes surrounding it. I notice the difference in brightness between the middle of the floor and the outer perimeter, lifting my gaze up to a dome vaulted ceiling high above. The sun shining brightly through the elegantly crafted stained glass.

Gold trimmed, limestone doric columns are placed on each side of large golden throne seats. Each one with a statue of Zeus holding a thunderbolt molded into the wall above them. The columns holding up a thick structure of stone that wraps around the perimeter of the room, columns similar to the ones at Apollo's Temple.

As I lower my gaze I find that most of the golden chairs are occupied with a woman or man sitting in them, some of their faces recognizable while most are not. I lift my gaze up to who sits in the center chair, designed to be larger and more intricately designed then the rest. My gaze flicks up to the crown atop his head, the golden staff of a lightning bolt at his side as he looks down at me. The tips of his moonlight blonde hair brushing along his shoulders, his golden gaze trained on me as Dionysus leads me forward.

Zeus watches me until Dionysus leads me to the middle, my gaze falling down at my bare feet at the golden sphere I stand upon.

"Take your seat, Dionysus."

I lift my gaze back up again, looking over at Dionysus as he lets go of my handcuffs. He says nothing as he walks over to an empty seat to Hera's right, watching as he lifts his gaze up to Hera as she deliberately turns her sharp gaze away.

"Afternoon, mother." Dionysus says to Hera as he takes his seat, looking over at her. I watch for a split moment as the careless, uninterested gaze he consistently fixes over his face slips as a flash of betrayal flashes over his eyes when Hera doesn't greet him back. I watch as he quickly smooths his face out, turning to stare ahead and acting like that didn't affect him.

I understand she's Queen of All Gods, as she's Zeus' husband and all, but what a bitch—

"Let us begin." Zeus says, interrupting my thoughts.

I glance at everyone seated before me, the golden chairs fashioned on either side of Zeus, curving with the circular formation of the room. I look to see Apollo seated to Zeus' left, and beside him his sister Artemis. She stares at me for a moment before I fix my gaze elsewhere, to the man seated to her left.

His eyes a piercing light blue, reminiscent of the endless vast seas. Set against rich, umber skin with tightly-woven braids traveling down just past his shoulders. Half of them pulled back into a bun, noticing the small gold hair cuffs placed throughout his hair. His gaze lands on me, roaming over my clothing then falling lower to my bare feet. My gaze halts at his sculpted arm and chest muscles on full display, exposed from his mint green robes.

He's…gorgeous to say the least.

"And who might our guest be, Zeus?" A woman seated to Dionysus' right asks, her voice radiating a calm yet definitive power to it. I look over at her and notice right away the bronzed chest armor that she wears, the only one armed aside from the man seated to her right while everyone else either wears robes or more casual clothing. Intricately designed gold breast plates and shoulder pads set against golden, honey brown skin with curly long black hair that falls well below her chest. Held in her hand is a long spear that extends down to the ground, the head of it sharp and pointed.

I lift my gaze up to her almond shaped, hazel eyes as they stare back at me. Her long eyelashes fan out as she blinks, her beauty striking even beneath all of the armor she wears. The weapon she holds by her side.

"And why does she have no shoes on?" Artemis says from the other side of the room.

"She looks as though she's being kept underground." The hazel-eyed woman says, lifting a brow.

"Because she is." Dionysus says to her as he leans in closer, lowering his voice.

"Silence." Zeus rings out, everyone around him going silent. He fixes his gaze back onto me, his chest sinking slowly as he exhales a beat of frustration. "As members of the council, I thought it was time to introduce a new face. A new ally to myself, and therefore to Olympia."

I keep myself composed and stand there silently as everyone exchanges looks with me.

"As you all know, I brought Dionysus onto the council when I knew he was ready to be a part of it. When he proved his allegiance to me, and earned his spot."

I glance over at Dionysus, not knowing that he was never a part of this council group to begin with. Wondering what it is he had to do to join, and why in the world he would want to when he appears to be so entirely bored he could fall asleep right here and now.

"As we expected because he is your son. But why her?" The man in the mint green robes asks.

Zeus stares at me before leaning his back into his chair. "Because she is my daughter."

I watch as people turn to look at one another, whispering. The only ones who don't seem to be phased are Hera, Apollo and Artemis. I notice that even though Dionysus doesn't speak a word, I watch the way his eyes widen at that knowledge. Realizing that he wasn't aware of exactly who I was.

Interesting.

"How did we never know about this?" The woman with the spear asks.

"Because, Athena, there were some…inconvenient circumstances that made it difficult to disclose such information until Melinoë was finally able to return home with me."

My blood threatens to boil as he refers to my mother as an *inconvenience*. Referring to my own autonomy and freedom as a nuisance. Somehow, I will myself to remain calm.

"And you, Hera. Are you her mother then?" Athena asks through a gaze of bewilderment.

Hera looks over at her, a stern gaze as she says plainly, "No."

"Then who is—" Athena starts.

"That is unimportant at the moment, as her mother is no longer a part of her life." Zeus interjects.

Keep it together. Keep it together.

"What is important is that I feel she can be a great ally to us all. As she possesses certain gifts that I believe to be unique, different from what any of us possess."

"And what gifts might those be?" Dionysus asks, his voice failing to remain aloof as a soft edge peeks through.

A wicked grin curves up Zeus' lips as he nods faintly, lifting his hand and lazily waving it until I feel something materialize beside me.

I gasp as I jerk my gaze over to the man standing next to me, his expression telling me he's just as shocked as I am. He looks wearily at me before shakily trailing his gaze up to Zeus. His hands slightly tremble as he works on a swallow. "Your Majesty, my apologies. I do not know how I ended up here. All I remember is a man bringing me here—" He stammers on his words as he looks up at Dionysus, recognition flaring in his face. "You. It was you who brought me here—"

"That's enough, Martin." Zeus holds up a hand, silencing the man. He lowers it back down to the armrest. "I asked Dionysus to bring you here. I've just willed you from a chamber I had you placed in."

Martin knits his brows together, looking away as he curtly nods his head. Confusion exploding over his face, feeling sorry for the poor man for being caught in one of Zeus' vile jabs at asserting his dominance. "Oh, I see, Your Majesty."

"Don't worry Martin, I will have Melinoë put you out of your confusion soon enough."

My head whips over to look at Zeus, speaking for the first time since entering. "What?"

Zeus looks down at me, keeping that same smirk on his face. "I want you to demonstrate just what you can do for the council today."

I shake my head slowly. "I—I don't understand." I glance over at the man. "What do you want me to do with him?" I take a step forward.

In a steady and eerily calm voice, Zeus says, "Kill him."

My eyes widen as I stare up at Zeus, disbelief suffocating me and causing my breathing to halt. My loss for words lasts for a few moments before I blurt out, "No."

A word that I didn't mean to blurt out, a word that he has not heard yet from me. A word that came from deep within me, at the core of who I am. Someone who does not hurt people just for the sick gain of another, or for amusement.

Zeus' smirk begins to fade as he stares down at me, his gaze hardening slightly as he tilts his head. After a moment, he begins to laugh. *Laugh.*

Martin begins to tremble beside me as I stand there, glancing at Apollo and then Artemis. Seeing nothing but impassivity fixed on their gazes.

"I apologize, Melinoë. I forget that you have far more humanity than me. Perhaps you need a little motivation to *inspire* you."

In the next moment, I watch as Zeus' gaze turns to Martin, feeling his power rush to the surface quickly as he says to him, "You will take this blade and will not stop trying to take Melinoë's head off with it until she has killed you."

I feel Zeus' power dissipate as I look over at Martin, watching as his eyes go from soft and slackened—from Zeus' mind compulsion, to harden with hatred as he turns to face me.

"She is evil, Martin. She is the enemy you need to protect yourself from." Zeus says to Martin.

A short sword materializes into Martin's hands, looking down at it before slowly lifting his glaring gaze up to me again. He begins breathing heavily as he takes a step towards me. "With pleasure." He says as a viscous smile curves his lips.

The second that Zeus frees the shackles at my wrists and ankles Martin swipes the sword at me. I quickly jump out of the way, rolling onto the floor before hiking back up to my feet again. I crouch down as I look up at him, knowing that no matter what I say to him, he won't be able to break Zeus' mind control. Not until either Zeus lifts it, or I kill him.

And I know that Zeus has absolutely no intention of lifting the compulsion.

Martin rushes towards me, quickly advancing on me with a burning hatred in his gaze as I immediately will my shadows to the surface.

A large barrier builds right in front of me, keeping Martin back from coming any closer. But whether it's because of the force of Zeus' compulsion, or the hatred he's instilled in his mind, he finds his way around my barrier.

I will my shadows to coil around the sword that Martin has, latching onto it as I tear it from his grasp. He snarls as he pounces on me, faster than a viper.

Is Zeus willing some immortal strength into this guy? How is he ganging up on me so fast?

We both fall to the ground with him on top, swinging at me and missing with the block of my arm covering my face.

I push him off of me as he falls backwards, landing on his ass before hopping up onto his feet again. In the next moment, another short sword materializes in his hand.

I glance over at Zeus and a rage erodes within me at that smirk on his face, perfectly aware of what he's doing.

Cheating bastard.

I look back at Martin, getting back into a fighting stance as I will my shadows to rip that sword out of his hand. Until another one materializes again.

And again.

And again.

"You are only delaying the inevitable, Melinoë. Might as well get it over with."

I clench my fists together as I feel everyone's eyes on me, watching as I constantly create a barrier in front of myself. My shadows latching onto the swords and pulling them from Martin's grasp.

After minutes of continuing to do this, I know that Zeus is right. He won't stop materializing new weapons for Martin, and will keep everyone here for as long as it takes for me to do what he says.

A fucking hate him.

I feel the anger well up inside of me. Threatening itself quickly to the surface as Martin takes another swing at me. A blast of my shadows attacks him, sending him backwards. But no matter what, he keeps swinging that sword at me.

So, if a show is what Zeus wants. If he wants me to show these other immortals what I'm about, then I'll show them.

Something overtakes me as I stand before Martin, narrowing my gaze on him as I infiltrate his mind. I seep into the cracks of his mental barrier, pushing my way inside until I see into his deepest fears.

I bring them to life in his mind, watching as the anger on his face suddenly turns to inexplicable fear as he suddenly drops the knife. He begins groaning in pain as he hallucinates being locked inside a small box, big enough to move a few feet in with no windows, no source of water.

A prison, nearly similar to the one I reside in right now. Except this one the size of a cave opening, the tiny pocket of air running out as he suffocates to death. He begins to hyperventilate, crouching down to the ground as his arms tremble.

And before I release my hold on his mind, I come across something that I don't think Zeus expected me to find.

I find the golden thread of his mind compulsion, the powerful hold it has onto his mind. Like a living, breathing entity drawing life from his thoughts. And through that thread of compulsion, I see a glimpse of what he'll do to Martin if I rebel against killing this man. What he'll do once he lifts the compulsion.

I peer deeper into it, an image of Zeus throwing Martin into a cell, similar to my own once he lifts the compulsion. That if I truly defy Zeus and do not kill him, he will lock him up for the rest of his life.

And at the reveal of what Martin's biggest fear is, I realize I would be trading one punishment for another for this innocent man.

Martin still crouches over on the ground before me as I reach into the darkest parts of myself, that reservoir of power that I'd said I'd never use to intentionally hurt anyone, and fulfill what is the more humane outcome for this man's life.

My shadows slither out from my fingertips and reach out for him. I will them to lift him up onto his feet, looking him straight in his eyes as I keep my hold on his mind. Never having tried it before, I slip a few words into his mind before I do what I have to.

You are going to be okay. I will visit you in The Asphodel Meadows soon.

Before his body can cease its trembling from my silent exchange, my shadows latch onto his neck and twist around it tightly. I watch as his eyes bulge out before I quickly snap his neck, killing him instantly.

I slowly lower his body to the ground, feeling the rush of a tear rising to my eyes but forcing it back down. Keeping it all together as I lay this man out on his back, staring down at his face for a long moment before lifting my gaze back up to Zeus.

"Excellent work." A tone that rings of being pleased with my obedience.

I glance over at the other gods, all of them staring at me with surprise and bewilderment on their faces. Whether it's due to the fact I just made this man hallucinate, or because of the shadows I produce, I don't bother to ask. I don't bother to try to read further into their expressions.

All I can think about is this innocent life I've just taken.

"How did you do that?" A red-haired, faired skinned man next to Athena asks. I notice he wears similar armor to hers.

I lift my gaze to Dionysus who just stares at me, blinking as if lost for words. I fight the urge to hide beneath all of their stares, their silence for what I've just done. Instead, I soak it all in.

"As you can see, she shares a similar gift to mine. Though hers can induce terrors rather than compulsion." Zeus exclaims.

Because through the weight of their gazes, there is one thing that has become apparent.

No longer do these gods perceive me as a weakness, but as a *threat*. And maybe, that's exactly what I need to be.

CHAPTER 41

My feet shuffle along the floor, my legs heavy and numb to the rest of my body as Dionysus guides me back to the dungeons. My mind fixated with the recurring loop of horror that was Martin's face seconds before I took his life.

His expression quickly shifted from seething rage to disorientation as my shadows latched onto his neck, the utterly sober and terrifying realization that his life was over. The only thing I could possibly do in that moment was by saving him the anguish of prolonging his pain any further, and snapping his neck.

They had all initially looked at me in silence, aside from Zeus. As the ringing in my ears and my head deafened their words, all I could make out in the long minutes as I stood there was an exchange of questions from the good-looking man next to Artemis.

"Is she able to infiltrate a god's mind and make them hallucinate as well?" He'd asked.

"Why don't you go find out for yourself, Poseidon?" Zeus had responded slyly.

After that, I had no idea what was said amongst the gods until minutes later after standing there, staring at the ground in front of me, I felt the rough grasp of Dionysus' hands on my arm. I forced my feet to move as he pulled me away from standing next to Martin's dead body, and led me out of the council room.

"Don't worry, the feeling will pass." Dionysus quietly says beside me as he opens the dungeon door. Not having a clue when Zeus willed the shackles back onto my wrists and ankles.

He pulls the door open, leading us both inside and down the twenty steps. The further we descend down into the dungeons, the further I sink into myself, hiding from the atrocity I've bestowed on that innocent man. Who never asked to be a part of an immortal's selfish feud. Who probably has a loving family and children at home, who will expect to see their father return home and become devastated when they find out he will never step foot in that door ever again.

I know Zeus' strategy to lock Martin up, had I rebelled, would've been both punishment for my defiance and also a manipulative tactic to place the blame and fault onto me for Martin's imprisonment.

An evil in exchange for a lesser evil.

We make it to the bottom of the steps, walking towards my cell door as my gaze lifts to the darkened cells that I pass. Glancing into them to see if I can see the woman I've exchanged conversations with while here. But all that stares back at me is pure and utter darkness.

"Before you are awarded a seat on the council, Zeus will make you do some…terrible things." Dionysus says as he goes to open the cell door. "It's just his way of knowing whether he can fully trust your allegiance or not."

Dionysus opens the door as he leads me inside, his pace not as hurried as he normally is to get rid of me. No—this time he's moving at a gentler pace, and even his voice is not the same smart-ass tone he usually has.

Accept a seat on the council? Why would I ever want to fucking do that? I would rather kill myself then ever stand by Zeus' side.

I stare at the wall ahead of me as the word death lingers in the recesses of my mind. The first human, the first life I've ever taken. A side of myself I have never seen before displayed just as quickly as I was led back down here.

Will Hades be able to see what happened when Martin crosses over to The Underworld? Will he be ashamed of me? Will my mother?

Those thoughts come just as quickly as they leave me as I look down at my hands.

A sudden snort creeps up my throat, getting caught behind my teeth until a laugh forces it out of my lips. I go to put my hand over my mouth to stifle it when the chains clank with the movement, forgetting for half a second that I had them on.

As if they're now a normal part of me now.

I look down at them as I begin to laugh so hard that tears begin to fill my eyes. I step over to the wall, allowing

Dionysus to chain me back up to it as I cannot seem to do anything else but *laugh*.

Dionysus peers his gaze up at me, staring at me as a splash of concern smooths out his face. "Are you okay?" He asks, attaching the chains onto my cuffs before stepping back.

I look at him, at the confused look on his face and how concerned he looks for someone that he's been a rude bastard to. Yet he has no idea that in a twisted way, I'm technically his sister.

I begin cackling, lowering myself to my knees as I clutch my hands to my stomach. Trying to soothe the aches that blossom deep in my belly from laughing so hard. Gods, there are so many secrets living under this palace it's no wonder Zeus keeps everyone at arm's length.

Tears stream down my cheeks as I look down at my hands, facing my palms towards me as Martin's face flashes in my mind. I wipe the tears dampening my cheeks away, the laughing beginning to subside as my fingers tremble faintly in front of me.

I lower myself down to a seated position, crossing my legs and placing my hands on my lap. I gently flex my fingers, staring at the creases in my knuckles as I shake my head. "How do you do it?"

"Do what?" He asks.

I lift my gaze up to him, finding him still standing inside the cell with his back to the bars. I lift my hands again to wipe the remaining dampness beneath my eyes. "Follow him blindly."

Dionysus stares at me for a moment before crossing his arms over his chest. "Because he's King of Olympia. Why wouldn't I blindly follow him?"

I shake my head slowly. "That's not a good enough reason to be loyal to someone."

His gaze lowers to my handcuffs, his gaze roaming over them before lifting it back up to me again. I watch as he works on a swallow, ever so slightly fixing his back straighter. "Because he's my father. What kind of a son would I be if I didn't stand by his side?"

I notice the way his fists tucked beneath his elbows flex once, as if gripping them tightly to keep whatever ruminating thoughts he has away.

I stare at him as I realize he has absolutely no clue what Zeus is hiding from him, no idea that he's been made to believe all his life that Hera is his mother. I think about Semele and what kind of anguish that must be to have to keep that hidden from her son. But why? Is Zeus threatening to harm her or Dionysus if she reveals who she really is?

I nod my head faintly, deciding to ask a different question. Asking it in a way that wouldn't be too suspicious. "I haven't seen Semele in a few days. Does she live here in the palace?"

He scoffs as he turns his head to the side, looking away. "Zeus gifted her with her own chamber long ago. I don't know why that is when my mother *fully* despises her, as do I."

I tilt my head slightly. "Why do you and Hera dislike her?"

He lifts his back away from the iron bars, lowering his arms from his chest back down to his sides as he slowly begins pacing along the cell. "Semele and my father had an affair for a long time. My mother knew about it, and it didn't take long for me to figure it out on my own." He lifts his gaze up from the floor, looking up at the wall ahead as he folds his hands behind his back. "My mother begged Zeus to end it, and apparently he did. Yet he tells me to just mind my business when I ask him why he allows her to live here in the palace, taunting my mother with the reminder that Zeus was not always faithful."

Well, faithful is definitely not the term I would coin for Zeus.

"I tolerate her at best. But I avoid her as much as my mother does." He looks over at me. "She's a constant reminder of what it looks like to be a homewrecker."

Fates, this guy has absolutely no clue what the real story is. That his anger is wholly misplaced.

"Once in a while I catch her staring at me though. It's creepy as fuck."

I nod my head, knowing there's really nothing to say without revealing what the truth is. "Yeah, I guess I'd be creeped out, too."

I lean my head up against the wall, hiking my knees up to my chest as I lower my gaze to nothing in particular.

"What did he promise you?"

I lift my gaze back up to Dionysus, knitting my brows together. "What?"

I realize Dionysus has stopped his slow pacing, standing at the cell door facing me with his hand on the bars. "When an allegiance is made between Zeus and another, there's usually something each gains from the other." He nods towards me. "He's made it obvious today in front of the council that he gains your unique gifts as a weapon to protect Olympia with. So what do you get in exchange?"

I stare at him for a moment, the words of what I want to say sitting right on the tip of my tongue. The *real* family I have back home, the love of my life that is waiting for me to come back home to him. The promise of a better life, one where I'm not imprisoned to chains and a severe lack of autonomy. The promise I made with him before I convinced him that his compulsion on me worked. The deal for both the people I love, and the people foreign to me. Both of which I would harbor any amount of suffering for as long as it meant that they were unharmed. All of those things strong enough reasons to play a façade for as long as I can until I'm no longer confined to doing so.

I blink at him as all of that puddles onto the surface, wanting to be expressed when suddenly all I can think of is how much I pity the man standing before me. Having no idea what his real life is, or the secrets that follow him in this palace. I look at him and find it hard to continue seeing him as an ungrateful bastard, always hiding behind a liquor bottle. Seeing the brutality of his insolence as a bandage for what's weighing heavily on the inside.

Yet instead of saying all of that, I settle with one word as a faint grin curves my lips. "Safety."

He studies me for a short moment before I hear a brief, soft noise. Trapped behind his closed mouth before he opens the door, stepping out of the cell. I watch as he goes to lock the door, turning around to walk up the steps when I call out after him.

"What about you?"

He halts, turning his head to the side.

"What do you get in return for your allegiance?"

He pauses before turning his head fully around. The dim glow of the fire atop the torch gently lights his face, highlighting the bridge of his nose and his gaze as he looks at me. I watch as a faint smirk curves his lips, nodding his head before he says, "Knowledge."

CHAPTER 42

Reimus

"Damn. That's…"

"A lot?" I say, finishing for Dimitri as his sentence trails off.

He runs his hand through his chestnut brown hair, exhaling a long sigh as he assimilates everything. Having stepped back inside to meet with him and Nora as Hades and Persephone asked if they could join me. I had agreed, though I can't lie. I was surprised.

I had imagined for them to want to return home to The Underworld after giving them such jarring and life-changing information. That they would want to process it all together. But as Persephone stands before me, more calm and steady now than she was fifteen minutes ago, it is clear to see where Melinoë gets her immense strength from.

That after every terrible occurrence that Persephone has been through, she continues to stand tall with her head held high. With an aura that stretches far beyond her title as Queen of The Underworld.

With her emerald eyes alight and steady, her cunning gaze able to pierce through the toughest of men's mental barriers. Revealing where their strength truly ends, and where their weaknesses begin.

A power that only a woman who has learned to become resourceful during times where help was finite, standing up against the abuse of control that many men use to dominate over women.

A woman who, whether she can witness it or not, is an inspiration to those around her.

"Yeah. I'd say a lot is an understatement." Dimitri says, glancing up at me before standing up from the leather sofa. He goes to stand near the fireplace, resting his elbow on the edge of it as he looks over at Nora who has gone silent.

I watch as her gaze raises from Dimitri's to Persephone's, a look of sympathy and apprehension resting there. I watch as she begins biting her inner lip, knowing all of the questions that are thrashing beneath the surface are begging her to ask them. So she settles for asking the one that is most obvious. "What will this mean for when Melinoë returns home?" She looks up at me, her chest sinking as she exhales quietly. "The prophecy spoke of Melinoë being his biggest weakness. What will happen when he finds out she's not under his compulsion, and she's no longer in his grasp?"

I stand there, knowing exactly what Nora is hinting towards. That when we finally make our move to free Melinoë, and Zeus finally finds out that she isn't able to be compelled by him, he will retaliate in a large way.

And because his ego and false ideal of control will be challenged publicly, he will go to drastic measures to regain it. In ways that will certainly cause destruction for the lives of innocent people.

Hades lowers his gaze to Nora, silent for a moment as the truth of what we all know settles in his gaze. His chest sinks faintly, folding his hands behind his back as he says confidently, "It means that we will need to prepare for war."

Nora's face—although knowing this is exactly what would have evidently happened one way or another, still flashes a look of worry. For what it means for her, for the people of Vulir. Elzwin. Lothario.

But as that worry surfaces on her face, so does the calm knowing that everything comes with a price. And freeing Melinoë—no matter how destructive the after effects of it will be, is still a necessary fight for justice in the end.

She takes a deep inhale in, releasing as she nods her head at Hades.

"How long after we bring Melinoë home do you think we'll have until Zeus makes his first attack?" Dimtiri asks, lifting his elbow from the fireplace mantel and stepping away from it altogether.

Persephone steps forward, narrowing her chin. "The specifics of how long is hard to say, but I presume soon after."

I watch as Persephone takes a few steps away from Hades, staring at the softly crackling fire. A silence stretching between us all before she says, "Though his paranoia causes him to act impulsively, he is highly methodical at his core. He's calculative and manipulative, always making counter moves behind the scenes and not just what is at hand. Apollo is also his closest ally," She looks up from the fireplace, glancing at each of us before landing her gaze on Hades. "With his gift of prophecy, I fear he has an even larger advantage at making moves we cannot even see yet."

Hades gives her a soft, knowing look. The silent exchange between them lasts a moment before Hades looks at me and Dimitri. "But that doesn't mean we cannot still play into his hand, and manipulate it to our advantage. We just have to wait for our opening, and use it when it is time. As for now," He lowers his gaze to Nora, giving her a steady yet soft gaze. "I would like the information that has been shared here to remain in this room. Aside from Hecate and Charon, which we will meet with after we leave here to discuss these developments with." He glances at Persephone, nodding once before training his gaze back to us. "I do not want to cause a rise of panic for the people of Vulir. That fear will only aid Zeus in succeeding what he thrives on: control."

"But what if Zeus makes it past the shield?" Nora asks as she fixes her gaze onto Hades. "I mean that in no disrespect," She says quickly, putting her hands up before continuing. "But who's to say that even though the shield is powered by your magic, that Zeus can't get past—"

I lower my hand gently to Nora's shoulder, pulling her gaze up to mine from her seat on the couch. I tilt my head slightly down at her, giving her a reassuring look. "Let's just focus on one thing at a time. Zeus will not get past the shield." I say softly, lowering my hand from her shoulder, looking up at Dimitri. "But should he ever succeed, we'll be ready."

Dimitri gives me an affirming nod before glancing over at Nora. The look in his eyes fierce and subtle all the same. A look deep within his gaze that he'll die at the hands of a god if it means protecting the girl he loves.

"Zeus will not be able to break through the shield." Hades says to Nora—to everyone as reassurance. "But that doesn't mean he won't still *try* by using bait to lure you both out." He glances at Dimitri and I.

Referencing the man that attacked Dimitri in the Sephyra Forest. Still unclear if that was Zeus just shapeshifted into a different form, or if it was someone else entirely. The answers of which are still unclear but prove that the extra security measures we've placed on Vulir are necessary at this time. "Dimitri and I continue to do extra security sweeps." I say aloud. "We will continue to remain vigilant and observant. But for now, we stick with no one entering or leaving Vulir until it is safe to do so."

Nora looks up at me, nodding her head as she forces a close-lipped grin.

"We will keep in touch." Persephone says as a portal opens up behind her and Hades. "For now, just watch out for one another. Stay within the borders of Vulir." She nods her head slowly before turning around, Hades along with her.

Nora stands up from the couch, walking over to Dimitri to quietly talk to him while I step towards the portal. "Persephone."

She turns around along with Hades. "Yes, Reimus?"

"Will you tell Makaria what you learned today?" I ask.

She stares at me for a short moment before fixing a soft grin on her face. "Even after already learning so much in such a short time frame, she deserves the truth. To not be hidden in the dark. So yes, I will."

Since before Melinoë was kidnapped, I haven't seen Makaria and though I have barely gotten to know her, I find that she is in my thoughts often. Wondering how she's faring and healing from having her whole life flipped upside down, hoping that she's able to somehow find solace through it all.

My lips curve into a ghost of a grin, nodding. "I think that is very wise. How has she been doing?"

The grin on her face creeps up a little higher at each corner of her mouth. "Now with the help of the right people by her side, she's doing better. Thank you for asking."

I nod once more, feeling grateful that she's doing better. "Of course. I'm glad to hear it."

Persephone nods her head, raising her hand to rest upon my shoulder. The weight of her hand comforting, a similar energy to the one that her daughter carries. A feeling of energy that I miss deeply. "We will return soon." She says as she lowers her hand, turning around as Hades does the same. As they walk through the portal I watch as colors of magenta and dark violet churn in the center, a misty outline of what looks like to be an open sky above a large terrain of land. As they vanish behind the wall of mist, the colors quickly shrink into themselves before the portal closes entirely.

342

CHAPTER 43

After Dimitri left to do the first round of security sweeps for the day, and Nora headed back to The Sanctuary, I eagerly opted to spend some time back out in the yard. Starting right back where I left off.

I climb up the ladder, carrying the first piece of steel roof covering up to the top of the structure. I lay it onto the roof support beams, lining it up so that the narrowed end on the side furthest from me lines up with the center of the roof. I lower my hand in my tool belt, pulling out my drill and a screw, drilling it in before drilling a total of five screws on each side.

I gently pull on the metal, making sure it's sturdy enough before climbing down the ladder and repeating the process with another roof covering.

I do this two more times until I feel a presence looming close by. I lower the drill into my tool belt as I climb back down the ladder, turning around to see Eiran standing behind me.

"It's beginning to look rather engaging out here." He says.

A soft chuckle escapes me as I go to grab a fourth roof covering. "My hope is that Melinoë will feel the same." I climb up the ladder, fixing it onto the support beams before lowering my hand to my drill.

"She will." He says calmly.

I drill the covering down on both sides, gently tugging on it to test its sturdiness before descending the ladder. I turn around to face him as I lower the drill into my tool belt. "Does it bother you?"

He tilts his head at me.

"To not be able to visit her. Do Zeus' wards prevent you from getting inside at all?"

He straightens his head, nodding slowly. "The dead are unable to get through, yes. And—" He pauses, taking a few steps closer to me. "Yes. I hate that I cannot get close to her at this time."

I look at Eiran and see what is plainly clear. Though he is dead and cannot be with her physically any longer, he cherishes seeing her still as he is now. Knowing that it is why he remains stuck here in the physical realm, not allowing himself to pass over completely to The Underworld quite yet. And because he sacrificed his own life to keep Melinoë safe, there could never be any amount of jealousy or callousness that would propel me to look at him as anything other than a heroic and noble man.

I lower myself down, grabbing another metal sheet as I look up at him. "I'm sure she feels the same." Giving him a soft grin before climbing up the ladder.

"She will need you most of all when she returns home."

I lift the metal roof covering onto the support beams, lining it up.

"But I think you already understand that by what you appear to be building here."

I pull out a screw, fitting it into the hole and drill it in. I pull another one out as I look down at what I've been building. Hoping for it to be a little space for Melinoë to find solace in our newly renovated yard. But I also hope it will be a reminder that her fears and turmoil become my own to carry as well. Because I will always walk beside her, and help her process the horrors that weigh on her heart with a comforting hand to hold. That I will also help guide her through them in any way that I can.

My twin soul. The love of my existence in this lifetime, and every other.

I fit the screw into the hole and drill that one in as well. "Persephone said she would spell the inside to be cool in the summer, and warm in the winter." I drill another screw in. "A small feature that I think she'll appreciate."

Eiran gives a breathy laugh as I finish screwing this covering down. "I fear you are right."

I finish drilling it down, descending down the ladder as I turn towards Eiran. "Do you think circumstances would've turned out differently? If Melinoë had made you not come with her, do you think…" The part of the poachers killing her instead of him hanging in the air between us. The sickening thought of what those men would've done to her if she had been alone churns my stomach.

Eiran shakes his head. "I don't think any persuading from Melinoë to get me to stay back would've worked. Even aside from how my fate was weaved, I think that my conscience would have driven me to accompany her to Vulir regardless."

"Did you feel wronged at all after you died?" Asking him genuinely not to try and pry but out of curiosity. Wondering if once you die, and are revealed your fate, if that messes with your mind or spirit at all. "I know you don't regret your decision, but do you ever feel…lonely?"

He blinks as he looks over at Alastor whinnying from the pastures. I watch as a grin curves up his face. "It isn't a sense of loneliness that a soul feels after they pass, but more so a loss of purpose." He turns his gaze back to me. "Even when I was revealed what my fate was meant to amount to—even before I was born, I still never felt unjustified in my human existence. It never felt unfair to me because I got to succeed in doing the one thing that brought me the most amount of purpose. And that was watching over Melinoë when at the time no one else did."

I give him a half grin, my heart warming at his words and how much he has done for the woman I—we *both* love. How greatly he has willingly sacrificed for her. I could never be anything but grateful for that. "What is it like? When you say being revealed what your fate was, what does that look like after you die?"

Eiran takes a step over to the side, looking down at where the crack in the ground used to be from Persephone's rage before she magically willed the foundation back to normal again. "It's a difficult concept to explain to a living mind. It's as if in the final seconds before you're dead, you're given this playbook in your mind of everything that's happened in your life. It feels like it extends for a long period of time but happens within a matter of seconds."

"And that is because time is a complex concept?"

He nods. "For me it was a little different. Since my existence was divinely orchestrated by The Fates themselves, it was as if all of the pieces that didn't connect before filled in all of the holes of the overall puzzle. As a spirit, you're just able to see things from all vantage points without the biases of a human mind to construe them. But when I died, I was revealed what my divine purpose was. To be a guide for Melinoë into her divinity, to you. Her twin soul."

I find my gaze drifting away from his, roaming over the spiritual body he possesses now. Though his voice has no hint of animosity in it, and I know he says it with just the reality of the situation, my heart still finds itself slightly caving into itself that a large part of his purpose was to bring Melinoë into divine union with me. However grateful I am for that, I still can't help but feel a rush of guilt for how quickly his life ended.

"I can feel the change in your energy. Do not feel guilt for the fate I was bestowed."

I lift my gaze to him again, realizing that he's right. If it was truly his fate to not only protect Melinoë when no one else did, but to also have brought her into my life, his fate would've been the same nonetheless.

And no matter what, it would've ended exactly how it was intended to. No matter how devastating, nor harsh that truth is.

I nod my head. "Thank you."

Without me needing to explain further, Eiran nods back. Smiling as he nods up to the half-way done roof. "So, what kind of lights are you planning on putting in here?"

A soft chuckle escapes out of me as I go to lift another metal roof covering. As I finish installing the roof, I tell Eiran the finishing touches I have in mind, including the types of lights I plan to install. And as the realization that my project is now coming to an end settles, I can only think about the nights that Melinoë and I will spend together here. The nights I will have her snuggled up next to me as I read entries inspired by her from my journal.

And as the longing for her deepens, I hang onto the hope that she'll be home with me soon. As hope is the only thing I have left at this point.

CHAPTER 44

Melinoë

The door opens at the top of the stairs, the warm glow of sunlight filtering in from above as a light pair of footsteps descends down into the dungeon.

Less than a minute later Bethesda appears at my cell door, lowering the key into the lock. "You've been requested." She says quietly before unlocking the door.

I stand up from the ground, knitting my brows together. "Who is requesting me?"

She steps inside, coming to unlock the chains at my hand and ankle cuffs. Silent as she begins guiding me out of the cell and up the stairs.

"Is it Zeus?" I ask her, her silence beginning to make me nervous.

She continues to deflect my questions as she guides me up the stairs. The warmth of the sunlight grows brighter and brighter the closer we get to the top, doing little to curb my growing anxiousness building within.

When we enter the throne room I look up to see Artemis standing at the center with Zeus by her side.

A long, thick braid travels down to the middle of her back as loose strands kiss the sides of her oval face. I narrow my gaze to the light freckles that I hadn't noticed before, dotting the bridge of her nose.

Bethesda guides me closer until we meet them in the middle, letting go of my wrists as she bows at the waist. "May I be excused for my duties now, Your Majesty?"

"Yes, Bethesda." Zeus says as he gives her a fake close-lipped grin.

Bethesda quietly leaves the throne room as Zeus fixes his gaze onto me. The royal blue robes he's donned in today highlighting the sharp curve of his jaw, the harshness of his watchful gaze. I briefly lift my gaze up to avert it from his, noticing that his crown is absent from his head today. Alerting me that this is an informal meeting.

I look over at Artemis, my gaze lifting to the silver bow and quilt of arrows strapped to her back. The sharp point of the arrow glinting from the sunlight reflecting on it.

"I don't understand why any of this is important." Zeus says next to her, jogging my attention back to him.

"Because if you want to use her as an *ally*, then you're not going to see the totality of what she can do down there." Artemis seethes as she shoots Zeus a quick glance before beginning to slowly circle around me.

"I've already seen what she can do. And since her...*unique* gifts are of no use to me right now, then she stays in the dungeon."

"Except you forget that one's gifts are like a musical instrument. You get better at them by practicing, strengthening it. So what happens when you need her *precious* gifts and she cannot wield the kind of power you seek in that moment to defend us?" Artemis studies me as she walks around me, her gaze roaming over me like a museum exhibit she's trying to decipher.

Zeus rolls his eyes. "Fine." He lifts a hand, willing the cuffs at my wrists and ankles to disappear. He begins to walk away when he says, "But keep her within sight. I have to step out for a moment but I will return shortly."

A wide grin curves up Artemis' face. "Oh, don't worry. She won't be out of my sight for even a second."

My gaze shifts to the portal that stands before Zeus, golden eather wraps around the frame of it as he steps through the middle. The portal vanishes with him a second later.

"So, you can make people hallucinate."

I turn my gaze back to Artemis, nodding.

She ceases her steady pacing around me, looking me over once more before meeting my gaze. "But have you ever tried it on an immortal?"

Thinking of that time at the cabin when I was able to get inside of Zeus' mind as he had his hand wrapped around my throat. Remembering the shock that splashed across his shapeshifted face, at the time knowing I revealed a part of myself that I kept hidden. But it was all worth it to see that look on his face.

I almost nod my head, but remember that if I said that, it would entail that I remember anything prior to coming here. So instead, I shake my head.

She takes a step back from me, keeping her sharp gaze pierced onto mine. "Well, try it."

My eyes widen slightly as I tilt my head. "On you?"

She turns her head around from side to side, looking over her shoulders before landing her silver gaze back onto me. "Does it look like anyone else is around right now, princess?"

I go to clench my fists at the use of the word princess, but watch as her silver gaze snaps to them quicker than a viper. Instead of letting her think it affected me, I leave them unflexed at my sides as I nod at the quiver of arrows strapped to her back. "Is this a trap so you have an excuse to shoot me with one of those?"

She chuckles as she shakes her head, lifting the bow and quiver off of her back and tossing them onto the ground in front of her. I look down, noticing the metal quiver has white vines that wrap around it with tiny leaves connected at the ends. At the center of the quiver is a small crescent moon. "I only use these for real threats."

Ouch, well isn't she just a ray of fucking sunshine.

"If you're going to be our ally, and defend Zeus and Olympia, then you need to be able to wield that special gift of yours against those like us."

The more that I hear the word ally used in the same sentence as Zeus, the more I want to crawl out of my own skin.

Artemis watches me like a hawk, those piercing silver eyes as if cementing me in place as she waits for me to do something. A wave of awareness alerting me that absolutely any microexpressions I were to accidentally let slip right now would definitely be noticed and scrutinized.

I lift my gaze back up to hers, nodding as I widen my stance and focus my gaze on her forehead.

I begin trying to pry into her mind, making a mental tether to hers and trying to find any gaps in her mental barriers. I focus, trying to find my way in but my frustration clouds my focus.

Artemis smirks at me. "I have perfected protecting my mental barriers for a long, long time. So you'll forgive me if they are hard to penetrate."

I sigh. "If you know I can't get past them, then why bring me up here and make me try anyway?" I pull back my energy.

She takes a step towards me. "I did not say you *couldn't* get past them, only that they are difficult to."

I sigh as I nod, centering into myself as I try again.

I stretch that thread of my power out to her as I keep my gaze centered on her, reaching for her mental barriers as I begin to push my way through them. I fall short against the thick barrier she keeps up around her mind, taking a long exhale out as I keep trying to break it.

I will my power to the surface, trying to penetrate into her mind from every angle. My breathing picks up as that frustration expands inside of me, obscuring my confidence and concentration. I try to quickly obliterate it by pushing harder against her mental barriers, straining myself against them.

"You're trying too hard. Relax."

I pull back entirely, annoyance exceeding any desire to want to try again. How was I able to slip into Zeus' mind so easily that one day? Unless he had his guard down completely and wasn't expecting it, and that was the only reason why I succeeded so easily.

I straighten my back as I lift my gaze back up to Artemis'. "Just give me a second." I pinch my index finger and thumb to the bridge of my nose, squeezing the frustration down before lowering my hand. "I'll try again." I say, unenthusiastically.

Artemis looks at me before lowering down to grab her bow and quiver, strapping them both to her back again. When I go to open my mouth she cuts me off.

"I think you need a bit of motivation." She says as she approaches me.

Her hand reaches out as she grabs my arm, a portal showing up behind her as she immediately pulls me through it. My bare feet stumble out onto a soft, damp ground.

I whip my head around to look at her. "What are you doing? He said not to leave the throne room?" I bellow out.

Artemis gives a faint smirk as she chuckles. "Actually, his exact words were to not let you leave my sight. Which I still have no intention of doing."

I go to open my mouth to yell at her when a soft breeze catches me dead in my tracks, caressing my cheek and blowing a loose strand across my skin. I stand there with my mouth slightly parted as my vision refocuses on everything behind Artemis. At what surrounds us.

I look behind her at the abundance of tall evergreen trees, my gaze slowly lifting high up to the clear sky as they tower over us. My breathing slows to a nearly non-existent rate as every anxious thought, every bit of frustration ceases inside of me, and I take everything in.

A piercing cry drags my attention over to a hawk flying overhead, his reddish-brown wings spanned out wide as he glides through the sky before landing on a nearby tree branch. I blink away the brightness from the sun shining high above, lifting my hand up to shield my eyes.

I slowly lower my gaze all the way down to my bare feet, sinking my toes into the grass. I almost let out a soft cry at the welcomed texture of it beneath the balls of my feet. My chest sinks heavily as I lower myself to the ground, reaching my hand out and sinking my fingertips into the grass. Deeper until my fingertips burrow beneath the soil.

A harsh cry threatens to erupt to the surface but it takes everything in me to hold it in, to remember that I'm not alone.

I raise myself back up to my feet, looking deeper into the treeline until I spot a line of soldiers standing at the edge of it. Each of them armored from head to toe with swords sheathed at their sides, creating a blockade along the woods. Standing with their backs to the forest as they face towards Zeus' palace only yards away, their hands on the hilt of their swords.

"They have only one purpose."

I turn around to face Artemis.

"Their jobs are to protect these woods, and the Casalas Mountains within them." She raises a hand behind her as I lift my gaze up to see we're standing at the base of large, towering mountains ahead of us.

My gaze fixates on the jagged slopes of the mountains, ranging from shades of deep green to grey. My gaze lowers down to trees towering above a running creek of water. The rhythmic, trickling sound of it stilling me for a moment.

The water, the birds, even the sound of the grass crunching beneath my feet as I take a step forward. The simple sounds of *life* blooming around me.

I take a deep breath in, soaking it all in.

"Now that I have your attention," Artemis begins before I hear her whistle.

I look at her as my brows knit together. I follow where her gaze is and turn to look at a large mountain lion slowly prowling towards us from a mile away.

My eyes widen as I whip my gaze back to Artemis. "Are you mad?" I demand.

She shrugs her shoulders. "You need motivation. And out here, I can give that to you."

I whip my gaze around, watching as the mountain lion lowers itself down to the ground, trying to hide itself within the tiny stalks of grass as it inches closer to me.

"She's been ordered to hunt you. Now you can either wiggle your way into my mind to interfere with that command, or you can become her lunch."

I seethe through my clenched teeth, balling my fists together. "I didn't hear you say anything to it." I whip my hand backwards towards the animal.

Artemis smirks. "I don't need to say anything. One look, one silent command," She taps the side of her temple. "And they know what their assignment is."

I loosen a ragged breath, looking back at the mountain lion before angling my body so I can face Artemis but still see the mountain lion approaching from the side. "Fine." I snarl.

I center into myself as I look over at the lion, half a mile away from me now. I look back at Artemis, exhaling a long breath before I begin.

"You already have the gift. So now use it to survive."

I will my power to the surface, focusing on her mind as I try to forget about the mountain lion slowly prowling towards me. I reach inside of her mind, meeting that same resistance as earlier. Instead of getting frustrated, I take a deep breath and keep trying.

I visualize what her mental barriers look like, appearing as shields of titanium surrounding her mind. Their walls glistening with a fortress of protection, searching for my way in until I spot it.

I slip myself inside and immediately suffocate it, taking hold as I try to imagine the one thing she would actually be terrified of. As she appears to be someone who isn't easily scared of much.

Apollo comes racing through the treeline with his bow and arrow at the ready, the determination on his face quickly shifting to confusion as he looks to see me out here with his sister. He lowers his weapon down. "What are you doing bringing her out here?" He demands, releasing the arrow from the nock and raising it back into his golden quiver. "If Zeus finds out—"

"Oh, don't be such a snitch. She's not going anywhere." Artemis says as she takes a step towards her brother, an amused grin on her face. "We'll be back in before Zeus returns."

Apollo rolls his eyes, approaching his sister as he looks over at the mountain lion. He notices the way that it has its sight latched onto me. "So you're tormenting the girl now. Nice."

"I'm giving her *incentive*." She remarks as she waves her hand lazily. "Beside, I'm not—"

In a split second the mountain lion changes course and pounces on Apollo, its mouth latching onto his neck and biting down hard as it pushes him backwards.

"Apollo!" Artemis screams as she races forward and whistles at the mountain lion, presumably a command to get it to stop hurting him.

It does nothing as it begins to feast on the god. Apollo's cries are deafening as he tries to pry the lion off with his hands, but is unsuccessful as the lion's teeth tear deeper into his neck. A second later severing his neck from his body completely.

A piercing scream erupts out of Artemis as she goes to pounce on the mountain lion when she ends up landing harshly on the ground instead.

She rolls over and hikes up onto her hands and knees, her hand immediately lowering to her hunting knife strapped to her thigh as her gaze whips to where Apollo and the mountain lion just were. Her ragged breathing simmers as she lifts her gaze up at me, a grin curving my lips as I point with my eyes behind her. She peers her gaze away from me, looking back at the mountain lion halted in its trek a quarter of a mile behind her.

Artemis quickly turns her gaze back up to me, watching as a flash of shock ripples across her features before it becomes a wide grin of pride.

I release myself from her mind, pulling my energy back entirely as she stands up from the ground. Removing her hand from hovering above her hunting knife.

"Well done." She says as she turns her head around, giving the mountain lion a look before it raises up from the grass, turning around and walking away from us.

"I could say the same. Are you able to control all animals like that?" I ask.

She faces me again, nodding. "While Zeus' dominion resides over Olympia, mine lies in the wilderness. I protect all that reside within, all that are wild and untamed such as myself."

She approaches me as I nod to the soldiers far behind us. "Is that why they stand guard out here? To protect what lives within?"

She huffs out a small noise as she grins. "In a sense. Or rather they try to keep everyone else out."

I shake my head, furrowing my brows. "Why would they want to keep people out of here?"

She stares at me for a short moment before smoothing her expression into neutrality. "Because these mountains now belong to Zeus, and he—well, let's just say he doesn't want any *unwelcome visitors* in them."

"Now—as in, these mountains belonged to someone else before?" I ask. Wondering why Zeus would want to acquire this land for his own. Wondering if it did not always belong to him, then who?

Artemis stands next to me as she straightens her back. Looking at the soldiers positioned outside of the treeline as she says, "It is unknown who. Now," She begins, changing the subject. "Before we head back inside I want you to close your eyes."

"Um, okay." I say, doing as she says.

"One thing that being in the wilderness will teach you is to hone in on your other senses, the ones that do not make you immortal."

I stand there with my eyes closed, listening to her speak as I suddenly hear the rustling of leaves ahead of us.

"Tell me what you hear."

I listen in as the rustling of leaves gets closer, louder. "I hear something moving."

"Good. Now focus on it. Does it sound like something large, or small?"

I listen in on the way that the leaves crunch beneath the animal, until the twig of a branch snaps beneath it. "It's large, but it doesn't sound heavy."

"What else?" She asks.

I hone in on the animal, noticing the pause in its trek towards us, a soft grunt-like noise emitting out of it. A moment later I hear the plucking of a leaf from somewhere nearby.

"It's a deer." I say.

"Are you sure?" She asks.

I open my eyes, looking ahead to see a doe chewing on a leaf from ahead of us. I look over at Artemis, a half-grin pulling up at my lips. "I'm positive."

She playfully rolls her eyes before she gently grabs my arm. "Come. Before Zeus gives me an earful that I am not interested in being on the receiving end of."

A portal opens up in front of us as we step through it, taking us back into the throne room. The only thought to float through my mind now is having been outside for the first time in weeks, knowing that Artemis didn't have to do that to truly get me to try harder at making her hallucinate.

But in an unconventional way, it was exactly what I needed. In more ways than one.

CHAPTER 45

Shortly after Artemis brings me back inside, Zeus appears in the throne room via portal. Placing the shackles back onto my wrists and ankles. He glances over at me before training his gaze onto Artemis. "Well?"

Artemis shrugs her shoulders. "Her gift is average. It'll need more practice to become stronger."

I keep myself from looking over at her. *Average*? I saw the way her face lit up with horror when she thought her brother was being mauled by that mountain lion. I saw the way her body locked up with tension as she tried to pounce on the animal to yank it off of him. A goddess who has been around for a lot longer than I have but was still influenced by my mind control.

I'd say my gift was anything other than *average*.

Zeus gives a chuckle as I witness Bethesda coming into the throne room with her gaze lowered to the ground. "As I suspected."

Artemis nods at Zeus, electing to give me a quick glance before making her departure from the throne room.

"You and Bethesda will carry out your normal chores." Zeus says before he makes his exit from the throne room as well, leaving me with Bethesda before she gently grabs my arm.

I allow her to guide me silently to the kitchen as I wonder why Artemis lied to Zeus. Not only about my ability to get through her mental barriers, but also at the fact that she took me outside. Though, as she made clear, he *technically* didn't say not to leave the room.

Though it still begs the question as to why she would go through the hassle at all? Why lie and—most importantly, why lie?

Bethesda and I reach the kitchen as she gets right to clearing off the kitchen island as I head into the cleaning pantry. I open the door, turning on the light as I go to grab the broom when something catches my eye from the top shelf.

I look up to see another water bottle left out with a sandwich this time. My eyes widened slightly as I nonchalantly look behind me, seeing Bethesda's back turned towards me as she hovers over the sink. I look back up at the sandwich and reach for it, immediately devouring it.

I close my eyes at the taste of mild cheddar cheese and warm ham as I chew it quickly, finishing the sandwich before reaching for the water.

I uncap it, taking a few long sips before placing it back onto the shelf. Grabbing the broom and wiping the sides of my mouth before stepping out of the cleaning closet.

It has to be Semele leaving that stuff out for me. Other than Dionysus bringing me those few trays of food those couple times, she's the only one who has brought me food any other time.

After some time of sweeping I hear the rush of little feet running into the kitchen. I look up to see a little girl with strawberry blonde hair glance at me, her weary brown eyes staring at me for only a moment until she rushes into Bethesda's arms.

"Maya, what are you doing?" Bethesda gently scolds the little girl as she rests her hands on her shoulders, peering down at her. She leans into Maya as she lowers her voice. "You know the rules. You must stay in the chamber while I work."

"I know, mama." Maya says in a sweet voice. She looks over at me again, catching a quick glance before looking back at Bethesda. "But I just—"

"No buts." Bethesda brings Maya in for a hug before pulling her away. She gives her daughter a smile as she tilts her head. "We will go for a walk in the courtyard as soon as I'm done, okay? But you must stay in our chamber until then."

Maya begins to frown as she steps away from Bethesda. "Okay, mama." She turns on her heels, her rose pink tulle dress swishing with her before she hurries out of the kitchen.

I look up at Bethesda, catching her gazing after Maya before she turns to me. She gives me a close-lipped smile as her chest sinks with her exhale. "Her father died a long time ago." She pauses as she goes to grab a dirty dish from the kitchen island. "It's just me and her now."

She brings the plate to the sink, understanding now her muteness and subservience towards Zeus. Why she does as she's told with no questions, and cleans the palace in exchange for a place to stay.

She doesn't do it because she wants to, but because she has to. For her daughter.

I begin sweeping again, piling the food crumbs and dirt into a small pile. "I'm sorry for your loss."

Bethesda rinses the plate before setting it onto a drying rack. She turns around, lifting her gaze up to me as she forces a grin. "Thank you." She grabs a cup with leftover milk in it as I see the yearning for a different life in her hopeless gaze. As if feeling like this is all that she has left to offer to her daughter.

"How old is she?" I ask, realizing this is the first time Bethesda and I have actually had a conversation together. Normally we work in silence together until she brings me back down to the dungeons.

"Maya will be seven next month." She rinses the cup under the water. "She is obsessed with being outside as of late. She wants to go for walks everyday." She chuckles as she sets the cup in the drying rack, turning around. "I'm only in my thirties, but sometimes I feel I have aged well beyond that." A tired gaze rests in her eyes before vanishing, a soft smile curving her lips. "I suppose it's good that she forces me to take her on walks everyday then. Fresh air is good for the soul."

I give her a grin back, nodding. After having spent what short amount of time I was gifted outside earlier, I find that my grin is real this time. "Yes, it is."

I watch as Bethesda looks down at the cuffs on my wrists, a frown pulling at her lips as her gaze lifts up. "I apologize, I didn't mean for that to be callous."

I shake my head curtly. "It's okay. It's not your fault I'm—" I stop myself, looking down at my wrists before fixing my gaze back at her again. I take a long inhale before exhaling, changing the subject. "I was the same when I was her age. I loved being outside, though back where I'm from we experience all four seasons. So I only had opportunities to be outdoors from spring to most of fall."

My hand wrapped around the broom flexes slightly, remembering all the time I spent in Hellen Park. Back during a time when life seemed both so simple, and miserable. A time when I had no idea who I was, or what my life amounted to. And as I sweep and mop the kitchen here, I find myself sometimes almost reverting back to that cluelessness. The part of myself who didn't know it was okay to stand up. Didn't believe her voice mattered.

A part of myself I've willingly had to succumb to again. Not for the sake of wanting to be silent, but for protecting the people I love.

But as I stand here now, would future me be proud of the strength and resilience of doing the hard disservice of being silent? Or would she be ashamed of reverting back to old patterns, even for the need for survival?

Sometimes, I wonder if this whole act is even worth it. Maybe I'm better off just saying fuck it and being my most unrelenting self. But even if I wanted to, I can't.

Because even after all of the years of abuse, my heart somehow still beats with compassion and softness. Even beneath the barbed wire cage that once wrapped around it, a defense that had been shattered when I met him.

Reimus.

With the warmth of his love, and his dedication to understanding and consoling me, he freed me from every suffocating bind that had been conditioned onto me. His complete acceptance of me was not only the key to regaining the ability to love again, but also learning to separate myself from the limiting beliefs that kept me from believing in myself.

Having promised myself once before that I wasn't willing to allow myself to be plagued by the binds of my past. By what Zeus made me once believe was real about me. And as I stand here now, I realize even through the act of fake obedience, I somehow found myself slipping into that version of myself again.

And as I stand there, I vow silently to myself.

No more.

I give Bethesda a nod, remembering she's still looking at me. "Though I don't believe I ever grew out of wanting to be outdoors, even at this age. Something about being in nature just...calls to me." I begin sweeping the pile into the dustpan before dumping it into the garbage. "So if she's anything like I was at her age, I fear you're stuck with her dragging you outside all the time." I chuckle as I go to set the broom down.

Bethesda chuckles softly. "I fear you may be right."

I go to retrieve the mop and bucket from the pantry, pulling them out before filling the bucket up with water. As I stand there waiting for the bucket to fill up, I realize how healing it was for Artemis to bring me outside today. Even in those fifteen minutes we stood out there, even if her intentions were just to get me to try harder to break into her mind.

It was what I needed to give me just that little nudge forward.

CHAPTER 46

Hours after Bethesda brought me back down here I hear the door swing open again, followed by a different pair of light footsteps as they make their way down the steps.

Semele approaches my cell door, tossing the key to my cuffs through the iron bars. My gaze follows the key as it lands on the ground next to me, my gaze lifting up to see her back already turned towards me. Before I can ask her the reason my gaze whips over to the bathing bucket appearing in my cell a few feet beside me. Light steam rising from the hot water within it.

"I need to be elsewhere in thirty minutes so make the most of it." She says, lowering herself to the ground as she leans up against the cell bars.

I grab the key, fitting it into the keyhole at my wrists and ankles. After unlocking them and removing them both, I take the key and bring it with me to the bucket. "Thank you."

She says nothing as I begin to undress, tossing my tunic and breeches to the side before I step into the water. Sighing contentedly, I lean back and enjoy the hot water for several minutes before I start washing my hair with the ivory soap left out for me.

"I heard you visited Apollo's Temple the other day."

I glance up at her back, nodding even though she cannot see me. "Yes, we did."

She crosses her legs at her ankles, her cinnamon brown hair flowing past her shoulders as she leans her head back against the bars. "Zeus only pays a visit there if there is something he seeks, so I cannot imagine you three went for pleasure."

My gaze glances up at her again, not breaking away from the natural movements of washing my hair at her statement. Knowing that any pause would be heard, and could signal that there is something to know, to hide. Regardless if she's been bringing me baths, or sneaking food out for me, she's still the one who helped Zeus kidnap me. She may not be entirely evil, but she still isn't to be trusted. So I decided to lie. Mostly. "He brought me there to see the Pythia. He wanted to know what she could see as far as my gifts and my allegiance for Olympia extends to." I lather the soap into the ends of my hair, lowering my gaze to the strands in my hands. "It was a short, and uneventful trip to say the least."

"Interesting." She says, the word enunciated in a slow manner.

A long moment of silence stretches between us as I finish lathering the soap in my hair, rinsing it out. I toss my hair over my shoulders as I begin lathering the soap over my arms, working my way down.

"The Pythia was once a mortal woman, similar to how that woman from that story I told you about was. Though each of them turned into an immortal for contrasting reasons."

I continue gliding the soap over my body, remaining silent as she continues to speak.

"The Pythia was already powerful as a mortal, and when given the opportunity by Zeus to be turned immortal, she didn't think twice. Imagine being able to tell the past, present and future of someone's life, a gift that very few other than The Fates can do. To then be given the chance to do that for an eternity."

I scrub the soap down my chest, over my breasts as I lift my gaze up to Semele. "I guess I wouldn't have passed up the opportunity if I were her either."

She makes a brief humming noise, a silent beat passing between us. "You would if it meant allowing someone else to have power over your autonomy."

I rinse the soap from my chest before standing up in the bucket, working the soap lower. "And you know this because of your close alliance with Zeus?" I query.

Semele chuckles lightly. "I have been Zeus' ally, his...*confidant* for a long time to know that his bargains always come with a price."

I lower myself back down into the bucket, letting the suds on the lower half of my body rinse off into the water. I peer my gaze up at the back of Semele's head, already knowing what she had to give up in return for bearing Zeus' child. But wondering what she would say anyway. "So then what do you think the woman in that story's price was? To bear Zeus' child and be turned immortal?"

Semele stays quiet for a moment as I see her head lower down towards her chest. I watch as she pulls out a necklace from beneath her collar, holding a gold locket in her hands as she opens it. "Zeus told me her purpose was only to bear his child, not to actually be a mother to the Twice Born."

I watch as her thumb traces over the picture held inside, and in that moment I know it's the same locket she showed me at The Sanctuary. With the picture of a young Dionysus nestled inside of it.

"But I demanded, for her selfless act nonetheless, that he allow her a place to live in the palace. That he owed her better living conditions then what she was afforded in Lothario, for bearing a child for him. So, he agreed."

I lower the soap to the ground as I rinse my body and my hair once more. So she hadn't lied about that part, being that she was originally from Lothario. And the locket she carried with her when she came to Vulir hadn't been fake.

Some of the things she shared with me were true after all.

Her gaze remains lowered to the locket in her hand. "She took it only with the confidence that she could still see her son, even if he did not know who she was. But as she started to witness the things Zeus would ask her son to do for him, to prove himself in exchange for one day giving him what he yearns for, that's when she made the ultimate sacrifice."

I squeeze the excess water out of my hair before I step out of the bucket. "Hadn't she already sacrificed enough?"

"You would think so. But for that boy," She pauses, shaking her head slowly as she lowers the locket beneath her tunic. "She realized when he was born what it truly meant to love someone unconditionally. That there were no limits to what she would do to protect him, even if she had to be a villain to those who did not deserve it."

I go to reach for the towel on the ground, wrapping it around my body as I dry myself off.

"See, the Twice Born does not know about his past. Does not know he was reincarnated from the womb of Zeus' mistress, and that not one but two souls live within him. Zeus loves his son, but respects him as much as he does anyone else."

So, essentially he doesn't respect him at all then.

"Hera knew what Zeus had done, and knew for a long time about the mistress. As The Goddess of Marriage and Childbirth, she demanded that he not embarrass her by letting the world know who the Twice Born's real mother was. That if Zeus told anyone, or continued seeing the mistress any longer, that she would seek harm against the offspring and mother."

"Damn…you really think she would've killed the son if he had?" I ask, lowering the towel to the ground before pulling over a clean white tunic.

"Hera fiercely protects women, particularly in their roles as wives and mothers. She is invoked by mortals for her blessing in marriage and childbirth, and it is a great honor to receive such from her. But she is not to be mistaken as a pious goddess. She will seek vengeance at her husband's infidelity."

I smooth the tunic over my chest before pulling on the light beige breeches. Looking up at Semele, wondering what she would've done had Hera come after Dionysus. Knowing that she cannot be oblivious to the way Hera looks at him, as if he were nothing more than an insect when he's been made to believe his whole life that the woman who despises him isn't his real mother. "So, the ultimate sacrifice she made then was her silence?"

Semele nods her head. "Her silence about the Twice Born's real past, about who his mother truly was, for the assurance of his safety. Though as he became older, it was as if the act of being reincarnated left an energetic imprint on him. He started to try and confide in Zeus about feeling different, even having surreal dreams about a little boy who was murdered."

Damn, that has to be grueling to say the least. Having no idea that they whole time it's a dream about how your first self was assassinated.

"But Zeus always assured him they were just dreams, that the divergence he felt within was just because he shared Zeus' powerful bloodline. But as time went on, the woman watched his behaviour change. Assumingly to numb out the noise that surrounded the inner walls of his head, to the past he had no answers to. That's when Zeus made a bargain with him."

I lower myself to the ground, picking up the key and walking back over to the wall where the cuffs and chains are.

I lower down to attach the ones at my ankles first, then move onto the ones at my wrists.

"When Zeus came forward to him one day granting him a seat on the council, the man denied his offer. Stating that he had no desire to be a part of the council. But when Zeus told him he hadn't been entirely truthful about his past, he had a quick change of heart. Zeus used the...*eagerness* of his son to know more about why he feels like an outcast, different to everyone around him, to fuel his dedication to also carrying out certain tasks Zeus would assign him. Promising him that if he carried out his duties, he would reveal the comprehension of his past. So he does what Zeus asks, but the woman knows better than to believe that Zeus will actually be forthcoming with that information."

I lock the cuffs onto my wrists, tossing the key as it lands behind Semele's back. The clinking sound chimes briefly before Semele lowers her head to the side, looking down at it. "So basically, he's just using his son for his own gain?"

She lowers her hand down, picking it up before she stands up from the ground. She briefly stretches her arms before turning around to face me, pocketing the key into her breeches. "The bottom line is that she realized not only did she sacrifice her silence, but in the end, she sacrificed giving her son a shot at a life that he truly deserved. Bearing a child with a man who—if she stepped out of her rose colored glasses at that time long enough, would've seen it was one of the biggest mistakes of her life."

My gaze roams over her face as understanding smooths over my face. "But you said she loves her son? How could she have regretted birthing him?"

"It is not having her son that she regrets, but with whom."

I blink at her as I nod slowly, narrowing my gaze as I lower myself to the ground. Reaching for the hair brush as I begin detangling my hair.

"I have someplace else to be." Semele turns around, taking a step away from the cell when I do the one thing that I never thought I'd do.

After everything she told me back in Vulir, about the son she cared for and loved very much, that she had with an abusive man. I begin to realize that maybe not everything was a lie. That having a child with a man who forbids you to tell your son who you are, who uses your silence against you is traumatic and disheartening enough. To live in, and share a palace with the son you bore only to watch the woman who gets your title look at him like he's nothing more than a fly on the wall. Unbeknownst to myself, I start to see Semele in a light I never thought I would after what she put me through.

Realizing that what she did to aid Zeus in kidnapping me was never entirely about me, but solely about protecting her son. That her actions were devious and barbaric, and I'm not sure if I will ever trust her fully again because of it. But a wave of finality hits me as I realize that I cannot fault her for doing inexplicable acts in the name of Zeus, all to make sure no harm comes to her son.

So as that realization hits inside of me, I speak two words that I never thought I'd say to her. "Hey, Semele."

She halts her stride, keeping her back towards me as she turns her head to the side.

"Thank you."

She turns around then, her gaze lowering to mine. "For what?"

I shrug my shoulders as I continue working the brush through my hair. "For bringing me baths." For a moment I pause. "For sneaking me food in the pantry." I say quietly.

She blinks at me before taking a step towards me. "You're welcome with the baths. But the food," She shakes her head as a faint smirk crawls up her lips. "I don't know what you're talking about."

A half-grin curves up my lips as Semele turns around and begins her ascent up the stairs again. Working the hair brush through my tangles until I finish detangling my hair completely.

And I realize in that moment, not once did I use the formal title of His Majesty when speaking about Zeus. Unsure if that will prove to have been a careless mistake on my end, or if it's just the beginning of my inability to hide behind the subservient façade any longer.

CHAPTER 47

Reimus

"You know what to do, Eileen." My father says.

I open my eyes, surrounded by the void of this same recurring nightmare. I look around, trying to find my mother and father but cannot see anything other than complete darkness.

"It must be done to save our people. To save our lineage. If he still holds the essence within him, they'll follow him until he is executed."

"Dad?" I yell out, walking forward as I try to find him. "Mom?" I begin jogging in a light sprint trying to find my bearings in the utter darkness.

I trip over what—I'm not exactly sure. I go to bring my hand to the ground when I feel dry dirt beneath my fingers. I scoop some of it up into my hands, studying it before slowly opening my hand and dumping it back onto the ground. I go to take another step when I feel my legs lock into place.

I try picking them up but cannot move a muscle. I begin to panic as I'm trapped in place when I feel a gravitational pull from the ground. As if beckoning me to submit down into it.

I hear chanting as tethers of vines shoot upwards, latching onto my wrists as energy courses through me. Causing my chest to heave forward as the force of its power overwhelms me.

My breathing picks up as I look all around and begin to see the darkness start to peel back. Crack by tiny, little crack.

"Mom!" I yell out, my gaze roaming wildly everywhere in front and behind me as tiny slips of light sneak through the cracks.

"It is time, Reimus. Remember."

I jerk my gaze over to the left, following where my mother's voice is coming from but only seeing a thin silhouette standing there. No distinguishing features, just the ghost of a body.

The vines at my wrists tug deeper into my skin, pricking me as I seethe at the bite of the pain. I watch as a trickle of my blood seeps from the surface of my skin, the vine coiling itself around it until a glowing light emanates from it. "What the—"

"The essence to be hidden beneath the soil from which we originate. Destined to be triggered back to life as he steps foot onto what belongs to us." She says, her voice carrying over all around me. "For until the time is right, the remainder of us hide in plain sight."

The vines loosen themselves as they uncoil from my wrists, lowering back down to the ground as my legs are no longer cemented in place. I look around until I see two people standing far away from me. I begin running towards them when I see the familiar face of my father as he looks down upon my mother.

"Dad!" I yell, rushing towards them.

He smiles down at her, raising his hand to her cheek as he gently brushes her skin with the backs of his knuckles. "He will make a great leader, you know."

My mother smiles up at him, leaning into his touch. "I know. I just wish I were going to be around to witness it."

"Mom, I'm right here!" I yell out, trying to close the distance between us but find that no matter how hard I pump my arms, no matter how fast I try to run, I don't make it any closer than a quarter of a mile away.

As if running on a treadmill, keeping me right in place with no progression of making it closer to my parents.

Callen nods his head. "I wish the same. Though we've known for a long time that we wouldn't be around to witness him coming into his essence." He slowly swipes a thumb beneath her eye. "I'm grateful for the time we have had with him."

Eileen nods her head, raising her hand to wrap around my father's. Tears begin to well in her eyes as a grin curves up her lips. "Me too."

Their figures begin to blur as I find the ground beneath me opening up, free-falling into a bottomless pit of nothing. I try to grab at absolutely anything when I hear the faint echo of my mother's voice.

"Remember."

I jolt upright in bed, sweat beading across my brow as the sheets pool down to my waist. My chest rises and sinks quickly as my breathing staggers, working on a swallow as I try to calm myself.

I wipe the back of my hand across my forehead before bringing it to the talisman around my neck. Gently gripping it for comfort as my breathing begins to slow back to a normal pace.

I lift the covers from me and walk over to the bathroom, turning on the light as I stand in front of the mirror. I turn the sink on, splashing cold water on my face before hovering above it with my hands on the sides of the basin.

My fingers grip the porcelain sink as my knuckles flex against my skin. Taking a shallow breath in before releasing it out.

It's always been the same nightmare for years, my mother telling me the same thing over and over again.

Remember.

I had always thought it was my own subconscious mind trying to continuously torture myself. To remember my mother before she was murdered by soldiers in the safe house I told her to go to. My father had been out defending our people with me when she had fled, demanding that he stay back with me to make sure our defenses were properly secured against the threat. I had slipped away for just a moment to run after a man making it past our defenses, heading in the direction to the safe house. I ran after him, tackling him to the ground when he pulled a knife out and—

No, that's not right. I was in my drago form when I attacked him. I set him on fire. But why do I remember the knife on my heart then—

I lift my hands from the sink, stepping back as I run a hand over my face. The blurry details of that day threaten to confuse me once again. An unfortunate side effect I'm sure from my own grief that prevents me from remembering each and every detail.

Though one detail I'll never forget is the look on my mother's face when my father and I went to secure the border. She had looked at him as if she had thought there might be a chance that we wouldn't make it out alive. And at the end of it all, she was half right.

As my father died defending our home, while I made it out alive. Whether by pure chance or luck, I can never know as both feel like a curse in their own respective ways.

I walk out of the bathroom, heading back to the bed as I lay down. I bring the covers up to my chest as I lean my head back into the pillow. Lying there wide awake, unable to fall back asleep.

I lean over to open the nightstand next to me, turning on the table lamp on top of it before reaching inside the drawer and pulling out my journal. I stare at it for a long moment, my thumb tracing over the spine of it as all I can fixate on is the empty spot next to me.

I open my journal to the next blank page, over a hundred pages already occupied by the verses of my enamoration for Melinoë. Knowing that I could fill a hundred more journals, detailing all of the ways that Melinoë is the greatest gift I've ever been given, and it still wouldn't show the lengths to how deeply she has a hold on me.

I tap the pen to the blank page, settling into myself as I try to let the words flow onto paper. Except as minutes tick by, the words I so effortlessly can convey about her fail me for once in my life. I tap the pen briskly against the paper, trying to distract myself from the empty space next to me. Frustrated by the growing number of days that her side of the bed has been left made.

Knowing that the pressure Makaria is surely facing, leaving the timing of when Melinoë comes home essentially up to her ability to come into her powers. I can't imagine how overwhelming that would be for someone.

So I have been patient, I have not gone out of my way to extract a new plan to bring Melinoë home quicker. But as my patience runs thin, so does the desire to follow the plan Eiran made clear we follow. So does any common sense that I try to maintain about how this time, I might actually need help in getting Melinoë free.

I set the journal back into the drawer, slamming it shut before rolling over onto my side. Facing Melinoë's spot as the day she'll return back home to me cannot come soon enough. The reminder of the cold, hard ground that they currently force her to sleep on blanketing me with a rage I've never known before. How I would give anything to trade places with her.

I would gladly suffer the discomfort of that dungeon ground for her to rest soundly in the safety of our bed.

I reach my hand out, resting it on her side of the bed where her back normally would be. My fingers grip into the sheets at what would be her hip as she sleeps deeply next to me, her long hair trailing down her warm back as I'd drown in the scent of her.

A memory surfaces as I close my eyes, allowing myself to drown in it.

I dip my head lower into her neck, my face covered in the long strands of her hair. The soft giggles she makes reverberates my skin like a delicate chill. She turns her head around to try and look at me when she belts out laughing. "Are you suffocating yourself in my hair?"

I lift my head up, some of her hair clinging to the bridge of my nose and my lip. I blow it off my lips as a chuckle escapes me. "Maybe."

Melinoë laughs as she turns onto her back, looking at me with those eyes that I'll spend the rest of my life admiring. She raises her hand, gently resting it on my jaw as her thumb sweeps across my skin.

I lean into her touch, kissing her palm as she says, "I love you."

The way she said it was so simple, like the normalcy of waking up every day and sitting down to drink a cup of coffee. The sweet, yet subtleness of those words like when I find her laying out on the balcony chair. Her hair flowing down her sides as she reads with the quietness surrounding her. And when I'd lean down to give her a kiss on the forehead, she'd greet me with the sweet song of her voice.

A simplicity that I will never tire of, so long as she promises to keep feeding me with it.

I lower my head down, pressing a kiss to her lips once, then twice before pulling away. "I love you." I say softly to her before I lower another kiss down to her chin. "Here," I bring my lips further down, pressing another kiss to her neck. "And here."

Her soft giggles against me turn into breathy moans as I lower my lips down to her breasts. Lifting my gaze up at her as I press a soft kiss against her hardened nipple. "And here."

Her soft gaze quickly turns heated as I continue lowering myself down, kissing every square inch of her breasts and soft belly until my lips hover above her pussy. I open her legs wider for me, lifting one up to bend at the knee as I press a soft kiss there.

I watch her squirm, her gaze alight on my lips as I lower them down, her pussy already glistening for me. "Especially here."

I lower my mouth onto her as I show her exactly how much I love her, not letting up until I've made her come not once, not twice, but three times. Drowning in the pleasure I'm eliciting for her with each cry I wring from her body.

I pull the comforter closer to my body, wrapping my arm tightly around it as the memory of Melinoë laying next to me ingrains in my mind. Knowing that when I wake up in the morning I'll remember that it was all just that. A memory. A silent escape to fill the emptiness beside me with the imagined comfort and bliss of her once more.

I arrive at The Sanctuary, pulling the front entrance door open as the aroma of banana bread hits me as I step inside. I make my way to the staircase at the end of the room, climbing the steps until I make it to the second floor.

I open the paneled wood door, stepping into the women's living corridors. A long hallway with enclosed rooms on each side, half of the women residing here occupy this floor while the other half occupy the third floor. I make my way down the long hallway, approaching the healers room. I knock twice on the door frame before stepping inside.

Nora looks up from a clipboard in her hands, a pen trapped between her middle and index finger. "Perfect timing," She begins as she turns fully towards me, handing me the clipboard. "Not as much to restock as last week, but we'll need more feminine toiletries as we're running low."

I look down at the list of inventory, scanning over the list of things we supply on a weekly, and monthly basis. Items such as feminine hygiene products, body and hair soap, toilet paper, food, beverages, blankets, towels, clothing, cleaning supplies and even toys and books for the children. Each week I meet with Nora to discuss what needs to be replenished, as well as any special requests from any of the women residing here. I try to make it so they don't feel like they live in a shelter, but rather a home. So if I get a special request that someone wants something we don't regularly restock, such as a new pan for baking or new canvases for painting, then I like to make it a priority to get those things for them as well.

It's important to me that after everything most of these women have been through that they feel comfortable here. Which is also why when I had this building built years ago, I made it different from a typical shelter. With every woman having their own inclosed room with a door, rather than staying all together in one massive room with no privacy.

After scanning over what we need, I lift my gaze up to Nora's. "I'll be sure to grab some more then. Are there any supplies you need at all?"

Though Nora mostly works with her hands to heal and tend to the women here, certain ailments still call for the basics such as bandages, gauze, and isopropyl alcohol to name a few.

She shakes her head. "I'll be good for a while yet."

I give her an affirming nod as I release the paper from the metal clip, handing Nora back the clipboard. I fold the paper up and tuck it into my pocket. "I will go retrieve everything now then."

Nora gives me a look as she slightly tilts her head. "How are you doing?"

I shrug my shoulders, both of us knowing that I'm miserable without Melinoë, but trying to make the most out of the situation anyway. "I'm as good as I can be right now."

She nods slowly. "When was the last time you had more than a few hours of sleep?"

A lazy chuckle escapes me. "Is it really that obvious?"

She waves her hand over as she guides me to her cabinet of herbs, opening the glass paneled doors open as she rummages inside of it. "You, my friend, have bags under your eyes. And in all of the years I've known you," She grabs two glass jars of herbs before she closes the cabinet. Shuffling over to a five-tiered shelf with supplies on it, reaching for an empty small jar. "Your perfectly sculpted face has never had wrinkles or under eye bags. So yes, it is obvious."

She fills the empty jar with a little of both herbs, sealing it shut before turning around and handing it to me. "Valerian root and lemon balm are gentle sedatives, so they should help you get some better sleep."

I look at the jar, inspecting it.

"I know it's not the kind of fix you're looking for, but for now it could hopefully help a little."

I lift my gaze up to Nora, giving her a faint grin. "I really appreciate this. Thank you."

"You're welcome." She sets both jars of the herbs back into her cabinet before closing it again. She turns around, placing a gentle hand on my shoulder. "If you need to talk about it, I'm here to listen."

I give her a nod. "Thank you, Nora."

She gives me a grin before lowering her hand and walking out of the healers room, exiting the room after her.

As I go to head back down the way I came, I notice something from the corner of my eye. I turn around, looking through the kitchen entryway at a stuffed bear left on one of the wooden kitchen tables next to a half-eaten piece of banana bread. I walk into the kitchen, looking around to see no one in here at the moment. I look back at the bear again, a half grin curving my lips as I recognize who it belongs to.

I approach the table, picking up the stuffed bear and exit the kitchen. I walk down the hallway to bring it to Carina's room when her daughter Elise comes running out.

"Mama! I found her!" Elise says as she comes running up to me.

I kneel down as I hold the bear out for her, her little hands coming out to clasp the bear before hugging it close to her. "Where was she?!" She exclaims.

I chuckle. "She was in the kitchen." I lean in a little closer, looking over my shoulder before facing her again. "I caught her eating some of the banana bread." I whisper.

Elise's eyes go wide as she gasps. "Really?"

My grin grows at her visible astonishment, nodding. "I guess Ms. Snuggles thought she could sneak some while you weren't looking."

A laugh bursts out of Elise as she looks at her stuffed bear. At the sound of her mother approaching, she turns around. Holding the bear up towards her mother. "Mama, Reimus said Ms. Snuggles was eating the banana bread!"

Carina approaches us as she gives her daughter a surprised look. "Did she now?" She lifts her gaze to mine, giving me a knowing look.

Elise nods her head curtly before taking off down the hallway to their room. Carina's gaze trailing along after her daughter.

I stand back up onto my feet as Carina turns her gaze back around to me. "Thanks for that. Now she will ask for me to make a plate for Ms. Snuggles from now on." Putting her hand on her hip, giving me a knowing look even as an amusement lights up her tone.

I chuckle. "My apologies, Carina. How are things going?"

Her honey-hued gaze holds mine as she lowers her hand from her hip, straightening her stance as she nods. "Good."

I give her a faint grin. "I'm glad to hear it. I'll be heading to the market to pick up the things we need. Any special requests?"

She scrunches her lips together, pondering for a moment until she shakes her head. "Nothing at the moment."

"Sounds good."

I make my way down the hallway when Carina calls out for me. "Reimus."

I turn back around.

She takes a step forward as she says, "When can we expect Melinoë to return from—you know." She narrows her gaze a moment before retraining it back onto mine.

As I stand there and have no concrete timeframe to give her, I tell her the only response I can give her at this point in time. "Soon."

CHAPTER 48

After I've gone to the market and picked up everything, I headed back to The Sanctuary to drop everything off. Stocking everything in its respective place in the supply room before making my way back home to cater to the backyard.

I lift the black double-hung window panel and set it into the wooden frame, aligning it and pressing it into the grooves so the sealant around the flanges can adhere to the wood. I check the grids to make sure no scratches are apparent before slipping shims under the window to keep everything centered in place. I move around to the window's exterior, drilling screws through the window flanges before making sure the windows slide up and down easily. I continue doing this until I have seven gridded windows fitted into the structure's openings, leaving the eighth and final opening for the installation of a black aluminum, full glass storm door. Marking my project nearly complete now.

After everything is installed I stand back, admiring what I've accomplished in building for Melinoë. Because if I am unable to do anything else at this time to help her, at least I am able to help with this.

I cross my arms over my chest, a genuine grin crawling up my lips as I peer through the glass door at the empty space within. All it needs now is just some lights, and some final touches to make the space complete.

"It's beautiful."

I turn around to see Persephone standing behind me, her gaze roaming over the structure I've built for her daughter. She steps around it as she observes it.

"Thank you." I say, uncrossing my arms.

"I came by to place the remaining plants and foliage down out here when I saw you placing the door on it." She turns her gaze over to me, an honest smile lighting her face. "It's clear to see not only the effort you took into building it, but also the thought of everything that went into it." She lowers her gaze back to the door, approaching it as she goes to pull the door open.

I watch as she looks down at the door handle, noticing that I chose one without a lock on it. A feature I intentionally implemented. "I think all that is left now is planting maybe some more foliage along the pathway."

Persephone lifts her gaze up to the roof, tilting her head as a low humming noise gets trapped in her throat. "I think there's still some more that can be done."

I stumble backwards as suddenly a large basswood tree plants itself into the ground, the towering branches hanging over the roof of what I've built. My gaze jerks over to the few terracotta potters now set along the perimeter of the structure, each with foliage planted inside. I watch as Persephone begins willing more basswood trees and foliage around the property, intricately planting them and further adding to the little oasis that we've both managed to create here. And when I think she's finished, she wills a cherry blossom tree onto the landscape. Next to the red-bricked path.

"That's much better." She says, coming to stand next to me as I gaze out at the stark difference between mine and Melinoë's land now. Having before just been a plain open landscape, now turned into a charming garden.

I look at what so accurately represents what's internal. Having felt empty and bare before Melinoë came into my life, to now having all of those dull spaces within filled with an abundance of life and vitality. Her ability to touch people in such deep ways without even doing much at all. To elicit the kind of joy and healing that regenerates someone from the inside out. Both remarkable and awe-inspiring.

"Makaria is becoming stronger." Persephone pauses for a moment. "She's making much progress with being able to portal. So, I imagine that it won't be long now until we can move in."

I look at her as a wave of relief washes over me at her words. An anticipation trickling itself down my back at her words. "That's good news."

She nods her head as she folds her hands in front of her lap. A slight grin curving on her face as she looks out ahead at the garden before us. "It is." She says softly.

At the sound of Alastor whinnying I look over my shoulder towards the pastures. He shakes his head as his tail flicks behind him, Gizelle grazing next to him.

"He misses her." Persephone says softly, her gaze turned towards the pastures.

"Every day he stands right there by the fence and stares out at the palace." I watch as Gizelle lifts her head up, looking at me now. "Even when he's preoccupied with Gizelle he always waits for her. If I didn't pour every ounce of free time I had into this, I knew I would be doing the same thing. Just waiting for her to come home."

I turn my gaze back towards the palace, lowering it to the red-bricked pathway that now leads to it. "I was going to ask her to marry me."

I feel the soft brand of Persephone's gaze as she turns towards me.

A long sigh escapes me as I lift my gaze to the tiered fountain ahead, a small bird bathing in the fiore basin below. "The day that Zeus kidnapped her, I told her I had a surprise for her. Waiting for her when she returned home from venturing into the Sephyra Forest with Semele. I tried to maintain a level of confidence on the outside, but internally?" A harsh chuckle escapes me. "I had never been more nervous in my entire life. Yet I couldn't understand why at that time. Why would I be so nervous?" I shake my head slowly as I watch the bird dip the front of its body into the water, fluffing its feathers as it bathes itself. "My love for Melinoë has been the realest thing I've ever known and felt. But I think in that moment, whether it was the twin soul bond speaking or just my intuition, I was being told that something was wrong. That even though she said she'd be right back, that I should've listened to that little voice telling me to not let her go. But I knew forcing her not to go would've been entirely against who I am with her."

Persephone steps in front of me, redirecting my gaze onto her as she narrows her chin slightly. "Because you know that Melinoë does not need someone to tell her what to do. That allowing her to have full autonomy over herself and her life is exactly why you are perfect for my daughter. Twin souls or not."

Persephone reaches out for my hand, holding it inside of hers as she gives me a warm smile. "And that is why you will make an excellent husband to my daughter."

I feel a surge of emotion rush over me to hear that word from her lips, to hear Persephone giving me her blessing to ask her daughter to marry me. Something I always thought that I would've asked her father for, but considering the circumstances, he can kiss both of our asses.

Husband. Even though I haven't had the proper moment to ask Melinoë to marry me yet, just hearing that title in the same sentence as her name makes me entirely too giddy on the inside. "Thank you." I say.

Persephone lowers her hand from mine, a wide grin creeping back up onto her lips. She gives me a nod before she says, "I will return as soon as Makaria is ready." A portal opens up behind her as swirls of magenta and violet brew together in the background. Tendrils of midnight shadows coiling and swirling around the center.

I nod, grinning. "I'll be waiting."

Persephone steps through the portal back into The Underworld, swallowing her whole as it vanishes with her.

CHAPTER 49

Melinoë

Bethesda opens up my cell door and steps inside. "Your presence is requested."

I watch as she pulls the brass key out, knitting my brows together. "For what?"

She lowers herself down to unlock the chains connected to my shackles, glancing up at me. "Council."

My expression smooths over, worry gnawing at me at the reminder of what happened the last time I stood before Zeus in the council room. "What for? I already met with the council members."

Bethesda grabs my chains, gently guiding me out of my cell. "Not that kind of council, Melinoë. Council with the village people."

A calm rage begins to form deep within my gut, not having signed up for this. Not having signed up for *any* of this.

The warmth from the heat of the sunshine sneaking through the doorway beats down on me the higher we ascend the steps. We reach the top and sunlight drenches me, pouring into every dark crevice in my body and lighting it up from its mute slumber.

Bethesda closes the door behind us as she guides me through the throne room, my gaze peering up to the top of the dais as Zeus sits upon his throne. I watch his gaze quickly pierce mine, as if to coerce me to shrink back into myself at the force of his stare. But as we continue walking, I keep my gaze trained on him as my head remains held high. A rippling assurance circling inside of me as it climbs higher and higher to the surface.

We reach the top of the dais as Zeus gives me a lazy nod. "Melinoë."

I stare at him as I give him a disingenuous smile, lowering myself down into a curtsy. Without saying another word, I turn to walk towards the cage and step inside of it. As I would rather endure the wrath of a thousand blades then to play fake nice in front of his face and ever address him by any title that he surely doesn't deserve.

Suddenly unwilling to play nice at all anymore.

Bethesda locks the cage behind me before leaving the room entirely as I watch someone enter the throne room from the corner of my eye.

I look up to see Dionysus entering from behind the dais, coming up onto my side as he looks up at me. His usual impassive expression flashes a hint of doubt before forcing his gaze away. I watch as he climbs the dais and makes his way over to stand on the right of Zeus.

"What a surprise to have you actually show up this time." Zeus says as he looks straight ahead, waving his hand as the doors at the end of the room open up. People filed into the room shortly after.

Dionysus shrugs his shoulders as he folds his hands behind his back. "I'm full of surprises."

Zeus scoffs at him as I watch a golden portal open up on his left. Apollo steps through it, closing the portal behind him. "Sorry I'm late."

"We have just begun, Apollo." Zeus says as I watch the sunlight glint off of his golden crown. Wanting to take the pointed edges of it and ram it into his neck.

I try breathing in deeply and exhaling slowly, trying to quell the anger that's ramping up inside of me but unseemly able to contain it as it pushes against every layer of my skin.

"Why is she in there?" Dionysus asks, catching a glance at me again as I peer over at him.

I lower my gaze to Zeus, watching him as he stares out at the people filing into the throne room. And for a split moment, I watch the slight upturn of the left side of his lips as he says, "To send a message."

I look away as that smoldering fire that's been teetering on burning out for weeks now amplifies briskly, scorching me from the inside out as I clench my jaw. I go to flex my fists inward when I quickly refrain from doing so.

I feel the gaze of Dionysus on my cheek before it finally lifts, assumingly to turn to face the small crowd of people gathered before the dais.

"Council is now in session." Zeus declares as he leans back into his seat. Looking as bored as he did the last time I stood up here next to him.

Nobody in the crowd moves or talks for several minutes until a familiar man emerges from within. He walks up to the dais and lowers himself into a deep bow. Those scarce grey strands peeking through his dark brown hair. "Your Majesty."

I notice the bags under Thomas' eyes have begun to worsen, signs of excessive time spent outdoors shown through the redness burnt onto his shoulders and cheeks.

"Thomas." Zeus says, giving him a nod. "What can I do for you today?"

I nearly shout at him in fury at his disingenuous response. Yet somehow, I remain level-headed.

"I would like to bring a concern to your attention, Your Majesty. I understand—per your instructions from the last council, that it was up to us to find alternative ways to water our crops. But even in the extra hours that I—as well as other farmers have spent outside, I fear that our efforts are not enough." Thomas brings a hand up to his chest, almost as if to suppress what he wants to say but forcing him to say it nonetheless. "Your Majesty, I hope that you might reconsider your previous conclusion and please allow for a few rainstorms to bless our lands. It is in my professional opinion that if our crops do not receive relief from this drought soon, then families will be severely limited with food in the near future."

I peer my gaze up from Thomas to Zeus, watching him intently as he stares upon the mortal man for a long moment. Almost wondering if he'll actually lower himself down from his immoderately filled ego. Instead, he shows myself and everyone the kind of man he actually is once again. "Is anyone else here experiencing this same dilemma?"

I look out at the crowd of people, begging in my mind for just one of them to speak out. To say something and not let this one courageous man stand up here alone, fighting for the rights and living conditions that they all live with. But as an agonizing long minute passes, I watch as some people turn to look at each other, some mumbling quiet words to one another, but nobody else comes forward.

No one else speaks out.

Zeus gives Thomas a look. "If there are no others addressing concerns for more water, then I'm afraid as I have said before, that others are managing fine with the resources they have. It may just be time for you to sharpen your farming skills, and perhaps take notes from others and how they're still finding success with their crops."

I watch as Thomas goes to open his mouth to say more, to potentially stand up against Zeus and demand for better. But as he looks around him, noticing no one looking at him and either looking at Zeus or the ground, he slowly closes his mouth and gives Zeus a defeated nod. "Of course, Your Majesty. I shall find other means." He says softly before lowering his gaze to the ground, stepping back from the foot of the dais.

I watch as this energetic blanket of despair weighs over him, his shoulders ever so slightly slumping forward as he keeps his gaze lowered. Someone who is willing to stand against the harsh dominion of an unfair king, to have the bravery and courage to speak out to only then be cast down after being repeatedly denied fair morality. I watch as he goes to turn on his heels, his posture slowly transforming from that of a confident individual, to a defeated one as he goes to merge himself back into the crowd. Retreating back into the recesses of remaining quiet and mute not out of choice, but for survival.

And in that moment, something ruptures within me as I witness a part of myself reflected back to me through Thomas. A part of myself that I have intentionally kept mute while I've been imprisoned here out of survival for myself, and for those I love. But as I stand here now, I realize that I have only perpetuated this harmful cycle that continues to repeat itself over and over again, aimed to keep the oppressed exactly that.

Until one individual is bold enough to stand up and speak out.

"For fucks sake." I shout.

Thomas' back goes rim-rod straight, turning around rigidly to peer up at me with both horror and shock in his gaze.

I look over at Zeus who has his gaze hardened onto me, threatening a cold chill to caress itself down my back. But I stand there and take it without a lick of fear.

I've fucking had it with staying silent.

"All your people fucking want is a little rain and you are so bent up in the throes of your ego trip that you won't even give them *that*?" A harsh laugh breaks out of me as that anger that's been welling inside of me for weeks now breaks through the barrier I've placed around it. Causing my body to shake with rage. "You have the ability to change the weather and help your people water their crops so they can eat, a *basic* human *right* and you want to keep that away from them? Gods, you are the most insufferable piece of shit I've ever had the displeasure of knowing."

Numerous audible gasps surface around the room, some of the people slapping their hands to their mouths as they whisper to themselves. Thomas just stands there wide-eyed, staring wholly at me.

I clench my fists as I try to will my power to the surface, to see if it would be strong enough to break the shackles. To move the overwhelming amount of rage coursing through my body in any way I can right now as I glare up at Zeus.

He stares at me as I watch the split moment when disdain plagues his gaze. Finally putting the pieces together, including his failed attempt to erase my memories.

I tilt my head to the side as a wicked grin appears on my face. I speak in an utterly calm voice as I say, "Surprised, are we?" A wicked laugh escapes me as I flick my gaze up to Dionysus. His eyes bulge slightly from their sockets as he stares silently at me. Blinking once before I lower my gaze back down to Zeus. "It was only a matter of time before someone outdid you with your own little *tricks*." I give him a wink as I turn around to look at the people staring at me.
"Your King does not give a fuck about you. And you all know this but are too afraid to say or do anything about it. So allow me to be the one to set the example—"

"Enough!" Zeus' voice bellows out as everyone lowers their gazes from me. He stands up as I feel the energy pulsate around the room, saying clearly with the help of his compulsion, "Council is dismissed. Forget everything that you all saw here today."

I watch as one by one, everyone's face smooths out into neutrality before they all begin filing out of the room.

I race to the front of the cage, gripping the iron bars. "No! Fight back! Damnit, fight back!" I scream after them as the cage door opens up.

"Yell all you'd like, daughter. They won't remember a thing." Zeus says as he advances onto the cage door, lifting his hand as he forces me to approach him with his power.

I try to thrash against his power but still end up in his grasp, with his hand around my throat.

He tilts his head down at me, assessing me for a moment before saying, "How?"

I thrash against him, glaring up at him as I spit at his face. "Go fuck yourself, *King* Zeus." I seethe with a well of anger that could surmount the most devastating destruction.

He stares down at me as he chuckles, his magic wiping away the wad of spit on his cheek before dragging me out of the cage by my neck. My throat constricted by the force of his strength. "Apollo." He says curtly.

I glance up at Apollo before Zeus drags me out of view from him. "Yes?"

"You know what to do. Give me a couple hours to deal with this first."

"Right away." Apollo says before I feel the energy of his portal appearing, quickly vanishing as Dionysus races down the dais after us.

"What are you going to do, father?" He asks, my face trying to look up at him but Zeus pushes my gaze back down to the ground.

"I think it would be informative for you to come with to find out."

Zeus and I land on the bottom before turning the corner and dragging me behind the dais. I manage to look up and see the door to the council room before it opens up to the empty room inside. Zeus shoves me onto the ground as the door slams behind us.

"I must say I am impressed to learn you were able to resist my compulsion." He looms over me as sparks of blinding orange light zap around him. His golden eyes swirling with eather as he stares down at me.

I hike back up onto my feet and go to charge towards him when a tether of his eather shoots out, latching onto the cuffs at my wrists and pulling them upwards. Restraining them above my head as I try to pull myself free.

"It's too bad your sister did not have the same advantage. How do you think she's doing now, by the way?"

I jerk my head towards Zeus as he begins to circle his way behind me. "You'll never find out." I seethe through my teeth as the zap of power feels like it's pinching my wrists. I flinch from it as I look up at Dionysus, a wicked grin curving my lips. "But it's good to see you're keeping the same tradition with your son."

Dionysus' eyebrows knit together as he shoots his gaze to Zeus. "What is she talking about?" He questions skeptically.

I laugh as I feel Zeus' power grab hold onto my feet, forcing me down onto my knees. I look up at Dionysus, shaking my head. "Don't you want to know why you feel so different? The real origins of your—"

"Silence." Zeus seethes as my back bows as a slash of fiery hot pain lashes at my skin. I scream out in pain as I try to move my arms down but his magical restraints keep them up.

I turn my head around to look back at Zeus, glaring up at him as I snarl, "No."

I feel my shadows begging to burst free from their captivity, to unleash themselves onto Zeus and show him that he has only seen the version I've wanted him to see.

But now, I'm no longer hiding.

I will not be silent any longer. And if that means I have to endure his wrath in order to be the muse for change, then so be it.

Dionysus' eyes widened, stepping towards me. "Who told you about that? How do you—"

Another slash of lightning hits my back, my jaw tightening stiffly to block out the pain when I realize—

He's *whipping* me. With lightning.

My back bows deeper as the sting of pain reverberates through my body, the burning hot blast of his lightning leaving a lingering effect as it trickles over my back.

"He's using you—" I manage to force out, taking another slash to the back. When I feel a cool kiss of air along my back, I realize that he's broken through my tunic, revealing my bare back.

Dionysus' wild gaze roams from me to his father, the perplexity of what to do overwhelming him until he says to Zeus, "Stop. This is not necessary, father. She already lives in the dungeon, isn't that punishment enough?"

"Your mother—" My words cut off from the agonizing pain of Zeus whipping me again. Screaming against the pain as I begin to pant, still unwilling to remain silent even in the face of the torture he's inflicting. Even as I begin to feel a trickle of blood run down my break from Zeus breaking the skin. "Is not Hera—"

"I said silence!" Zeus roars.

"*No!*" I scream back, feeling my power rushing to the surface but inhibited from the chains around my wrists and ankles. "I will die before I ever give you the satisfaction of remaining silent again." My chest rises and sinks deeply as I breathe through the pain.

Dionysus lowers his shocked gaze down to me, opening to speak another word when Zeus cuts him off.

"Speak another word of this, and you will face her same fate. Do you understand?" He bellows angrily at his son.

I watch as Dionysus shifts his gaze from me to Zeus repeatedly, the look of uncertainty clear in his face. All of the questions he has bubbling to the surface, the boy inside of him begging to know the truth to what has plagued him for years. But after a moment, I watch as all of that vanishes as he smooths his expression out. "Understood."

"Good." Zeus lashes another whipping at me, crying out in pain.

I hear Zeus tsking at me from behind, a moment of silence stretching between us before I feel the restraints pull me up from my knees, forcing me to my feet. "At the clear display of your treason, I wondered what I might do with you. As leaving you in the dungeons is no appropriate form of punishment."

He whips me again.

"But that was until you brought a rather productive idea to mind."

And again.

"One that I think will fit right into my plan all along." Zeus says, chuckling before lashing a whipping at me once again.

My back bows deeply as I cry out in pain. My mind instantly tried to pull myself back into the recesses of my memories, wanting to hide me—numb myself from feeling the pain. To protect me from this cruelty. But even in the face of his excruciating torture, I don't allow myself to hide. I take every lashing, every brute force of agony, as I would rather feel everything than to subject myself to another moment of numbness again.

Because when I have my moment of revenge, I want to remember this moment for what it was.

The start of my beginning, and his end.

"Dionysus, go make yourself useful for a couple hours until I call you back here."

I feel the chains between my wrists lengthen as he forces my arms to widen above me. Widening them until they're both hanging at my sides above my head, the golden thread of his power latching onto my wrists tightly and keeping me locked in place. I feel coils of his power wrapping themselves around my ankles, completely locking me in place.

"Melinoë will stay here for the time being."

I look at Dionysus as he catches a quick glance. A beat of hesitation keeps him cemented in place before nodding his head, forcing himself to exit the council room.

And as I am left alone here with Zeus, I do not give him the satisfaction of seeing me shed any more tears.

CHAPTER 50

Reimus

After hours of working on some of the final touches to the yard, and spending some time with Alastor, Gizelle and Arion, I come inside to finally shower.

I walk down the hallway and before I can ascend up the stairs, I feel an energy surge behind me. As I turn around, I see both Hades and Persephone standing before me.

As I look upon Persephone's steady gaze, I see the flicker of worry residing there. "What's wrong?"

Persephone steps forward, her shoulders tense. "Hades and I have been called to council."

I tilt my head slightly, furrowing my brows as everything inside of me goes silent. "Why would Zeus call you both to council if he has Melinoë in his possession, knowing you two would try to extract her?" I step towards them. "What is the reason for—"

"We do not know." Hades answers calmly, noticing the lick of concern flaring in his expression. Something that I rarely see from The God of The Underworld. "But something did happen yesterday."

I step towards them, a calm storm beginning to swirl within me. "Tell me."

"A soul named Thomas passed through to The Underworld yesterday, and when we looked at his soul, to judge him," Hades says, pausing. "We saw how he died."

I shake my head. "I don't understand—"

"It was Melinoë, Reimus."

I turn my gaze to Persephone.

She loosens a breath. "Thomas was killed by Melinoë." She says quietly.

Suddenly I feel like the floor has been swiped out from beneath me. Denial immediately rushed over me. "Why? How could she have killed him if—"

"The man was brought to Zeus' palace by Zeus, and was used as bait for Melinoë to show what her divinity entailed to Zeus' council. She—" Hades hesitates before he continues again, "She resisted ending his life but...Zeus was never going to allow him to live a normal life. I saw what his compulsion entailed. He would've kept him prisoner along with Melinoë had she resisted."

I take a step back and narrow my gaze to the ground. He'd forced Melinoë to kill someone? She must know that it's not her fault. She has to know that.

Gods, I hope she does.

I lift my gaze back up. "But why would he call you both there? Won't he fear that you'll—" I shake my head as ruminating thoughts of what it could be begin to plague me.

Is calling them both there a trap? Does he know that Melinoë isn't affected by his compulsion? What is the reasoning—

"Reimus," Persphone says, resting a hand on my shoulder.

I lift my gaze up to hers, trying to take a deep breath in but feeling it go nowhere.

"We will return as soon as we're able to, with the answer that you and I both are searching for." She assures me.

I feel the talisman send me a burst of energy, bringing my hand up to it to try and stifle the potency of the vibration.

I watch as Persephone's gaze lowers to it, slowly trailing it back up. "Promise me you will wait for us to return."

I fixed my gaze on her, knowing exactly why she felt the need to say that. At what she's insinuating. I nod my head as I lower my hand. "I'll be here."

She lowers her hand as she steps back, a portal willing behind both of them as she gives a faint nod. I watch as Hades reaches out for her hand before the portal swallows them whole, vanishing entirely.

I quickly step away as I rush to the one room in the palace I do not use. I rush into the center of the room, the torches on the wall lighting up upon my arrival.

I lift the talisman from beneath my shirt, holding it up in front of me as it begins to glow beneath my palm. "I need you to do something for me."

It blinks at me as if to state its understanding of my plea.

I lay myself down onto the ground, my back flat against the hardwood floor as I take a deep breath in and out. Centering into myself.

I know why Persephone asked me to stay here, as we don't know the strength of what the talisman is capable of when cloaking Melinoë or myself behind it. But that's a risk I'm willing to take right now as something in my gut feels horribly wrong.

And technically, I'm not leaving. My spiritual body is.

"Keep me protected and cloaked in invisibility. Take me to Melinoë." I close my eyes as I try to wash out the worry of why Zeus is calling council, and needing to see it for myself.

So I steady my breathing over and over again until finally, I fall asleep.

I wake up, standing above my physical body laying on the ground as I look around the room. The flames of the torches bright but dimmed with a graying hue.

I look down at the talisman necklace, whispering to it as it glows brightly. "Take me to Melinoë."

After a few moments, I watch as a portal opens up a few feet beside me. I look through it, seeing swatches of bright gold and white illuminated through it. I approach it, assessing the midnight swirls around it. Entirely similar to the ones I've seen Melinoë wield around her portals before. I take one last breath before I step through it, coming out the other side and stepping out onto a polished floor.

I look up to see golden chairs at the far wall, men and women seated in them—

Immortals, I realize.

My vision catches a glimmer of blinding white and orange light, coaxing me to lower my gaze to who stands in the middle of the room when all the anger inside of me threatens to flood to the surface.

I instantly go to rush to her side when the talisman gently burns my skin, wincing at the sting of it. I look down at my chest, watching as it glows brightly. When I go to try and take another step forward, it vibrates against me.

Taking that as my sign to stay put, I force myself to cement my stance into the ground as my gaze roams over the golden eather keeping Melinoë's wrists restrained above her head. The front of her body facing towards me as her back faces the immortals and Zeus at the center seat.

Before I can stare long at him I feel energy pulsate beside me, watching as a portal opens up and The Queen and King of The Underworld step through it.

I watch as Persephone looks to her daughter immediately, a churning rage brewing beneath her as Hades peers up at Zeus. "Zeus, what is—"

"Thank you all for coming today." Zeus says, interrupting Hades. "It appears I have made a regretful mistake in forming an allegiance with Melinoë. As she has proven to be a traitor all along."

My eyes widen as my gaze shoots to Melinoë, pain lancing her face as she lifts her gaze up to Persephone. Giving her mother a wink.

I watch Persephone's expression as it remains unchanged, the fury that lies beneath it remaining intact as she steps forward. "Release her, Zeus." She says far too calmly. A warning for the dangerous wrath that brews beneath the surface.

He chuckles as he tightens the restraints on her wrists. "You should be grateful, Persephone. I brought you here so you could have one last look at your daughter before I kill her."

My entire body numbs itself with ice cold rage.

Persephone shakes her head. "You wouldn't." She insists.

"Oh, but I should. Considering she so publicly disgraced me in front of my people." Zeus begins as he steps down from his seat. "I feel it's the only correct punishment for her rebellion. What do you think, Melinoë?"

I watch as a bright orange whip appears, lashing out at Melinoë's back as I scream out for her.

Her back bows harshly as she takes it, enduring the torture as she lifts her gaze to her mother. "I'm fine. I can take it—" Her words end in a harsh cry as Zeus whips her again. My entire body quaking with anger as I have no choice but to stand there and watch.

Persephone's gaze roams wildly over Melinoë, her chest sinking harshly as she advances on her daughter but is blocked by an invisible wall willed by Zeus' magic.

She whips her gaze up to Zeus. "Stop—I'll give you whatever you want. Just stop!" She lowers her gaze frantically to Melinoë. And as understanding blankets her gaze, I realize in that moment what she's about to say before she even says it. "I'll give you Makaria in exchange for her to stay alive."

Zeus' attention flickers to Persphone, keeping his whip at the ready as he waits. "Go on." He drawls.

Persephone lifts her gaze up to him, working on a swallow as she pauses. "My bargain is I bring you Makaria, in exchange for Melinoë to remain living. *Safe*."

Zeus cocks his head slightly. "You would bring your only other child to me, to save her life? While you live with none of your children in your vicinity?"

I watch as Peresphone lifts a gaze up to Hera, then to Dionysus. Pausing for a moment as she takes in who truly sits in that seat, in that body. I watch her keep herself together as she raises her gaze back to Zeus, curtly nodding. "I would do anything to keep my children safe."

Zeus pauses for a long moment, contemplating while everyone in the room remains silent. It isn't until a few moments later that the whip vanishes and he says, "Meet me back here in two hours. So I know that you won't try any escape plans."

Persephone nods. "I'm surprised you didn't offer for us to meet in Lothario."

Zeus watches her.

Persephone shrugs her shoulders. "That way if I truly have something up my sleeve, Melinoë will be far away and as we will all be within your vicinity then—well, there's no chance of us trying to free Melinoë."

He gives her a slow nod. "Then we meet in Lothario. Bring those fire breathers so I know exactly where they are. I know he'll come, so I expect to have him right where I can see him. Otherwise you can forget our bargain."

Persephone nods her head. "Understood. I will go retrieve Makaria." She lowers her gaze to Melinoë, glancing at her once before turning around.

I watch as Melinoë lifts her gaze to Hades, shaking her head violently. "No—leave Makaria out of this!" She yells, trying to thrash herself out of the restraints. "Don't do this—"

"It's already been done." Zeus says as he looks to all the other gods and goddesses. "You're all dismissed."

I watch as they begin to disappear as my gaze lowers to Hades, feeling a sudden pull of energy reaching towards me. I begin to back up when I feel it slither into my mind.

We told you to stay where you were. Hades says into my mind.

I watch as him and Persephone open up a portal behind them, giving Melinoë one last look before they both vanish.

When I go to try and advance towards Melinoë again I feel the talisman jerk me backwards into my own portal, invisible from anyone else seeing. It pulls me backwards as I fall back and land on the wooden floor of my palace, next to my physical body.

A moment later I'm forced to merge with myself once again.

CHAPTER 51

My palms push against the hardwood floor as I jerk upright into a seated position, looking down at the talisman hanging from my neck.

No longer casting a vibrant glow as it idly rests against my skin.

"Do I even want to know why you're laying on the ground in the dark?"

I lift my gaze up to Dimitri as he leans against the doorway. The slightly knit brows begin to straighten out as I hike up onto my feet, walking towards him. "Actually, yes. You do."

He steps away from the doorway as he follows me out of the room. "What's going on?"

I stride quickly down the hallway as I send a message down the Guardian's channel to Charon. *I need you to maintain surveillance of the outer perimeter for the next few hours.*

As Dimitri hears the command down the Guardian's channel he looks at me, concern flashing in his gaze. "Rei." He challenges.

I continue making my way to the living room, knowing that at any moment Hades and Persephone will be returning. "We're moving in. In less than two hours."

Dimitri walks beside me as we make it to the living room, the concern once on his face now gone as determination begins to settle in.

"I went into the astral realm to see if I could see what was going on in Zeus' palace, to see why he just called council. He knows that she hasn't been under his compulsion this whole time, and he's threatened to kill her." I clench my fists together. "But that's when Persephone offered Makaria in exchange for saving her life."

Before Dimtiri can even open his mouth I watch as a portal opens up, Hades stepping out of it as his gaze falls on me immediately. "A careless fucking move. You're damned lucky that Zeus didn't pick up on your energy." The portal vanishes behind him.

"I know what I did was risky, but I needed to know. I needed—"

"What you *needed* to do was wait until we returned, like we had *told* you." Hades seethes, stepping forward as he approaches me. "Zeus may not be able to see the deceased, or those in the astral realm, but he can still very well feel when an energy is present." He briefly glances at the talisman. "It may have saved your ass this time but don't let that convince you you're suddenly invincible."

I meet his stern gaze. "I get it, but no amount of whatever you say now would've deterred me from still trying in the first place." My voice steady and carrying an edge to it.

Hades lets out an exhale, shaking his head. "Look—none of this matters right now anyway," He begins, taking a brief moment of pause. "Zeus might've caught us at a moment when we weren't exactly ready to move in, but it ended up being what we needed and Persephone used it to our advantage."

"Where is she now?" I ask.

"She went to retrieve Hecate. She should be here any moment now."

"What do you mean Persephone used it to her advantage?" Dimitri asks, chiming in so he can understand what just happened.

Hades lifts his gaze to Dimitri. "We've been in a state of waiting for Makaria to learn to tap into her gifts, to at the very least learn how to portal. But the plan had always been mostly the same: use Makaria as a way to lure Zeus out, so that Hecate and Dimitri can move through the Casalas Mountains to retrieve Melinoë from the palace while the rest of us preoccupy Zeus. Even with presenting Zeus something that he can't refuse to turn away from, Persephone and I discussed how intricately the ruse would have to be to lure him out as he wouldn't believe that Makaria just came of her own willing accord to see him. Especially not after getting her memories back and being lifted from his compulsion, therefore knowing what he did to her."

My gaze lifts to the space beside Hades, a portal willing there before Persephone and Hecate both step through it.

"So when Persephone and I arrived at council, and saw Melinoë, we both knew that he was aware of her façade. And we both knew this was the best opportunity for us to extract our plan."

The portal closes behind them as Persephone steps forward. "I had to make him believe that I was desperate to do anything to save Melinoë. If there is anything that fools a man like Zeus easiest, it's a show of weakness. I had to be convincing that I knew he would not save Melinoë unless I gave him the one thing he wanted. But in a twisted turn of fate, that talisman," She nods to the crystal hanging from my neck. "Aided us in retrieving the knowledge of the prophecy from Melinoë, which Zeus is still unaware of at this moment. So I knew if the prophecy were true, that he wouldn't actually kill her. But I couldn't allow him to know that."

I look down at the talisman, wondering how we were fortunate enough to still find it in the Sephyra Forest instead of being destroyed. How one night's intuitive feeling guided me to put it on, to then realize it was not only connected to Melinoë but myself as well. Where it aided as a tool for me to still see Melinoë and learn everything we know now.

"But what about Makaria? Is she ready for all of this?" I ask, lifting my gaze up to Persephone.

She looks at me for a beat of silence before she says, "I'm afraid she has no choice but to be ready."

"But if you two are going to be there, then why can't you just portal her out of there when we've retrieved Melinoë?" Dimitri asks beside me.

Hades looks at me. "Because if something goes wrong, we need her to be able to leave on her own."

I give Hades a knowing look. "As in if Zeus gets wind of our plan and retaliates, you two won't leave."

Hades nods slowly, glancing over at his wife. "This fight has been a long time coming." They both share a silent exchange with one another before they both turn to face me and Dimitri again. "We both have no intention of backing down this time. Especially if his retaliation involves endangering the people of Lothario."

"They may not be *our* people, but they are innocent bystanders nonetheless. Hades and I will still ensure their safety should a feud arise." Persephone says as she glances a look at me. "And also because when the time comes and he learns that this was all a plan to extract Melinoë, he will immediately try to kill you Reimus."

My gaze roams over Persephone.

"This is where we come in." She says, looking at Hades standing beside her. "We won't let him get the chance to hurt you."

The sudden realization that this is finally happening overwhelms me both with a rush of high adrenaline and determination. Seeing Melinoë restrained at her wrists like that, bound above her head as he *whipped* her—

I feel the heat inside of my body ramp up until I feel a bead of sweat on my brow. Moving my hand up to wipe it away when I flinch away, the heat branding from my palm nearly burns me.

"Are you alright?" Hecate asks, coming to stand in front of me.

"Yes—fine." I say frustratedly, not sure why that keeps happening but having no desire to analyze it at the moment. The only thing that's on my mind now is freeing the love of my life, and bringing her home.

And I won't be returning home until she's safe with me.

I shake my head as I try to simmer the rage building within as the vision of her back bowing surfaces in my mind. Instead of shoving it down this time, I use it to fuel me. Enliven the rage I've felt since Zeus took what belongs to me. "Dimitri, as soon as you and Hecate have Melinoë in your grasp let me know."

Dimtri nods his head as he looks over at me, watching his gaze glance down to my hands briefly before trailing back up. "We won't leave until Melinoë is with us."

I give him a look back, nodding my head before fixing my gaze back onto Hades. His gaze held steadily but finding him glancing down at my hands nonetheless. "Once I get word from him down the Guardian's channel I'll give you a nod. Letting you know we're ready and then Makaria can portal out of there while I go and meet them in the Casalas Mountains."

Hades gives me a nod. "Chances are Melinoë may be too weak to portal herself. If that's the case—"

"I'll fly us back home." I stare sternly at Hades. "Whatever it takes."

Hecate looks over at Dimitri. "I'll portal us back."

He looks over at her, nodding before training his gaze onto Persephone. "But if Zeus is expecting both me and Reimus to be in Lothario with Hades and Persephone, then how am I able to help you extract Melinoë?"

Hecate looks at Dimitri as a slow grin curves up onto her lips. A look of her own secret plan brewing beneath. "That is where *my own* little trick comes in."

As Hecate tells us about what she's been working on, and what the addition to our extraction plan is, I feel everything else in my life around me go utterly quiet as my focus hones in on freeing Melinoë. My every sense is on high alert as I'm gripped with the awareness of what I've hoped and longed for finally becoming reality.

As Persephone leaves to return to The Underworld, both to retrieve Makaria and tell her of what's going on, I wait impatiently as that lingering heat in my body idly sleeps at my fingertips. A fire that is unwilling to simmer itself and retreat back to wherever it comes from within me.

CHAPTER 52

Melinoë

"Put her back in her cell. Stay down there with her until I've returned."

The restraints around my wrists vanish as I fall to the ground, nearly face-first before I block the blow to my face with my arm. The vibrating aftershock of the pain in my back lingers as I push myself up onto my hands and knees, grimacing at the pain as my arms tremble violently. I manage to get myself back onto my feet as I look at Dionysus. His gaze honed in on me before fixing it on Zeus. "Why do you need me to stay with her?"

Zeus glares at Dionysus, ire glimmering in his gaze. I realize not ire for his son, but for the change of events that have threatened his hold on control. At his lack of being able to compel me.

I realize this is my opportunity to get myself out of here, so if Dionysus is going to be the one to look after me, then I'm going to need to do it in a pretty harsh way.

As Hades stood in front of me with my mother, I felt the gentle brush of him sneaking into my mind. Slipping itself beneath my mental barriers to tell me just a few words before they vanished behind their portal.

We're coming for you. Be ready.

I knew that my mother would never give Makaria up like that unless there was a hidden reason why. I knew when she didn't retaliate right then and there in the council room, that there was something already being brewed amongst them. And when Hades gave me that confirmation, it took everything in me not to sag into myself with the relief that surmounted my body.

It took everything in me to still play my part, to yell at my mother to not get Makaria involved. Because I knew that if I'm actually going to get out of here, I need to put on the best show to succeed.

"Do as I say." Zeus says before turning away from us entirely, walking with Apollo out of the council room until it's just us two.

Dionysus looks at me, his gaze lifting to my back before grabbing the chains and guiding me out of the council room. He says nothing for a long moment, our feet shuffling across the throne floor as guards begin to pool into the room. Stationing themselves in a single file line at each entrance, including in front of the dungeon doors.

I huff out a lazy chuckle. "Jeez, such excessive amounts of protection for someone who's shackled to these." I lift my hands up.

Dionysus lowers his gaze to them, looking ahead again. "I assume they just want to be prepared. But while I'm around, you won't get away with anything." He declares.

The door to the dungeons comes closer into view as the soldiers standing in front of it move out of the way for us. Each of them clad in golden full-body armor, their hands laid against the pommel of their swords strapped to their sides.

I look up at Dionysus. "Because if you keep doing what Zeus asks then he'll finally tell you about your past, right?"

Dionysus says nothing as we approach the door, opening it up as he guides me in front of him as we descend down the steps.

"We both know that he's never going to tell you the truth."

"Quiet." He seethes as he pushes me forward, forcing me to move faster down the steps.

I chuckle as I reach the bottom, Dionysus coming to my side as he guides me to my cell. "You're seriously willing to be his bitch just to get nothing in return—"

"My father—*our* father, has done a lot for me." His chest puffed out as he steps in front of me, his gaze hardened onto mine. "I'm sorry that you two had a rough relationship, but don't project that failed relationship onto me." His chest sinks as he finally exhales, turning around with his hand on my chains as he pulls me forward.

"What exactly has he done for you other than make you his bitch and feed you with empty promises?" I challenge as he shoves me inside of the cell.

I stumble inside before turning around, Dionysus shutting the door and locking it as he stands there glaring at me. "I do things for him because I respect him. Not because I'm his bitch." Anger rising in his words.

Good. I'm getting a reaction out of him. This is what I need. Actually, what he needs as well if he's going to be able to lift the rose-colored glasses off and see the reality of his situation.

"Respect is earned for a man who deserves it. Zeus won't even give your people fucking *rain* to water their crops just because he doesn't deem it as a big enough issue. Because you people have food in this place that could last you months, while your people are on the brink of experiencing a shortage of food because your *King* is a selfish, ego-centered prick."

"Shut up!" He bellows as his hands go to grab the iron bars, his fingers gripping into them. I watch as he clenches his jaw briefly before relaxing the muscles there again.

I shake my head as I study him, watch how the wheels in his head begin to turn violently. Watch the confusion and shame center around him as the truth of these thoughts are ones he's thought of before.

And as the anger begins to subside to some degree, I witness as empathy begins to cloud my judgement for just a moment as I look upon the conflicting expressions on Dionysus' face. As confusion clashes with denial, as anger clashes with the years of unacceptance that have taken over his identity and purpose.

I step towards the cell door, saying in a voice a notch lower, "Hera is not your real mother, and I think deep down you know it."

Dionysus keeps his gaze on the ground, shaking his head. "I don't know what you're talking about."

I tilt my head, that damn empathy in me building as I look at the anguish on his face. Remembering what it felt like to be deceived, to not know the truth of my past and how much it discombobulated my thinking and what everything even amounted to. I look at the face of someone who has had to build defensive walls up not because they wanted to, but because they felt there was no other way to protect themselves.

And whether it's because of the look on his face, or because he's my brother, in that moment it makes me rethink my whole strategy.

I keep my gaze on him as I step forward. "I can tell you the truth. Of everything Zeus has kept from you."

He finally lifts his gaze, watching the flames from the torch above highlight the different colors in his eyes. Never having really paid attention to them until now.

As my gaze hones in on the colors blended together there, I realize not only are his multi-colored eyes a rich shade of emerald green, but of sapphire as well.

The same color irises as my mother, and Semele.

A low humming noise briefly gets trapped in my throat as I look at my brother. "Your eyes are two different colors."

He huffs at me. "Yeah. They're blue and green. Your point?"

A faint grin curves my lips. "Not just blue, but sapphire."

He watches me for a long moment, not understanding yet.

"Who else in this palace has sapphire colored eyes?"

He knits his brows together, pondering over the different individuals who live here until realization hits him like a train. His eyes widen as he steps back from the cell, lowering himself to the ground as his gaze lowers to his hands on his knees. "It can't be." He says breathlessly.

I walk up to the cage, lowering myself down to my knees as I try to guide his gaze back up to me. "Your real mother, Dionysus, is Semele."

His gaze remains trained on the ground.

"You knew that Semele had an affair with Zeus. You told me you were aware of this." I say gently.

He remains silent as I watch him internally trying to put all of the pieces together.

"You've had to live this whole life thinking that your mother hated you, but Hera doesn't look at you that way because you're her son. She looks at you that way because—" I pause, wondering if saying it is too harsh or not.

"Go on."

I bring my gaze back to Dionysus, realizing he finally lifted his to mine. "Say it." He says.

I work on a swallow as I continue. "Because you're a constant reminder of Zeus' infidelity."

He blinks at me before he huffs out a broken laugh. "So it's true then." He shakes his head as he looks away. "I'm…the Twice Born."

I lean my head forward, tilting it. "You know about that?"

He slowly nods his head. "It's a tale no one speaks about, saying that it would grant those who speak of it bad luck. But I heard a few people at a tavern whispering about it one day. The story about how a mistress loved a man so much she bore a child for him. Except it wasn't just any child, it was to reincarnate the same soul again. In a new body."

All I can do at the moment is just blink and remain silent as he speaks.

"I asked Zeus about the story, he said it was a made up fairytale for the village people to believe in. But after that day, something always made me want to come back to it. Like I felt drawn to understanding it deeper. And the more that I tried to shove it all down, the louder it beckoned me to pay attention to it."

I lower my hands over my knees. "Do you know who your first mother was then?"

He looks up at me, shaking his head.

I sigh. "Your first mother was Persephone, Queen of The Underworld." A beat of silence passes between us. "My mother."

He looks at me for a long moment. "So...we're related then?"

I nod my head. "In a twisted sort of way, yes. I believe we are."

He exhales heavily as he shakes his head. "You know, hearing you say that. I feel like my reaction should've been this huge blow out of denial and trying to prove you wrong. But as you say that now, something familiar comes over me." His gaze bores into mine. "I felt it when I watched him whip you."

I look away, still feeling the effects of his brutality on my back. Not even wanting to know how it looks right now.

"I was standing there wondering 'What makes this okay?' and 'I should do something to help her.' I felt this odd sort of spark of protectiveness over you, and for the first time I felt true anger towards Zeus. I shoved it down thinking that I couldn't possibly go against my father like that, but when I saw your skin splitting open? It made me think if he's willing to do this to his own daughter, then how am I any different?"

I tilt my head, lifting my gaze back up to him. "I wish that I could tell you that you are different. That he won't treat you the same as he did me and Makaria, but I think deep down you realize the abuse he's enacted upon you. But it terrifies you to admit to it so you allow yourself to remain blind to it."

He stares at me for a moment. "Who is Makaria? I heard that name in the council room when your mother spoke of her."

"She's my sister. Well, technically our sister I guess." I corrected.

"And she knows you are here?"

I nod my head.

"But they're going to offer her up to Zeus in exchange for keeping you alive?"

I nod again.

He sighs as he runs his hand through his light brown hair, blowing out a long breath.

I bring my hands to the bars as I lean closer. "Dionysus. I know you're feeling a lot of emotions probably right now, and processing it all at lightning speed. But you don't have to continue letting this be your life."

He looks up at me, knitting his brows.

"If you let me go, I can take you with me."

He jerks his head back. "Why would you do that? You don't even know me."

I faintly grin at him. His reaction to my gesture reminding me of a time when I didn't know there was better out there for me. That people could be *good*. Feeling subjected to a life that I didn't want for myself, but was too broken to find the way to demand better—to *allow* myself to have better.

And as I witness the pain in his two-toned gaze, I am reminded of how far I've come. Having been in his shoes once before. "I think I know you a lot better than I even imagined to."

He stares at me for a long moment before shaking his head. "I'm sorry. I—I can't."

I sigh as I bring myself away from the bars. Seating myself down onto my rear as I look at the torch above the wall. The flames dance together, reminding me of the flames I'd sit and watch in the fireplace back home. Curled onto the chaise lounge as Reimus reads me another page of poetry, written for me.

And as I sit here, I let Hades' words slither through my mind once more. At his promise to avenge my freedom, trusting that whatever plan they have will work.

I look over at Dionysus and realize that with or without him, I'm breaking out of this cell today. Even if I have to use the darkness of my powers against anyone that stands in my way.

CHAPTER 53

After an hour of Dionysus and I sitting down here in silence, my patience quickly thins out as I grow restless. Zeus' instructions for Hades and my mother to meet him two hours after their council meeting, to bring my sister as a peace offering for my life, blare in my mind.

And as that two hour mark creeps closer and closer, I find myself unable to remain seated as I slowly pace along the cell door.

I look over at Dionysus who has taken to standing again. "I've told you everything you needed to know. There's no reason for you to continue doing what Zeus asks of you, yet you still stand by his side. Why?"

He looks up at me, blinking once before turning his gaze away. Crossing his arms over his chest and remaining silent.

"Even though I hardly know you, I'm still giving you an out. But I can only do that if you meet me halfway and let me out of here."

A small noise gets trapped in his mouth, akin to a light huff as he shakes his head. Seeing the levels of denial litter themselves across his face.

I sigh as I lean my head closer to the bars. "You don't have to be afraid anymore—"

"I'm not afraid." He smolders.

"Well what are you then? A coward hiding behind a father who doesn't respect you enough to tell you the truth—"

"Enough!" He bellows as he advances onto the cell, his arms coming up to grab the bars and glare down at me.

I watch as his chest rises and sinks heavily, his nostrils flared as all of those years of pent up anger simmer on the surface. The years of debilitating loneliness and obscurity of who and what he truly is. I watch as his hardened gaze smooths out, his hands slowly lowering from the bars as he steps back into his post.

I go to step away from the bars as well, wincing as my hand comes up to my back. Gently pressing my fingers there when I feel the open gash of my skin, a chill creeping down my back as I lower my hand back down.

Dionysus watches me, his gaze flickering to my hand at my side as he steps forward. "You're bleeding."

I lift my hand up to see crimson fluid on my fingertips. "I figured as much." I go to wipe my hands on my beige breeches, staining them.

His gaze roams over me as I watch his chest slightly rise, lowering just as quickly. A tick in his jaw drawing my attention as he clenches it shut.

I sigh. "I've been where you are now."

He redirects his gaze back onto me.

I narrow my chin slightly as I say gently, "I know what it's like to wonder if your whole life has been a lie, to wonder if your father ever cared for you at all."

I watch as he works on a swallow, remaining silent.

"I know what it's also like to blame yourself. To think that you should've noticed the signs had you been just a little less naive, a little less trusting. But none of this is your fault, Dionysus."

He loosens a staggering breath as he unclenches his jaw. Shame washing over his face as he says roughly, quietly, "I've done some terrible things."

I shake my head slowly. "We've all done terrible things. What matters now is how you handle the information that I've given you. You can either allow it to destroy you, continue drinking yourself into oblivion and continue doing bad things for him, or you can decide against that."

His gaze bores into mine, siphoning my every word.

"You have the ability right now to prove that you aren't like him at all." I lift my wrists up, displaying my chains. "You can make the choice right now, to not only do the right thing by freeing me, but also by giving yourself permission to unshackle yourself from him."

Dionysus stares at me for a long moment, the silence between us deafening as all I can do is try to get him to do the right thing. Hoping that if he doesn't see through the manipulation that Zeus has inflicted upon him, that I'm still able to see my way out of here.

After a long beat of silence, Dionysus goes to open his mouth when he snaps his head up towards the door at the top of the steps. The vibration of feet shuffling across the throne room floor echoes throughout the dungeon. Until a moment later we hear the sound of wailing from the soldiers above.

The door slams wide open as the screaming of men pierces the walls around us, the dim lit dungeon suddenly glowing with the rays of the sunlight filtering in. The sound of someone running down the steps lasts briefly before Semele rushes towards the cage, her gaze shooting to Dionysus before me.

"Something's happened up there. They need your help." Her gaze fixated on Dionysus again. "I'll stay down here and keep watch."

Dionysus can do nothing but stare at her for a long moment, the truth of what I've told him plaguing him from any verbal reaction until Semele snaps him out of it.

"Now, Dionysus!" She shouts.

He glances over at me quickly, hesitating for a moment before rushing up the steps and into the throne room.

I look at Semele, approaching the cell. "What's going on?" I say, trying to act confused and worried, trying not to sound hopeful that this is it. This is my ticket out of here.

She looks up the steps, the sound of men screaming still echoing its way down here. I begin to feel the ground tremble beneath me, looking down to see tiny pebbles beside my feet ricochet gently off the cement ground.

"He knows now, doesn't he?"

I lift my gaze up to Semele, my brows knit together. But as I see her pull out the key from her breeches, and quickly fit it through the lock, my brows quickly smooth out as the screaming in the throne room above quickly silences out as I fixate on what she's doing. "What are you—"

"Melinoë, we don't have time right now." I listen as the locking mechanism clicks, Semele pushing the gate open as she hurriedly steps inside. Moving quickly over to me as she grabs the cuffs around my wrists. "Answer my question. Does my son know who I am?"

My gaze tracks over her as I nod. "I told him everything."

She nods her head curtly. "Listen to me carefully." She unlocks the chains from my wrists, watching as they clink to the ground. "I need you to take my son with you. Force him to, if you must."

I lower my gaze to her as she kneels at my feet, unlocking the cuffs at my ankles. A gentle breeze of air glides along the skin there as she stands up again, looking at me as she rolls her eyes. "Did you really think I didn't know you weren't under Zeus' compulsion?"

I go to open my mouth, shaking my head slowly.

"I knew this whole time your memories were intact. I thought if I helped you understand the story of the mistress—*me*, that you would understand why I had to do what I did." Her gaze bores into mine as she tilts her head. "When I yanked your talisman off, I felt the familiar power that radiated from it. A power that I had felt when Dionysus was in my womb, an essence that bores not one, but two souls. So when I felt the protective magic that Hecate spelled on it, I knew it would aid *both* of you." She shakes her head. "When Zeus ordered me to destroy it, I knew I had to leave it where Hecate would find it. So I buried it in the Sephyra Forest, and told Zeus it had been destroyed."

I had wondered how it was still intact after I was kidnapped, how Reimus was still able to visit me in the astral realm. And this whole time—

Semele had been trying to help me. The food, the baths. But it still begs the question. "Why? Why would you go to all this trouble to help me but still kidnap me in the first place?"

She glances up at the stairs before training her gaze back onto me. "Because it was supposed to be Dionysus who kidnapped you."

My brows knit together as I shake my head.

"After Dionysus failed to extract you the first time, he was ordered by Zeus to make a second attempt. But when Dionysus told Zeus he was unable to get through Vulir because of the protective shield around it, Zeus was angry with his failure and told him to extract you by any means necessary." She works on a swallow. "And I knew when Zeus said by any means necessary, that he would've let his own son get injured just to get to you and your sister."

"His first attempt? I—"

My eyes widen as the memory of Dimitri getting attacked resurfaces. Having little recollection of what the man looked like outside of the shield, all of us having assumed it was Zeus just shapeshifted into another form.

I've done some terrible things.

Dionysus' words alarm themselves inside my mind and what he meant by them.

"I told Zeus I would take Dionysus' place instead, that I wouldn't fail in retrieving you. So Zeus agreed, and released Dionysus of his duties. I knew that I would only be granted access to Vulir if I made myself convincing, as I learned that those who have ill intentions are kept out. So, what I spun to Reimus and Charon that seemed like a lie was actually the truth."

Her story of running from an abusive relationship, where the father still had her son. It was all technically the truth. That's why she was still granted access into Vulir because even though her deeper intentions were to kidnap me, her anguish for her son and the life she shared with Zeus was all true.

"I never wanted to see this happen to you, but I meant what I said, Melinoë. I will do anything for my son. And right now, that includes seeing him get far away from here." She grabs my arms as she jolts my attention to focus on her. "But you must act *now*. Hecate can't hold them off for long up there."

Hecate…is here—

My throat threatens to constrict as I will myself to remain focused, nodding to Semele. "Thank you."

She guides us quickly out of the cell. "Zeus is in Lothario preoccupied with your mother and all of them. I already checked, Reimus is there along with Dimitri. You, Hecate, and my son need to exit through the throne room entrance, and out to the Casalas Mountains."

A choked cry threatens to burst out of my throat at the sound of Reimus being nearby. No longer just in his astral form, but physically nearby.

We hurry past my cell when I yank her back. "Wait."

She whips her gaze back to me. "Please don't tell me you actually want to stay here—"

"I'm not leaving without her." I say, nodding to the darkened cells to the left.

Semele steps towards me, tilting her head as confusion furrows on her face. "Her? Melinoë, who are you talking about—"

"I believe she's referring to me, cupcake." A sultry voice slithers out from the cell next to us.

I watch as Semele's face blanches with fear, her eyes widening as she says, "Melinoë, you have no idea what you're letting out if you—"

"I'm *not* leaving her." I roar as I feel the weeks of anger, the humiliation, the restriction that's been imposed on me—on *my* magic rises to the surface. It expands quickly inside of me, forming faster than ever before. The overwhelming sensation is akin to getting pulled along a violent current with no other choice but to allow it to swallow me whole. "Open it. Now." My words sharper than a blade piercing flesh.

Semele hesitates before nodding, lowering a key to the lock and unlocking the cell right next to mine. The door slowly creaks open as Semele steps back, the ruffled sound of something expanding within causing me to take a step back as well.

A moment later I watch as not a human woman, but a creature emerges from the darkened cell.

My gaze roams over her large, jet black wings spanning out wide behind her before the sound of clicking coaxes my gaze down to her feet. I watch as a long, sharp talon taps against the cement floor, the noise I remember hearing from her cell the times we did speak. I trail my gaze up her bare legs, darkened like the rest of her body and having similar features to that of a human. Knowing full well that she is anything but.

I fixate on her flexing her claws at her sides, cracking the knuckles there as if readying herself up for what is above us. I lift my gaze higher to the face of a predator, her bright yellow eyes stealing my breath for a moment before noticing the horns jutting from her forehead.

I stand before this terrifyingly beautiful creature, finding myself unafraid and instead welcoming everything that she is. A creature that is unafraid of showcasing all of the worst parts of itself, and instead embracing exactly who they are. Reminding me that as The Goddess of Nightmares, that I am not all light and bliss. That the power that lurks beneath me can be dark and destructive, fueled by years of abuse.

Years of suppression and silence.

Years of having my power stripped away from me.

And as I stand before the creature now, that darkness welling inside of me begs me to let her out.

So, I finally do.

I give her a wicked grin, my shadows eagerly pooling at my fingertips. "Are you ready to have your *treat* now?"

She gives me a wide grin back, the points of her sharp teeth showing through her lips. A low chuckle slithers out of her as she says in a voice filled with smoke, "I have been waiting for this day."

We both begin our ascent up the stairs, Semele following behind us as I watch my shadows lick the steps below me. Coiling around my ankles, kissing the sore skin from where the cuffs used to be. They whisper sweet words of revenge to me, and I beckon their call gladly.

We reach the top step as I hold my palms out at my sides, stepping through the doorway to see some of the soldiers being suffocated by a dense fog. Their golden armor like sunshine being swallowed whole by the darkness of the night, their muffled screaming the only noise I can focus on. Satiating that well of anger inside of me like a siren's song.

And as I stride into the throne room, I do so not just as Melinoë.

But as The Goddess of Nightmares.

"The Keres! She's out of her cage!" One soldier shouts in a panic to the others. The fog quickly creeps up to his ankles, just missing him as he turns away to run.

The Keres shoots up into the air as she soars above the soldier running away from her, honing in on that fear intensifying from him as a nervous sweat profusely beads along his brow. I watch as she taunts him, playing with her food before banking downwards and latching her mouth onto his throat. His wailing being cut short as she tears the head from his neck, his body thumping to the ground as blood drips down her jaw. Her hand latches onto his face, her claws digging into his skin as she drinks the blood dripping from the shredded tendons in his neck before tossing his head onto the ground.

"Melinoë!"

I hear the sound of Hecate's voice ring out from across the room, but as my sights lock in on the soldiers advancing towards me, all I can concentrate on is one thing.

I lift my palms up as my shadows shoot out from my fingertips, willing them to attach themselves to each of the soldier's necks. I watch as they drop their swords, clawing at my shadows constricting the air from reaching their lungs. I smile wickedly as I watch their faces turn blue.

And with the snap of my wrists, all of their necks crack like a symphony of notes.

Their bodies crumple down to the polished floor as my shadows release themselves from their necks, and slither back towards me.

My gaze lifts to what's at the top of the dais, the seat placed above it. My gaze momentarily drags itself to the cage beside it, my calm fury boiling over. All of that power that's been stifled to remain inside of me pours over the wall I've kept it behind, and I let it fill every crevice of my body as I unleash it.

CHAPTER 54

Darkness swarms the entire throne room, suffocating the remaining soldiers as they claw at their necks. Trying desperately to fight for the air that I no longer allow them to have.

A blast of power eradicates the cage at the top of the dais, shattering it into a million pieces. Never to be used on another innocent soul again.

I watch as one by one, soldiers drop like flies onto the polished floor as I suck the life right out of them. The very breath from their lungs snuffing out like the flames on a torch.

I look down to the headless man's body, smirking to myself as I wield my shadows to lift his headless corpse up into the air. I move him up onto the dais, placing his body onto Zeus's golden throne. Extracting my shadows back to me as I watch crimson pool down to the floor, staining the gold-flecked floor with a river of crimson.

I feel the hands of Hecate on me as she pulls me into her embrace. "Melinoë." She whispers into my shoulder.

I gasp into her arms as I hug her tightly against me. Tears welling in my eyes at the velvet touch of the amethyst robe around her. "Hecate—"

"We don't have much time."

I pull myself away from Hecate to look at Semele.

She nods towards the throne room's main entrance. "I'll stay here to create a distraction for Zeus when he returns. But you must leave *now*."

I step away from Hecate as I step towards Semele. My mouth opening and closing, failing to find the words for her shocking assistance in helping me escape. Instead, I nod as I ask, "What will you tell him?"

I watch as a grin appears on her face before willing a bruise under one of her eyes. A purple bruise appears on her cheek a second later. "That you escaped, of course."

I look around the throne room. "Where's Dionysus?"

Semele shakes her head. "I don't know. I'll figure it out. Just *go*." She urges.

I nod as I look at Hecate, grabbing her hand as we book it out of there. Before we can make it to the door I feel a looming presence soaring above me. The Keres lowers herself down in front of me, halting me in my hurried stride.

The Keres nods her head, dipping it low enough as if to assert a bow. "Thank you, Melinoë. I will remember your kindness for an eternity."

I nod. "You deserved freedom as much as I did."

She grins, blood still dripping from her mouth. She soars up as Hecate and I pull the door open, and she flies straight out of the palace. My gaze follows the darkened figure as she glides across the sun-drenched sky until I ram into a hard body.

I look up to see a familiar chestnut brown haired man grabbing my shoulders. "Dimitri." I say breathlessly.

He gives me a quick grin before looking over his shoulder at the soldiers making their way towards us. "I'd love to exchange greetings right now, but I'm afraid right now is not the time."

A portal opens up beside Hecate as she waves Dimitri and I over. "Let's go."

Dimitri and I step right through it and are transported deep within the Casalas Mountains. The portal closing up behind us, the soldiers with it.

I turn around to the sound of soldiers from the edge of the forest making their way towards us, their swords at the ready.

"I told him we're here."

I whip my gaze over to Dimitri as the breath leaves my lungs momentarily. My knees suddenly become weak at who he's referring to. At who is nearby.

Reimus.

"I'll handle this." Hecate says as she stands in front of us. I watch as a whirlpool of energy charges the air around us, the leaves from the trees whipping past our heads as a thick fog begins to flow along the forest ground, making its way towards the soldiers.

They immediately fall to their knees as soon as the fog comes into contact with them. Clutching onto their legs as the armor from their legs *melts* off, leaving their skin exposed from the knees down. Large, painful blisters appear on their ankles and travel up to the rest of their bodies as the fog suffocates them from the chest up. Their anguished cries stifle out moments later as their bodies fall limp to the soiled ground, Hecate pulling the fog back.

I turn to Hecate, tilting my head. "Poison?"

She glances at me, smirking. "Indeed."

I turn to see soldiers closing in on us from all directions, a group of them from my right quickly closing in. I will my shadows to the surface, but it's too late as one of them advances on me—

Just as he was about to lift his sword to strike me he halts in place. His body quivers as he drops his sword to the ground, watching as blood begins to pool out of his eyes, nose and mouth. He stands there unable to move for only a second before he falls to the ground. Revealing Dionysus standing behind him.

He strides over to me as I stand in a defensive position, unaware what his intentions are for being out here. Whether to stand beside us, or to imprison me once more.

But as he looks at me, I see the finality of what's already written on his face as he says, "I believe a thank you is in order for saving your ass there."

I stare at him for a long moment before a faint grin forms on my lips. "*Thank you*." I say mockingly.

He approaches my side as I see for the first time a grin appear on his brooding face.

"Wait—I know you." Dimitri says from beside me, moving to stand in front of Dionysus. I watch as first recognition registers on his face, followed by anger. "You." He seethes, pushing Dionysus.

He hardly stumbles back as he gets in Dimitri's face. "Look, I had no choice."

"What's going on?" Hecate asks casually, as if she's not propelling a mass amount of fog towards the soldiers coming towards us.

I sigh audibly. "This is Dionysus. My brother."

Hecate whips her gaze over to me, then him. I watch as Dimitri does the same, only slightly lessening the rage he has for the man who attacked him in the forest. "What?" He asks.

"Listen, it's a *long* story. I'll explain everything later but for now," I say, raising my hand up as my shadows whip out at two soldiers closing in on us. I snap their necks instantly before dropping them to the ground. "We need to get out of here. Where is Reimus?"

Dimitri stands by my side as he goes into a defensive stance, looking over at me. "He's coming."

My heart trips up inside of my chest, realizing that for right now I'll have to set that excitement to see him aside. As now we stand completely surrounded by men in gold armor.

I watch as a sword materializes in Dimitri's hand, turning my gaze over to Hecate who is still fending off the soldiers with her fog.

"Try anything against Melinoë and I won't hesitate to gut you." Dimitri snarls at Dionysus, holding the sword up and at the ready. "And I promise what I do will be far kinder than what Rei will do."

My heart leaps out of my chest at the sound of his name. My mind wants to pull me away, to focus on the fact that he's *right here*, so closely within reach.

But as my power lashes out at a soldier, I'm forced to remain alert to the growing numbers surrounding us.

Dionysus sighs beside him as his gaze hones in on the soldiers advancing towards us. "I thought my display a few seconds ago was enough to tell you what side I am on—"

"Wait—" I interrupt Dionysus, looking over at Dimitri. I knit my brows together as I say, "Semele told me you'd be in Lothario with Reimus. She said she saw you there."

Dimitri and Hecate give each other a smirk before glancing back at me. And before they can tell me further, my power lashes out as we get ambushed.

CHAPTER 55

Reimus

I stand beside Hades, Persephone on his left. I watch as village people meander around on this bright and sunny day, most of them wearing rags for clothing. I look directly in front of me where Makaria stands. Her long hair flowing down her back, the blonde strands as bright as moonlight against her porcelain skin. She stands there unafraid, unshaken, as we watch Zeus walk towards us with another at his side.

No soldiers flanking him. Which means he's ordered them all to stay back in case anything goes wrong, and to keep an eye on the palace. On Melinoë.

His golden piercing gaze falls onto Makaria right away, a grin curving his lips before lifting his gaze up to Hades, Persephone, then me.

He stares at me for a long moment, a revolted expression lining his face before looking at Dimitri beside me.

The sun-kissed god with the golden bow and arrow beside Zeus looks upon Makaria before lifting his gaze to me. His glance over me is noticeably different from Zeus'.

A curiosity in his gaze.

"Glad to see you've stayed true to your word, Persephone." Zeus says as he stops his stride, only a few feet separating us. He lowers his gaze to Makaria. "Good to see you again, daughter."

I watch her back threaten to stiffen before she calms herself enough to keep it relaxed. Instead, she lowers her head into a quick bow. "Happy to see you again, father." She says sweetly.

"I'm so glad that we could come to a peaceful resolution today." The grin on his face showed anything but welcoming.

Persephone gives Zeus a forced grin, seeing her holding back her temper.

We have her. I repeat, we have Melinoë.

At the sound of Dimitri giving me the confirmation I was waiting for down the Guardian's channel, I look over to Hades. When he looks towards me, I give him a nod. And in the next second, that brief silence stretching between all of us quickly erupts into chaos.

I look over at the figure standing beside me. Eyes begin to melt from his face, sloping down his cheeks like shriveled up berries until his shoulders cave into himself. The skin on his arms solidifies and runs down his legs like ice cream melting under rays of heat.

A spell Hecate put on an inanimate object. To resemble an identical replica of Dimitri, but not him at all. Just to give us enough time until they had Melinoë, and enough time to persuade Zeus that we were all here in accordance.

I watch as a portal quickly opens up for Makaria, the swirls around the center of it matching the color of her hair. She quickly steps into it, and just as quickly closes it behind her.

The rage on Zeus' face causes his skin to redden before emanating a bright orange hue. And as his sights land on me, like we knew it would, Persephone shoots a blast of her power at him. Forcing him to stumble backwards as Hades surrounds him with a field of darkness.

"Now!" He shouts.

I immediately shift into my drago form and ascend quickly into the sky, banking fast for the treeline that I know will lead me to the Casalas Mountains.

That will lead me to Melinoë.

I propel my wings harder than I ever have before, flying quicker than the speed of light to get to her. And when I see her far below on the ground, fighting against soldiers swarming them, everything in me breaks wide open like a dam.

I soar across the sky, producing a loud piercing cry to let them know I'm near.

That I'm coming for her.

From this high up, I can hear her choked cry as if she's standing right next to me. The sound of her at all rattling me entirely from the inside out as I bank downward into the treeline.

She looks up at me as a man next to her stays fighting off soldiers surrounding them. Her eyes welling with tears as she gasps violently at the sight of me.

As I reach the ground I shift back into my human form, looking up to see Melinoë having turned around to shoot blasts of her shadows at the soldiers swarming her. One of them manages to swipe his sword out at her, but she manages to duck in time. She rolls onto the ground as she holds her hand up, blocking his blow with her shadows. But my gaze catches on her back, at the angry wounds that mar her skin.

I clench my fists together as fire-hot anger infiltrates my entire body. The temperature in my body rises to dangerously hot levels as I go to take a step towards her when my foot gets stuck.

I look down, noticing vines surfacing from the soil and latching onto my ankles. "No." I whip my gaze up to her. "Melinoë!" I shout.

She blasts two soldiers back before looking back at me. Her gaze lowered to the ground before stumbling over to me. "Rei. What's happening?" She cries as she goes to rip the vines out. She quickly jerks her hands up as they nick her skin.

The vines wrap around my ankles as visions violently resurface themselves into my mind. Memories of me standing in this very soil many, many years ago.

"The essence to be hidden beneath the soil from which we originate. Destined to be triggered back to life as he steps foot onto what belongs to us." My mother says, her voice carrying over all around me as people begin to form around me. "For until the time is right, the remainder of us hide in plain sight."

I watch as each of them takes a knife and makes a slit into their palms. The crimson liquid spilling and pooling down into the earth, watching as it seeps deep below the soil. "For until the time is right, the remainder of us hide in plain sight." They all say in unison.

I look down to see myself doing the same thing, my blood dripping down into the soil as I kneel down. I lay my palms flat onto the earth as I feel the charge of my energy leave my body.

Not my energy, but my essence.

I look up at my mother smiling down upon me. "I am so proud of you, my boy."

I smile up at her, feeling the true essence of the Draghi bloodline leave my body. Temporarily, until the day comes when I can reclaim it back. When the day arrives when I can reclaim the land my people once called home. "How will I know when it's the right time to come back?"

My mother smiles down at me, resting a gentle hand on my cheek. "You'll know."

I lean into her touch. "And I won't remember any of this?"

She shakes her head. "Not until you step onto the soil, and reclaim what is yours."

I nod my head in understanding, looking up at my father standing next to my mother. I take a deep breath in, feeling the essence pool itself out of my body and return itself back to the ground. A familiar heat that we've managed to keep secret, to keep protected but must relinquish for the secrecy of our people's lineage. To be hidden for now. "When the time is right, I will reclaim our home." My gaze lifts to the golden palace miles away.

To the King who sits upon that throne, who we know is making plans to take over what belongs to us. To reclaim it as his own as he has done for his father's throne.

My mother nods her head, taking a knife to her own hand. But before she makes a cut, a smoldering fire lights up her hands as she grins down at me. Having no idea that her, as well as all of these people, would never see this side of their lineage—their power again.

"We will have just enough in our blood to go to war with, but the remainder will slumber below." My mother says.

The memory of the war resurfacing, seeing that I was not in my drago form when I set that man on fire. I was—

"Rei!" Melinoë yells, pulling me from my resurfaced memories just as the vines around my ankles uncoil themselves from my skin. Where suddenly, the essence of who the Draghi truly are now flows through my veins. The pieces of my forgotten, blurry past entirely clear now as I look upon her face.

Her emerald eyes cement me in place, the tears that line them threatening to shake me to my core. But at the reminder of what I saw on her back, at what *he* did to her—

All I see, and feel, is red.

As soldiers begin to swarm us I step in front of Melinoë, keeping her close behind me as I feel that heat ramp up in my hands. No longer feeling perplexed by it and using it for exactly what it's intended for.

I feel the overwhelming amount of essence rushing through me like a welcomed reacquainting as I lift my hands out, and unleash myself onto the soldiers surrounding us.

As fire erupts from my hands and scorches the soldiers into a burnt crisp.

CHAPTER 56

Melinoë

I stare at Reimus as he blasts fire onto the soldiers from his *hands*, obliterating them to ash when more swarm us from his side. He wastes no time in lifting his left hand out, sending waves of scorching fire onto the men. Burning them to a fine crisp.

I watch as anger—as *vigilance* highlights his face. His determination to kill and light on fire each and every soldier that inches their way to us. And each time I try to move from behind him, he shoots me a warning look to stay back.

I've never seen him so fiercely protective. I never knew he could shoot fire from his hands. I—

Reimus steps forward as his gaze hones in on a soldier who initially advanced on us, but now begins turning away as he sees his men burnt to a crisp.

"Oh, I don't think so." Reimus says in an eerily calm voice, nothing like I've ever heard before.

He lifts his hands, shooting a blast of fire out onto the man. I stare at Reimus as he watches him burn to death, his chest rising and falling swiftly before he looks around to see the remaining soldiers having fled from us. Retreating back to the palace.

"Rei." I say quietly, calling out for him.

At the sound of my voice it's as if everything in him snaps out of his rage filled trance and he whips around towards me. I watch as his chest sinks deeply before pulling me close to him.

A choked cry escapes out of me as I sob against his hold. That familiar patchouli smell of him lights up every lost part of me as I weep in his arms.

He cradles me to him as our knees give out, both of us falling to the ground. He tugs me closer to him, making sure to not wrap his arms around my back and instead my shoulders. Keeping the force of his hold away from the wounds on my back.

I pull myself away from him, holding his face in my hands as I realize there are tears streaming down his striking blue eyes. My lips quiver as his hands come up to my cheeks. "I tried to tell you when I visited you." He says roughly. "In the astral realm."

I watch as he pulls my talisman out from beneath his shirt, the onyx crystal shining and pulsating between us.

"I knew you couldn't hear me, but I hoped you knew that I was coming for you." His thumb caresses beneath my eye, wiping the tears away. My chest caves wide open as I stare into his eyes now, the feel of his thumb pushing my hair away from my face lights up every nerve, every darkened crevice within me. I nearly shiver at the feel of his touch, like reuniting with the other half of myself all over again.

He looks at me for a long moment, a shuddering breath leaving him as a grin curves up his trembling lips. "Let's go home."

I take a shuddering breath in at those words.

Home.

I nod curtly as he brings my face in, his lips crashing with mine. Oh, the way I missed the feel of his lips. Ones that could bring me back from the dreariest of places.

And they have, time and time again.

He forces himself to pull away, leaning his forehead against mine for a moment before ushering us both up from the ground. He looks down at me, grinning as his hand lowers to hold mine. The weight of it a much, much needed refuge I've yearned to return back to. A normalcy that I've yearned for each and every day.

As we both turn around to face everyone else, I watch as he looks up at Dionysus, knitting his brows together before leaning in towards me. "Who's he?"

I chuckle softly to him. "Remember what I told you of the prophecy? About a first born son?"

I watch as recognition flares in his gaze as he wipes the remaining dampness beneath his eyes. "The Twice Born." He looks down at me, blinking. "Your brother."

I nod, grinning. "I've offered for him to come back home with us."

Reimus lifts a brow. A look of non-opposition, but curiosity nonetheless.

I glance over at Dionysus who has taken to talking quietly with Hecate. Probably to distract himself from the fact that Dimitri keeps passing glances over at him. "He deserves a better life than what Zeus has awarded him." I say, turning my gaze back onto Reimus.

Reimus lowers his brow, lifting his other hand to run his fingers through my hair. He narrows his gaze to the strands laid on my chest, feather lightly tugging on the ends until he raises his gaze back up to me, nodding. He turns his gaze over to Dimitri, tilting his head towards me. "Should I know why Dimitri keeps looking at him like he wants to kill him?"

I hum softly. "Yeah, there's a lot of explaining that needs to be done. When we get home."

Reimus looks down at me, smiling. A gorgeous smile that I thank The Fates for blessing me with. He nods his head before movement in the trees snaps his head up to my right. He immediately goes to stand in front of me when he lifts his hand up, and without hesitation, shoots blasts of scorching fire out from his palm.

I watch as it quickly billows upward into a wall, unaffecting whoever he's unleashing it onto as they maneuver the fire away from them. I step around him to see Apollo holding an invisible shield in front of him. His gaze lowered to me. "Melinoë."

Without hesitation I will my shadows to the surface, standing in a defensive stance when I unleash them onto him.

He blocks my blow with the swift wave of his hand, ricocheting them away from him while still keeping Reimus' fire from reaching him. "Melinoë, I am not your enemy."

"I may have *acted* pious and naive while under the guise of Zeus to survive, but I can assure you I am not." I say as I lash out at him again. This time landing true on his neck.

Since he's also maintaining the shield, he is unable to bring both of his hands up to his neck. As I watch his free hand come up to pull my shadows off, I lash out again at him. This time aiming to keep his arm tethered down to the ground, the shadows coiling over his fist to keep it closed. I begin to constrict the shadows tighter around his neck when I hear more rustling through the woods.

"Don't do it, princess."

I look to see a silver arrow nocked and ready, Artemis aiming it right for my chest as her gaze remains honed in on me. "I don't want to hurt you, but if you kill my brother, I will."

I let her words filter in one ear and out the other as I fix my gaze back onto Apollo. As I turn my gaze away from her, I will my shadows to constrict tighter around his neck.

In a flash, I hear Artemis whistle as movement travels around the perimeter of the woods. I look over to see an array of wildlife revealing themselves, ranging from mountain lions to coyotes. They all lower themselves to the ground, each of them aimed to attack either myself or Reimus. I watch as Hecate and Dimitri go into a defensive stance as they become targeted as well.

"He's right, Melinoë. We're not your enemies."

"Shut up." I seethe.

"If you let go of your hold on him, he can prove it to you."

I look over at her, tilting my head. "With what? His words?" I force out a harsh laugh.

"No, with this." She points at the center of her forehead, to her mind.

I look back at Apollo, his gaze wholly on me as he tries to form words. Instead, he rests his free palm on his forehead. A gesture that the Pythia did when she read the prophecy from him. I watch as he blinks at me, his face beginning to turn blue at the loss of air reaching his lungs.

I look back over at Artemis as she nods towards her brother. "We are on your side. Trust us. Allow him to *show* you."

I look back at Apollo, realizing that as a god who has mastered his gifts far more than I ever have, has been around in his godhood for eons before me, that he could probably just as easily push the fire back onto Reimus instead of just keeping it out in front of him. That as I watch my shadows around his fist begin to dissolve, as if willed to dissipate by his magic, that he still hasn't retaliated against me yet.

I unleash my hold on him as Artemis releases her arrow from aiming at me. Apollo taking a giant breath in, rubbing his hand around his neck as he looks up at me.

I look over at Reimus, his stern gaze wholly on Apollo before redirecting it onto me. "It's okay." I say, nodding for him to lower his defenses. He gives me a look before stifling the fire from his hands, retracting that power back into himself as he lowers his hand entirely.

I look over at Apollo as he lowers his shield, straightening his back before walking towards me. His steps unhurried and tentative, as if to still be cautious of those who are around me, that I know will defend me.

I walk towards him as Reimus follows close behind, meeting him halfway until we're only inches apart. I glance at the golden band across his bicep, similar to his sister's before lifting my gaze to his face. The golden halo around his irises churn brightly as he lowers his hand to mine, lifting it and bringing it to his forehead. "Close your eyes."

I look over at Reimus who has taken to standing directly behind me, unwilling to venture far just in case. He gives me a nod, a confirmation that he will assess everything that happens. And will make the judgement call to pull me out if anything goes wrong.

I turn to face Apollo again as he flattens my palm to his forehead, a light energy pulses to my hand and travels down my arm. Like an idle buzzing sensation similar to what I feel in the astral realm.

As Apollo lowers his hand from mine, I tentatively close my eyes and breathe in and out deeply. And as everything around me quickly begins to fade away like watercolor paint to a canvas, I'm transported to a memory of him and his sister.

I look around to see that everyone other than myself and Artemis has cleared away. Standing in a different part of the Casalas Mountains, I look up to see Artemis with her back facing me. The sound of a twig snapping sends me looking in the other direction, watching as Apollo walks towards his sister. Walking right past me as I am a passenger in his own memory.

I turn around and watch him stand by her side, folding his hands behind his back as they both look upon the tallest mountain in the valley. "He's given the heart to Semele." He pauses for a beat before saying, "The process of reincarnation is now underway."

I watch as Artemis remains facing forward as I walk closer to them, positioning myself at Artemis' left as I look at the impassivity on her face. A slow nod follows her beat of silence. "It has begun then."

"Yes." Apollo says quietly.

My attention snaps to a dark-haired couple walking through the forest beyond the valley, deepest into the mountain range.

"Which means she will be born within the next year or two if all goes according to the prophecy." Artemis says, watching the couple as the man puts his arm around the woman, my gaze lowering to her extended belly. Presuming she's not far along from giving birth now.

Apollo nods his head as he watches the woman. "It is as The Fates have willed it, and so shall it be."

I take a step closer, watching the way the woman's face lights up when she smiles. The man leans in to give her a kiss, his sharp jaw brushing up against her chin before pulling away. I watch as the sunlight through the valley shines across his face, across his eyes.

Icy blue eyes that could cement someone in place—
Eyes like Reimus'.

"Zeus has begun to express his…indignation to the land." Apollo says, nodding to the couple down in the valley. I watch as deeper out, more people surface in and out of the treeline. Until my gaze lifts up to a large figure with wings soaring above the mountains.

"As we had expected." Artemis says matter of factly.

"It will be quite some time before he makes his move, but it would be wise for them to start preparations now." Apollo lifts his gaze above to the drago soaring in the air. "When the time comes for the essence to be hidden, we will need to preserve those left somehow. To protect their bloodline."

Artemis lifts her gaze up before following the drago lowering himself back down to the ground. "I see less and less of them shifting into their drago forms. Staying hidden in the mountains." Her gaze watches as the drago shifts into a man. "I believe they are already aware that something is coming."

Apollo and Artemis stand there in silence for a beat of a moment as a deer steps out from behind stalks of grass. Inching its way over to Artemis, her hand lifting out to pet it. "And at the right time, you will tell her?"

Apollo nods as he looks at the pregnant woman far out. "For the survival of her son, whose soul will be shared with whom heralds nightmares, will be alerted to the fate of their land when it is time. That the only way to save it, and the people who shall remain, is to hide her son's essence into the land's soil. To be reclaimed by him when the time is right, receiving his title as leader over the land. Over the Draghi bloodline."

Shit. The pregnant woman is Reimus' mother, and when he had spoken about her being able to see premonitions of the future, he had no idea that she was being awarded these prophecies by Apollo himself.

"It is with both him and her, that they will not only bring harmony to the lands North and South, but a new reign of power will emerge from their union. But Zeus must believe that he's eradicated all of them, which means the remaining essence must be hidden below."

The deer beside Artemis begins to walk away from her, merging itself back into the forest. A faint grin curves up her face as she says, "And those who survive will be hidden in plain sight until the time is right."

"Precisely." Apollo says, watching the deer vanish. "He knows they draw their power from the Earth, from their homeland. When he takes it over, he will need to believe that the power has been stripped from them. That their power only lies in shifting, but not of wielding fire with their hands."

I watch as Artemis sighs, turning to face her brother now. "The people in Olympia will not survive under Zeus' rulership. He will dry them completely of their sources, leading them to starvation and eventually death."

Apollo looks at his sister, his gaze reading of compassion and earnestness as he says, "That is why it must be her. She is the only one who can do it. As when she finally accepts herself fully, she will accept the gifts that Zeus unknowingly passed down to her." He shakes his head. "As even though he tried to damn The Fates by taking Hades' fate of having children, The Fates damned him in return. Granting Melinoë not only the gift of darkness, but of light. Of shadows and lightning."

I shake my head as I watch this all play out in front of me. It can't be—

A memory surfaces of being in the throne room, practicing with Zeus. Testing the strength and capabilities of my gifts. I remember twice seeing sparks of light filter through my shadows, thinking it had been just an after effect of my shadows absorbing his magic.

But they weren't absorbing it because it was foreign, they were absorbing it because it was familiar. *Because I already possess the similar abilities as Zeus.*

Artemis nods her head slowly. "A fate of shadows and fire."

Apollo takes a breath in, exhaling as he nods. "Indeed."

My eyes widen as I go to take a step back when I'm transported into another memory of Apollo's. One where he stands before the Pythia in that small room below his Temple. My gaze lowers to the cauldron between him and her, idle as smoke ceases to form there. "He has requested you speak of the prophecy."

The Pythia raises her gaze up to Apollo. "I am loyal to you, before I am to any other god. So how you would like me to proceed is what I will follow."

I step around to Apollo's side, looking up at him as his face remains neutral. "You will have no choice. You will have to give him the prophecy."

She tilts her head. "Which one?"

There's more than one?

"Only the one that speaks of him and his children. Of his fate. The other prophecy does not belong to him, so we shall keep it that way."

The Pythia nods her head. "And the girl?"

Apollo pauses for a moment before saying, "It must only be revealed to her when he reclaims his power back from the land. At which point, she must be the one to come seeking it."

The Pythia nods again. "Very well then."

I feel the energy around me vibrate as my body is sucked backwards until suddenly, I'm back in front of Apollo.

In the Casalas Mountains.

I open my eyes, lifting my gaze to my hand still on Apollo's forehead. I glance back at Reimus as I shake my head slowly, in complete awestruck.

"Melinoë."

I turn my gaze back to Apollo as he lowers my hand down from his sun-kissed forehead. The golden halo around his irises churning brightly as he asks, "Do you understand now?"

I blink at him, nodding my head curtly as I say breathlessly, "Yes." I look over at Artemis, who's standing nearby watching me. "I do."

He nods his head before stepping away from me. "You all need to leave now before Zeus makes his way back. I will return for you when the time is right."

I feel the energy of a portal opening up behind me, assuming either from Dionysus or Hecate. I stand there, blankly staring at Apollo before he puts his hands on my shoulders. "Melinoë, you must leave. *Now*."

A sudden boom sounds from far away, my gaze lifting to beyond the treeline to a cloud of darkness hanging over a village of small buildings. I give Artemis and Apollo a knowing look before turning around with Reimus in tow.

Hecate stands beside the portal, waving us to step inside of it. Dimitri and Dionysus step through it first as I look through the center at what lies inside, at the palace I've longed of being reacquainted with. And as I step through and my foot lands onto the plush rug of the living room floor, I feel everything crack wide open inside of me.

Reimus steps inside behind me, followed by Hecate before she closes the portal entirely. I lower myself to the ground, reaching my hand out to feel the texture of the rug. The softness of the material, lifting my gaze to the soft sounds of the fire crackling in the fireplace next to me. I take a shuddering breath in as the aroma of my home settles within me.

I crumple to the ground and lay there, tears welling in my eyes before streaming down my cheeks. Reimus is at my side instantly as he brings me into his lap, curling myself into him as I clutch onto his shirt. Digging my nails into the soft fabric as I remind myself of the knowledge that I'm home.

I'm free.

I'm safe.

I repeat it over and over in my mind as suddenly, the mental anguish that I've been keeping locked inside, stifled into the pit of my soul, overwhelms every bone in my body until I'm forced to succumb wholly to it.

The exhaustion of having to bottle everything up sends me into a deep sleep, for the first time in weeks.

CHAPTER 57

Reimus

I watch her chest rise and fall softly, steadily as she sleeps beneath our covers. My hand lifting to caress her hair back from her face, a comfort in her touch that I can't fathom to be away from right now.

As we walked through the portal I watched the way Melinoë gravitated towards our living room floor. Everyone around remained silent as they watched Melinoë silently break apart. Overjoyed to be back home, but under the physical and mental exhaustion of what she went through nonetheless. Knowing that it was only a matter of time before her mind and body demanded to finally rest, after spending weeks being imprisoned and in a constant state of hypervigilance.

I lower my hand from her face, my gaze falling to her shoulder. To the wounds I know are still on her back. Wounds that Hecate and Nora have both already agreed to treat and heal when she had finally awoken. Both of them asked if I had wanted them healed while she was asleep, but

I had declined. Not wanting to make any slight movements and risk waking her from her slumber.

We arrived back home three hours ago and I have not left her side once. After I carried her up to our bedroom, I gave one look to Dimitri as he already understood what I was going to ask of him.

To give Melinoë and I privacy as she begins her road to healing, to mourning a traumatic event.

He's communicated with me a few times through the Guardian's channel, the first time to alert me to Nora arriving. Asking if I'd like Melinoë healed while she slept. The other time to just check in, to see if she was still sleeping. A half grin had lifted onto my face when he asked, sensing the true genuine concern in his voice. Not just concern for his best friend watching his girlfriend undergo a traumatic event, but for a woman who has suffered a great deal.

And holding genuine worry for her wellbeing.

I still have no idea what the beef is with Dimitri and Dionysus, knowing at some point I'll need to be filled in on that. But for right now, I have no desire to worry about anything else other than who is before me.

My gaze lowers to her feet at the end of the bed, the movement underneath the dark grey sheets lifting my gaze back up to her face as her eyes groggily peel open. I seat myself to the edge of the chair, leaning over her as I give her a warm smile. "Hi." I say softly, my voice barely above a whisper.

She peels her eyes open, those emerald irises staring back at me. Gods, am I grateful to be able to witness those eyes again.

She lifts a hand up to her face, wiping the tiredness from her eyes before looking at me. "Hi." Her voice carrying a tired rasp.

I lift my hand to her forehead, checking to make sure she's not running a fever. Not sure why she would be but feeling like a protective and overly cautious boyfriend nonetheless. "How are you feeling?"

She pushes herself further up until she's seated against the headboard. She winces and pulls away, remembering her wounds on her back.

"Nora and Hecate have agreed to heal those when you're ready."

She lifts her gaze back up to me, watching her chest sink deeply. She stares at me for a long moment before she says, "I know there is a lot that needs to be filled in still—"

"Don't." I shake my head, coming to sit on the bed next to her. "You have been through a great deal. Nobody expects anything of you right now."

I watch as tears well in her eyes, moving my hand to gently wipe them away. My gaze lowers to her hand on the bed, curling her fingers into the sheets before releasing again. I watch her do this twice before she speaks. "I can't allow him to have control over me." She rasps as she shakes her head. I watch as something changes in her expression, going from exhausted to completely wide awake as she takes a steadying breath in. "I have been sitting down for weeks, immobilized to a cage—"

She cuts herself off before the hand clutching onto the sheets pushes them away from her, forcing me out of the way as she stands up from the bed. "I need to be moving." She says, heading straight for the closet and opening it up.

As I am about to open my mouth and tell her what she needs to do is rest, my words die off at the tip of my tongue as my gaze lowers to her back. To the wounds that I know still lie beneath her silk robe.

She lowers the robe from her naked body, not even wincing as the material slips down her back. She pulls over a black loose-fitted shirt, smoothing it out over herself before pulling out a clean pair of underwear.

I watch her still for a moment, holding them in her hands as her fingers gently rub the material. She slips them on before pulling out a pair of leggings. "Is everyone still downstairs?"

I come closer to the closet, standing in the doorway. "Yes. No one has left yet."

"Good." She says, turning the closet light off and making her way to head out of the closet. "We have much to—"

I gently grab her by her shoulders, halting her for a moment and forcing her gaze up to mine. I watch the way her chest rises and sinks quickly, her breathing mimicking the eagerness I feel in her energy. The hyperalertness in her gaze as it roams over my face, unable to settle in one spot.

My hands raise up to gently cradle her face into my palms, watching as she takes a staggering breath in. "Okay.

We will go downstairs and discuss everything at hand. But first, just pause for a second with me. And *breathe*."

I watch her chest sink as she finally releases the breath she's been holding onto. I lower my hand down to lift her hand up to my chest, laying her palm flat there as I breathe with her. "Focus on nothing else for a moment, but what you feel right here. And breathe with me."

I watch Melinoë intently as I take a long breath in, watching her chest rise with mine to a silent count of four. Her gaze settled over my face as we exhaled together, repeating it again and again until I felt a faint tremor in her hand. Her skin no longer locked into stiffness and softening once again. The hardness around her eyes easing more and more as she breathes with me.

Intentionally guiding her back to the present, reminding her that she is with me. That she is safe again.

After several minutes of this I watch as her shoulders loosen the tension there, her fingers curling into my shirt as she steps closer to me. Her chest rising and falling at a steady, controlled pace now.

She raises her hand up to my jaw, rubbing her thumb along my cheek as she softly grins at me. "I needed that."

I bring both of my hands to hers, pulling it away from my face and pressing a kiss at the center of her palm. "I will bring you back as many times as you need me to, Melinoë. Your troubles are also mine, and I will devote as much time as needed to sit through them with you. To heal them, together."

Her eyes rim with dampness once again as her grin deepens. She lowers her hand from mine as she brings both of her hands up to my face, pulling me down closer until her lips press against mine. Her tears run down her cheeks, trickling past my lips as I cup my hands beneath her jaw.

I pull my lips away just enough to whisper into the space between us, "I love you."

She smiles against my hold. "I love you." She whispers as she kisses me again. I fall deeply into the feel of her lips against mine, allowing them to ground me into what is right now.

My twin soul.

The love of my life.

My goddess.

She pulls away as she looks up at me, watching as a vibrancy of life restores back into her gaze as she whispers, "Thank you."

I nod to her, stepping away as my arms fall at my sides. I grab her hand, cradling it in mine as I say, "You ready?"

She takes a steady breath in, releasing as she nods. "I'm ready."

We walk out of the closet, out of our bedroom, and make our way back downstairs. Her hand held snugly in mine, acting as the anchor to keep her tethered in the present as she prepares to reunite with everyone.

CHAPTER 58

Melinoë

As we walk into the living room my gaze falls on everyone seated around, waiting for when I would make my appearance after being asleep. The first person to make eye contact with me is my mother, her gaze widening slightly as she stands from the couch, facing me.

She rushes to me as I wrap my arms around her, her hands coming up to my shoulders as she gently squeezes me. Making sure not to press them against my back, against the wounds I still have yet to heal.

It's not that I don't want to heal them, it's just that suddenly they don't affect me as they once did. They don't hurt as badly now that my body has begun to heal them, though with Zeus' eather, he made it so that it takes far longer for them to heal. Even as a goddess.

I'll get to it later. Right now, there is a lot that needs to be talked about in regards to what is ultimately pending against us.

War.

My mother pulls away, tears rimming her eyes as she pushes a strand of my hair back from my face. She says nothing as she looks over my face, her mouth opening when Makaria rushes to our side.

Her eyes already reddened and puffy, her lip quivering as she pulls me into her. My arms wrapped tightly around my sister as we shed a few tears together.

I feel a tremor in her body ripple against me as she whispers into my ear, "I'm sorry it took me so long. I really tried to sooner—"

"Hey," I say gently as I pull her away, shaking my head as a tear trickles from my eye. "Don't do that to yourself." My voice lowering. "Don't allow *him* to manipulate you to feel that way." Narrowing my gaze on her.

Her golden gaze roams over my face before nodding, wiping her tears away as she forces a grin. "You're right." I watch as her back straightens a little taller, glad to notice the life simmering in her gaze again even through our tears. Hoping that that means during this time away from each other, she was able to find the peace that is owed to her.

I pull away as a familiar copper-headed woman makes her way to me. Instead of giving me a hug, she grasps my hands into hers as a warm smile lights her face. "It's really good to have you back, girl."

I nod curtly. "It's good to be home."

I continue to exchange greetings with everyone else, starting with Hecate and ending with Dionysus. "Sorry, I know this must be a lot."

His sapphire and emerald gaze locks onto mine as he vaguely shrugs his shoulders. "It's been different to say the least." He glances over at Dimitri who, for the first time, is not looking at Dionysus like he wants to kill him.

I give him a faint grin before I face everyone in the room, Reimus making his way back to my side, standing a foot behind me. My gaze roams over everyone here, those who are blood related and many who are not.

All who I know will fight for what is right, and will fight by my side.

"Thank you, for everything you've all done to get me back. I don't take what any of you have done lightly." I say, my throat threatening to choke up at those last words. "I understand that by now, everyone in here," My gaze lowers briefly to Dionysus. "Aside from Dionysus, knows about the prophecy. But as we were in the Casalas Mountains, I was given more information on where Zeus' allies truly lie. I was made aware that there are many in his palace that have done what I've done. Have persuaded to make him believe they are on his side, when there is a greater fate at hand."

"And you—" Dimitri says, stepping closer to us as his gaze hones in on Reimus. He briefly lowers his gaze to his hands. "You didn't even shift. You were able to shoot fire from your *hands*. The Draghi bloodline has never had that ability."

Reimus takes a step forward, nodding his head. "When Eiran had spoken with us, stating that we must follow Melinoë's extraction plan, I didn't understand why it needed to be followed through to each detail. Until I stepped foot onto that soil."

He looks over at me briefly, stepping closer to me as the memory of him blasting fire from his hands resurfaces. Never knowing that Reimus could do that before, knowing that we haven't had a chance to talk about it yet. Part of the reason why I wanted to meet with everyone right away so *everything* could finally be discussed at once.

"When I stepped foot onto that soil, I was transported to a memory of mine that had been long forgotten. Had been long buried, hidden with the essence that once ran through my veins." He looks over to Dimitri. "That runs through the Draghi bloodline's veins." He takes a calm breath in, releasing. "Before the Casalas Mountains were home to Zeus and his people, they were the ancestral home of the Draghi. It is where our people originated from."

"What?" Dimitri exclaims, shaking his head as confusion creases his face. "That's impossible. I would've—"

"Remembered?" Reimus asks coolly. When Dimitri says nothing, he nods slowly. "You do not remember because for your protection it was stripped from you, as was your essence. My mother and father, leaders of the Draghi bloodline, did this intentionally in case Zeus or any of his allegiances came sniffing for the truth of how far a drago's power extended to. It was a tactical move meant to preserve the power of our bloodline, to make Zeus believe we could only wield fire when shifted into our drago forms."

I watch as Reimus holds his hand facing up, an ember of fire lighting from his palm and smoldering calmly there. I watch it rise higher from his palm, willing it to dance along his skin before snuffing it out completely. "We all knew war was coming, but my mother was tipped off by a god who encouraged her that the only way to save our bloodline was to temporarily hide our essence in our land's soil. For me to one day reclaim, and awaken our people."

I turn to face Reimus, looking up at him. "It was Apollo." I say, looking at everyone else again. "When we were in the mountains, Apollo came for me. I thought he was coming to bring me back to the palace, but he showed me a memory of his. Of him and his sister, Artemis, watching over the Draghi in the mountains." I look back over at Reimus, "It was of both of them watching over your mother and father when your mother was pregnant with *you*."

He looks down at me, blinking once. "What else did it show?"

"It was of Apollo and Artemis talking to each other, asking when they were going to tip your mother off about Zeus' plan to take over their land. Your mother wasn't prophetic, she was given the fate of your people from Apollo."

Reimus looks at me for a beat of silence before I continue.

I turn around to everyone else in the room. "Apollo confirmed that for the survival of Reimus and the bloodline, that the essence was to be hidden until he reclaimed it. But he also said something else." My gaze roams over Dimitri. "They kept talking about how those who survive will be hidden in plain sight. So..." I look up at Reimus.

"You mean to tell me that there are more of our people out there?" Dimitri exclaims, both relief and concern on his face.

"I believe there are, as when I was given back my memories from taking the essence back, I received similar visions. It was a ritual of me giving my essence back to the land to hide it, but everyone around me who participated in the ritual chanted the same. That they were to be hidden in plain sight until the time was right."

I watch as he shakes his head, relief pooling in his features but the rigidness of *where* they are floods his gaze. That somehow, Artemis and his mother and father figured out a way to possibly preserve anyone's bodies who survived the war on their land. That instead of it just being Dimitri and Reimus left, there could be more out there.

Waiting to be brought home again.

I go to grab his hand, directing his gaze back to mine. "We will find them. Together." I remind him.

He lowers his gaze to mine, nodding before lifting it to everyone else.

"So Vulir isn't where the Draghi originate from?" Nora asks from her stance near the fireplace.

Reimus shakes his head. "Vulir has always remained what it is. A home for those seeking refuge and solace. When I arrived here with Dimitri, we were granted immediate access by Charon. When asked about what the protocols are for keeping the people here safe, that's when the title Guardian was awarded to us. Before that it was as if

Vulir was hidden from a map. No one knew about it except for the people who resided within it."

I look over at Hades standing near my mother, his gaze wholly on Reimus until he looks at me. "Is that true?"

Hades nods. "Vulir has been around for many, many years. Yet no one safeguarded it until they arrived. Before that, it was just the shield I maintained around it as nobody really knew about Vulir."

I look at everyone and watch as the whirlwind of information seeps itself into their gazes. Dionysus looking as if he's just been revealed an entirely alternate reality to the one he's been living in, been hidden away from. Hecate's gaze is steady, yet curious as she processes it all.

"Did you see anything else?" Reimus asks from beside me.

I look up at him, hesitating before nodding my head slowly. "There was discussion between them in the memory of you and I bringing harmony to the lands both North and South. That with our union a new reign of power would rise. I didn't understand what she meant by union though."

I watch as Reimus' expression changes, glancing over to the rest of the room.

I tilt my head. "What am I missing here?"

"Oh, this will be interesting." Hecate says from where she stands.

Reimus lowers his gaze to me, taking a breath in before telling me what he found out while I was gone. That when they realized that my talisman protected him too, that Hecate dug into the why of it.

I stare at him for a long moment, blinking before words can form again. "Twin souls?" I say breathlessly.

I had only heard of that term once, from a fairytale book that my sister read when she was little. A phenomenon that two people who were fated to be united together shared one soul, split into two vessels. Two bodies.

My mind swarms with what Eiran told me a while ago, something that always stuck with me but had never understood its meaning.

You meeting Reimus happened for a reason. You may not be ready yet, but you will see soon that he is the catalyst in more ways than one.

Our paths crossed for a reason, but yours crossed with him for an entirely different one.

"The prophecy—" I begin, looking up at Reimus. "It said that my soul would be shared with the one who heralds fire. It—makes sense."

"I'm still a little lost here." Dionysus chimes in as everyone looks to him. "What prophecy?"

I watch as my mother's gaze pierces into his for a moment, something settling over her features before forcing herself to smooth it out.

I lift my gaze to Dionysus, and tell him what I was told by the Pythia.

After I finish, his eyes widen as he looks over at my mother—his *first* mother. He stares at her for a moment before saying, "I lived my whole life turning a blind eye to Zeus' cruelty. Not because I wanted to but because it was easier to…" He trails off as he shakes his head. "I am very sorry for what he has done to you."

Persephone steps towards him, her chest sinking as she stares upon the man who holds her first born's soul inside. She approaches him, tentatively reaching for his hands as he allows her to grab them. I watch as her back trembles as she clasps his hands in hers, loosening a shuddering breath before willing her composure over again. They exchange a moment of silence together before my mother nods her head, stepping back from him again.

Watching as that interaction alone healed something within her. Not at what Dionysus said, but at the chance to hold her son's hand again. Knowing that though he's been reincarnated, that she can still feel his energy from just a simple touch.

"So…" Makaria says as she loosens a long exhale, her gaze fixated aimlessly before shifting it to me. "Where do we begin?"

I look up at Reimus as he nods. "My mother was given the Draghi bloodline's fate from Apollo himself, which tells me that his alliance—along with his sister's, truly doesn't align with supporting Zeus. If there are more of our people out there," He exchanges a glance with Dimitri. "Then we need to figure out how to bring our people back. Before we begin to prepare to take back our land."

Hades locks gazes with Reimus. "While Zeus is still King, he will never willingly allow you to have claim over that land again."

"Correct." Reimus looks down at me, already knowing what he's about to say. Maybe that fact alone proves that we're truly twin souls. That I could just give him one look and he'd understand what it is I would say if I were the one speaking right now. That silently, we're both on the same page.

He turns his gaze back to Hades. "Which means if we're going to take back the land of the Casalas Mountains, then we must take over Olympia."

Nora and Makaria both jerk their heads back in surprise as Hecate's eyes widen. But it's Hecate that speaks out first. "Take over Olympia?" She repeats slowly.

I nod at her. "The prophecy spoke of me being Zeus' greatest threat. I thought it was just because our gifts are so different, but that was until Apollo let me see into his memories."

I fix my gaze onto Hades as he watches me, listening intently. "When I was—" I hesitated for a moment before continuing, Reimus reaching for my hand and squeezing it gently. "Zeus initially would have me practice with him. I thought he was just trying to see to what extent my gifts—my shadows lied, but that was until I realized with Apollo's memory he was trying to see if it were true. That I possessed similar powers to his."

My mother steps forward beside Hades. "And what is that?"

I lower my gaze to my hand as I lift it up. I take a breath in, releasing as I will myself to remember in my mind.

I am not him.

This does not mean I am anything like him.

As I will my power to the surface I watch as everyone's eyes widen at what dances along my fingertips. Not the shadows gathered there, but tiny sparks of lightning.

I lift my gaze up. "When he took your fate," I say, looking at Hades. "He damned not only your chance at having children, but also The Fates themselves. As we were not meant to be Zeus' children."

I lift my hand a little higher, willing the sparks of lightning to form into pointed spikes as tendrils of shadow billow out from my fingers. Intertwining themselves together. "But The Fates then in return damned him. Giving me not only the gifts I should've inherited from Hades, but Zeus as well."

Hades watches my hand in awe as he stares at the two different powers colliding together.

"There was a reason why Zeus despised me the most. It was because even though he manipulated that prophecy for his gain, I still came out with the qualities of who my father should've been. And that greatly angered him, but also why he kept me close because he suspected that if I had both his and your powers, I would be a great threat to him." I will the shadows and spark of lightning away, retracting that energy back into myself. "It is why it must be me who kills him."

Hades lifts his gaze from my hands to my face, shock and understanding both settling there. But as I look at him, I watch something else swarm his gaze.

Pride.

"I have strong reasons to believe that Zeus' first method of attack will not be on Vulir, but will be on the people of Elzwin instead. I'd like to immediately start working on portaling everyone here to Vulir, where they will be safe inside of the shield."

Dimitri steps forward as he exchanges a glance with Reimus. "Where are we going to put everyone? We're already stunted on the amount of land and housing we have left."

"I can extend the shield."

I look over at Hades as he speaks.

"With the extension, we can will more housing down." My mother says as Hades steps to her side. "Melinoë is right. Zeus won't come here outright. He'll retaliate against Elzwin first."

Dimitri nods his head then. "What can we do?" He says looking to Reimus. "What will we tell our people?"

I look at him dead in the eyes as a faint grin curves my lips. "The truth."

I look up at Reimus, feeling the brush of his arms as I say, "Once you all brought me back home, there was no turning back." I look over Makaria then Nora, my gaze roaming to everyone before me. "The inevitable has already begun. This is the beginning of war."

CHAPTER 59

Twin souls.

Those two words float themselves around my mind, bouncing off of the walls and blaring their presence again. The truth of that statement seemingly feels so right. So…guided.

I hiss as I scrunch my shoulders together at the brief sting.

"Sorry," Nora says tenderly from behind me, my arms folded beneath my chin as I lay on my belly. "These wounds are pretty deep."

"Shouldn't be much longer now." Hecate gently reassures as she works beside Nora.

After meeting with everyone—and then finally explaining to Reimus and Dimitri the backstory of Dionysus, I was ordered by Hecate to allow her and Nora to heal me before we did anything else. At the sternness in her gaze filled with worry, I agreed.

"Semele told me she purposefully left my necklace for you to find it." I say over my shoulder to Hecate. "She said she knew it would help one way or another."

Hecate continues using her eather alongside Nora's healing abilities to heal the open wounds on my back. Her concentration wholly on my back as she says, "So she knew it was spelled to protect you?"

I nod my head as I lower it back to the tops of my hands. "She said she felt its power, that it was tailored for not one but two souls. She knew you'd try to do a locator spell on it."

"But she still helped Zeus kidnap you." Nora reminds me.

I stare at the headboard to mine and Reimus' bed, loosening a breath. "That she did."

"Are you insinuating that you forgive her?" Nora asks.

The disbelief I felt overcrowding my heart and my gut that day in the forest plagues me again momentarily. To look at Semele and wonder why after everything we had done to help her in Vulir, feeling so confused and betrayed by her actions. A part of me still does.

But after hearing her story, to the small acts of sneaking me food and bringing me baths, my lens on her behavior has shifted as a clear reasoning for her actions became apparent.

"No, I don't." I grimace at the feel of my skin closing over on my back. A feeling that isn't terribly unpleasant, but isn't enjoyable either. "I just see from another perspective why she did the things she did."

"What if she comes back? To see Dionysus." Hecate asks.

All of these solutions come forward in my mind. Ones where I lock her up, to see how she enjoys being manipulated and broken down to just a woman shackled to a cage. Another solution where I match blow for blow, hoping to hit as hard—if not harder, then she did that day.

But as I lay here now, I can't even begin to allow myself to ruminate on what would happen if she came back. Would I be angry at her again? Would I be more forgiving because of her underlying intentions for just trying to keep her son safe?

Yet all that matters at this very moment is getting the people out of Elzwin and over here to Vulir. The rest can wait. "I don't know, honestly."

A while passes until Hecate and Nora finish healing the wounds on my back. When I stand up I notice the tautness that was once there is now gone, the reminder of those whips against my back no longer a memory on my body.

Now only a thing of my mind.

I lower my hand to my back, feeling the smooth skin there before giving them both a nod. "Thank you."

They both give me a smile as Hecate says, "Are you ready?"

I take a long breath in before releasing, nodding as I smooth my shirt down. "Ready."

And with both of them at my side, we exit out of the Guardian's Palace and make our way to the village hall. Where Dimitri and Reimus have gathered all of our people so I can inform them of what is to come.

"Thank you all for coming on such short notice. I promise I will not take up much of your time here." I say aloud to the people of Vulir. Each of them standing in the village hall with their eyes on me as Reimus and Dimitri stand guard at the entrance doors.

"As some of you have noticed, I have been away for a period of time." I pause, feeling my nerves rise within me as I look down the hall to Reimus. His gaze already on mine as he gives me a soft grin, his presence stilling those nerves from overriding me. Giving me that small boost of confidence, of grounding energy, to keep going.

I look back out onto the crowd of people. "During which time I was taken prisoner by he who is referred to as The King of Gods. My father."

I hear whispers float around the room as soft gasps go off.

"As you can see, I have escaped with the help of those close to me." I give Reimus a small half grin. "But though I have escaped, it unfortunately does not mean that this is over yet." I steady my voice as I straighten my back, saying clearly, "As Zeus will retaliate, and we are to make the necessary, cautionary preparations in light of what is to come. Which is war."

I listen as people turn towards each other, their whispers turning into talking. Their gasps turned into fearful, widened gazes. Seeing the beginning stages of worry settling in. Knowing this was inevitably going to be the reaction, but hoping I can ease it with what I say next.

"I do not tell you all this to frighten you, to ensue panic amongst you all. I tell you the truth, because as someone who has lived in the shadows most of her life, I know how crucial honesty is. How important having the veil lifted from one's vision is, and to see the raw truth of what is right before our eyes instead of being lied and deceived to. Because true power does not lie in oppressing others, it lies in feeding them the knowledge they deserve to know to survive."

I watch as several people's heads turn towards me. Their words dying in hushed tones, silence sweeping over them as they watched me curiously.

"The King and Queen of The Underworld are outside at the perimeter right now, extending the shield of Vulir. This will allow us more land to build homes for those in need, for those who need our protection now more than ever. As though the times ahead may still be uncertain, one thing we can always count on is the shield that Hades instills for our protection. That no other village is blessed to have but us."

I lower myself from the podium, bringing myself closer to the floor as people begin to open up for me. Creating a cleared passageway for me to slowly walk through as I continue to speak.

"One would say that a community, first and foremost, is only as strong as its leader is. That only then can the strength of a leader inspire and invoke courage upon the people that follow them." I take a few steps forward, merging myself deeper into the crowd as silence surrounds the room. "But I say that's false."

I lift my gaze to Reimus, seeing his gaze piercing onto mine as pride swims in his grin.

"There is absolutely nothing more powerful than a community of people who can, at all of the odds and uncertainty presented to them, still find a way to fight for change and for what is right. All it takes is just one person to stand up, for everyone else to find that same courage within themselves to do the same. And when we all band together, we all fight together. As *one*. So I understand your impending worries, and I promise that I will care for them as if they are my own. Because though Vulir has only been my home for a short amount of time, there is nothing I won't do to keep everyone who resides in it safe."

I stop at the center of the room, the middle of the walkway paved for me as I roam over each and every single person in attendance. "So as we put down these new homes, and merge people over from a village that is currently in danger, all I ask is to open your arms to them as willingly as you have opened yours up to me. Some of them—if not all, will be frightened just as you all are. They will be confused, and will most likely be grieving a home they are forced to leave behind." I pause for a moment. "So let us all come together as a community, and *unite* together to protect what is our basic, individual right. To *live* peacefully."

As everyone in the room has their eyes on me, I do the one thing I was always adamant about keeping a secret. No longer feeling the need to run from who I am, and what I bear any longer as I let who I am slip intentionally.

My divinity, no matter how dark or terrifying, makes up who I am. The darkness within encompassing all that I have survived, all that I have faced to get to this point now. To stand in a room full of people and not cower from who or what I am, but to embrace it as what it is.

A strength.

Shadows begin to slither out of my fingertips, falling to the ground like mist as gasps sound around the room. Coiling around my feet and remaining close to me as I stand tall before these people, revealing myself completely to them. "Because I vow as Guardian of Souls, Goddess of Nightmares, that anyone who threatens what you have all maintained for centuries, will find judgement by my hands. And I will show them no mercy."

I stand there as everyone remains silent for a long time, noticing that Reimus hasn't stepped forward at all yet to say a few words. But by the look on his face, I can see it in his eyes.

That I do not need him by my side to make my point across to our people.

But as I look at him now, I watch as his grin remains in place as he slowly lowers down to one knee. Raising his right hand over his heart, he bows his head slightly but still keeping his gaze on me.

My breath hitches as I watch Dimitri lower himself down next to him, emitting the same gesture as people in the crowd turn to look at them.

They don't need to do that, it's not necessary—

My gaze catches on Quinn, a soft grin curving his lips as I notice he's already lowered himself down to one knee. Holding his right hand over his heart and his head slightly bowed.

I watch as each and every person in here does the same, all of them slowly lowering down like dominoes until I'm the only one left standing.

"Guardian of Souls." One woman rings out. "We honor you, in all realms and timelines, as Guardian of Vulir."

"Guardian of Souls." Everyone else in attendance repeats after her. "We honor you, in all realms and timelines, as Guardian of Vulir." They say in unison.

Unable to help the dampness that's formed in my eyes as I watch everyone stay kneeling, that even with what I've bore to them that they have all deemed me as worthy and deserving of such a title.

Claiming me as a Guardian of Vulir, as one of their own.

CHAPTER 60

I step outside onto the cobblestone road as the soft words of the village people follow behind me, their steps hurried with determination and purpose as they all meander away from the village hall.

"I have some woven blankets on hand." One seamstress replied when the village butcher announced he was able to give out an excess of beef to those in need. My heart swimming with warmth at their immediate effort to begin preparing for the arrival of the people of Elzwin.

I look out past the strip of shops lining the cobblestone road to the array of cottage homes where I watch pillars of wood being placed down. Wooden pillars begin to form a gable roof before hickory colored bricks cover it. Bay windows fitting themselves in the open grooves on the lower level as casement windows line the top half of the cottage.

I turn around to face Reimus. "I'm going to see if they need any help."

He nods, his gaze roaming my face. "I'm going to make sure the perimeter is secured. Dimitri will help where he can here and I'll meet you over there when I'm finished."

He raises a hand to my cheek, gently swiping his thumb there as he smiles. I lean into his touch as my lashes flutter open, nodding into his touch.

His gaze traces over my face as if taking in every crevice, every groove of my skin and framing it to memory. His smile deepens as he says, "You are *extraordinary*, Melinoë."

He leans down and kisses me, the moment quick but taking my breath away nonetheless. His lips hover above mine as he whispers, "Never forget that."

He steps away as his hand slowly lowers from my face, turning around and leaping into the air as he shifts into his drago form. The large swipe of his tail nearly knocking out the water fountain at the center of the village.

I chuckle to myself as I turn my gaze back over to the cottages, willing a portal open and stepping through it.

I step out to see Hades with his hands out, his palms facing towards the homes as he wills the foundation down with large wooden pillars. My mother standing a few feet from him as I watch her will windows into an already built home. A wooden mahogany door installed at the front of the cottage, clear-beveled glass panels willing into the top half of the door.

"Need any help?" I yell out.

My mother turns around to face me as she gives me a wide grin. "There might be something you could help with, actually."

I approach her side as she lowers her hands, the cottage in front of us now finished. "Come." She rests her hand on my back as she ushers us forward.

We step inside to complete emptiness as my mother leaves the door ajar, walking further inside as she stands in what I'd presume to be the living room. "Hades and I are off to a great start. We're confident that we can have enough houses done by nightfall, ready for the people of Elzwin to move in first thing tomorrow."

I watch as my mother begins willing pieces of furniture down into the room around us, starting with the room we stand in. A light beige couch appears behind me, taking a few steps back as a low-rise coffee table appears where I was just standing. She begins willing all of the appliances necessary for a kitchen—a stove, refrigerator, sink, light daffodil colored countertops and cabinets. I hear a ruffle of furniture being arranged on the floor above us, assumingly placing beds and dressers above.

I watch as she wills a metal chandelier at the center of the dining room. Beautiful champagne-colored, dusted glass bulbs with unlit light bulbs screwed within.

"I can magically arrange for electricity to be powered into each and every cottage."

I look over at her, tilting my head.

She gives me a faint grin as she steps closer to me. "Or you can power it yourself."

It takes a brief moment for what she's saying to register. The realization I came to that after all this time of disconnecting myself from Zeus entirely, I still held some of the same gifts he has. Having conflicting emotions about whether I'm okay with that or not, the point still stands.

I shake my head slowly. "I haven't learned—*allowed* myself to fully tap into that power yet." I bring my hands together, facing my palms up at me as I stare down at them. "I'm still coming to terms with the fact that I share it at all."

My mother gently grabs my hands, forcing my gaze onto hers. "The gifts that flow in your blood do not determine who you are, but you can choose *how* you use them."

I sigh as I let her words sink in.

"Utilizing the gifts that were bestowed upon you does not mean you are anything like him." She ensures, softly squeezing my hands. "You can either run from the fact that you share his thunder, his lightning. Or you can decide to use it for *good*."

She steps back away from me as she walks closer to the chandelier, looking up at it. "I had always wondered if any of my children possessed the same gifts as him. Whether that be shapeshifting, or the power to wield lighting." I approach her side as I lift my gaze to her face. "But I never for a second imagined one of them to possess the same gifts as Hades. And even in the fucked up situation of it all," She pauses as she turns to look at me. "You possess what Zeus never imagined possible. Powers that belong to two Kings in two vastly different realms. Shadows of darkness, and the fire of lightning."

She faces fully towards me as she places her hands on my shoulders, narrowing her chin. "Remember, it is not about where your power originates from, but how you use it. All you need to do is let go of the fear that surrounds it, like you did when you worked with Hades to let go of the fear around utilizing your shadows."

She steps back as she folds her hands in front of her lap. I glance up at the chandelier, studying it as my palms begin to dampen with the nerves in my body. A coiling tension blossoming from deep in my chest at the thought of having more similarities to Zeus then I ever wanted to have. But my mother is right, power is just that. It doesn't mean that I'm still anything like him—

No. Zeus uses his power to manipulate others. To *control* the people of Olympia and those closest to him. And I—

I am nothing like him.

I put the needs of people before myself, sometimes to a depleting fault. I use my voice not to berate others, but to build people up. To enliven strength and courage in the people of Vulir, and soon to be Elzwin. Because who I am is the kind of person who sees people as individuals, not self-serving objects.

The kind of person who spends her days tending to offerings left behind in the cemetery of those who have passed on. Because even in the afterlife I believe the souls deserve to be remembered, to be protected. Because even in death, their lives still matter.

As I look up at my mother, I take a steadying breath in as I will my power to the center. Focusing not on those thick tendrils of shadows, but on the sparks of lightning they absorbed once before. Reclaiming as their own.

I lift my palms up, feeling the power begin to slighter and crackle gently beneath my skin. Feeling as if tiny pricks are bubbling to the surface as I will it higher to the surface.

After a few moments of steady breathing and trying to pull it forward, I watch as sparks of light form at my fingertips. My eyes widening slightly as I look up to my mother, her gaze wholly on my hands with a soft grin on her face.

The sparks become bigger, brighter as they zap between my fingertips like electricity coursing along my skin. I smirk as I look up at the lightbulbs, raising my fingers and pointing them up as I will that energy to move from me. Extending it outward.

I watch as those sparks lift off my fingertips, shooting out towards the bulbs and merging themselves within. It happens within a blink of an eye but shortly after, a warm glow emanates from the once unlit glass bulb.

My breath hitches as I look down at my mother again, the glow of the light above us that I produced casting along her face. Her grin deepens as she says, "Want to try the other cottages we've already put down?"

As a wide grin of my own forms, I nod eagerly as I leave the cottage with my mother.

And as Hades and my mother continue to lay down more cottages, I will electricity into every single one of them.

CHAPTER 61

Reimus

I soar through the sky as I pass the shield, heading into the Sephyra Forest. Wanting to make one final sweep and stop before I met back with Melinoë.

I glide over the treeline, looking down below for one particular area that I know he'll be in. And when I see him down below, I begin swooping downwards. Shifting right before I land onto the forest floor.

Sage looks up at me, chuckling as he turns around. "Nice of you to pay me a visit, Guardian."

I give him a half grin as I say, "I figured it was only right for me to check in with you. And to also give you the news that Melinoë is home."

His face smooths over as he looks at me, stepping towards me. "Our Lady of Vulir has made her safe return home. That is splendid news."

"It is." I say, the eagerness to get back to her ramping up in my body suddenly. "Though the fight does not end there, I'm sure you'd imagine."

Sage chuckles as he goes to seat himself down on a log crafted into a chair, armrests protruding at the sides as he rests his pale arms down. "I imagine he is not thrilled at her escape, and his anger will be catastrophic." He looks at me for a moment of silence. "I imagine this means you are here to offer me, once again, to join you on the other side of the shield."

I nod my head. "I cannot guarantee your safety out here, but I can within the border of Vulir. We are making arrangements to evacuate the people of Elzwin."

I watch as a hawk lands on a branch up above, ruffling its feathers before tucking them in behind him. His beady little gaze narrows down onto me, tilting his head as he stares at me. Observing.

"I appreciate your offer, but I will remain where I am. But do not fear for me, shifter. I am not alone out here." He narrows his chin.

I lift my gaze up to the hawk again, lowering it back down.

"Besides, she's already warned me of such…impending destruction."

I tilt my head at him. "Who?"

"She who hunts. She whose wild nature matches those who dwell in this forest and beyond."

My brows knit together as I open my mouth to speak, Sage cutting me off as he lifts a hand up. "I would appreciate a visit from Melinoë whenever she is willing, however. When it is safe to do so." He lowers his hand back down, a calmness etched into his features. "I do miss what joy it is to be in her company."

I close my mouth, taking that as a sign that Sage isn't willing to come with me and is not budging on leaving the forest. At his words, I simply nod my head as I say, "I will be sure to tell her. Be safe, Sage."

Sage nods his head as the hawk above lifts himself off the branch, spreading his wings as he flies away. "Likewise."

I turn around, shifting back into my drago form and take to the skies. I make my way back to the village, over to where I see numerous new cottages laid down, grinning at the impeccable progress made so far.

I swoop down, watching both Hades and Persephone's gaze lifting to mine. Shifting before I've reached the ground. "Your tail was this close to swiping out this roof I just installed." Hades states.

I chuckle as I approach him. "Sorry, I'm not used to having an abundance of new homes here. I'll try to be more careful."

He scoffs at me, lifting his lips into a half grin as he nods to a nearby cottage. "She's inside there."

"Thanks." I say before turning to head towards the nearby cottage.

"Reimus."

I turn back around to face Hades.

He gives me a softened look as he says, "Forgive Persephone, but she told me of what you planned the day Melinoë was taken."

I blink at him as my mind wanders to the velvet black box, sitting at home tucked deeply away in my dresser drawer. Having wanted to present it to her as soon as we got back and after she awoke, but wondered if the gesture would've seemed rushed and forced. "I don't know if right now is the right time. She's been through a lot."

Hades gives me a look, a grin curving up his lips. "No one moment will ever be the perfect time." He looks over to his wife, a soft longing gaze forming. "Life is unpredictable, it's chaotic and messy. When you find someone willing to weather both the storms and the euphoria of it, then time becomes nonexistent when love prevails every waking moment together."

I look over to Peresphone, too far away to hear what he's saying but looking over at him nonetheless. She gives him a warm smile as her features light up just by his gaze alone. A subtle glow radiating on her face before she faces the home she's willing a roof onto.

He turns his gaze back to me. "It would be wise to assume that things will get worse before they get better." Knowing he's referencing the fate of the realms, to the villages. To the war that is impending. "There will always be reasons that make you feel like you should wait. The demands of being a leader hanging over both of your heads." He pauses for a beat of a moment. "But at the end of the day, when you two are together, that's all that truly matters in the end. Twin souls or not, that kind of love prevails every challenge you will ever face together."

I let his words settle inside of me, stirring a storm of emotions that encompass the turmoil of wanting to ask her to marry me, and also wondering if I should wait. But he's right.

I don't want to wait. I want to ask the woman I love to marry me *now*.

To make her into my fiance.

Because with the unpredictability of life, tomorrow is not always guaranteed. There will always be reasons to wait, and I have no desire to any longer.

I look back over to the cottage that Hades said Melinoë was in before shifting my gaze back to him. "If Melinoë asks for me, can you tell her I got caught up in the village?" A ridiculously wide grin curving my lips. "Tell her that I'll meet her at home. Maybe...keep her occupied here for another hour or so?"

Hades gives me an approving nod as a grin of his own forms. "Will do."

I give him a nod. "Thank you." I say before turning on my heels and shifting back into my drago form.

I hurry my way over to The Guardian's Palace—our home, to put something together for Melinoë for when she returns.

The whole time my heart racing and beating wildly inside of my chest. A giddiness ensuing within as I put all of our impending worries on the back burner for now.

CHAPTER 62

Melinoë

I step out onto our bedroom floor, the portal closing behind me as I go over to the closet to change when I halt. A note on our dresser catching my eye as I walk over towards it. Smiling at the familiar handwriting.

Meet me downstairs when you're ready

I grin at the note as I set it back down, heading back over to the closet to change out of my leggings and shirt. I pull out an ankle-length, pale yellow tiered skirt, setting it aside as I grab a black long-sleeved shirt. I make my way over to the bathroom, taking care of my personal needs and freshening up before getting dressed.

As I pull on the shirt I immediately feel the edge of the cotton sleeves rubbing against my wrists. Even at the softness of the fabric I take a staggering breath in, my pulse picking up as I can only focus on the tightness around my skin.

I go to wrap my hand around my wrist, rubbing the skin there and reminding myself that my wrists aren't bound any longer.

It's just a shirt.

But at the tightness of the sleeves, I quickly pull them up to my elbows. Feeling relief immediately wash over me as the air kisses my wrists.

I look at myself in the mirror, taking a few deep breaths in and out as my palms rest on the bathroom counter. The rough stone wall I'd become familiar with replacing the smooth marble surface beneath my fingertips. A taunting phantom smell of that dark cell threatens to cement me in place when I force it out, shutting it all down.

I'm free.

I'm home.

I'm safe.

The words I repeat inside of my head do little to soothe the panic blossoming in my stomach. As I go to straighten myself I feel the bones in my back softly cracking, pulling my hands away from the hard surface as I lift one beneath my shirt. Pressing my fingertips to my bare back.

"They're gone." I repeat out loud to myself, closing my eyes as I take a deep breath in. Feeling the smooth skin there that has replaced the open wounds left by Zeus' whips of lightning. "I'm free."

As I continue to settle my breathing, focusing on my wound-less back, I hear the sound of birds chirping outside. Opening my eyes and lowering my hand from beneath my shirt as I walk out of the bathroom, closer to the sound.

I look over to our balcony door and see a bird fly past the window. Never having heard them outside there before, but knowing that birds only chirp in environments where it is safe.

Because here, with Reimus, I *am* safe.

A faint grin curves up my lips briefly before I make my way downstairs, wondering where exactly Reimus wanted me to meet him. I don't have to wonder for long though as when I reach the main floor, I see Aven standing there waiting for me. "Good evening, My Lady."

I chuckle softly to him. "Aven, what has Reimus got planned now?" I ask, raising a brow.

A wide grin—probably the most genuine smile I've ever seen on Aven's face appears. And as a man who is always jolly and in high spirits, that's saying a lot.

He takes my hand, leading me away from the stairs and down the hallway. "You shall find out." He leans in, speaking softly as the hint of excitement is evident in his voice.

I peer at him with a mischievous grin. As I open my mouth to ask him what's going on, I feel the presence of another waiting for me towards the end of the hall.

Reimus.

My twin soul.

He stands there with his arms tucked behind his back casually, dressed in mostly his usual attire. Though this time instead of a white shirt over his black pants, he wears a matching button-up black shirt. The buttons at the top of his collar undone and open. His hair combed and slicked back aside from the few strands hanging above his brow.

As we approach him, he gives a satisfied look to Aven. "Thank you, Aven. I'll take it from here." He says steadily before reaching for my hand from Aven's.

Aven gives him a nod before turning on his heels, walking in the opposite direction down the hall.

I turn my gaze back to Reimus, tilting my head. "What is all of this?"

He comes to my side, tucking my hand between his elbow as his hand lightly rests against his chest. He guides us through the open doorway, stepping into the hallway that leads to the back terrace.

At the thought of the terrace, and the pastures at the end of it, my breath hitches as I think of—

"Alastor." I say breathlessly, jerking my gaze to Reimus. I take a shuddering breath in before quickly releasing. "You knew I'd want to see him." I lower my gaze down to his attire, still perplexed.

"Yes, but that is not the only reason why we're going outside."

As we make our way down the hallway the setting sun casts its golden, orange rays through the windows on our left. I glance over, knitting my brows at what I could easily see through clearly the hand beveled glass windows now seeming to be blocked by something—

"I never told you the story about the day I met you at the shield." Reimus says as his other hand comes to mine tucked beneath his elbow. "You were what I thought was this girl trying to gain access to Vulir, to the refuge that we offer to our people." He looks over at me. "Little did I know that you would amount to far more than that."

As we reach the middle of the hallway I hear those same birds chirping again, this time coming from the end of the hallway leading to outside. I grin to myself at the welcoming sound, at the words Reimus speaks.

"But as I looked upon you, I was curiously drawn to you. It was as if a magnetic weight had pulled me towards you, until suddenly I was finding myself taking any excuse to be near you." His hand lightly squeezes mine. "To feel your touch."

I give him a warm grin.

"But the first night you came home from mentoring with Hecate, and I saw the look on your face—your energy, I knew." We step closer to the door leading outside when I get a strange whiff of something.

Lavender, mingled with the gentle sounds of water running. I lift my gaze up, wondering if there is a leak somewhere when I lower it back down.

"I knew that by how protective I immediately felt towards you, that you would change everything in my life. In the most soul-widening, most predominant ways. And as I sat with you while you drifted off to sleep that night, I immediately saw the reward in everything I had faced prior to you."

Tears begin to well in my eyes at the thoughtfulness in his words, the weight that they carry. His poetic way of speaking love into my life, into me.

We near the terrace entrance when that soft sound of water falling intensifies, growing louder as I look through the beveled glass door and gasp at a large dark object situated outside of it. My other hand comes up to my mouth as he opens the door.

"And I knew that I would spend the rest of my life showing you what a true gift you are. How valued and treasured you are to me."

The door opens up as the breath from my lungs gets trapped in my throat. My gaze landing on the object I saw through the glass doors. A large, limestone tiered water fountain. The water I heard running off the edge, splashing and falling into the large fiore pond below. I watch as birds perch on the edge of the basin, dipping themselves into the water and ruffling their feathers as they bathe themselves.

I lower my gaze to the red brick laid beneath my feet, at what used to be all grass. I stare at it for a long moment before lifting my gaze up to Reimus, tears in my eyes. "You did all of this?"

He gives me a wide grin as he says, "You haven't even seen the rest of the garden yet."

Garden? I—

Suddenly the scent of lavender catches my attention again, turning my gaze to where it came from. And as I look up, my breath catches in my chest again at the pathway leading out to the rest of the terrace—

No, no longer an empty terrace at all.

The red brick beneath our feet leads up into a curved pathway as foliage and plants line the walkway. My gaze lifting even higher at the basswood trees planted all along the landscape, filling the emptiness that was once before. Sweeping lavender bushes are intricately placed throughout the garden as trimmed bushes and shrubs are tucked against the exterior wall.

I go to take an aimless step forward when the birds draw my attention to them again, noticing something that I didn't before.

Situated around the fountain are two black garden benches with plush cream-colored cushions. I blink at them as I realize—

He'd given me a little area for me to sit out here and read, just like I had told him I would be interested in had I lived here and redecorated.

He places his hand over mine as he guides us deeper into our garden, my gaze tracking over every little detail that he put into it. Hyacinth planted near asphodel flowers with little bird feeders strategically placed throughout. My chest sinks heavy as a tear falls down my cheek, feeling blown away by this man's kindness. By his utter devotion to wanting to see me happy, to show me he loves me.

And gods I have never known love to be so beautiful, so effortlessly reciprocated to me, than when I met him.

I look up at him as we walk through our garden. "You did all of this while I was away?" I ask, my words ending on a choked cry.

He nods down at me. "I knew that there was a set out plan that we had to follow to ensure your safest return home, but I found myself incredibly restless to say the least. Even…unsure of my competence at times."

My heart breaks at his words as I stop walking, turning towards him as I free my hand from his elbow and place it onto his chest. I shake my head as more tears stream down my face. "You are not incompetent. You *helped* me while I was there."

I watch his chest sink as he lifts a hand to the tear running down my cheek, wiping it away.

"When you visited me in the astral realm, your presence alone helped give me that spark I was beginning to lose there. *You* saved me, Rei."

I watch as he works on a swallow, emotion clouding his gaze as he grins down at me. He brings his lips to mine, losing myself in the feel of his touch. Melting into his presence.

He pulls away as he glances up behind me. "Come, I have one more thing to show you."

Anticipation clouds my mind as he turns me around, guiding us both deeper into the garden when I halt completely.

"As I put all of this together for us—for *you*, I realized there was one more thing that I needed to build. A space that I hope can aid you in feeling safe after some time."

I release my hand from his grasp as I walk towards it, my mouth hanging wide open as I look at it in its entirety. I reach my hand out to touch the red mahogany wood, my fingertips gliding along a window that fills the entirety of the wall. With seven more of them to wrap around the entirety of the structure.

Around the little garden house, the little gazebo that Reimus built me.

I lower my shaken gaze to the door, pulling the handle and going to step inside when I halt. I look down at the door, searching for the lock when I realize there isn't one.

"I made sure I installed a door that did not have one."

My hand trembles from the door as I turn around to face him.

"When I would visit you in the astral realm, I quickly knew that small spaces would be triggering for you for some time. As would dark spaces."

My chest heaves at his words, staring at him as a tear rolls down my cheek.

"I knew in my heart that I wanted to help in any way that I could, to help you through whatever harrowing thoughts you would have once you came back home to me. So," He begins as he steps closer to the gazebo. "I installed it with large enough windows. To not only let in lots of light, but also to help you feel not as if you are closed off in a cell, but connected to our little oasis. To the rest of the world." His hand extends to our garden surrounding it.

He lowers his hand as he taps the door. "A door without locks, and if that is even too much I will remove the door myself. Whatever it takes to help you feel safe. And inside," He lifts his hand to what awaits us inside of the gazebo.

I turn around to see a small crystal chandelier hanging from the center of the roof. The warm, orange light casting itself onto a small wooden shelf set to the side. White pillar candles set on top of it as their steady flames mimic the warmth from the setting sun outside.

From the warmth blooming in my chest.

My gaze lowers to the beige sofa and wooden coffee table below the chandelier, saffron throw pillows set neatly against the sofa. And then, at the last—but still thoroughly thought out detail, I notice the clear vase of bacarra roses at the center of the table.

"A space where we can sit together in, or you can slip off to by yourself. When you need a break from the demands of life, or from your thoughts when they try to trick you into believing you are still trapped."

I turn my body to face Reimus, tears streaming down my face now as my heart cleaves wide open. The thought, the attention to detail in this entire space meticulously planned out.

Something that no one would have ever thought to do for me, except for him. And he is *everything* I've ever needed.

The catalyst to my life in more ways than one.

I watch as Reimus begins to lower himself down to one knee as my eyes widen, gasping as he lowers his hand to his pocket. Pulling out a black velvet box and opening it.

"This," He glances down at the box before training those breath-catching blue eyes back onto me. "Is what I had planned for us that day."

I lift my hand up to my mouth as I look down at the ring inside. The floor beneath my feet suddenly felt nonexistent.

"I thought it was best if I waited, to give you time to heal. For us to figure out what is coming towards us. But I don't want to waste another moment, Melinoë. Because gods forbid if something were to happen and I lose my chance at asking—" His word ends on a choke as a tear streams down his cheek, working on a swallow. "If I lost the opportunity to ask you to be my wife, then it would be by far the greatest loss I've ever experienced."

My legs numb themselves in place as all I can do is stare down at him. The raw emotion in his gaze, the second tear that streams down his face. At the slight tremble in his hands as he presents this ring to me.

Presents his *love*.

"Melinoë, will you do me the greatest honor in marrying me?" He says through glistening eyes.

I shakily lower myself down to my knees, my lips trembling as I nod my head. "Yes. Of course I will." I say through a harsh laugh, love pouring out of every crevice and every ounce of me.

I watch his shoulders sink as he exhales, as if he had been holding onto his breath until I've answered. He gives me the widest smile I've ever seen before lifting the ring and placing it onto my finger.

I glance down at the marquise cut diamond, gasping at its beauty before lifting my gaze up. His hands come up to my face as he brings me into him, our lips clashing with one another's in a moment of utter passion and longing.

His lips caress over mine as I fall deeply into him, my hands coming to tangle themselves in his hair. And in this moment, not even the golden sunlight streaming in from the glass windows could compare to the warmth that he ignites in my soul each and every day.

My twin soul.

My fiance.

My soon to be *husband*.

All of those words merry themselves inside my head as we kneel on the floor of the gazebo he built for me, kissing one another as if we have all the time in the world to love each other.

Because we in fact do.

CHAPTER 63

After spending some time sitting in the gazebo together, sharing sweet nothings and spending a lot of time kissing as night quickly came, we finally ventured our way back inside to have dinner.

In which Aven was especially gleeful to serve this time. Constantly cooing and admiring my ring. Oh, how I missed his joyful spirit.

As I stand in our bathroom now—after both of us having utilized it to shower and do *a lot* of touching, I grab my hair brush and make my way back into our bedroom. My damp hair trailing down over my black silk robe as I bring some of it forward to brush.

I seat myself on the edge of the bed as I brush through the tangles in my hair, feeling relieved to have been able to take a real shower after having been bathing in a large bucket.

I work the brush through my tangles, my mind roaming to how it felt to brush my hair in that cell. Alone, in the dark.

I release a shuddering breath as I work the brush through my hair faster, pulling at my hair and wincing at the snag of my hair.

Reimus comes over and gently places his hand over mine, stilling me and drawing my gaze up to him.

"Where are your thoughts?" He asks, taking the brush from my hand and seating himself next to me. He motions for me to turn around.

I do as he says and turn away from him, exhaling slowly as he begins gently weaving the brush through my hair. "When I was imprisoned there I wasn't awarded much, as one would expect. I wasn't even given a brush for my hair for a while, until Semele gave me one."

I release another long exhale as I continue.

"I spent every single day leaning up against that stone wall. I can almost still feel the grooves imbedding themselves in my back—"

I go to reach my hand up to check, to make sure they aren't there when Reimus catches my hand. Gently squeezing it as he continues brushing my hair with the other. "Can you feel this?"

He squeezes my hand again, his calloused skin pressing against mine as I nod my head. "Yes." My breathing begins to slow already.

He lowers my hand back down as he finishes brushing through my hair in silence as I unload everything piling to the surface.

"When I put on that long sleeved shirt today, I had to roll the sleeves up. I—" I shake my head. "I couldn't bear to have the fabric touching my wrists."

Reimus tenderly weaves the brush down through my hair, finishing untangling the strands. "I noticed." He says quietly.

I take another deep breath in, releasing again as he lowers the hair brush to the nightstand. His hand comes to my chin, caressing the skin there as I lean into his touch. I lift my gaze up to him as my lashes flutter open. His touch electrifies every nerve in my body, as if waking them up from a slumber as the thoughts of that cell begin to dim away.

"I said that I would bring you back whenever you needed it." He says as his hand lowers from my chin, his fingers lightly tracing themselves down along my neck. Pimpling the skin there as I inhale sharply at his touch.

His fingers lower themselves beneath my robe, slowly slipping it off my shoulder before it falls down my back. Exposing my breasts to the chilled air.

His fingers continue their slow exploration down my back, sending a thrill through my blood as he brings his hand over to my chest. Lightly grazing the back of his hand against my nipple.

"So let me do that for you."

He leans in, bringing his lips up against my neck. But instead of kissing me there, he just traces his lips across my skin. Inhaling sharply at the pleasure eroding my body.

"Do you feel this?"

I exhale raggedly as I hiss out, "Yes."

"Good girl. Now," He finally presses a kiss to my neck, slowly lifting his lips from my skin before lowering them down to my collarbone. His lips travel further down to my breast as he lowers himself down from the bed, kneeling down before me as his icy blue eyes lift to me. "And here?"

His lips slowly close over a hardened peak, arching my back into him as his hand lowers to open up my robe, letting it pool down at my sides as his fingers trace themselves down my belly. Down to my hip where he traces featherlight circles there, tension coiling tightly below. "Yes." I hissed.

He lifts his mouth as he travels down my belly, opening my legs wider for him. His fingers pressing into my thighs as he lowers a kiss next to his hand, a moan slipping from me. "You still with me?" He says, his voice smooth like whiskey.

"Mhmm." I say through pressed lips.

A watch as a smirk lifts one side of his lips as he lowers himself down, pressing a kiss to what I already know is glistening.

My back bows off the bed as he inserts his face between my legs, pulling me closer to the edge of the bed until I'm forced to hold myself up by my elbows.

"And what about now?"

A cry wrings out of me as his tongue flicks out, devouring and savoring the wetness there as my hands grip the silk sheets. His hands firmly on my hips as he keeps me in place.

I writhe against his face as that tension springs loose, coming undone as he drinks every last drop of me. Moaning out his name as the grip on my hips tightens until he releases entirely. His gaze remains on me as he raises himself from the ground and pushes me further up the bed, climbing on top of me as he lowers his sweatpants off his legs. His hard cock pressing against my pussy as he lowers himself down.

"All I want you to focus on right now is the fact that you're laying in *our* bed," He pushes my hair out of my face as he gazes down at me. "Feeling *me* touch you."

He lowers his head down, capturing my lips with his own. My hands coming up to his face as I bring my legs up, hooking them around his waist and urging him down.

He lifts his mouth from mine, lowering his hand down and pressing his cock to my pussy. I let out a frustrated cry as he teases me, rubbing his cock in my wetness before slipping himself inside. "Focus on how I *feel* inside of you, little spitfire."

He pauses as he begins to fill me, letting only the tip press in. He slowly sinks himself deeper as his lips come to my neck again. His warm breath sending me deeper into a dizzying need. "How I stretch and fill your pretty pussy."

He thrusts all the way to the hilt, burying himself completely as he says, "Focus on nothing but that."

He descends out of me just to slowly thrust into me again, the torture of it exquisite. All-consuming and not enough at the same time. He flicks his tongue out, gliding it slowly along my neck. The same pace as him thrusting inside of me.

"Feel my tongue and my cock worship you."

For a while he moves in and out of me slowly, soft moans turning into cries of pleasure the closer that I get to coming undone once more.

"Please—" I say as he lifts his face from my neck. His gaze falling on mine. "I need you. I need more—"

Before I can even finish my sentence Reimus starts thrusting into me hard, grinding in and against me as his movements become feverish. As his need along with mine intensifies.

I run my fingers along his back, pressing them into his skin as I grind my hips against him. His lips capture the moans escaping from my lips before his own whimpering falls between us.

"Fuck *me*—" He says as he holds me to his chest, hauling me up as he shifts himself to lay down onto the bed as I straddle him. He groans out as he grabs my hips and plunges me down on him over and over. "*Nothing* feels fucking better than you."

My hands lower to rest beside his head as I roll my hips onto him, his hands gripping deeper into my hips as he fucks me hard.

"Rei—" I scream as my release nears me.

He pistons in and out of me until another orgasm rolls through me, stealing every part of my awareness and breath onto this moment.

Reimus buries himself inside as he whimpers his release, feeling his body tremble beneath me. Both of us staying like this until he lifts me off of him and I lay myself down next to him.

I go to lift my hand up to his face when he grabs it, pressing a kiss to my palms before leaning over me. He guides me onto my belly as he hovers over me, his hand gently caressing down my back as I feel his lips pressing themselves against my shoulder.

He presses another to the top of my back as his other hand comes to my rear, gently gripping me as his kisses slowly press into every corner of my back. Caressing every crevice of new skin there where the wounds used to be.

"Let my lips replace the scars hidden beneath." His hand on my rear lifts my hips up, gasping as a finger slowly descends itself down until he's slowly rubbing the wetness pooling there. Shared with what he left behind, dripping out of my pussy. "Let me heal you."

As he continues to press kisses all along my back, his finger moves inside of me with an intentional slowness. Moving in and out of me patiently, decadently, so there is absolutely nothing else I could think about other than the sweet bliss of him fingering me.

He lifts his lips to press themselves against my neck as he wrings soft moans from my lips. I feel him glide his lips up to my ear, sending a chill down my spine as he nips my earlobe. The sound of his own heavy breathing and his erection pressing against my rear taking center stage in my thoughts.

And for the rest of the night, nothing else occupies my mind but the sound, and feeling of him.

CHAPTER 64

Reimus

"I don't want to wait."

The tips of my fingers lightly trail themselves down her arm, occasionally lifting them to run them through her hair. Pushing those midnight black strands away from her face as she gazes up at me.

Having been unable to stop touching her since we laid in our bed last night. Even when we both fell into a deep sleep, our arms and limbs remained tangled in one another.

My gaze lowers to her lips, slightly swollen and reddened from hours of exploring her mouth with mine. Aside from our moans and her cries of pleasure, we made up for our time spent apart with everything but our words.

More of last night's memories resurface of her bright emerald eyes lifted to mine, her soft plump mouth wrapped around my cock, taking all of me deeply down her throat as if she'd never get the chance to again. My body trembled as she took her time on me, sucking me, pleasing the ever fucking life out of me. My gratitude ran down the side of her lips as she swallowed every last drop.

I lift my gaze to her forehead, leaning down to press a soft kiss at the center as she adjusts her arm over my chest. "Then we won't wait." My voice groggy from sleep, and coming several times last night. My cock grows hard at the reminder as her leg brushes up against mine. But I know that with what we have ahead of us today, there's no amount of hiding in this bed that would keep us from it.

"Our lives are going to be too unpredictable for the foreseeable future," She begins as her fingers on my chest idly trace circles along my skin. "And with fall weather here, I definitely don't want to wait and have a winter wedding."

I chuckle beside her as I tuck her closer to me. "I don't think I would like that either." I brush her hair back for the millionth time as I look down at her. "We have to find a venue. Somewhere memorable."

Melinoë lifts her chin to look up at me. "Or we can have it here…in our new backyard." Her lips lift into a grin.

"Are you sure you don't want to have it indoors? With gorgeous tapestries, elegant and—"

"I don't care about any of that." She chimes in, shaking her head. Her smile deepens as she says, "I only care that the people closest to me are there, and that I get to marry you. Nothing else matters."

She lifts herself up onto her elbows, hovering over me as she presses a kiss to my lips. Her hair pools over my chest as she leans back. "Well, I also would like to have a beautiful dress made but *then* that's all I want."

I chuckle beneath her as I nod my head. "I fear you just want our wedding outside in the garden so Alastor can also be in attendance."

She giggles. "I would also like that." Her grin begins to smooth out. "I want to go see him. Before we leave."

I nod, having expected nothing else. Knowing that we were going to see him yesterday but caught up with our—well, everything. "He'll be very happy to see you."

Her eyes glisten as she exhales, lowering herself down to kiss me again before sitting up from the bed. The black silk sheets pool down to her waist before she lifts them away from her, stepping onto the floor from her side of the bed.

A sight that I will never take for granted.

She heads over to our closet to change when I hear Dimitri down the Guardian's channel.

Can we talk? If you're not busy. I'd hate to disturb you if you're—well, you know.

My chuckle slithers down the channel as I respond back. *Are you at the palace?*

Yes.

Okay, I'll be down in a few.

I stretch my arms up as I lift the covers from me, making my way over to the closet to join Melinoë in searching for something to wear. "The people bowed to you yesterday." I say as I step inside.

Melinoë looks up at me as she pulls on a pair of underwear before slipping a pair of black leggings on. "They did. They also called me a Guardian of Vulir."

I step to her side as I flip through my hangers of shirts, pulling a long-sleeved one down. "They did." I look over at her as I pull it over my head. "How do you feel about that?"

Melinoë shrugs her shoulders. "I care about the people who reside here, and wondered if after some time of us being together, that people would begin to see me as the same as you." She pulls out a long sleeved tunic, pulling it over her head.

"Us being together has nothing to do with them titling you their Guardian."

"It doesn't?" She asks, my gaze lowering to her rolling her sleeves up to her elbows.

I shake my head as I pull on a pair of boxer briefs before slipping on a pair of black pants. "When I became a Guardian of Vulir, I earned the title from the people first. Only then did I take my Guardian's Vows. But when they do title you as such, it's seen as a big deal." I button my pants as I narrow my chin. "After your speech yesterday, you showed them not only what kind of a leader you are, but an *honest* one at that. And they greatly appreciate that."

"Do you think they're expecting me to take those vows then?" She asks before stepping out of the closet.

I turn around and watch her head over to the vanity. She lifts the hair brush and begins working the tangles from her hair as I approach her from behind, stilling her movement momentarily. "You don't have to. They don't expect it." I kiss the top of her head. "They will still call you their Guardian whether you take the Guardian's Vows or not."

She looks up at me through the mirror, a faint half grin pulling up at her lips. "I would take them." She says softly.

I move from behind her to lean up against the vanity table, my hands pressed against the edge. "You don't have to if you don't want—"

"Actually, I do." She says as she sets the brush down, inserting herself in between my legs as she wraps her arms around my neck. "When you and I first evolved into more, the thought didn't really cross my mind. But something's changed since I've been here." My hands go to her waist as she smiles up at me. "I feel protective of this place, of Vulir and those who reside in it." Her emerald eyes churn vibrantly. "I'll do everything in my power to keep them safe. So yes, I want to take the Guardian's Vows."

A wide grin curves my lips as I pull her into me, my hands roaming to her rear, skimming up to her lower back. "Is it strange that I found that extremely attractive?"

She giggles, feeling her breath dance across my lips as she leans hers in closer to mine. "Well, you had once claimed you were a strange man." She leans in for a quick kiss.

"Correction, I said that if strange is what grabbed your attention then that is what I would be." My hands roam up her sides as I lean in and press my lips to her neck. Feeling her pulse skitter beneath my touch as she moans softly beneath me.

"Same thing." She says breathlessly. She jerks a little as I press another to her neck, the reaction sending a dizzying heat to my head and my cock.

Fuck, it's only been a few weeks that she's been apart from me but I feel like a fucking starved animal for her. All I want to do is just bury my face against her skin, in between her legs. But before I can think longer on it, she pulls away from me.

She forces my gaze to hers as she says, "I'm afraid we don't have time for that right now."

I exhale slowly. "I know."

She takes a deep breath in, her chest sinking as she exhales.

I move my hands from her waist to her arms around my neck, narrowing my chin. "We're doing the right thing." I reassure her when I sense her building anxiousness.

"I know." She says, loosening another breath. "I just hate to take them from their homes. To have to uproot them like this, but it's for their safety." She shakes her head. "Some of them may not even come."

I lift my hand to her cheek, gently caressing my thumb there as I say, "Then that would be their choice. Which you cannot then take responsibility for."

She leans into my touch as she nods her head, her gaze drifting away. "I know." She lifts her gaze back up to mine. "Remind me that if the time ever comes."

I nod my head. "I will." I press a kiss to her lips before she steps away from me. Slipping on her shoes as I lean away from the vanity. Melinoë exiting our bedroom to spend a few moments with her horse as I head downstairs to meet with Dimitri.

My gaze lowers to the smoldering fire beside me, the embers similar to what can be wielded from the tips of my fingers. The palms of my hands.

I lift my hand up now, willing a spark of fire to rise from my palms. The flame steady in place as are now the memories of my past, the sacrifices that were made to keep the Draghi bloodline safe from those who tried to wipe us out. The part of the ritual—and what Melinoë saw in Apollo's memories striking me once more.

To be hidden in plain sight until the time is right.

I shake my head as I ponder over that phrase. All of the Draghi except for Dimitri and I had been wiped out during the war when they took over our ancestral land—

Zeus took it over.

His name became apparently familiar once my memories served me again, though having no idea about his children. About Melinoë or any of the other atrocities that he has performed. The Draghi had always just suspected something vile about him, about how he would lead as King to Olympia.

And we were right about our intuitive hunches.

"It has to be done there." I say to Dimitri, shaking my head as I train my gaze up to him. "For you to gain back your essence, your innate power as one of the Draghi. We have to regain it from the land we originated from. That is what I remember."

"But we were just there? I was standing on the soil I—" Dimitri slowly shakes his head as confusion creases his face. "Why do you think it didn't work for me?"

"Because the essence couldn't be reclaimed back into your body until I had claimed it for myself. Until I reclaimed my title as leader of the Draghi. Now that I have regained what I buried beneath the soil years ago, the remaining essence that belongs to each Draghi left alive can now be reclaimed." I shake my head as I shrug my shoulders. "I don't know why it was orchestrated that way but that is what I remember about the ritual."

Dimitri's chest rises then sinks again. I understand completely where he's coming from, and his concerns about retaining what belongs to him. To also be caught a little off guard at the truth of our lineage and our kind. "What has Melinoë said about it all?"

I pause for a moment as I step away from the mantel. "I have not brought it up to her yet."

His brows knit together, he goes to open his mouth when I hold a hand up, stifling his words and the confusion I already knew he was going to spew.

"We will be going back."

His brows smooth downward as his mouth closes.

I step closer to him, placing a hand on his shoulder as I say, "We will retrieve what belongs to you. Just give me a day or two to discuss it with her, and also have a word with Hecate. If we're going to go back, we'll need her aid as that area will be heavily guarded."

He nods his head. "Understood. But why would we need Hecate's help?"

"To see if she can perform a cloaking spell on us while we're there."

"Okay. Yeah, that's probably a good idea." A moment of silence stretches between us before a half grin lifts one side of his face. "Congratulations, by the way."

Unable to fight my own grin as I say, "Thank you."

"Does this mean I get to be your best man?" He tilts his head as I lower my hand from his shoulder.

I chuckle. "Actually, I had thought to ask Aven."

A flash of surprise dances across his gaze before giving me a look, rolling his eyes. "Okay, not funny."

We share a laugh together, one of those moments that seem to come as quickly as they go. A short moment in time that feels more significant when later looking back on it.

"Where do you think they are?" He asks, referring to what the prophecy spoke of. What I saw in my memories, as well as what Melinoë saw in Apollo's vision. "Do you think there are any alive out there?"

I shake my head slowly, exhaling. "I don't know." I lift my gaze up to his. "But I hope so."

CHAPTER 65

Melinoë

I walk through the garden, training every detail of it to memory as a wide grin lights up my face. Turning into a full-blown broad, beaming smile when I reach the end of the garden and see Alastor across the way.

His head immediately lifts up to see me, a loud whinny emitting from him as he begins pacing anxiously along the fence. His tail swishing violently from side to side.

My breath hitches at the sight of him as I begin running to the pasture, my eyes swelling with tears as my heart cleaves open. Alastor lightly galloping to the pasture gate as he waits for me.

I make it to the pasture gate, unlocking it and slipping myself inside as Alastor advances on me, sniffing me as he nudges my chest. My hands come up to his face as I press kisses along his forehead. Tears slipping down my cheeks as I whisper to him, "I missed you so much." My words ending in a choked cry.

His whinnying turns into a low nicker as he tries nibbling on my sleeves, wringing soft giggles from me as I pet down his neck. Feeling for any build up of dirty or loose fur. Instead finding his coat to be really shiny and clean. "I see that Reimus has been keeping up with brushing you at least."

He huffs at me as he lowers his head back down to my chest, sniffing me. I bring my arms up to his neck, giving him a hug as I embrace this moment with him.

But as I feel the presence of another behind me, I still against him until a wide grin blossoms on my face. "I was wondering when you would visit me."

I lower my arms from Alastor, turning around to see Eiran standing before me. A faint grin on his face as he says, "I needed to check in with you. See if you are okay."

I go to reach for him, feeling silly that I obviously can't feel him. I pull my hand back as I nod. "I'm doing okay. I'm really glad to see you again."

"As am I." Eiran says, glancing at Alastor.

I make my way over to the barn to grab Alastor's grooming bucket, something that I missed doing very much. Alastor follows behind me as Eiran glides to my right. "So your explicit instructions for them to follow, to free me."

Eiran lifts his gaze up to mine, the sunlight above shining through his spirit body.

"It was because of Reimus, wasn't it?"

We reach the barn door as Eiran folds his hands behind his back, nodding. "He needed to step onto the soil in order to regain his memories, and also re-inherit his powers."

I grab Alastor's grooming bucket and walk back outside, him waiting patiently for me. "And the Draghi; are there any of them left beside Reimus and Dimitri?"

I lower the bucket to the ground as Eiran lowers his gaze away from me, silent.

I nod as I press my lips together. "Right. The Fates—you can't say."

Eiran lifts his gaze back up to mine, his shoulders slumping forward somewhat as he says, "I presume you met some of the gods that reside in Zeus' palace. One of which including your brother, Dionysus." He says, changing the subject.

I nod my head. "I can't believe this whole time Zeus had another child, that he reincarnated him—especially when that's not his role to do so. Even Apollo and Artemis," I say, pausing. "That they aren't true allies to Zeus?"

Eiran shakes his head. "They are not."

"So who even are Zeus' allies? Truly?"

"Assuming you met the council members, I can tell you that Poseidon remains a true ally to Zeus. He resides and rules over mainly the Aegean Sea, a body of water that borders east of Olympia."

"And what can you tell me about him?" I ask, lowering down to grab a grooming brush before standing up straight again, running it along Alastor's side.

"Poseidon is fiercely protective over the sea, and can be a cruel god when angered or provoked. But he tends to stay out of reach, sticking to the seas and rarely making an appearance in Olympia unless Zeus calls for council." Eiran says, stepping closer to me as I brush Alastor. "They, along with Hades, are gods that have been around the longest. So with that comes boredom, and the tendency to do things out of impulse rather than sound logic."

"Hmm. Wouldn't have guessed." I say dryly. I lower my gaze to my wrists, momentarily needing to remind myself that the chains are gone. That I'm no longer shackled and bound.

"Hera is loyal to him as well, but it appears it is more due to an arrangement to keep his infidelity from being publicly shared. Though everyone knows his habitual nature to...*wander*." An enunciation on that last word. "But Hera, like Zeus and Poseidon, can be conniving and cruel when angered as well."

"So basically, Poseidon and Hera are on the loyal list for Zeus. Got it." I run the brush along Alastor as I remember that one goddess I'd seen in the council room. "What about Athena?"

"Athena is loyal to Zeus, but she is an independent goddess first and foremost. Which means she has been known to challenge his decisions a time or two before. Acting against his wishes when it was deemed necessary for the people of Olympia, who she is fiercely protective over."

I look over at Eiran. "I find that hard to believe. Considering Zeus denies doing something as simple as changing the weather so his people don't run out of crops, I can't imagine someone who is *fiercely protective* over the people would be okay with that."

Eiran tilts his head. "It is unclear if she's aware of that or not as the people do not express their concerns to her, but to him."

"But would they? Express their concerns to another god or goddess if given the opportunity?"

He shrugs his shoulders. "It has never been an option before."

I scoff at him, shaking my head. "That's honestly pitiful," I pause for a beat. "And...heartbreaking."

"How so?"

I make my way over to Alastor's other side, standing patiently as I groom him. "Because what it sounds like is Zeus is the only one who can actually make decisions for Olympia—which, fair. Being *King of Gods* and all." I roll my eyes at that last part. "But that just means that those people will never have a fair shot at...anything then. And I know I'm not the only one who thinks that." I look up at him. "Apollo showed me his memories in the Casalas Mountains. Artemis told him long ago that she knew the people of Olympia at some point would starve out and die under Zeus's rule." I shake my head at him. "How do you know that knowledge, and not do something about it?"

"Maybe it's not that they do not care to do anything about it, but that the opportunity to has not arisen."

"Maybe." I say, all while feeling like that's still bullshit. My mind trains on something else about my time there. "You were trying to tell me about her. About The Keres, weren't you?"

Eiran looks at me, hesitating first before nodding his head. "Though I did it in such a subtle way, it would still be considered crossing a line with The Fates."

A moment that meant so little at the time when Eiran jokingly mentioned sending The Keres to me. Mentioning that they were creatures that fed on bloodshed and violence. Not only had he known that fate would lead me to being captured—which is something that I can't hold against him, but that I'd also run into her there.

I look up at him. "Did you know that I would free her?"

"No. But," He pauses for a moment. "I knew your compassion and integrity would not allow you to rest if you had left her there."

He's right. I wouldn't have been able to be okay with myself if I left her there to rot in that cell.

My mind then reverts back to Thomas, the only one who came forward about the dying of their crops. My mind unable to focus on anything other than his bravery being shot down, and how much that disappointment on his face still affects me to this day.

CHAPTER 66

"It's gorgeous!" Nora exclaims as she turns my hand to the side.

I chuckle as she *thoroughly* examines my ring, her widened gaze glittering with the awe of my announcement. "I suppose he did okay."

She looks up at me, smirking as she rolls her eyes. "I'd say he did *more* than okay." She lowers my hand and brings me in for a tight hug. "I'm so incredibly happy for you both."

I wrap my arms around her as a gentle breeze brushes my hair back from my face. "Thank you."

"So who is your maid of honor then? What of your bridesmaids?" She pulls away from me, giving me a side eye as one side of her lips turns up.

I chuckle once more. "Well…" I begin, trailing off intentionally as a half grin kicks up my face. "I mean, *I guess* you could be a bridesmaid."

She lightly swats at my arm as she gasps. "You mean it would be an *honor* to have me as one of your bridesmaids."

I turn my shoulder out of the way as I chuckle, sighing contentedly. "Nora, it would be a most impeccable honor if you would accept being one of my bridesmaids."

She grins mischievously as she says, "Now that's more like it."

The sound of footsteps from behind me draws my attention before a hand rests itself on my shoulder. Reimus leaning down to kiss the top of my head. "Everyone is in attendance, I see. And then some." He goes to stand beside me, smiling.

As I stand in the center of the village, I'm surrounded by those who more than agreed to help me merge the people from Elzwin over today. Hecate approaching from my left, her amethyst robe billowing behind her as the sunlight casts her skin a warm brown. Nora standing before me, no longer wholly focused on my ring but now looking behind her to those showing up.

The people of Vulir begin merging into the streets. Some of them emerging from shops on either side of us, some of which coming from the west side where most reside. All of them—nonetheless, coming out to assist in any way they can.

Dimitri approaches Reimus' right, looking over to me as he gives a half grin. His gaze falls on Nora for a brief moment before looking out towards the people.

At the presence of someone to my left, I look over to see Dionysus. I lean my head in towards him. "You don't have to do this if you don't want to. Nobody will feel otherwise if you don't."

"I know." He says, his gaze glancing at me before roaming over the village ahead. "I want to."

I turn towards him, lowering my voice so only him and I can hear. With the exception of Reimus who stands close by. "Then I will presume I need not have any worries about where you stand now. That I do not need to worry about you changing sides, and potentially putting my people at risk."

Dionysus raises his gaze back to mine. "You can rest assured I have no intention of going back." He shakes his head as he clenches his teeth momentarily. "That there is nothing there worth persuading me to change my decision."

I nod slowly, keeping my gaze on him. "And what of your mother?"

He stays silent for a moment, my gaze lowering to the sudden tick in his jaw before it vanishes a moment later. "Not even her." He says flatly, though I hear the faint grief in his tone.

As if he hasn't fully accepted that part of his story yet.

I nod again. "Very well then."

I face the front as I step closer to Nora who has turned to talk to a villager. "When you see a portal open up, begin directing everyone to their new homes. If the people would like to help, allow them in any way they're willing to."

She nods her head curtly. "Got it."

"We do have a few rooms available in The Sanctuary as well. Should any women with or without children feel more comfortable staying there then allow Dimitri to help them get set up. Elzwin is a low-populated village, there should be no more than one hundred that come through." I pause for a moment. "That's if they all come through."

Nora nods her understanding again, forcing a smile. "We got this."

I step back next to Reimus as Dimitri approaches Nora, talking softly to her as Hecate and Dionysus come closer to us.

"When we arrive, we'll begin immediately." I say to them. I look over at Reimus, exhaling. "We don't know when he'll attack Elzwin, so every moment counts."

Reimus gives me a nod as he reaches out for my hand. "You ready?"

I nod. "Ready."

I will a portal open before us, listening to some of the people around us gasp and whisper to themselves. I look through the opening, seeing the familiar book shop staring back at me. The fuzzy outlines of people meandering about in the village, some of their bodies halt their strides as they see a giant portal open up in their village.

A type of sorcery they've all been made to believe is forbidden and dangerous.

I take one last breath in, exhaling as Reimus and I step through the portal first. Dionysus and Hecate following behind us.

My foot steps out onto the familiar gravel road, the familiar scent of my home wafting towards me as I hear the first round of gasps.

I look up to see Jester standing several feet away from me, his wide eyes locked onto the portal behind us. His hand stills on the door to his bookshop as if having seen us through those casement windows, and running outside to get a better look.

I lift my gaze to other village people walking about, stopping to stare at the portal, then me. I watch as a mother grabs her small child, bringing him closer to her as her arms and shoulders tense.

I begin to slowly close the portal behind me, watching as some people turn around and head for the homes nearby. Going to bang on their front doors to get them outside to witness too what is going on.

Exactly what I had hoped they'd do.

As the portal closes permanently behind me I feel the nerves inside my belly expand and coil tightly together. My breaths come in less than steady waves.

I feel the weight of Reimus' hand against mine, pulling my attention to him and back from the anxiousness whirling inside of me. He lowers his head near me as he says quietly, barely above a whisper, "They are used to believing in a certain way of life. Don't let the worry of that negate what you've come here to do."

I take a long breath in, releasing as I let his words cement themselves inside of me. He's right. I'm nervous because I know they've been raised to believe magic and spirits and mediumship to be dangerous. They blame what happened to the women that were massacred here years ago on that. So I can't blame them all for being terrified by us showing up through a portal.

But what I can do is explain. And do exactly what I did with the people of Vulir. I can give them the truth, and allow them to make their own biases and opinions from that.

"Hello." I say, nodding to everyone crowding around us now as more people filter from between shop alleyways. "Some of you may know me. My name is Melinoë."

I look over at Jester, the hand above his mouth slowly lowering as he releases his other hand from the door. Stepping fully outside as his gaze sweeps over me.

"For those of you who do not, I lived here my whole life before I…left. So I remember what was instilled upon me at a young age, as many of you." I take a moment to breathe, pausing before continuing again. "In order for me to explain why I am here before you all today, and why I have shown up the way I have, I must explain how what we were made to believe was a scare tactic meticulously planted. That we have been given a version of a reality that is not sound and true."

I watch as some people turn to each other, whispering softly as more people join us in the street.

"Many years ago, a group of women were massacred in this very village. It was said that their execution was because of their involvement with witchcraft and mediumship, and I am here to tell you all that's a lie. That the reason why they were murdered is for something far more nefarious."

A round of gasps echoed in the air around us again, and as their eyes darted over to me after looking at one another, I told them the truth.

I tell them why those women were murdered, and by who. That it was all a scheme not entirely to deceive the people of Elzwin, but to deceive me. I tell them how that man's cruelty does not end there, and what he has done to me. To my family.

I tell them what I have witnessed myself while being held prisoner in his palace, how he treats his people and the state of condition they live in. I tell them who my mother is, and who I am. That I am The Goddess of Nightmares, Guardian of Souls. But that my intentions are only to keep the innocents safe, as that is what I've come here to do.

I tell them what it cost for me to be freed, and what I believe to be in danger because of my freedom. And at the mention of their village, a place that was once my home, I watch as eyes widen both in disbelief and fear.

As I speak to the people of Elzwin, I occasionally feel the gaze of Dionysus on my left cheek. Most of what I shared today was him hearing for the first time. And at the mention of how Zeus has treated my mother, and his nefarious reasons for it, I swear I feel a pulse of energy from him as he gazes at me.

A brief detection of power that feels heavy and light at the same time.

Anguish and acceptance.

"I understand that what I have shared with you all is a lot to take in. I am well aware that there will be questions that I am willing to answer, but I'm afraid time is not on our side for that at this moment. As my priority is first getting you all merged over to Vulir, where you will all be safe. Vulir is a village that is surrounded by a protective barrier called a shield. It allows us to remain invisible to most, aside those with neutral or pure intentions. If we all stay within those borders, I believe that we will have a real shot at keeping you all—"

"Safe?" A man rings out. His familiar voice draws my attention, my breath hitching as he emerges from the crowd.

Terry stands before me, his brows furrowed in bewilderment beneath his baseball cap snug on his head. "Coming from the girl who *stole* from me. You expect us to uproot our entire lives at the perceived threat that can't be proven aside from—what, your story?" He snarls, drawing a few people's attention to him.

My heart sinks at his obvious skepticism—and resentment for taking Alastor in the dead of night. Stealing him, actually.

I release a steady exhale as I keep my shoulders straight, saying in a clear voice, "To ensure you all are kept safe, yes."

He huffs out a harsh laugh, lifting his cap from his head and running his hand across his head. He shakes his head as he lowers the hat back on. "Listen, girlie. I sympathize with what you're saying, but I highly doubt any of us are willing to just leave everything behind." He turns around, looking at some of the people standing near him before facing me again. "I mean, what am I gonna do with my horses? My barn? Heck, we have our *whole lives* here."

People whisper amongst themselves. As a nervousness coils within me, Reimus gently squeezes my hand. Reminding me of the power of truth.

"We have homes available for immediate move in, with extra supplies and food to at least get everyone started. I cannot begin to imagine what you all are thinking right now, and I know how scary this must be. To be forced to leave behind your home." Guilt threatens to burrow itself a place in my chest but I don't allow it to. I stay firm in what I'm aiming to do here. "I am certain that if you all do not leave Elzwin, you will die."

People whip their gazes up to mine, some with shock written over their faces. Some with alarm that I would be so blunt.

But right now, time is of the essence. And I do not have the luxury of waiting for them to get on board.

"If you think what you've seen today is frightening, is alarming," I wave my hand behind me to where the portal was. "Then I'm here to tell you that that is only a fraction of the kind of magic that a god or goddess can wield. And if you linger here in Elzwin, you will not survive what comes your way."

I watch as Terry works on a swallow as he stares at me. As they all do.

"I will give you all a half hour to retrieve what you can from your homes before we begin moving you over. Take only what truly matters, leave the rest. I will make it my mission to make sure you all are as comfortable as you can be during your transition to Vulir. But if you truly do not want to come, then I will understand." A twinge of worry settles inside of me for what those will face that do not move. "It is your choice at the end of the day."

My gaze roams over them, noticing a woman with tears in her eyes. Dampness settling on her cheeks as she steps forward. My heart lurches for her and the devastation that all of this must be on her. But when she speaks, I'm wildly taken back by what she says.

"I believe you." She shakes her head slowly. "No one gives a story with that much detail and still lies." She wipes beneath her eyes, turning around to look at those behind her. "Think of your children, your sisters, your brothers. Your wives and husbands. Think of your *life* as if it matters."

Some of the people looking at her smooth their expressions into less fear, and more understanding.

"She could've left us to fend for ourselves. Instead, she came here to warn us. To give us the opportunity to still survive." She turns her gaze back around to me again. "Can you show us?"

I tilt my head at her request.

"Show us what a goddess can do. Prove it to us."

At her request I look at Reimus, letting go of his hand as I will my shadows to the surface. I hear a chorus of gasps, followed by quick silence as I will my shadows to slither themselves along the ground. Some people backing up as they watch them creep closer.

"What are you all doing just standing there!"

A man shouts, rushing hurriedly to the front of the crowd as he catches my attention. He keeps his hand lowered to his thigh as he glares at me. "You can't sweet talk us. I know exactly what you are—"

He quickly unsheaths a dagger from his pant pocket, rushing towards me when he's immediately blasted backwards. My gaze lowers to the burn mark now on the hand that held the dagger, his other hand clutching it tightly as he yelps in pain. His chest rising and sinking quickly as he breathes through the second degree burn.

"Make a move against her again, and it won't just be your hand I burn." Reimus warns the man.

I look up at him as he hones his gaze onto the man, watching him as he retreats back into the crowd before Reimus says, "Make no mistake. Melinoë has been gracious in giving you all a warning, in trying to give you all safer living conditions as *each* and *every* one of your lives are at risk." He steps away from my side, straightening his gaze as he says calmly. *Too* calmly, "But if you so much as raise your hand at her, the fear you feel today will pale in comparison to what I will do."

I stare at him for a long moment, never having seen this protective side of him. Feeling both wholly consumed by it, and incredibly aroused.

He turns his gaze back to me as he steps back to my side. "You were saying, my love."

I blink at him before I turn my gaze back to everyone before us. Their gazes wide-eyed, their mouths clamped shut as silent beckons them. "As I said, you have thirty minutes. Meet back here and we will begin filing everyone through."

As everyone looks at me for a long moment, I wonder if they'll just stand here and stare at me. If they'll forget that they have legs and feet, if they'll suddenly be numb to the rest of their body as they process everything before them. But then, I watch as the woman who spoke up turns around, retreating quickly through the alleyway to her home.

I watch as one by one, people begin rummaging through the crowd back to their homes. Slowly but surely, deserting the crowd into an almost nothingness.

Terry stays behind as he approaches me. Reimus stepping in front of me as he comes closer, the tension in Reimus' back coiling before I rest a hand on his shoulder. Quickly subsiding it with just my touch. "It's okay. I know him. He means well."

"Though I shouldn't, girl. You took my damn horse." He says, standing in front of me now.

Reimus watches him intently but loosens the defensive strain in his body.

I exhale, frowning. "I know. I'm so sorry Terry. It—" I exhale again. "It's complicated to explain, but it was for a reason. I promise he is alive and well."

Terry's gaze roams over my face, studying me for a moment before saying, "You really mean it? That we're in danger here?"

I nod my head. "I promise I wouldn't have come unless it was necessary."

Terry looks at me for a moment before nodding. "Well, then I sure hope you have some place where I can house the horses. You know I wouldn't leave without them."

My gaze catches Jester retreating back into his bookshop, closing the door for only a moment before stepping back out with a stack of books in his hands. He makes a quick glance over to me, giving me a curt nod before turning around and walking towards the direction of the village homes.

For a moment sorrow cleaves at my heart, at everything these people have to leave behind. I even wonder for a moment if I should visit the cabin, if I should take this final chance to grab anything I might still hold dear.

But as soon as that thought comes it leaves just as quickly. Because there is nothing left in that cabin worth remembering, nothing I want to hold onto. As my life truly didn't start until I came to Vulir. Everything I'll ever need is there, or in The Underworld.

I train my gaze back onto Terry, fixing a half grin up my lips as I say, "I might have made some arrangements."

CHAPTER 67

Reimus

Almost a half hour later people begin crowding back into the village, all of them traveling with just what's on their backs. Some of them with small children clinging to their legs, or pets curled up in their arms or standing beside their feet.

I look over at Melinoë as I nod my head, facing the people again as she wills a portal open beside us. A short moment later, Charon appears next to the opening. Judging by some of the gasps they were not expecting to see another immortal stand before them.

Especially not one who wears midnight black robes that disintegrate at the ends and looks—well, like someone who has risen from the dead.

"This is Charon. He is our gatekeeper for Vulir, and will judge each of you upon entering the portal. Should any of you be deemed as hostile or have ill-intentions towards myself, or anyone here including the people of Vulir, you will not be granted access into Vulir." I lower my hand to the side. "Let's begin."

As people form a somewhat single-file line, I look over at Melinoë who watches them intently. Assessing everyone who reaches the portal, and those who get granted access to enter. So far, everyone receives the green light to pass through to Vulir. But by the looks of it, we still have around eighty-five people to go.

I watch as her beady eyes scan the crowd, as if looking for someone. But before I can open my mouth to ask who, a wave of relief crashes into her when a man and a woman rush over to her. Opening their arms to her and dropping their things on the ground.

I lower my gaze to the hunting bags that lay on the ground now, filled to the brim with flannels peeking out of the flap opening. Fishing wire and all sorts of hunting materials noticeable.

"I'm so glad to see you again. I had worried so much when I didn't hear from you or Eiran that something terrible happened."

An awareness spreads over my entire body, realizing that these two must've been very close to Eiran. Feeling my heart cleave for them that they're about to hear even more heartbreaking news.

I watch Melinoë's expression, seeing her trying to wield a neutral look when a silhouette drags both of our gazes to her side.

Eiran stands there, glancing at the man and woman in front of Melinoë as a smile curves his lips. He looks back to Melinoë and says, "Tell them that I've found peace."

My heart sinks for him as I watch him pass a tender glance at the two people before us.

"Don't tell them that I still linger, they won't be able to move on otherwise. Shauna and Mac deserve to know the truth, but they have worried much for me since I've left. I want them to heal, and finally be able to move on."

Melinoë then grabs both of their hands, and tells them how their friend died. Sacrificing his life for hers.

I watch as both of their faces crumple up with grief, tears streaming down their eyes as Shauna nods. "Thank you. We both wondered if—" She looks over at Mac. "If something happened but we didn't want to believe it. We had hoped that we were wrong but now we know."

A tear runs down Melinoë's cheek as I look over to Hecate and Dionysus, both of them standing at the portal and helping the mortals inside.

"And you know he's at peace?" Mac asks as he wipes the tears from his eyes.

I look up at Eiran still standing there, tilting his head to Melinoë as he watches her give them the closure they need.

Melinoë nods her head. "I am able to walk amongst the souls of The Underworld. He has already drank from The Lethe, so his memories and his pain from how he died have been erased."

I watch as she works on a swallow, loosening a shaky breath.

"He resides peacefully there, with the rest of the souls in The Underworld." She forces a faint grin.

Mac nods his head curtly, squeezing Melinoë's hand. "Thank you." He lowers his other hand on top as he says, "I know he would've chosen to die no other way. He loved you very much."

Mac lowers his hands from Melinoë as does Shauna, they both give a final nod before retrieving their things from the ground and making their way back in line.

I turn to Melinoë, watching her chest rise and fall as I place a hand on her cheek. Wiping the tears away. "They can find peace now. This is good."

She nods her head as she looks over to Eiran.

He smiles at her as he lowers his gaze to her hand, his smile widening even more as he says, "Congratulations." He lifts his gaze to me. "Both of you."

Before we can both say our thanks he vanishes entirely.

She glances at all of the people walking through the portal. Watching as she does a head count of who is still in line. "Ten." She looks up at me, sighing. "We're missing ten."

I glide my thumb across her cheek, tilting my head. "We knew that there would be some who would not want to leave." I say gently.

"I know. I just...before it was only a possibility. It's different now that it's reality."

"I know." I say softly as I lean down to kiss her forehead.

I look up to see that mostly everyone has now entered through the portal, knowing that Dimitri and Nora are assisting everyone into the village on the other side. As some of the remaining village people make their way through the portal, Terry hurries over to us.

"Alright, girl. They're all ready."

She grins at him as she looks over at Hecate, watching her and Dionysus guide the last two people through. "We'll meet you both back in the village once we're done."

As the last person walks through the portal, Hecate glances up at us. Smirking as she says, "We'll be here." She walks through the portal as Dionysus walks in behind her. Melinoë closing the portal entirely.

"Alright, let's go round 'em up." She says as we go to Terry's barn.

⌒

As we get there Melinoë wills a portal open by the barn entrance where the stalls are. Terry jerks back for a second, a laugh escaping out of him a moment later.

"Forgive me, but that'll take some getting used to."

"Trust me, I understand." She says.

The three of us waste no time herding the horses through the portal, coming out the other side to a fenced in pasture down a ways from a newly built cottage.

The home features a barn and a few acres of land so the horses can roam with ample amount of space. A request that Melinoë had put in for Hades to build in hopes that Terry would willingly come to Vulir.

"Damn, this is nice." Terry says as he walks through the portal tentatively, his gaze roaming the pasture before unhooking the lead rope on the horse. He looks over the entirety of the property before his gaze settles on the outline of shops at the heart of the village.

As I step through the portal to herd another horse in, I halt in place. My fists balling up at my sides. "What are you doing here?"

Melinoë rushes to my side as she looks at Apollo, standing at the entrance to the barn.

"I came to make sure you were getting everyone moved into Vulir." He says, lifting his gaze up the barn door before bringing it back down again.

She tilts her head. "How did you—"

He simply taps the side of his forehead.

Melinoë nods her understanding. "What are you doing here?"

"I came to warn you." Apollo says as he steps closer.

I go to stand in front of Melinoë when he chuckles softly, shaking his head. "I thought I made it clear that I am no threat to either of you."

"Well, one can never be too sure nowadays."

Apollo tilts his head slightly. "Even after I told your mother long ago how to preserve the essence? To save the Draghi bloodline?" He straightens his gaze. "To save you."

I say nothing as a tremor ticks through me.

"What do you mean warn us?" Melinoë says, stepping in front of me and changing the subject.

Apollo lowers his gaze to her. "Zeus is planning something. What it is? I do not know. Ever since you escaped and Dionysus with you, he's become even more paranoid than he already is. Keeping his plans to himself."

Melinoë lifts a hand to the portal. "I've already cleared the people out."

"All of them?"

Melinoë slams her mouth shut as she says nothing.

"You need to clear them all out, Melinoë."

"I can't." She remarks. "I can't force someone to go if they don't want to."

He lifts his chin as he says, "Yes, you would be correct." He goes to turn on his heels when he stops, turning his head over his shoulders. "I will be in touch soon. Though should you ever need to get ahold of me, all you need to do is have me summoned."

A portal with bright gold eather trailing around the edges opens up, Apollo walking through it as it closes behind him.

"Why does he think we'll need him? To summon him?" I ask her, curious.

She shakes her head. "I don't know." She raises her hand up to her face, lowering her index finger and thumb to the bridge of her nose. Pressing them together there.

Terry comes out of the portal, looking over at us as he says, "Well y'all said to get moving. What are you doing just standing around?"

Melinoë lowers her hand as we put what Apollo said to the wayside for now while we finish herding the horses through.

CHAPTER 68

After a long day of merging people from Elzwin to Vulir, and getting them situated into their new homes and essentially their new life, all I can ponder over now is what Apollo said earlier today.

Zeus is planning something.

The knowledge that not even Apollo knows what that something is slightly jarring to me.

I raise my hand up from leaning it against the living room mantel, lifting my whiskey to my lips as I take a generous sip. The awareness of someone standing behind me raises my senses.

I turn around to see Dionysus standing in the doorway of the living room, his gaze briefly lowering to the whiskey in my hands before saying, "I don't mean to intrude. Melinoë said I could stay here. For a while until I—" The words of *until I figure something out* hanging in the air between us. He clears his throat as he continues. "I promise you'll hardly know I'm here."

I look at him, knowing that if he weren't related—in some twisted fashion, to Melinoë, then I would've scorched him on fire for what he did to Dimitri. I would've shown him no mercy as he hadn't for my best friend. But as I stare at him now, I see the understanding of the situation that he's in. That just like the people we merged over from Elzwin, this is new territory for him.

And he's basically all alone in this with no one familiar to turn to for comfort.

I shake my head. "You're welcome to stay here as long as you need." I say, lifting my glass up. "Drink?"

I watch as an awkward tension releases from his shoulders as he steps further into the living room, forcing out a weak chuckle. "That would be great, actually."

I walk over to the credenza, lifting the decanter of amber-hued liquid and pouring some into an empty glass. I hold the glass up for him.

"Thanks." He says, taking it and downing it in one swig.

I lower my gaze to the empty glass, huffing out a soft chuckle as I lift the decanter. Adding more to his glass. "You did need a drink."

"It's been a…weird few days. Few weeks, actually." He says, sipping it this time.

I turn away from the credenza, facing him as the fireplace behind me warms my back. "I'd imagine so." I pause for a moment, letting a beat of silence stretch between us before I say, "I apologize for Dimitri, by the way. It's in our blood to be…unforgiving when us or one of our kind has been harmed."

Dionysus shakes his head, his light brown wavy hair shuffling vaguely with the movement. "Honestly, I don't blame him. What I did was unforgivable." He exhales softly before he says, "I don't excuse what I've done, but I was only doing what Zeus told me to do. What—"

The words of *my father asked me to do* dying at the tip of his tongue.

I lower my gaze down, his fingers beginning to turn bone white as he grips the glass. When he sees where my gaze has fallen he loosens his grip, sipping the whiskey. "I knew Zeus was an overly-domineering King, but after Melinoë, after the things I learned today," He looks up at me, shaking his head as his lips curl slightly. "I don't want to be anything like that."

His multi-colored eyes churn brightly before me, noticing the contrast of both emerald and sapphire in his gaze.

I lift a shoulder. "Then you only need to make the conscious decision to not be like him. Each and every day."

Dionysus nods his head before downing the rest of his whiskey.

"So that trick of yours," I begin as I lift the decanter, pouring him another glass of whiskey. "That you used on that woman in the forest that one day. Is it willing people to bleed—or produce wine from the inside out?"

He sips the whiskey again. "That is what part of my divinity is. God of Wine and Vegetation." He lowers the glass down. "Amongst other things."

"What other things?" I ask, sipping my whiskey.

He gives me a look. "Pleasure."

"As in you can evoke others to feel pleasure?"

"No, not like that. I mean—not in a nonconsensual way at least." He chuckles. "More like when mortals are around me they feel inspired to divulge in the pleasures of life. It's an energy that I carry that rubs off on others. Sometimes pleasure looks like dancing and eating. Sometimes my presence entices people to find pleasure with others. With themselves."

"Interesting." I drawl.

"And it's more like making people hemorrhage wine from the inside out, replacing their blood with it."

I raise my eyebrows, grimacing. "I can't imagine that is pleasant."

Dionysus curls his lips as he says, "It's not."

A beat of silence passes between us before he says, "I think I'm going to retire for the night. Melinoë said there was a spare room on the second floor, but that I should probably pick one on the third. As it's bigger?"

I crease my brows together as I wonder why Melinoë would say that when the rooms on the third floor are no bigger than the ones on the second. But then I realize since our bedroom is on the second floor, it makes sense why she would tell him to stay on the third.

So our...*noises* don't keep the poor bastard awake.

I fight a grin from appearing on my lips as I hold back a chuckle, nodding instead as I look at him. "Pick any room and make yourself comfortable. You are welcome to join us for mealtimes if you'd like as well. Aven is my chef, and his cheerfulness will surely make you feel right at home."

Dionysus downs the rest of the whiskey before setting the glass on the credenza. He forces a smile before he says, "Thank you. I will keep that in mind."

As I watch him turn on his heels and exit the living room, I wonder to myself if Semele misses him.

If she will one day come looking for her son again.

As I near our bedroom I hear the faint sounds of rustling within. The faint scrape of hangers being pushed across the closet rod drawing my attention.

I step inside to see Melinoë standing in our closet, lifting a dark brown sweater from a hanger and slipping it on. She lifts her hair from beneath the collar as I lean against the door frame. "Going to the cemetery?"

She looks up at me, giving me a faint grin as she says, "I know it's late, but I won't be gone long. I just…need to go for a little while." She lowers her gaze briefly as she slips on a pair of shoes.

I step away from the door frame as she walks past me, going to adjust her hair in the mirror when I approach behind her.

She turns around, lifting her gaze up to mine as I lower down to give her a kiss. I pull away enough just to say, "I understand." I lean down to kiss her once more before pulling away entirely. "Take your time. I'll be here waiting for your return home."

She smiles at me before a portal opens beside her, the darkness of the night showing through the center with rows of headstones set beneath sweeping trees.

A place that I know brings Melinoë a deep sense of comfort she can escape off to. A place she feels both protective of, and also welcomed in.

She walks through the portal, closing it behind her as I go to change out of my clothes. Putting on a pair of black sweatpants before I lay myself on our bed, and wait for her return home.

CHAPTER 69

Melinoë

The dead of night surrounds me as I step out onto the cemetery grounds, the utter silence encompassing what I feel when I'm here.

I walk forward through the darkness, the moonlight above the main source of light to guide me. I lower my gaze to the headstones ahead of me, slowly passing each one until I stop to find something needing to be tended to.

I approach a headstone with a gold-framed picture toppled over, the glass facing the soil. I lift it up, leaning it up against the granite surface as I look down at what lays inside of it.

A picture of a woman and a man, their arms interlocked together as they smile widely at each other. I squint my gaze further and recognize the man and woman in the photo.

Irene and her husband, the man I helped cross over to the afterlife.

I lift my gaze to the writing on the headstone, reading aloud quietly to myself.

"Embris." I enunciate, reading the words that display beneath his name. "May he rest beneath the moons and the stars."

I grin at the words, remembering what he told me to tell her the day he passed. That he loved her more than the moon and the stars. A sweet sentiment.

"She had that added recently."

I look up to see Embris standing behind me, a wide grin curving his lips as he nods to it. "You should've seen how her face lit up once they were finished carving it. That glow that she once had when I was alive sparked in her face again." He pauses as I stand up from his grave. "Gradually each and every day, I begin to see more of it."

I smile. "She'll find the fullness of that spark again. Eventually."

He gives me a look. "And what of you?"

My brows knit together as I tilt my head. "I don't understand."

"I can see it. You're happy but…something has changed." He nods towards my chest. "Something weighs on you now that didn't before."

I loosen a soft breath as my brows smooth back straight. Shrugging my shoulders vaguely as I say, "Some things have changed since we last spoke."

Suddenly the edge of the sweater feels suffocating around my wrists, keeping my gaze on Embris as I go to roll my sleeves up. Releasing the breath I've held in as the cool night air kisses my skin.

"And you," Embris begins as we walk side by side together through the cemetery. "Do you feel changed?"

I hesitate for a moment, already knowing the answer to that but not having admitted it to myself yet. But as I say it out loud now, it feels both unsettling and freeing as the word slips from my lips. "Yes."

"And do you think you've changed for the better?" He asks.

I loosen a breath, thinking about the things that I did to those soldiers after being freed from those dungeons. The acts that I committed upon them without a hint of remorse or hesitation. Something that I would've never dared to commit upon anyone.

But as I step fully into who I am, I connect myself wholly to that innate darkness that flows in my veins. That settles deep within my spirit.

That while it is strengthened by the trauma and abuse of my past, the anger of injustices I've faced. It is also my armor wielded by my own strength, a bond that seeks to keep me safe. Albeit in ways that are not deemed as pleasant.

But sometimes, I don't want to be pleasant. Sometimes it is necessary to make those who seek harm against me pay.

To be angry, to *fight*.

And no matter how empowered I am by that new mentality, I also feel the way my darkness has latched itself onto me. Unsure if that is a good thing or not yet.

"In a way, yes." I look over at Embris. "I do."

He gives me a grin as he says, "Then that's all that matters." I watch his smile fade slightly as he looks up in front of us. Nodding before turning to me again. "Someone has been waiting to see you."

In the next moment Embris vanishes from me entirely. When I look up in front of me, I see a familiar alabaster entity standing before me. The shadows around him coiled around his midnight black robes and feet.

"Keeper." I whisper, grinning faintly.

He gives me a nod. "I had wondered when I would see you again, Goddess of Nightmares."

We both begin to walk in step with one another. "I had been...preoccupied. But it is good to be home again."

"That is an interesting way to put being imprisoned."

I turn my head over to him, my eyes widening slightly at him before I face forward again. Keeping my tone neutral. "How did you know?"

"Eiran came to visit me while you were away. Told me where you had gone, or rather where you were kept."

I loosen a breath as I look at the sweeping branches of a tree up ahead. Trying not to hyperfixate on my wrists as I say, "Then you must know what is to come."

He nods his head. "It was wise for you to bring them over to Vulir."

"Not everyone came, though."

"I imagined so." He pauses for a moment. "I sense the toll that has on you as well."

I softly huff at him, even though his calculation isn't wrong. "I have to remind myself that I can only do so much. They must also meet me halfway if they want to ensure their safety."

"But do you truly believe that?" He asks.

I let a moment of silence pass between us before I admit, "No."

"What a gift and a curse it is to care so deeply for others. Especially when you have not always received the same in return."

At Keeper's words, I feel a tremor work through me as dampness rushes to my eyes. I stop walking altogether as I try to shove it back down. Trying to quell the storm that rushes through me.

But as I stand in the dead of night, in the cemetery with no one but Keeper around to hear me, I remember that for the last few weeks I had been forced to carry it all inside of me. To keep it locked far beneath so it was inaccessible for me to pay attention to. A decision I knew was—at the time, the best for my survival.

But as I look down at my wrist, lowering my other hand to it to rub the skin there, I feel that small box that I locked everything away inside of me break wide open.

As everything comes rushing out.

Tears stream down my cheeks as I sob beneath the moonlight. My shoulders heave forward as I fall to my knees and *weep*.

The chains around my wrists.

The cage beside the throne seat.

The whips. Oh, the sting of those whips—

I lower my hands to the ground and curl my fingers beneath the soil, desperately trying to ground myself into the present. To remind myself that I'm here, and not *there*.

I feel the hair on the top of my head stir as a large figure hovers high above me before slowly gliding downwards. The sound of large wings flap against the air before he lands on the ground, quietly walking towards me.

I feel him lower down onto his knees beside me, his familiar scent of patchouli wafting towards me as my back trembles with my grief.

My anguish.

He remains silent as he lowers his arm to my back, pulling me towards his chest as the weight of his calloused hand anchors me to the present as I weep at his side.

And for a long while, I let the tears run freely as I allow myself to feel it all. Working every shudder, every tear out of my body.

Reimus remains silent as he holds me tightly to him while I purge everything I'd been keeping locked away inside me.

CHAPTER 70

I hiss through my teeth as I feel the sharp poke of a pin stabbing my waist.

"Sorry, dear." Bellinda says kneeled below me, the seamstress of Vulir. Her hazel eyes lift up to mine through a lens of sympathy. "I'm almost finished."

I try to let out a deep exhale but am slightly restricted by the tight fitting bodice that is being fitted in place.

Five days have passed within the blink of an eye. Having spent most of my time getting the people from Elzwin acquainted with their new home—their new life. And the other majority of the time either getting our final wedding arrangements in order, things that I wouldn't have thought of. But I guess that's been a great advantage to having Nora around and as one of my bridesmaids.

In Nora's words, *I* needed her help. As I was totally fine with just getting my wedding gown and making sure we had enough food for everyone. Let's just say her and Hecate have both taken the liberty of getting everything else in order.

I ease my weight from one foot, leaning onto the other as Hecate comes walking into the bridal suite. Clasping her hands over her mouth. "Oh dear, you look stunning."

I smile as I say, "Thank you. Bellinda is doing an incredible job."

Bellinda looks up at me as two pink splotches faintly color her sun-kissed cheeks. She lowers her gaze back down, finishing tailoring the final touches.

Makaria steps into the room as her reaction similarly mimics Hecate's. Her eyes glowing with a vibrancy that I haven't seen in a while. Warming my heart at the sight of it.

She grins deeply as she says, "I can't believe my sister is getting married." I watch as her eyes glisten, going to bring her hand up to her face.

"Oh gods, please no more tears. I've expelled enough of them already." I say, chuckling as Makaria steps up closer to the stool I'm standing upon.

"Fine. No tears…for now." She says, a giggle escaping out of her.

Hecate looks over at Makaria, resting her hand on her shoulder as she grins widely. "Wait until you see the veil."

"Oh, I would very much like to see it now."

"Hey, it's not finished yet." Bellinda chimes out, peering her gaze up at the two. "Plus, it's all lace so it's very fragile. It will only be coming out when it is time to put it on this one's head." She says, nodding up to me.

"*Yes, Bellinda.*" I say.

"Okay so it looks like the only thing that we have left to do is figure out seating arrangements." Nora says as she looks down at a list in front of her, situated on a clipboard.

"Our mother said she would handle that." Makaria says, looking at me. "That's one of the many perks of being a goddess. You can just will things into existence."

We share a brief laugh together as Nora shoots me a glance.

She goes to open her mouth when I silence her with the lift of my hand.

"But," I begin as she closes it. "I told her that you wanted to set up most of the decorations, and plan most of the wedding with Hecate instead. So she promises *only* to will the seating."

Nora bows her head as an approval grin curves her lips. "Thank you."

"You know, if I ever get married, I'll have you coordinate my wedding too." Makaria says.

Nora tilts her head as she smirks at her. "Does that mean there is a mister in your life currently? Or are you just playing with my emotions?"

I watch as faint splotches of pink show up on Makaria's cheeks, trying to keep the grin on her face from surfacing when she says, "A lady never tells."

Nora gasps as she lifts her hands into the air, following Makaria out of the bridal suite as I hear her voice echo on the way out. "You can't just leave me hanging like that, Makaria."

I giggle to myself as Hecate steps forward. "You'd think that she was the maid of honor with how thorough she has been with helping plan it."

Hecate chuckles as her golden gaze lifts to mine. "She has certainly taken a lot of the headache of planning it away."

A moment of silence passes between us.

"Thank you, by the way."

I tilt my head. "For what?"

Hecate smiles as she says, "For asking me to be your maid of honor."

A smile curves my lips as I say, "There was no one else I would've asked."

Because it's true. When I came to Vulir I wasn't looking for a friend. Someone that I could bear my soul to and find acceptance in. To form a bond with who not only uplifts me, but also reminds me to soften and let others in.

But I found all of that, and more, in Hecate.

"So, you're sure it'll work?" I ask.

She nods her head. "I felt the essence in him. I believe that if I act as a bridge between them, I can transfer Dimtiri's share of the essence to him."

I nod my head, Bellinda standing up and stepping back from me to observe and assess her work. "I think it'll give Dimitri some peace of mind if we can."

The following day after going into the cemetery, Reimus and I met with Hecate to discuss what we thought was needed in order for Dimitri to regain his essence. That it needed to be regained from the land, and if she'd be willing to assist by cloaking us from the soldiers—and from Zeus, as we stepped onto the soil of the Casalas Mountains.

She'd suggested that she could just transfer the essence to him. And after doing a spell on Reimus to locate it, she confirmed that it was possible.

Which is great news, as I have no intention of stepping foot on that territory again unless absolutely necessary.

In the days that have passed there have been no warnings, no news of any attacks made by Zeus. I've found myself fidgeting at the lack of action happening, but as Reimus had reminded me before, it's probably another intentional move.

Meant to keep me anxious and on my toes, waiting.

Hecate chuckles softly. "I imagine it will." She looks up at me. "How is he around Dionysus now?"

I shrug my shoulders. "He tolerates him, but he still hasn't completely warmed up to him yet. I don't expect him to."

"Neither do I. But in time, he may. Especially if Dionysus continues being active in the community."

After a few days of Dionysus staying at the Guardian's Palace, he came to me asking what he could do to contribute around here. That the thought of just sitting around would make him go stir crazy.

And boy, do I understand what he means.

So Reimus offered for him to help with assisting the villagers from Elzwin as they got acclimated.

I grin faintly. "Yes. He might."

"Okay, what do you think? I will need to tailor off the excess fabric, but otherwise she's finished."

I step down from the stool as I turn to look in the mirror. My eyes widening as my mouth parts open, my breath hitching as what Bellinda has created for me.

"Bellinda—it's…" My gaze roaming over the gown as my words trail off. "It's perfect."

I see Bellinda smile widely through the mirror, clasping her hands together. "Oh, good. I'm so glad you love it."

As I look down at the gown, a wide smile of my own lights up my face as the knowledge that Reimus and I will be married in three days surfaces.

A day that cannot come soon enough.

CHAPTER 71

Reimus

"You ready?"

Dimitri gives me a curt nod, extending his hand out to Hecate standing between us. "Ready."

I look up at Melinoë, giving her a slight nod before extending my hand out to Hecate.

"This should not take long," Hecate begins as she looks between both Dimitri and I. "I will fully retract myself from both of you when it is done."

She extends both of her hands out to Dimitri and I, giving Melinoë a nod before she clasps onto our hands.

Melinoë steps back from us, wielding her shadows to the surface as she begins to build a wall around us, cloaking us from everything else. Her palms face outwards as she extends the barrier around us, keeping the edge of the perimeter far enough away from us that it's not suffocating. But close enough to keep the energy that Hecate wields at a close range.

Hecate closes her eyes as she begins to mumble a series of chants to herself. Her hand firmly held in mine as I feel the essence ramp up inside of me. Uncoiling itself from the base and springing upwards.

My body bows slightly backwards as I feel Hecate's power coaxing it out of me. The sensation akin to gravity pulling me upwards from the inside, working to expunge the essence to the surface.

I look over at Dimitri who has his eyes closed, his chest rising and falling deeply as he holds onto Hecate's other hand. My attention jerks down to my chest, to the beam of light emanating from it.

A faint orange glow of energy that slithers along my veins, pulsating out of my pores as the brightness intensifies. I watch as the essence detaches a portion of itself from the rest, watching that sliver of light slowly crawl itself over my arm. As it attaches itself to Hecate's hand, I feel the subtle loss of it.

A distinct knowing that it never belonged to me to begin with.

The essence leeches its way up Hecate's arm as the light highlights her brown skin, giving it a golden hue. Her hand stays firmly clasped to mine as the chanting continues, the essence spider webbing itself to her shoulders before it lowers down to her chest.

Her body acting as the bridge to both Dimitri and myself. A crossroad of safely guiding the essence to who it belongs to, ushering it with the will of her power.

I watch as it slithers to her other arm, inching down her skin until it comes into contact with Dimitri's hand. And as it latches onto Dimitri's fingers, coiling itself around his skin, his body jolts forward as he takes a sharp breath in.

I watch as the essence molds itself to him like a parasite claiming a host to feed off of. The essence pulsating as the faint orange glow travels up his arm, extending to the rest of his body. And instead of becoming energy that controls him—

It becomes an extension of him, as it was always meant to be.

The glow suddenly begins to dim rapidly, the light stifling completely as Hecate lets go of both of our hands. Her soft chanting ceasing as she opens her eyes. "It is done." She says, looking over at me first before glancing over at Dimitri.

Dimitri keeps his eyes shut for a long moment, his chest rising and falling sharply as he stands there silently.

"You may lower the shield now." Hecate says to Melinoë.

I watch as the inky tendrils of shadow begin slithering down the large border she put up for us. The wall surrounding us lowering further and further to the ground until they pool along the grass and inch themselves back to Melinoë.

With her fingers lazily pointed downwards, I watch as her shadows retract themselves back into her skin. Until suddenly the grass beneath our feet is a rich green once again.

She looks up at me, grinning softly before turning to Dimitri.

I follow her gaze as Dimitri finally opens his eyes, a look of awe and starstruck in them. He blinks once, then twice before I watch the sudden fall of his chest.

I step around Hecate, going to his side when I ask quietly, "How do you feel?"

Dimtri finally pulls his gaze from staring at nothing to looking at me, a moment of silence stretching between us before he works on a swallow. "I remember it." He gazes down at his hands. "The ritual."

I say nothing as he continues speaking.

"I remember giving my essence back to the land—to our home." He lifts his gaze back up to mine. "I remember agreeing to having that memory stripped from me. To protect our people and what essence flowed through our blood. To keep *him* from learning it." He clenches his jaw as a tick runs along the sharp edge of it, his words a notch lower when he says, "I remember…"

As he lifts his hand up higher, his palm facing the sky, I watch as a small tendril of fire appears above his skin. Raising up an inch from his palm as it dances there. A grin curving his lips as he says, "It feels really good to be back."

I chuckle softly as I nod. "Yes, it does."

Dimitri lowers his hand, the flame stifling with it as he looks at Hecate. He turns his body fully towards her as he grabs her hand. "Thank you," He says, kissing the tops of them before lowering them back down. "Truly."

Hecate smiles as she says, "You're welcome."

Dimitri trains his gaze on Melinoë, giving her a half grin. "And I promise I won't use it on Dionysus."

She chuckles as she nods. "That would be greatly appreciated."

"Unless he does something to deserve it. Then I won't hesitate." He cuts in, smirking.

Melinoë gives him a raised brow as she leans her head to the side. She goes to say something when I interject.

"I think what Dimitri means to say is," I step closer to Melinoë as I give Dimitri a look. "That he's willing to give Dionysus a second chance, and begin anew until proven otherwise."

I watch as Dimitri's mouth falls open, a burst of frustration dancing across his face. "Okay, that is not what I'm saying at all—"

Melinoë gives him one look, raising her brows ever so slightly. Causing him to sigh heavily as his expression smooths out.

"Fine." He forces out as he lifts a finger. "But only because he's your brother—or whatever. And…" He trails off for a long moment before continuing. "Because he was only doing what he was told to do."

Melinoë gives him a reassuring and approving nod.

"But I still don't trust him." Dimitri cuts in.

Melinoë chuckles softly as she says, "I don't expect you to. I only expect you both to behave yourselves when you're forced to stand in the same room as each other in just a few days."

A warm, vanilla feeling comfortably nulls itself inside of me. The preparations that have gone into our wedding day have filled me with the most amount of joy I've felt in a long time. Promising Melinoë—and Nora, that I wouldn't take over too much of the wedding prep. Only a few things in particular that Nora agreed I could handle and manage.

A laugh surfaces inside of me at the memory of Nora finding out about the engagement, and discussing the layout of the wedding with her.

"Eww, and you think *that* screams elegant and ethereal?" She'd said when I asked her how she thought about putting a silk runner down along the garden pathway. "No—there will be *flower petals* scattered along the walkway with twinkle lights hung in the tree branches above the walkway. That way when the guests arrive and walk through it, they'll be transported into a wonderland of mysticism and *class*." She'd said, peering at me sidelong.

I laughed as I'd said, "You're right. That sounds much more charming."

"I'll *behave*." Dimitri groans out, bringing me back from my thoughts.

I watch as Melinoë approaches his side, lowering her hand to his shoulder as she leans her chin on top of her fingers. She smiles as she says, "You're the best."

I watch as the harshness from Dimitri's shoulders and gaze soften, a grin kicking up the corners of his mouth as he shrugs his shoulders vaguely. Trying to shrug off the warmth that she suddenly brought to his features though the effect of her words remains.

As the care he's developed for her blossoms on his face. Knowing that even though he doesn't care for Dionysus very much still, that he would settle his own dislike of him if it meant doing it for her.

She steps away from him as she comes to me. "So, do we know what Aven is making yet?"

A chuckle escapes out of me as I am reminded of the glee of his face when I told him I would be honored if he made our reception dinner. He'd said he'd need to bring on some help, in which I agreed.

I lower my lips to the top of her head, pressing a kiss there as I say, "All I know is that it's going to be a *feast* like we've never seen before, as he put it."

She chuckles beside me as she wraps her arms around me. "Well whatever it is, I'm sure it'll be perfect."

I give her a wide grin as the finality that I'll be marrying the love of my life in just a few days settles. The idea of perfection having little to do with the decor and the food, and all to do with who I will be sharing this moment with.

Who I get to share eternity with.

CHAPTER 72

Melinoë

The next day I made it an effort to spend some time in The Underworld with the souls. When they asked where I've been, I decided to just tell them I had been busy with other things.

Not wanting to burden them with the truth of where I've been, especially as time creeps closer to my wedding day.

I spend much of my time in the Asphodel Meadows, letting Irwin and Shayla debate with me about who has grown the most tomatoes since they've last seen me. Giggling as Shayla glares at Irwin in a playful manner, as if to tell him *if you don't agree that I have grown the best tomatoes then you might find your garden suddenly dismantled.*

After spending some time with them I visited Elana where she insisted, upon the news of my engagement, that she bake me fresh muffins. I obliged as I sat in her kitchen, listening to her talk about the Transmigration that will be happening in a few months. The process where souls who've decided to reincarnate again get to be reborn, living out another existence on the earthly plane in new bodies with new life missions to be guided towards. When I'd asked Elana if she'd ever reincarnate, she told me she was happy being where she is now.

That even though she cannot remember anything from her past life—due to drinking from The Lethe prior to her arrival in the Asphodel Meadows, that she feels at peace here and is content with an eternity of baking and resting.

I now sit in the grass with my sister by my side, just as we had done shortly before everything happened.

I look over at her now, her gaze trailed up to the cyprus tree towering over us as a hummingbird hovers above a branch. Its tiny little wings flapping at rapid speed as the pink sheen coloring the underside of its neck shines visibly. His light green belly camouflaging with the tree leaves as he darts into them, hidden from us now.

"I came here a lot when you were gone." My sister says, bringing her gaze down to the stretch of land ahead of us. "Many times I found myself envious of the life that surrounds this place. How they could still find such exuberance in a place meant to be your everlasting end. Drowning in my own grief of a part of myself I found hard to get back."

I look over at my sister, a frown forming on my face.

"After a while I finally found it in me to talk with the souls. The irony that they find total peace in complete disremembrance of their former lives while I felt…plagued by knowing the truth of mine. It was hard for me to feel safe again, to grapple with the truth of who I am. With the core traits that I've embodied since I was young that Zeus took advantage of."

She finally looks over at me as a faint upward turn of the corner of her lips appears. "But you inspired me, even in your absence, to be brave and *own them* in the turmoil of it all. That he only continues to control my actions if I allow him to."

I give her a warm grin as I say, "You are perfect the way you are, Makaria. All of the warm and bright characteristics that you hold make you who *you* are." I shake my head. "Don't allow him to shape that for the worse. Don't give him that power."

She nods her head as her grin widens. "I know that now."

She leans into me, wrapping her arms around my shoulder as I hug her back. I take a long inhale in, releasing when the charge of energy drags my attention forward.

I look up to see Thanatos standing before us, taking a step forward from his portal when he halts abruptly. His pearl white hair shining starkly against his midnight wings as they tuck themselves closely to his back. His gaze lowers to mine as his gray eyes widen slightly. "My apologies," He begins as Makaria pulls away from me, looking up at him. "I didn't know you were here, Melinoë. I will…"

He looks over to Makaria and I watch as twin splotches of pink form on both of her cheeks. Her gaze lowering away from Thanatos as a smirk deepens on my face.

Oh, I missed *something* around here.

"No, stay. I was actually just getting ready to leave." I say as I stand myself up from the ground. Makaria whips her gaze up at me, her eyes widen briefly when she sees my smirk. "I need to see Hades before I return home anyway."

Thanatos nods his head as he passes a quick glance at Makaria. "Of course. He should still be at the edge of the courtyard."

"Thank you." I say as my sister stands up. I look towards her as I say, "Well, I'll see you in two days then?"

A wide grin appears on her face as she nods. "Wouldn't miss it for the world."

We give each other a parting hug before I pull away, willing a portal open as I step inside of it. Looking over my shoulder as the two walk towards each other. Noticing the look of longing and admiration on Thanatos' face.

A look similar to the one that Reimus gives me.

I huff out a nearly silent noise before stepping through the portal, coming out the other side to the palace courtyard. I close the portal when I see a dark hair above a tall back standing up ahead, his gaze fixed on the souls far below him.

I walk the short distance towards him, standing by his side as I say, "So, can I assume that you are aware of Thanatos and Makaria spending time together?"

Hades huffs out a short laugh. His hands remain folded calmly behind his back. "I am aware, yes."

I nod my head, a moment of silence passing between us. I go to open my mouth when Hades cuts me off.

"You have nothing to worry about." He ensures. "If it were any other god I would be cautious. But I have known Thanatos for eons. He is good."

I closed my mouth, stifling the question I was going to ask about Thanatos. But as he quells my curiosity—and protectiveness for my sister, I say instead, "Good to know."

Hades turns to face me, the soft look in his features smoothing the harshness that usually is there. "Are you ready for the big day?"

I nod. "I am."

"Good. I know your mother is very excited to watch you get married."

A pause of silence stretches between us before I say, "Can I ask you something?"

He nods. "Of course."

I take a deep breath in. "Did you...know?" I lift my hands up, wielding a few tendrils of shadow to the surface. "Did you suspect that The Fates had defied Zeus by making me still like you?" I let the shadows fall away as I lift my gaze back up to Hades.

He looks at me for a brief moment before saying, "I hadn't been sure, as I truly did not know about the prophecy until you had told Reimus. Told us. But that day, when I asked you to show me what you could wield,"

I nod my head. "When you were training me."

His gaze roams over my face. "When both of our shadows connected, I felt..." He trails off as he shakes his head. "Familiarity. And in that moment, I had begun to wonder if The Fates put some of my essence inside of you. Shared my same gifts with you. But I never knew for sure."

"Does what you know now anger you?" Asking about the part in the prophecy that Zeus was not supposed to be the one to bear Persephone's children, Hades was.

He stares at me for a moment, watching the ridges of his sharp jaw clench briefly. "Yes." He says honestly, not bothering to lie to me which I appreciate. "It does. Greatly."

I loosen a breath as I shake my head. "He has ruined so much. For all of us."

My hand comes to my other, gently gripping the sides of my wrist. Feigning the reminder of the loss of chains there. I take a long breath in before releasing. "He cannot take anything else from us. But I know what is on the horizon." I lift my gaze back up to Hades. "And I would be a fool not to admit that I am afraid, even in my determination to end him."

Hades glances down briefly to my wrists. "War is unpredictable, and there is no guarantee that everyone who fights with us will still be standing at the end of it."

The feel of his hand on top of mine stills my fingers gripping into my skin, the weight of it blanketing over the sudden anxiety rising.

"But I will do everything in my power, Melinoë, to keep you safe. Even if I have to give my life to ensure it."

I lift my gaze up to him, knitting my brows together.

"Because you may not be my daughter through blood, but I view both you and your sister as such nonetheless." His gaze narrows briefly. "The children I was not able to give life to."

My brows smooth down as a frown pulls at my face. I slowly lower my hand from my wrist, lowering both arms down to my side.

"I would like to show you something. If you have the time."

I nod my head. "Sure."

Hades nods as a portal opens beside him. I gaze through it as my breath hitches at what lies in the center. A deserted stretch of land before towering slate grey mountains, wafts of fog hovering in the air around them.

I gasp as I lift my gaze up, looking over to the far end of The Underworld. That stretch of land that I had asked Hades about before.

"I know trust does not come easily to you," He begins, drawing my attention back to him. "But I promise you will always be safe with me, Melinoë."

I glance between him and the portal, knowing that for whatever reason he wants us to venture there must be a good one. That he is right, trust does not come easily to me. But I also hold no doubt of belief that he means what he says.

That I am always safe with The King of The Underworld.

I nod my head. "I know."

Hades extends his arm out as I usher mine around his. "Do not show fear while you are here. You have nothing to be afraid of."

And as we stepped through the portal to Tartarus, I held no fear for where we were going.

CHAPTER 73

My feet step out onto ashen, cold ground. Splinters of cracks deviating within the stone surface, spider webbing towards the mouth of a cave. The air around us pitch black aside from the glow of the sky above.

Those same magenta and fuschia hues in the sky yet darker and more dull here.

I lift my gaze up to towering peaks of mountains, realizing that we're at the center of them. Dense fog coils itself against the dreary slopes as a heaviness settles in the air around us.

Hades gently squeezes my arm, pulling my attention back as he guides us closer to the opening of the cave.

"As you know, Tartarus is a place in The Underworld where I keep the worst of the lot. Those who have committed vile acts of treason, and things of the like."

I hear the skitter of something move across the ground as my foot bumps it, my breath hitching as I look to see where it went. But as my gaze stays lowered, I watch as thick tendrils of shadows form on the ground beneath our feet.

Following closely to us as Hades guides us closer to the cave. I almost wonder if I'm willing them accidentally when I look up at Hades.

Realizing the shadows are coming from him.

I watch as they cling loosely around his legs as they follow us deeper into the abyss.

"It is a place where that innate well of darkness in myself gets to come out. With no restriction on how I wield it. To judge how those imprisoned inside are to spend the rest of their eternity." A moment of silence passes between us. "An abyss of pure, and unfettered terror not for me, but for those who reside inside."

As we approach the opening of the cave, I peer inside to total darkness. Unable to see even a flicker of light until a torch suddenly appears beside Hades, hovering over his shoulder as it follows us forward. I look at the flames dancing above it, feeling my hands begin to dampen with the resemblance of the one in that cell.

My chest begins to rise and fall quickly. "Stop—"

Hades stops his stride as he turns to look at me.

I keep my gaze lowered to the ground, unwilling to look at the torch and be reminded of that place. Unwilling to become overwhelmed with those memories.

Suddenly the blow to my back stings me, the flare of fire scorching my skin as my skin peels open. I jerk my hand to my back, hissing through the pain as I groan through my skin splitting open.

The image of Zeus standing behind me with no remorse for whipping his daughter. While all of the gods and goddesses just watched, not one of them was willing to enact retribution for my sake.

Not one of them stepped forward at the cruelty of his actions.

Suddenly I feel the weight of hands on my shoulders. Not Zeus' but his.

Hades.

"Melinoë, listen to me." He says steadily. "This is all a figment of the memories that plague your mind. You are not there anymore."

I keep my eyes squeezed shut, unknowing when exactly I shut them. Breathing in and out deeply, trying to get the pain on my back to go away. But the fire scorching my skin won't subside, it won't—

"You have escaped. You are free from him."

I take his words in, trying to settle them deep within me but unable to still shake myself from the feeling of those whips against my back. The harsh lash of pain they inflicted upon my skin that I can still feel as if I were still in that moment.

Standing there before all of those people as they just watched me.

In the next moment, I feel pressure along my wrists followed by a kiss of icy wind along them. I take a staggering breath in when I begin to focus on that instead, finding the coldness against the skin there to be borderline unpleasant with the brisk coldness.

I finally open my eyes as I lower my hand from my hand, bringing it in front of me to see his shadows lightly floating around them.

Not coiling tightly, but free and floating unbound.

I take a few deep breaths in and out, finding my breathing steadying as the pain on my back dissipates. I look up at him as my gaze lifts to what hovers beside him now.

No longer a torch, but instead a ball of bright silver light.

I feel his shadows slip away altogether, the coolness lifting with them as I look up at him. Standing up straight again after hunching over and curling into myself. He gives me a moment to gather myself, allowing me to be the one to break the silence. "Thank you."

His head tilts slightly as the sharpness from his features softens again as he looks at me. "We can take a moment before we enter—"

"No," I begin as I take one last steadying breath. Feeling centered and in my own body, and in the present once again. "I'm okay."

He stares at me for a moment before nodding his head. He lifts his arm up again as I interlock mine with his and enter the cave of Tartarus.

We walk through a long dug out corridor, the limestone walls curving at the top and forming a tall arch. Silence no longer accompanies us as the faint sounds of wailing slither in and out of the corridor. Pimpling the hair on my arms to stand up.

"One soul in particular that I was most *eager* to judge, was one who went by the name of Broderick Willard."

Hades guides me further down the corridor, those wailing sounds creeping closer and closer to us.

"When he was alive, he had a special interest in *taking* what he wanted. Sometimes these were trivial means such as petty theft, but other times, it included far more nefarious acts. And most of the time he was not alone. He usually had the assistance of his companions, Tavius Jallar and Deacon Lancis."

The ball of light to Hades' left begins to reveal a series of openings on either side of the walls ahead of us. Both openings with an iridescent prism acting as a shield to the opening.

Acting as a gate to keep whatever is inside imprisoned.

"When Broderick died, his soul remained lost for a short while. He thought he could use this to his advantage to take care of some unfinished business as he put it. But when his body was finally scorched to ash, his soul was left with no choice but to enter the gates to The Underworld. To finally pass through and receive judgement from me."

Everything inside of me hollows out as we approach the first corridor, the inside not being very small at all. My gaze tracks over the jagged ground before lifting up to who is bound inside of it.

A man with a familiar goatee curving along his chin.

The breath that leaves me feels like it goes nowhere as I look upon the man who killed Eiran, and tried to rape me in the astral realm.

"When I judged Broderick's life, I knew his punishment would have to be special because of what he attempted on you in the astral realm. I was greatly infuriated by the act to say the least." An edge to his tone following his words.

My eyes widen as I witness Broderick's hands being chained up to the ceiling of the prison, stretching his body up until he's standing on his tiptoes. His body completely nude as his head hangs downwards, tension causing the veins in his neck and arms to starkly stand out.

I only lower my gaze when I see the top of another's head, noting the similar haircut. I lower my gaze further and I sharply inhale at what I witness.

"I figured if they could stand by each other's side through all that they committed while alive, then they can be together in death, too."

The nude man beneath Broderick holds a knife to his cock, slowly rocking the blade back and forth at an agonizingly slow pace. Watching as each shred of skin gets tethered by the blade, watching as it sinks halfway down into his shaft when Broderick wails a piercing cry of pain.

As I stand there I watch the man below him cut through his cock, finding not the alarm of disgust rock through me, but the utter calmness of approval.

"The one below him would be Tavius, while the one standing behind him is Deacon."

Not even noticing that another was standing in the room at all, I lift my gaze to Deacon positioned behind him—nude as well. I knit my brows together as I watch him hold something to Broderick's back. "Is he—"

"Stabbing him in the back? Yes, he is." Hades says coolly.

I watch as the tip of a blade comes out of Broderick's chest, a trail of blood seeping out of the wound before it begins pooling down his chest the further the blade surfaces.

And as Broderick's screams intensify, I watch as Tavius saws through the last bit of flesh of his cock. Watching as it shrivels up and falls to the ground, blood spurting out of the open wound.

I step away from Hades, approaching the prism gate as I halt.

"They cannot see you. Only if I allow them to."

I let the breath I held in escape then, slowly leaving my lungs as I watch a burst of magic spark within the corridor. I watch as the shriveled up dick hovers up from the ground, reattaching itself to Broderick and the blade through his chest pulling backwards and out of his skin. The blood pooling there retracts back into his body as the blood spurting from his sawed off cock ceases as it reattaches itself back on.

Without saying another word, I stand there and watch as it happens again.

And again.

The whole time that my gaze is watching the events play out before me I feel a part of myself latch onto the satisfaction that is Broderick's pain, his agony. A wounded part of myself that never came back with me after that man killed Eiran.

Because from that moment on, added onto the restrictiveness that I felt all my life growing up, I felt even more powerless because of what this man did to me. Took from me.

Who made me feel even more weak than Zeus ever did before.

But as I watch him be brutally tortured by his own *brother* as he'd called him, I feel that wounded part heal itself over. A woundedness that only intensified after Zeus kidnapped me, forcing me into a state of quietness where I never spoke out.

That final, lingering part of my shadow that wanted nothing more than to be accepted for what it was.

Pain.

That wanted to be nurtured but I never had an idea how to mend her back together. Never knew how I could merge her back into the wholeness of my being without feeling the tremendous shame and guilt that came with it for not better protecting her.

Until now, as I watch that retribution I've longed for play out before my eyes.

Realizing that the restrictiveness I've felt around my wrists started well before Zeus kidnapped me and chained me to a dungeon. That the first time I was held against my will was with Broderick pinning me down. That maybe the reason why it had affected me so much was not just because of the physical chains once placed there, but the magical ones that once were as well.

I feel hotness blanket my gaze as tears rush to my eyes, the warmth in my blood mimicking the rage of that little girl inside of me who just wanted to live in peace. Who just wanted to be accepted, and treated fairly as everyone else.

Tears stream down my face as my body quivers with her rage, with the injustices that we've faced together. And as we both silently shed tears together, I experience a profound wave of healing that threatens my knees to buckle in on themselves. But as I force myself to remain standing, that I would never again bow beneath someone's feet again, the totality of what Hades has just shown me settles inside of me.

That justice *can* be enacted for me. That unbeknownst to myself and without knowing it, it *has* been.

And whether Hades realizes it or not, his judgement for these men healed those remaining fibers of my soul that believed I could not be granted a fair outcome.

That fate would not serve me a just, and swift grace of dignity on my behalf.

I turn away from the corridor, looking at Hades through red-rimmed eyes as I say to him, "Thank you." My words shaken by the force of the energy coursing through me.

Healing energy.

I rush myself into him, wrapping my arms around him as my tears cease themselves in his arms. Hades tentatively goes to wrap his arms around me, but when he does, he relaxes into my hold.

As we both stand there for a long moment, I feel the calm buzz of warmth settle over my skin. Replaced by the rage of her pushing against my skin, and instead with the comfort of her feeling safe once more.

As I mentally witness her get back up from the cold ground, standing up on weak knees again as she smiles up at me. That inner child of mine walks over to the neatly made bed and slips herself beneath the soft cashmere covers, laying her head back down on the pillow once more.

A wide grin curving up the corners of her mouth as she closes her eyes to finally rest.

CHAPTER 74

Reimus

I steep the tea bag into the hot water as the sweet and spicy aroma of honey and turmeric wafts itself towards me. A wispy steam rising from the ceramic mug.

I grab both mugs and make my exit from the kitchen and head outside. The warm orange glow of the setting sun greeting me immediately as I step out onto the red-brick pathway. The gentle sound of birds chirping surrounds me as I follow the trail deeper into our garden.

I come to the end of the trail, looking up to see Melinoë tucked away inside the gazebo. Her legs hiked up close to her chest as she rests her back on the cream-colored cushion. The ends of her long inky strands flowing over the edge of the sofa as she holds my journal up to her face. Her gaze slowly sweeping over the words displayed within.

I open the door and seat myself beside her feet, handing her the mug. "It's probably a good thing I haven't written my vows yet."

A grin curves up her face as she closes the journal, looking up at me as she seats herself up on the sofa. "I'm sure if you did you wouldn't have been so willing to let me read it." She sets my journal down on the coffee table as she takes the mug from my hand. She takes a deep whiff of the tea before making a low humming noise and taking a drink.

"You'd be correct." I take a sip from my mug, setting it down onto the coffee table before I lean back into the sofa.

When she came home today from being in The Underworld, I'd noticed the lingering redness beneath her eyes. The puffiness in her face as if caused from expending deeply held emotions and grief from within her. When I asked her if everything was alright she said yes. And as a grin curved her lips, and I saw the tension from her shoulders ease, I believed her.

When I asked if she'd like to talk about it, she nodded her head. When she asked if she could also read any new poetry I'd written in my journal, I happily obliged. Handing her my journal to soothe her in any way she needed while I made us both some tea.

I lift her legs up and lay them over my thighs, caressing my hands down to her feet as I slip her shoes off. Massaging her feet as she leans up against the back of the sofa. Her tired, yet vibrant emerald gaze latched onto mine.

"Hades took me to Tartarus today," She begins as she loosens a breath. "I saw where he keeps the prisoners detained there." She pauses for a moment. "I saw him."

A storm builds inside of me at who I already know she's referring to. A fire of anger lighting up inside of me at what he attempted on her.

"His name is Broderick—or was, whatever." She takes a ragged breath in. "I never knew his name up until then. I had only known him for what he did to Eiran," She works on a swallow. "Almost did to me."

I continue gently massaging her feet, not letting the anger inside of me cause me to cease their determination to lift any more tension from her body.

"Before today, I thought that I had healed and moved on from all of that. It still haunted me in ways, of course. But I thought I had moved past that. Because he didn't succeed in what he was after with me. But," Her gaze flicks away. "I realized it wasn't what he *almost* did that still affects me, but the *control* he had over me in that moment. That I felt utterly defenseless and weak, unable to free myself from the restraint he had over my wrists."

If I could burn his body alive again I would. Better yet, if only I would have been able to get my hands on that fucker when he was still alive. I would've made him pay so severely, burning his hands so tremendously he'd never be able to use them again.

Scorching his face so his presence alone would turn everyone in the opposite direction.

"When I was imprisoned, I was yet again shackled at my wrists. Except this time they were physical. And because they were bound by magic, it depleted my powers to a nothingness so I couldn't tear myself free from them." She lifts her gaze back up to mine. "And once again, I was left feeling defenseless and weak. Especially—"

She clenches her jaw as she looks away. I gently bring my hand up to her chin, guiding her gaze back to me. "Anything you ever tell me will never cause me to look at you in any other way than what I see you now, and have always seen you since the moment I first met you."

Her eyes glisten as she looks at me.

"As a beautiful, courageous, and *resilient* woman. Someone who is capable of standing up again and again even when circumstances around her challenge her willingness to keep fighting." I lower my hand from her chin as I coil a strand of her hair around my finger. "A brave, and powerful warrior."

Her gaze roams over my face as a weak smile lifts her lips. It slowly falls away as she continues speaking. "He kept me in a cage right beside his throne. He'd hold council with the village people, with me caged inside of it." She takes a long breath in, releasing. "It was humiliating. Degrading. And he knew it."

A tick along my jaw forms at how hard I'm clenching my teeth. It takes all of my willpower to loosen it as this moment is not about my anger for her father's constant injustices towards her. It's about her feelings regarding it all, and giving her the space to express the turmoil of what she felt.

"Numbing my emotions was the only thing I could do to survive through it. Something I swore to myself I'd never do again, but it was necessary to make him believe that I was under his compulsion. And to do so felt like I was back at that cabin all over again. Being ignored by him but still controlled in micromanaging ways." Her emerald gaze churns brightly. "I thought once I returned home that I would be an emotional mess. Drudging everything up and processing what I had to force myself to drone out. And I am." She gives me a faint grin. "I am because I feel safe enough to. With you."

I lower my hand to the one in her lap, clasping it into mine as my thumb trails idly over her wrist in soft, sweeping motions.

"But seeing Broderick in his eternal prison today, it mended something inside of me." She gazes at me as she pauses for a moment. "It made me feel powerful in a way that I felt lacking in for a long time. In situations where—like my father, others have manipulated their selfish gains over me."

I watch as a shift settles in her gaze. Fueling the conviction in her words.

"It was the spark I needed to remind me that my darkness is to be wielded how I see fit. For my protection."

I feel the air thicken around us as her power charges.

"Now, there is nothing that I won't lay waste to in order to see Zeus fall. To kill him for everything he's done to me, to my mother. To everyone he's taken advantage of." Her words end in a harshness I've never heard before.

She takes a few sharp breaths in and out before stifling the energy around us completely. A calm sureness etched into her face as she states clearly, "The prophecy spoke of me being his greatest threat, so I will prove The Fates right."

A fire lighting up in her gaze as she looks at me. "Next time, I won't hold back. He will get the worst from me."

I gaze at her as I continue gliding my thumb over her wrist, feeling nothing but pride for the woman seated beside me. The growth that she has made since I first met her, the vengeance that pools in her gaze currently.

And I will make sure she gets what she deserves.

I nod slowly, a half grin kicking up my face. "As you will it so shall it be, my Queen."

The fierceness in her gaze lingers as she smirks at me, nuzzling herself closer to me as she lifts her hands up. Wrapping them around my neck as she exhales slowly. "I do love it when you call me that. Almost as much as your other nickname for me."

I chuckle as my hand lightly skims up her waist. "Is that so, little spitfire?"

I watch her grin deepen before she leans in to kiss me. "Though, I realize I don't have any nicknames for you. Shall I call you…oh! How about loverface?"

I knit my brows together, chuckling. "Okay, that is one I actually have never heard of before."

She giggles against me. "Okay, hmm…" She lifts a hand to her face, pressing her index finger to her full lips. Her eyes widening briefly as she quickly pulls it away. "Oh! I know," She lowers her lips to the side of my lips, pressing a quick kiss there. "*Little shifter*." She wiggles her eyebrows at me.

A laugh bursts out of both of us before I pull her hand close to my lips. "Honestly, I don't care what you call me at this point." I press a kiss to her hand. "As long as I'm yours." I bring her hand to my chest, splaying it out as I rub my hand along hers.

A wide smile lights up her face as she lowers her gaze to the ring on her finger. The warmth in her gaze intensified. "I can't wait to marry you in two days."

"Me neither." I say, letting her feel the beat of my heart beneath my flesh. A steady rhythm that belongs to her, and her alone. "In this lifetime, and every other."

She lifts her gaze to me, her smile deepening as she nods. "I am yours."

Melinoë crawls herself into my lap as she shows me just how much she is mine. With everything but her words.

As I greedily, *eagerly* return the same sentiment.

CHAPTER 75

Melinoë

"Which one?" The Pythia asks as she tilts her head.

Apollo's golden gaze stares at The Oracle of Delphi as he says, "Only the one that speaks of him and his children. Of his fate. The other prophecy does not belong to him, so we shall keep it that way."

The Pythia nods her head as a shift of understanding settles within her gaze. The cauldron before her is still, empty. "And the girl?"

The golden ring in Apollo's eyes churn vibrantly as he levels his chin with hers. "It must only be revealed to her when—"

The dream begins to shift and slip away as darkness falls in its place. Both Apollo and the Pythia melting away as—

I jolt awake, my eyes springing open as I gaze up at the ceiling above me.

Nestled in our bed alone this time as Reimus stayed in one of the guest rooms upstairs. Because today—

Today I get to marry the love of my life.

As if my thoughts were interlinked with Nora's, I hear the rush of her feet against the hallway floor before she's swinging the bedroom door wide open. "Rise and shine, sweetcheeks. It's time to get you prepped and ready."

I sit fully up in bed as I look over at the balcony glass door, noticing the soft glow from the sun streaming in. I lower my gaze to a clock on our bedside table, squinting as I say, "It's eight o'clock." I lift my gaze back over to Nora as I wipe the sleep from my eyes.

And that dream…I remembered the first time I had seen those same events play out. When Apollo let me into his memories to show me them.

"Which one?"

Those two words alarm themselves in my mind as I realize that the prophecy about Zeus isn't the only one that the Pythia was asking about. But what is the other one?

Before I have the time to think longer about it, Nora jumps onto the bed. Startling me from my thoughts. "Yes, but—" She crosses her legs beneath her. "We have much to do before the ceremony in…" She looks down at the clock. "Seven hours."

I chuckle as I shake my head. "Nora, all I have to do is put on my dress, do my hair and makeup. What am I going to do for the remaining… four hours?"

"I'm glad you asked." She says in a chipper tone, sliding me a mug of coffee that I didn't even realize she was holding. "You will be *relaxing,* and *enjoying* yourself as you leave all of the stress of your wedding day shenanigans to me." She gives me a wide smile. "And…spending time with your bridal party, of course."

My gaze lifts over to the doorway as I see both Hecate and Makaria walk into the room, both of them lighting up with excitement. Behind them I see Euphrosyne, Thalia, Aglaea, and—

"Sage." I chime out as I get up from the bed, setting the mug down on the nightstand.

I rush over to him as I give him a big hug, having only been able to visit him once since I've been back home. I had invited him to the wedding but wasn't sure if he would come or not.

I'm really happy to see that he did.

He pulls away from me as he says, "Contrary to my stubbornness to not leave the forest, I wouldn't miss this for the world. Well, unless I were dead. Then I suppose that'd be the only way."

I raise my brows, nodding slowly. "I suppose so." I drag out. My gaze trails to everyone standing behind him, rushing over to my sister before hugging everyone else.

"So when does the dancing begin?" Aglaea asks, her long champagne blond hair flowing like strands of silk.

Her sister Euphrosyne chuckles beside her. "During the reception. *After* the ceremony."

"Oh." Aglaea says, a hint of surprise in her tone.

I laugh as Hecate comes to my side, pulling me into her before willing a bottle of champagne into the air. "After enough glasses of this, you may find yourself doing a bit of dancing before the ceremony."

Before the bottle can land in Hecate's hands Nora snatches it away. "No way am I having the bride getting herself drunk before she's walked down that aisle." She goes to set the bottle down on the dresser, looking at all of us. "The last thing we need is Melinoë getting so drunk she doesn't remember her special night. And—there is nothing tackier than a wasted bride before we've all even sat down to eat. So," She approaches me like a mother hen, her hazel gaze full of seriousness beneath that excitement for coordinating my wedding. "*No* alcohol until the ceremony is complete." She peers her gaze at me.

"Yes, *mother*." I say sarcastically.

A smirk curves up her lips as she wraps her arms around my shoulders, sighing contentedly into my embrace. "This is going to be the best day ever. I will make sure of it."

I lean my head into hers, feeling a surge of bubbling giddiness and warmth rush through me at the day ahead of us. Incredibly curious to see what decorations Nora has put together, knowing that they will be with the utmost effort and taste.

"So," I hear Sage drawl out, a hint of mischievousness in his tone. "This is where copulation happens."

I lift my head from Nora's and whip my gaze over to Sage. His hand lightly glides over my sheets as he smirks up at me.

"Um, what does copulation mean?" Euphrosyne asks, her innocence admirable.

Her sisters giggle beside her before Thalia says, "It means having sex."

"Fucking. *Aggressive* canoodling." Sage says, winking.

"I don't think…you know what—" I chuckle as I say, "Let's just get today started with."

"Is this what you're planning to wear tonight?" Sage asks now from my dresser, having moved over there faster than I could even blink. He reaches into the drawer and pulls out a black lace lingerie set, holding it up. "It's quite dashing."

I rush over to him, snatching it out of his grasp as he giggles. Causing not only me to laugh, but everyone else.

As the room around me is surrounded by not only love, but mutual excitement for what lies ahead.

Hours later after getting something to eat in me and letting the three sisters fight over how my hair should be done—and then come to an agreement and style it, my mother and Hades appeared in the living room. Reimus keeping himself to the third level with Dimitri and Dionysus.

I sure wonder how that is going.

My mother gives me a warm hug as she says, "You look marvelous, Melinoë." Her eyes glistening as she pulls away from me.

Her jet black hair is swept up into a low bun as face-framing pieces hang loosely next to rosy cheeks. A periwinkle, flower hair pin tucked into her hair to match her gorgeous agave green gown.

A floor-length silk gown with a draped, off-the-shoulder cowl neckline exposing her shoulders and the top of her chest. The bodice corset snatching her figure pristinely as a front slip raises up to her mid-thigh. Exposing her silver open-toed heels.

"And you, mother…you look beautiful." I say in awe.

"That she does." Hades says as he steps to her side.

Donned in an all black suit, the color choice one might assume was picked for this special occasion. Yet if they knew him, they'd know this was the only color he wears.

Persephone lightly swats at Hades' shoulder as he leans in to kiss her on the cheek. "Always with your sweet words, darling." She grins against his touch before she looks around her, to the windows showcasing outside. "So, are all of the decorations in order?"

"Almost." Nora says as she comes down the hallway, having said she wanted to speak with Aven to make sure everything is prepared and ready for tonight's dinner. Apparently, she also wanted to introduce herself to the extra help in the kitchen that were gracious enough to help Aven tonight.

Her floor length gown the color of rich cabernet, the satin pooling down at her feet like a mermaid emerging from the water. Her straight, orange copper hair barely touches the smooth fabric draped over one shoulder, one side of her dress elegantly cinched to one side of her waist. The ripples of fabric drape down beside her bare leg as it pokes through the high slit. A pair of similar silver heels to my mother's fashioned on her french-tipped feet. "I have just about everything set up, except—"

"The seating. Yes, yes. I know." My mother says as she chuckles, lifting her gown up as she goes to take a step. She looks over at me first, smiling as she says, "We'll see you out there."

I nod to both of them as I loosen a breath. "See you both out there."

My mother gives me a parting hug as she turns around, picking her dress up again. "Show me where I need to set them down, Nora."

They both walk out together, the sound of both of their heels clicking against the hardwood floor as I look at the women reclining in the room around me. The color of their dresses an intentional feature I can only assume Nora was very specific about as each of the sisters wear the same dress as Nora. Each of them with their long blond hair cascading down their backs in half-up styles.

I look over at Hecate in her cabernet-hued dress, hers bearing the same silk material and snatched waist but completely sleeveless. Her hair is pinned back as it sweeps down in long dark curls along her back. Her golden gaze softly latches onto mine as a thought passes through me, wringing a soft chuckle from my lips.

She tilts her head at me.

"This is probably the first time I've ever seen you without your amethyst robe."

Hecate chuckles as she says, "I thought for a special occasion as such that I could part ways with it for one night."

"Do you feel strange without it?"

"I could lie and say no, but truthfully, yes. At least a little." She chuckles as she nods to Hades. "It would probably be like him if he were to wear anything other than black."

He lowers his hands down to his attire, lifting a brow. "I wear other colors."

"Yeah? Like what?" She asks, arching a brow.

Hades ponders over it for a few moments before huffing out a brief laugh. "Dark grey."

"So, essentially black."

"Yeah, pretty much." He says.

I laugh as Hecate comes to my side, pulling me in for a hug as footsteps sound from down the hall. My heart begins to race as I wonder if they're—

Dimitri enters into the living room, halting as he looks upon us. As he stares upon me.

He blinks at me before he can finally formulate words to escape his mouth. "Melinoë, you look…incredible."

I nod my head. "Thank you." I lower my gaze to the black bowtie fashioned to his white button up shirt. A striking black jacket pulled over and buttoned at the center. A pair of matching black pants to complete the suit. "You clean up nice yourself."

A half grin kicks up his face.

"Is he…here?"

Dimitri nods his head. "He just ventured his way outside to greet the rest of the guests. I came by just to check on you."

I loosen a breath as I nod. I go to open my mouth when he cuts me off.

"And yes, I have been *cordial* with Dionysus." He says plainly.

I chuckle. "Good."

"Okay, we're just about ready—" Nora calls as she sweeps into the room, her heels clicking against the ground. "So that means everyone outside and into position except for these two."

My gaze remains on Dimitri as I witness him starstruck in Nora's presence. His mouth slightly parted open as his gaze slowly falls over her, starting from her hair and ending at her feet. He takes in every curve of her, every trace of her body through not a heated lens—

But one of immense fondness.

I look over at Nora, nodding my head. "Alright, you all heard the woman." I watch as my words bring Dimitri back to life, clearing his throat.

As everyone clears out of the living room, but not before giving me a hug and complimenting my dress once more, I now stand in the room with just myself and Hades.

"Does he know he's in love with her?"

A snort escapes me. "He knows. He's just…"

"Afraid?" Hades asks.

I turn towards him, hearing the subtle sound of violins and harps coming from outside, the faint echo of people talking. My pulse kicks up as I loosen a shaky breath. "Yes."

Hades lowers his chin, resting a hand on my shoulder. "And you," The weight of his palm oddly calming me down. "Are you feeling afraid?"

I exhale heavily, shaking my head. "No—I just can't believe in a way that this is really happening. That someone could…love me enough to want to spend the rest of their life with me."

Hades watches me as I continue speaking.

"There was a time when I would have scoffed at the idea of marriage. At spending my time with anyone really, for that matter." I look down at the bridal dress I wear now, trailing a hand along the fabric at my waist. "But that was also during a time when I believed that love was not possible for someone like me." I lift my gaze up to Hades, smiling through the warmth blossoming in my chest. "And now today, I'm surrounded by it."

Hades grins softly, those harsh features in his face softening as he says to me, "You have *always* been deserving of it, Melinoë. And in the end, no matter what life throws at you, that is how you win amidst it all. Because you have the one thing that Zeus will never, ever have."

I tilt my head. "Which is what?"

"*Real* admiration and acceptance. *Real* love."

I feel my chest cleave open as I let his words sink in, that heat settling there uncoiling and blossoming even further.

"So let today remind you of the love that you rightfully deserve, and allow yourself to drown in it."

Heat rushes to my eyes but I stifle it back, not wanting to smudge my makeup. At least not yet, knowing that Reimus' vows will most likely do it for me then. "Thank you." I say, nearly choking on my words.

His hands gently squeeze my shoulders before lowering them back down to his sides. "You're welcome. And what you asked of me,"

I watch as a warmth of his own begins to light up his features, pulling his grin into a wide smile as he says, "I would've never asked that of you as I know that I'm not…"

A frown pulls slightly on my face as I see The King of The Underworld, for the first time since I've known him, have a hard time expressing his thoughts.

"I didn't want to pry as that is something very personal. But after you asked me to walk you down the aisle, it was one of the greatest honors I had ever been granted."

I grin at him as the memory of leaving Tartarus surfaces. Before I made my way back home, I told Hades it would be strange not to have my father there to walk me down the aisle. As that is something that every daughter looks forward to. But the more that I spent time with Hades, I began to grow a likeness towards him. One that feels more familiar, more safe than I ever felt with my biological father.

So when I asked him if he would walk me down the aisle, I held no doubt in my mind that it was the right decision.

As Hades had always accepted me for who I was, something that Zeus never could do. And even though Zeus took his fate of having children away from him, I thought I owed it not only to him to have the honor he never thought he'd have, but to also owe it to myself to see that I still get walked down that aisle.

By the man who should've been my father.

I feel the energy thicken beside us as my mother portals into the living room, gazing at me then Hades. "We're starting."

I give her a nod. "Perfect. Thank you, mother."

She nods her head before portaling back outside.

"You ready?" He asks as he lifts my veil up, gently placing it over my face before he extends an arm out for me.

I take one final deep breath in, releasing it. "More than ready." I loop my arm into his, smiling. "And thank you."

We make our slow exit out of the living room as the melody of the violins and harps changes into a slower pace. "For what?" He asks.

I stare at the hallway before us, the sunlight pooling through the windows directing us to where we're headed. "For being you." I say simply.

And as we enter into the hallway, I feel the weight of my gown pooling behind me like cascading rivulets of water. Feeling more strong, and more sure of anything I've ever felt in my life before.

Because in a way, Reimus was wrong the other night. The moments I felt strongest weren't when I had to fend for my survival. Weren't in the moments when I had to figure everything out on my own.

Sure—those all required a specific kind of strength from me. But the times I felt my strongest were when his utter devotion poured into me like it was as simple as breathing. When his words of love lit up every crevice in my body, lifting me from the shallows of what I suffered. His simple acts of kindness—such as sitting with me when I was suffering mentally from healing from my past, or just taking my dirty dishes from me when I was finished, and not asking for a simple thing in return.

It wasn't the turmoil of my past that truly made me strong, but the consistent current of his irrevocable love for me. That in return, allowed me to pour unconditional love back into myself.

And just as much as I deserve this, his love that was entirely worth waiting for, he deserves my love just as much.

Not an ounce of fear or doubt lingers in my bones as I make my way outside with Hades by my side, eager to marry the love of my life.

My twin soul.

My other half.

The catalyst in more ways than one.

CHAPTER 76

I step outside as that soft melody weaves through the garden closer to me. Bright and lush notes of a harp harmonize with the slow bass of a cello as the slow, sweeping resonants of a violin fill my chest with warmth and fullness.

A rich, beautiful melody.

Hades and I walk past the tiered water fountain, moving deeper into the garden when I lower my gaze to the glass lanterns lining the edge of the walkway. White pillar candles nestle within them as steady, golden flames cast a warm ambiance against the ferns and shrubs behind them. White rose petals lay scattered along the red-bricked pathway.

I look up to tall wooden arches positioned every few feet along the walkway. Each of them showcasing gorgeous white roses, hydrangeas, and lush greenery. My gaze lifts to the sweeping basswood trees, finding small golden lights gleaming from the branches that follow us along the walkway.

This is…more than I could've expected.

My chest sinks as emotion clogs my throat at the thought that Nora put into my wedding, down to every small detail. She really did what she said she would. That she'd give me an ethereal wedding and make it feel magical.

As Hades and I make our way closer to the gazebo, the final point before we turn towards the wedding party and down the official aisle, I take a deep breath in. Releasing slowly through my nose and blowing the lace-trimmed veil forward an inch.

Hades remains facing forward, his elbow steadily nestling mine as he asks quietly, "You alright?"

I take another staggering exhale out as I say, "Yes. I'm just moved by the decorations."

Hades chuckles softly as I hear the music—just on the other side of the remaining arch now, slowing its tempo as I hear everyone stand up from their seats. The sound causes a quick flutter in my chest as we step closer to the arch. My view of the ceremony is obstructed by tall shrubs lining each side of the arch.

My palms begin to dampen as Hades and I turn the corner, stepping in front of the final arch as my breathing starts to pick up. Gods, why do I have to be a naturally anxious person? I'm not nervous in the slightest to marry Reimus, nor am I afraid.

But knowing that a small sea of people are waiting on just the other side, even though I know everyone in attendance, still gets the nerves inside of me restless nonetheless.

As I take one final breath in and out, I let those anxious feelings go as we round the corner and step in front of the final arch. My breath seems to go nowhere as I see what awaits me.

More arches stand before me—except these ones are fashioned from tall tree trunks that rise high above us. Each one framed with bouquets of white roses and hydrangeas, foliage pouring out on the sides as saffron orange ribbon keeps them bundled together. Large, sweeping white drapery connects from each bouquet, both sides attaching to the middle of the top of the arch. The fabric creates soft ripples as it hangs loosely from the center, falling down the sides of the tree arches.

My gaze lowers to the backs of dark walnut chairs. Draped with smaller bouquets and saffron colored ribbons. Not even noticing who stands in front of them as I finally lift my gaze to the end of the aisle.

My gaze locks with Reimus and I feel the breath leave my lungs entirely. His hair slicked back with only one loose strand hanging in front of his forehead, his icy blue eyes sharp as they track my every movement. Watching his chest suddenly rise before he clenches his jaw as emotion swarms his gaze.

I forget for that moment in time that Hades is still walking me down the aisle, that his elbow is connected with mine. I forget everyone standing in attendance on either side of me, what anyone is wearing and the soft whispering as they watch me walk down the aisle.

Everything completely drones out from existence as I look upon Reimus and can't see, nor focus on anything else, but him.

My twin soul. My *husband*.

I smile beneath the veil as I watch Reimus' eyes glisten beneath the shining sun above us. His hands folded neatly in front of him beneath a sharp black suit. Looking as handsome as ever as his gaze does not falter from mine.

I regain feeling back in my legs and feet again as Hades and I stop at the end of the aisle, Reimus slowly making his way to us as he stops before me.

Hades lowers his arm from mine, the weight of his hand lifting mine and setting it into Reimus'. The immediate warmth I feel from him a familiar comfort as a shock of awareness flows through me.

Hades leans into me, pressing a kiss to my cheek before turning away and seating himself down.

Reimus and I take the few steps forward before we turn towards each other. His gaze sweeping over my face, and then my dress. "You look…otherworldly." He whispers.

A wide smile curves my face as the officiant steps closer to us. "Today we are gathered here to witness the special union of Melinoë Khthor, and Reimus Kallias. We are also gathered here today to witness Melinoë sign her loyalty, and pledge to become an official Guardian of Vulir."

Reimus keeps his gaze locked onto mine as the officiant continues speaking. The sounds of the birds just moments ago completely silenced out as my entire focus trains on him.

"Melinoë, if you would please raise your right hand and place it over your heart."

I follow the officiant's instructions, placing my right hand over my heart.

"Now lift your left palm up."

I do as he says as Reimus smirks at me. Him having prepared me already for how the process goes, knowing exactly what to expect.

"Repeat after me, and let the first drop be drawn."

I watch as Reimus lifts a dagger, pressing the tip of the blade to the center of his palm. Gliding it along his skin as crimson beads to the surface.

"I, Melinoë Khthor, vow with my life to protect the people of Vulir to the best of my immortal ability. That neither friend nor foe will come between my allegiance to their safety, nor their right to live peacefully."

I repeat the words as Reimus lowers the blade of the dagger to my left palm, pressing it in and cutting open my skin. Crimson bleeds out of the superficial wound as Reimus lowers his palm to mine.

I feel a spark of energy course through me, but more than anything, I feel the weight of Reimus' skin against mine.

"With this vow, I bind myself to this promise. And swear it with integrity, and honesty. So mote it be."

I repeat the words as I finally lower my gaze to our conjoined hands, watching as the blood trapped between our palms begins to drip down from our hands. But in mid air, I watch as that droplet of crimson floats back up to our hands, and merges itself back into our skin. A pulsing warmth flows through my hand as I feel my blood—as well as the trace of Reimus', merge back beneath my cut before the skin closes over itself.

"I now pronounce you, Guardian of Vulir."

Reimus is the first to let his hand go, seeing that no blood or marks are left behind on either of our hands. I go to lower my hand back down to my side when I feel a nudge along my mind.

Not the kind of nudge of someone trying to intrude on my thoughts or memories, but something softer. Less invasive and far more familiar.

Now I can whisper sweet nothings without needing to speak them out loud, little spitfire. His voice wrapped in smoke and velvet, heating my blood.

A wide smirk crawls up my lips as I send back down the Guardian's channel. *Careful, there are others that can still hear us.*

A moment later I feel the brief nudge of Charon down the bond. A light and airy feeling as if to resemble a light chuckle.

"Now, shall we continue?"

I look over to the officiant, nodding.

"Reimus, would you like to share your vows first?"

Reimus nods as he continues keeping his gaze on me. I fully expect him to pull out a piece of paper from his breast pocket, but as his lips begin moving again, I realize he's memorized his vows by heart. Needing not a piece of paper to passionately articulate what he feels for me, effortlessly.

"Couples say that it is hard work to maintain a relationship when you love each other. That there will be hard days to go with the great ones. That if you both love each other you'll stick by each other's sides, even when that spark between you two threatens to burn out. And as I stand here before you today, I have never disagreed with something more. Because loving you is *far* from hard work. Loving you is as easy as breathing, as fluid as the blood that circulates through my veins. That as vital as I need oxygen to flow into my lungs to survive, I need the warmth of your love to keep my heart beating. As it belongs to nothing, and no one else."

The tear brimming at the surface of my eyelid falls down my cheek. My lips tremble before I press them together.

Reimus' eyes glisten with tears as he blinks them back, one slipping free and rolling down his cheek. "I can stand here today and vow to love you through sickness and health, or say 'til death do us part. But not even death will erase my devotion for you. As I will wander and search this earth for you, in each and every lifetime after this one. Because *you*, Melinoë," He chokes on his words as he clears his throat, starting again. "Are not hard to love. You are a *gift* to me, and to everyone around you. And I will spend the rest of my days showing you how valued, and how effortless it is to be your partner. Your husband."

Reimus' face crumples up with emotion as my heart yearns out for him, wanting to wrap him up in my embrace as I shed hot tears of my own. My lips tremble once again as I loosen a breath, his hands gently squeezing mine in between us. Feeling the faint tremor work through his skin.

I don't know if I can possibly love this man anymore than I already do, but gods. The way my heart splits more and more open when I am with him surprises me all the same.

"And you, Melinoë."

I pull myself from my thoughts, clearing my throat as I begin. My gaze trained wholly on Reimus in this moment—*our* moment, together.

"When I was a little girl I learned early on to not ask questions, that everything is the way it is and nothing can be done about it. I was conditioned to believe that the scales of sacrifice always outweighed reward, and it was unrealistic for me to ask for too much. As I had been given shavings of crumbs most of my life."

A tear runs down his cheek as he gently squeezes my hands nestled inside of his.

"When I met you I was forced out of familiar territory, out of the comfort that I had falsely believed belonged to me. I began to peel back all of these layers within me, and the exposure to that rawness stung at first. But you kept feeding my starving heart with your simple acts of kindness, healing that malnourishment of what I lacked so deeply. Where suddenly I wasn't drowning in the heaviness of lack, but in the lightness of reward. I get to witness every single day now that love can be *safe*, can be more than kind. It is through you, Reimus, that I will always feel alive through the warmth of your irrevocable love. As there is nothing more special, more rewarding, than being intertwined with your love. And I will spend every day showing you how much of a true gift you are to me."

Reimus and I stare at each other as I watch a tear slip down his face, his eyes glistening with *love* and utter adoration as he gazes at me. My lips tremble as he tentatively lets go of my hands, reaching for my wedding band from a decorative ring pillow.

"With this ring," Reimus begins as he holds it up to my finger. His voice thick with emotion. "I vow with my soul and my life, to never stop loving you as fiercely as I do today. As I will love you, and protect you, even after my final breaths. I vow to shelter you through any storm, to shower you with laughter when you have been swept away from droughts of anguish."

He slides the wedding band along my finger, keeping his hand there. "In this lifetime, and every other."

I take a staggering inhale in as I lift Reimus' wedding ring, holding it up to his finger. "With this ring, I vow with my soul and my life, to never let a day pass us by where you are not reminded of how much I love you. As there is—and will never be, no other than you who has my heart completely."

I slide the ring onto his finger, sniffling as tears brim my eyes.

"In this lifetime, and every other." I lift my gaze up to his. "I am yours."

I watch his chest sink suddenly as a gentle warmth pulsates through me from his hands. He notices it when my gaze lowers to his hands, and tries to pull his hands away from mine but I keep mine firmly clasped to his.

You can never hurt me, Rei. I am never afraid when I am with you, because I am always safe with you.

I watch his eyes widen slightly as he sends a warm nudge along the bond. The feeling similar to a purring cat when they rub up against you, the warmth of their fur gliding like silk along your skin.

"I now pronounce you husband and wife." The officiant looks over to Reimus as he smiles. "You may now kiss the bride."

Reimus lowers his hands from mine as he lifts the edge of my veil up, his gaze lowering to the lettering tailored at the bottom above the lace-trimmed fabric. A wide grin curves his face when he reads the letters.

In this lifetime, and every other.

He lifts the veil over me until it flows down along my exposed back. The length of the veil flowing down my dress and to my feet.

Reimus in the flash of a second twirls me into his arms as he leans me down, and kisses me. His arm holding my back up as my leg hikes up.

Suddenly, a chorus of clapping reminds me that people are standing before us. A few whistles ring out, one of which I can identify coming from Dimitri.

And for a small eternity, it's just Reimus and I. With nothing but the feel of his lips against mine. His familiar scent of patchouli, the welcomed brand of his hand against my skin.

As his lips tentatively leave mine he brings me back up to a standing position. A wide smile gracing both of our faces as we both turn to face the guests, holding hands.

I look to see my mother and Hades seated in the front row along with my sister, Hecate, Nora, and Dimitri. They all give us ecstatic smiles and cheers, even catching a glimmer of dampness from my mother's and Makaria's cheeks.

But before we walk down the aisle, my gaze catches on what is beside them. A single special request that I made to Nora for the wedding.

For her and my mother to keep one seat in the front row empty, to be reserved for a special someone who I'd hoped to attend.

As I look over at that empty seat now, I see the silhouette of Eiran's body standing in front of it. Gazing at me with genuine happiness as he claps for Reimus and I.

I look over at Reimus as he looks down at me, smiling as he sees who made it to our wedding.

We both turn back towards the crowd, walking down the aisle to make our way to the dining tables set out down the aisle and to the far left. An array of tables set out with beautiful floral centerpieces on white cloth. As I look over at mine and Reimus' table, I see a vase in between our plates.

Filled with bacarra roses.

I smile as I feel Reimus lower his hand from mine, lowering them to my legs as he sweeps me up. Causing me to giggle as he carries me the rest of the way to our table. The silk of my gown flowing down over his arms as he presses soft kisses to my cheek.

And as I look up at the decorated tall arches with sweeping drapery, the twinkle lights peeking through the trees, I find myself believing in fairytales after all.

CHAPTER 77

Reimus

As I look over at Melinoë, at my bride—

My *wife.*

Gods, I don't think I'm going to ever tire of saying that. I might even find myself now letting Melinoë pick petty disagreements with me just so I can have a reason to watch that fire burn in her gaze as I call her my wife.

The gown Bellinda crafted for her is more than anything I ever thought it would be. Mainly because I never thought I could find Melinoë more beautiful than I already do. But when I first saw her today upon walking down that aisle, I swear the floor went right out from under me.

As I felt utterly weightless in her proximity.

As Melinoë talks to Nora beside her, I lower my gaze to the satin pooling down her legs, a slit of lace poking through to match the lace hanging off her shoulders and traveling down her arms. Noticing that Bellinda hemmed the material to stop at just beneath her elbows, my heart cleaving at the small—yet large, detail of it.

Lace trims just the edge along her corset, the satin fabric cinching her waist before it pools like flowing water down her legs.

I actually wouldn't mind right now if all of these people left so I could take Melinoë inside and show her just how exquisite she looks. Matter of fact, maybe I'll just dismiss everyone now.

Okay, maybe I won't actually do that. Not just because there are a sea of guests here, but mainly because of the glow that's radiating off of my wife's face from mingling and talking with all of the people.

All of these people who came to show us love. Show *her* love.

"Isn't that right?"

Nora's voice pulls me from my thoughts as I lift my whiskey to my lips, lowering my free hand onto Melinoë's thigh. "I fear I am far too distracted by my wife to have heard anything you said just now."

Melinoë lifts her emerald gaze to mine, smirking as a heat dances in her eyes.

"What I was saying is that I told Melinoë you thought the decorations were beautiful, too."

"Oh, yes." I say as I look up at her. "They are indeed lovely, Nora. Thank you once again for doing all of this for us."

She nods her head as she dips into an enthusiastic curtsy. "My pleasure."

Melinoë chuckles beside me, the sound coaxing a brief flutter in my chest.

The music begins to dwindle down to a slow, intimate melody. I watch as some guests on the raised wooden platform step away from it, moving back to their seats.

I set my glass down on the elegant white table cloth, tealight candles hidden within glass vases glimmer against the now-dusk sky. I step out of my seat, holding a hand out for Melinoë. She looks up at me.

"May I have this dance, my wife?"

Her grin matches my own as she places her hand in mine, and I guide her out to the dance floor.

We step onto the wooden platform as I guide her to the center, turning her in front of me. The hanging lights above glint off of the small jewels embroidered onto her veil trailing down her back.

I pull her close to me, her right hand laying flat on my chest as I keep her other held firmly in mine. I lower my chin to her cheek as everyone around us blurs out.

As if just the two of us.

"I realize we never discussed our honeymoon." I say softly.

She giggles against me. "That is because I don't care to go elsewhere. As long as we have three days uninterrupted together, I don't want to spend it anywhere else other than our bedroom."

I hum against her. "That can surely be arranged." I grin against her cheek.

I feel her heartbeat kick up a little, sending a dizzying heat to my veins.

"Am I allowed to guess how you'd like to spend those three days, wife?" I purr against her.

"I could think of a few things." She says huskily.

"Do tell. And do be *very* specific." My voice lowered a notch.

Suddenly I feel a cool tingle slither from beneath her palm, gliding down my chest before dipping below my pants. It takes everything in me to continue willing a neutral face as I feel a tendril of her shadows lower itself further and further down—

I squeeze her hand, stifling the sudden jerk reaction as that tendril caresses over the tip of my cock. So featherlight as she teases me.

A second later I feel that tendril of shadow pull back into her palm, quicker than the blink of an eye. Our bodies too close together for anyone to have seen or noticed.

"I think I'd rather just make you wait and see." She lowers her lips closer to my ear as she whispers even quieter, "I do like it far more when you're whimpering for release." She lowers her face back down, feeling the curve of her smirk gliding along my skin.

I chuckle against her, low and throaty. "Careful, little spitfire. I have no problem sweeping you up into my arms and taking you back inside regardless of our guests in attendance." My hand on her bare back glides up and down slowly, feeling goosebumps raise along her skin beneath my touch.

She chuckles against me again. "You know I wouldn't make it that easy for you."

The music tempo begins to pick up a hair faster, signaling the change of a song. I pull my head back, looking down at her now before lowering a kiss to her lips. I pull myself back, raising my hand from her back and pulling both of her hands to my chest. Kissing the tops of them as my gaze stays on hers. "Then know that I will be eagerly waiting when you're ready to venture back inside." A smirk playing up my face as my thumbs caress over her knuckles.

We gaze at one another for a small eternity, soaking each other in as if storing this moment to memory.

"I love you." I say softly to her before lowering her hands back down.

She smiles up at me through painted soft red lips, her emerald eyes contrasted beautifully against her darkened lashes. "I love you."

At the sound of the rest of the world around us coming back into focus, I turn my gaze to someone stepping onto the wooden platform. Actually, more like three someones.

I step back from Melinoë as Euphrosyne, Aglaea and Thalia rush up to her. Each of them looking as lovely as ever with wide grins on each of their faces. "Okay, you two have been up here for an eternity. Now it's our turn."

I laugh as Melinoë turns towards them, Thalia gently grabbing her hand and twirling her into a spin. Melinoë laughs vibrantly before Sage comes in to join them in their dancing.

I make my way back to my seat when Dimitri comes up to me, bringing me in for a hug. "I'm so happy for you, man."

"Thanks, brother." I say as he pulls himself back. "Still feeling okay?" I nod to his hands.

Since I transferred Dimitri's essence back into him with the help of Hecate, I've checked in on him every day just to make sure he wasn't having any strange side effects. Or were feeling overwhelmed in any way with obtaining the power of the Draghi again.

"I feel great, actually." He says, and the expression on his face makes me believe it. "It's still taking a bit to get used to having it again, but I feel whole again. I can't explain it otherwise."

I nod, giving him a grin. "Good. I'm glad to hear it."

I watch as Dimitri catches a glance in Nora's direction. Her back being turned towards us as she talks with Hecate. He averts his gaze back to me as I watch some of that great feeling slip from his expression.

"Ask her to dance."

He lifts his gaze up to mine, widening his gaze some.

I shrug my shoulders. "Nora loves to dance. And she hasn't been on the dance floor yet." I catch a glance in her direction. "Maybe she's just waiting for the right person to ask her."

What I expected was for Dimitri to deny what I'd said, or to argue that she's busy talking with Hecate and that he shouldn't bother them. But unknowing if it's because of the type of event he's surrounded by presently, or because obtaining his essence did give him some kind of confidence boost to be a little bolder, he gives me a faint grin as he pats my shoulder.

I watch as Dimitri turns around and walks towards Nora, approaching her side as he nods his greeting to Hecate. He holds his hand out, his mouth moving with words I cannot hear from where I'm standing. But as Nora takes his hand and he guides her out to the dancefloor, I feel a surge of joy beam in my chest.

Okay, now *we're getting somewhere!*

I stifle a burst of a laugh as Melinoë chimes down the Guardian's channel, her enthusiasm echoing through her words as I look over at her.

She gives me a smirk as she looks at Dimitri. Winking at him.

He rolls his eyes but a grin shortly follows as he takes Nora into his arms, and guides her into a dance.

And as I take my seat and look out all of those attending, at each and every one of them enjoying themselves, I find my gaze falling back onto Melinoë as I watch her face light up with pure joy as she dances with the sisters.

I find in that moment that there are few moments in life that I would pay my soul to witness for the first time again. My beautiful wife dancing with the friends that she's made here, in a wedding dress worn as she married *me*, being one of them.

CHAPTER 78

Melinoë

I'm not sure how much time had passed since I first came onto the dance floor, but I know that once I finally made my way off of it, it was pitch dark out with now the twinkle lights around us being the only source of light aside from the moon above.

After being pulled into dancing with the sisters I went to retrieve my wine glass from Reimus and I's table when Sage presented a new one for me. He'd handed it to me before pulling me into a twirl, impressed I hadn't spilled any on my dress.

It wasn't long until Hecate and my mother joined us, along with Nora after having her one-on-one dance with Dimitri—which I was *very* pleased to see. When I saw the faint pink splotches on her cheeks when she made her way over to me, I could do nothing but grin. She'd rolled her eyes at me but I knew.

I knew.

As I finally take a moment to sit down I look up to see Dionysus walking towards me. His light brown hair combed back, exposing the angular plains of his jaw.

"I came to give my congratulations, and to tell you how great you look tonight." He says as he steps next to me, smiling.

"Thank you." I nod, grinning up at him. I lower my gaze to the water that I've seen him babying all night.

He catches my gaze and says, "I've spent a lot of my time drinking."

I lift my gaze up to him.

He shrugs his shoulders. "It was always as a way to numb myself to my surroundings, to what I was dealing with. Both externally and internally." He lifts the glass up, tilting it to the side as he glances down at it. "It appears I don't always feel that urge to drink now…since being here. I guess I have you to thank for that."

I sigh as I give him a faint smile. "I'm glad I could help, then."

He gives me a genuine grin before he leans himself down, pressing a soft kiss to the top of my head. He pulls back as he says, "So, does this mean I'm supposed to call you sister for now on?"

A brief laugh bursts out of me. "You can if you'd like."

He huffs out a soft noise before looking over to his side. To where both Makaria and Persephone stand, talking to one another.

He stares at them for a moment before looking back at me. "I know I should say more to them. I just…find myself coming up blank." He runs his free hand through his hair. "I'm still adjusting to it all, you know?"

I slowly nod my head, watching as my mother turns to glance over to us. Giving me a wide smile before darting her gaze to Dionysus. Her gaze lingering for a brief moment before turning back to my sister.

"They will welcome you as if there had never been any time spent apart." I say, lifting my gaze back to him. "They won't treat you as an outsider."

He watches me for a moment, understanding in his gaze as his chest sinks from his exhale. He gives me a slow nod before he says, "Thank you, Melinoë." He stands up straight again. "For everything."

I watch as he turns on his heels, his grip tightening around the glass briefly before he makes his way over to them. My mother's gaze sharpens on him momentarily before forcing herself to smooth it over. Makaria gives him a wide smile as he approaches them. I watch as he nods his greeting to Persephone and Makaria, and continues to stand there as he makes conversation with them.

A small, yet big step.

"I saw we had a special guest today." Hades says as he approaches the table.

I lift my gaze to him, grinning. "I had hoped he'd come today. I'm glad he did."

He gives me a smile as he says, "I don't think he would've let himself miss it."

I look over to that empty seat now, over by the aisle. "Do you think that's why he didn't want to fully cross over?" I look back over to Hades. "Because he knew this moment would come and he didn't want to miss it?"

Hades tilts his head slightly. "I don't think so."

I knit my brows together. "How do you figure?"

"Because part of being King of The Underworld means that I also have an affinity for being able to read souls. Both ones that have crossed The River Styx, and those who wander the earthly realm. Unwilling to fully cross over." A moment pauses between us. "I read his soul, and he still feels…unfinished. As if he's waiting for something else to occur before he makes his final descent to The Underworld. But what? I cannot be sure."

A frown pulls at my lips. "Do you think he feels unfinished because…" My words trail off as I glance over at the rest of the reception.

"Oh, no. Not in that way, Melinoë." Hades shakes his head, calming my fear of Eiran feeling unfinished with me having moved on. I know that's a silly thing to think as he's told me time and time again that I was meant to find Reimus, that our time together wasn't meant to advance further. But still, the thought still roamed through me. "It's a feeling as if he's waiting for something else to fall into place. That's why he still lingers."

"Oh." I say, having no idea what else it could be. Unless Eiran is waiting to see what happens with Zeus, and is lingering around to help us through the war. Regardless of what it is, there's a selfish part of me that enjoys having his familiar presence around.

Knowing that he won't remember me at all once he finally does drink from The Lethe. And I'd like to think that I will accept his final goodbye, because I've already mourned his death. That this extra time together has been a blessing and I've taken it as such.

Though a part of me feels like saying our final goodbyes won't be as easy as I want to believe.

"Have you heard anything about his whereabouts?" I ask.

Hades shakes his head. "Nothing yet."

I nod as Hades lowers a hand to my shoulder.

He looks at me as he says, "We have other days to worry about that. But tonight, just enjoy yourself." He smiles.

I match his smile. "I will."

He lowers his hand as he turns around and merges his way back to the rest of the party.

I look over to see Reimus talking with a guest—Carina, a woman from The Sanctuary. She wears a pale pink dress that flows down to her mid-calf. Her daughter Elise runs up to her after dancing with Nora for some time, gently tugging on her dress. Her tulle dress a pale blue, matching her sparkly silver mary-jane shoes.

I smile as Carina lowers down to pick her daughter up, holding her against her hip as Elise rests her head on her shoulder. I catch Dimitri walking towards me from the corner of my eye.

And when he approaches the table, he immediately puts a hand up. "Don't even start."

I laugh as he goes to take the seat next to me. "I wasn't going to say anything." I lied.

I totally was.

He snorts as a laugh gets trapped in his throat, shaking his head. "Whatever."

My laugh dies down as I look at him, watching him stare at Nora from across the way as she talks to Dionysus. I watch as an edge sparks to life in his gaze.

"Why are you so afraid to tell her how you really feel?"

He doesn't move his gaze away from her, tracking Dionysus' every move. A protectiveness ensues in his energy as he watches her intently. "I don't know." He mumbles.

I watch him for a moment, remembering the grief that racked through him when I helped keep him preoccupied months ago while Nora healed his wings. I remember the love, and deep sadness he held in his gaze when his mother showed up after I'd called out for help. The tremor that racked in his body as she stepped up to him, telling him how proud she was of him.

I look at him now as I see that similar edge in him that I used to have myself. A wall that can only be brought up when you've suffered through great loss, and don't want to ever feel it again.

"You're afraid to lose someone you love again."

I watch as that edge lessens from his gaze slightly.

"It feels safer to keep her at arms length, because if something ever happened to her it wouldn't hurt as badly."

He loosens a heavy, long breath. "Losing my mother was…soul crushing. It happened unexpectedly," He shakes his head slowly. "Even though I grieved her death, I feel a part of me never came back."

I nod slowly. "Or maybe it's still there, but you just are afraid to reclaim it."

He finally tears his gaze away from Nora to look at me.

"I know you're aware of Eiran, and who he was to me. What he meant, and still does to me." I pause for a moment. "After he died, I never thought I'd let myself love again. I felt like I wasted so much time being afraid of the idea of love because of the abuse I grew up with, that I missed out on actually experiencing it when it was *right* in front of me." I loosen my breath. "So when he died, I blamed myself for that too. For not noticing what I had sooner."

Dimitri remains quiet as he watches me, listening.

"When I met Reimus, I—" I broke out into a short burst of a laugh, shaking my head. "He turned everything I thought I knew upside down. Completely shattering that guard I had up for everyone around me." I lift my gaze over to him now, smiling as I watch him continue in conversation. "There was nothing I could do to stop myself from falling deeply for him. Regardless of us being twin souls, he…made me believe in love again. Not only that, but that I could forgive myself and try again."

I turn my gaze to Dimitri, tilting my head. "Death is always unexpected. We are never truly ready to say goodbye to those we love. But if I were to say anything right now, it would be that I hope you find the courage to open yourself up to love again. That yes, there will be a time when the both of you are separated as it is inevitable." I pause for a moment as I watch something light up in his eyes at my words. "But you need to ask yourself; will your life still feel purposeful if you continue to stand off to the side, harboring these feelings for Nora but never saying anything to her about them? Or will you die feeling like you missed out on something beautiful because you were afraid of getting close to her, to some day lose her?"

Dimitri blinks at me as he stares at me for a moment, seeing the wheels turning in his mind as the subtle edge to his expression completely smooths out. A long moment of silence passes between us before he says gruffly, barely above a whisper, "I love her." He shakes his head slowly as he stands up a little taller. "I…"

His words trail off as he stands up from the seat, looking over towards Nora who has now taken to talking to Euphrosyne. He stares at her for only a moment before stepping away from the table, and striding over to her.

I watch as Euphrosyne tears her gaze from Nora, looking at Dimitri and guiding Nora to turn around. Her brows knit together, her mouth going to open to probably say some sarcastic retort when Dimtiri advances on her.

His hands cup her jaw as he pulls her to him, and presses his lips to hers.

I watch as Nora stands there stunned only for a brief moment before she wraps her arms around his neck, pulling him closer to her as they share their own small moment of eternity together.

A wide smile lights up my face as I watch Nora and Dimitri relax into each other's embrace, as if it were a moment that had been building and building for a long time that they were finally allowing themselves to experience together.

Reimus comes to my side as he presses a kiss to my cheek. "Well, this was unexpected. But I am thoroughly pleased, nonetheless."

As he seats himself back down next to me, I find a short laugh bubbling up my throat at his words. And as he puts his arm around me, I nuzzle myself into the best thing that unexpectedly happened to me.

CHAPTER 79

As guests began to make their departure, Reimus and I made our way back inside after everyone cleared out. My mother, Makaria and Hades making their way back to The Underworld, the sisters back to The Sanctuary, Sage back to the forest, Dionysus back to his chambers on the third floor, and Dimitri and Nora…well, I have no idea where they went.

As I lift the veil from my hair, I feel the hands of his on mine.

"Have I told you yet today how magnificent you look?" Reimus asks, trailing his fingers along my skin as he replaces my fingers with his. Releasing the veil from my wavy hair.

I chuckle as his hands return to my hair, gently running his fingers through the strands. "About twenty times actually."

I watch through the vanity as he smirks at me. "Twenty does not feel like enough."

His fingertips lower themselves down my back, sending chills along my spine. I feel his hands stop at the zipper on my dress. "When I watched you walk down that aisle today, I had many thoughts run through my mind." He lowers the zipper an inch down. "The first being what good karma had I done in a past life to be given such a gloriously, beautiful bride in this one."

I feel him slowly lower the zipper down, the tightness around my chest loosening.

"The second was the atrocious acts I would *gladly* bring forth to anyone who laid their hands on what is mine."

My chest rises as I feel his hands lower down my back, the zipper along with it. The satin dress falls down my chest as my breasts bare themselves before us.

"The third," He pauses, chuckling as he lowers himself down to his knees, guiding the zipper down until it reaches below my ass. His hands slipping inside, gently working the rest of the dress down. "The third was whether I wanted to tear this gown off of you tonight, or keep you in it while I fuck you into the early hours of tomorrow."

His hands come to my underwear, slipping them down my legs as heat floods my pussy.

"But then I realized, if I were to ruin your gown, then I could never have it hanging in the closet as a reminder of whatever good deeds I had once done to deserve you. To be able to call you mine."

I feel his hand caress up my hip as he presses a kiss on my inner thigh. My pulse humming as my breath hitches.

He slowly lowers himself back up, his hands gliding up the sides of my body as he does. He removes his hands from my skin as he moves them to untuck his shirt.

I turn around, catching his hands as he watches me through a heated gaze. I slowly lower them to his sides as I lift his shirt from beneath his pants. His abdomen clenched as I slowly unbuttoned his shirt. "I appreciate you being so…considerate. Bellinda worked very hard on my attire for tonight."

His shirt opens up as I lower it off of him, watching it fall to the floor. I move my hands down to his pants, keeping them there for a moment as I feel the tension rise in his body. "However, I fear you are not the only one who is feeling considerate."

"Hmm. Is that so?" He says through a voice as smooth as whiskey.

I lower the zip from his pants and begin gliding them down his waist. I lower myself down with them until they pool at his feet. I look up at him. "Yes."

I lower my gaze to the bulge from his briefs, a smirk crawling up my face as I bring my hands to them and slowly pull them down. I hear him curse under his breath as his hard cock is now only a few inches in front of my face.

I will my shadows to the surface, just a few tendrils as they snake themselves up his legs. Willing them to feel like soft kisses along his skin and watching his breathing begin to quicken.

A wispy tendril travels up his thigh until it glides over the shaft of his cock. I watch Reimus jerk forward as I will it to coil around him until the ends of the tendril are lightly brushing along the tip.

"Fuck." He rasps, his chest rising and falling rapidly.

I watch through wicked desire as pearly white liquid beads at the tip, my mouth leaning in as I lick it off. Reimus shudders beneath my touch before I lean back again. "Do you like how that feels?" I ask huskily.

Reimus nods his head curtly. "Yes." He hisses.

I lower my gaze to watch as the tendril glides lightly along the tip, causing Reimus to begin thrusting his hips slightly forward.

I will another tendril to rise up and glide lightly along his balls before cupping them.

"Oh, gods." He moans as that liquid I love to taste so much beads at the tip again. "Please—"

His words cut off as I tilt my head up at him. "Please what?" I ask, feigning an innocence.

Please—" He shudders beneath the touch of my shadows. "*Please* let me sink my cock down your throat."

Heat rushes to my pussy at the desperation in his voice, trying to tease and prolong him as long as I can. But my own patience dwindles at the direness of his need.

I will my shadows away from his cock as I press a kiss to the tip, licking his cum before wrapping my lips around him. I pull back, making a popping noise as I look up at him. "Like that?"

"Deeper." He grounds out.

A breathy laugh escapes me before I give him what he wants.

I descend my mouth on him as he thrusts into me to the hilt, his cock slipping down my throat as I take all of him.

His body trembles as his hands go to cup my jaw. "*Nothing* feels fucking better than you." He slowly begins fucking my mouth as I take him greedily.

I will my shadows to retract completely as Reimus glides in and out of my mouth, slowly to start. But as I moan my own satisfaction of having him deep in my throat, it cracks his restraint wide open.

He begins fucking my mouth fast as I gag on his cock, cum dripping down my throat.

"You look so good with my cock in your mouth, little spitfire." He purrs, a wickedness to his tone. "And you take me so good."

I moan against him again, causing him to throw his head back as he bucks into my mouth. Taking every long inch of him eagerly.

I feel his body tense up before he pulls out of my mouth, hiking me back up onto my feet in one swift movement. His lips coming to mine as his body presses up against mine. The hardness of his cock against my belly.

I moan, grinding against him as I want more. *Need* more.

He lifts me up until my pussy is gliding along his cock, my cries of pleasure getting caught between his lips.

He moves us to the lounge chair as he seats himself down, my legs straddling him as he pulls his lips from mine.

I go to sink myself down onto him when he grabs onto my hips, halting me.

"Not yet," He says raggedly, leaning his head back as he looks up at me. "Let me just touch you." He rocks my hips against him, my wet pussy rubbing up against the shaft of his cock. "Let me feel that wet pussy on me before I sink myself deep in it."

My hands come up around his neck as I rock against him. Moaning against the delicious hardness of him.

"Make me beg for it."

So, I do what he asks.

I grind against him as wetness pools from me, rubbing my clit against him as my own dizzying release rises. I moan against him as his hands grip my hips, dragging me against him as his chest rises and falls.

He lowers his mouth to my breasts, sucking on a hardened nipple as I cry out. I ride him as I soak his cock with my wetness, my orgasm rippling and coiling tightly until it breaks loose and sends me over the edge.

"That's right, baby." He says as he lifts his lips from my nipple, his lashes lifting as he gazes up at me. "Let me hear you."

I cry against him as my orgasm rolls through me, soaking him as he groans out in pleasure. Liquid beading at the tip of his cock as I rock against him.

"Okay—*please*. Let me fuck you now." He says hoarsely as he whimpers. "I can't wait any longer."

And because I can't wait any longer either, I lift my hips and sink myself down his shaft. His body shudders as he groans out his pleasure.

I waste no time riding him as he lifts my hips up, pistoning me down onto him over and over again.

"Be a good boy and cum for me now, Rei." I say against him.

He leans his head back as he says, "I promise I'll be good."

In the next moment he holds me in place as he tilts his hips, ramming up into me hard and fast. I feel him lock up inside of me before he pulls me down flush to him. His own release spilling inside of me as he holds me in place.

I move his hands and put them up above his head, leaning into him as I grind my hips into him.

"*Fuck*—that feels so good." He whimpers as I ride him through his release. "Don't stop." He groans out.

I grind my hips against him as I feel him spill himself inside of me. Every last decadent drop as I take what belongs to me.

I slow my hips as I catch my breath, lifting myself off of him when he carries me to the bed, laying me down on my back.

He pushes me up further onto the bed, spreading my legs open as he lowers himself down onto me.

I feel liquid drip out of me as he pushes my hair back from my face, pressing a kiss to my forehead and then to my lips.

My body tingling as I look up at him. The man I get to share my whole life with.

My twin soul.

My husband.

I push the loose strand of his hair back from his face, smiling weakly.

"I was made to worship you, Melinoë." He says thickly.

He lowers his hands from my face down to his cock, repositioning himself at my pussy again. He sinks himself in again, already hard once more. Wringing a moan from my lips as he stretches and fills me.

He lifts one of my legs up, bending it at the knee as he hooks it over his shoulder. He presses a kiss to the side of my knee before locking gazes with me again. "Let me prove it."

He thrusts fully into me, wringing a moan from my lips as he does exactly what he says.

CHAPTER 80

Reimus

As I lay next to Melinoë I admire the soft breaths she takes as she sleeps, the way her mouth parts open ever so slightly. Unable to keep my hands off of her all night, neither of us had gotten any sleep up until a couple hours ago when we were both too tired to move.

I'd woken up for whatever reason, but hadn't been able to fall back asleep again.

So, I just lie awake and watch her. But as this dizzying need continues to keep resurfacing, so does my willingness to please her in more ways than one.

I lower my gaze to her breasts, her nipples still hard even in her sleep. I lower myself closer to her, sinking myself under the covers as I trail a hand up her belly. Inserting myself in between her legs as I lower my lips to a nipple.

I press a soft kiss there, moving my hand down her side until my fingers brush along her pussy. Still wet, so soft.

I lower my finger along her wetness, slipping it between her lips as I press another kiss to her nipple.

I watch as she takes a sudden breath in, her body moving ever so slightly as her eyes remain closed.

I smirk as I press a kiss to her other nipple before lowering myself down her body.

I open her legs up wide for me, looking down at the prettiest pussy I've ever seen in my life.

I lower my mouth, flicking my tongue out as I lick along her center. Tasting what's been left over for me.

I feel her stir awake as she takes a sharp inhale in. "Rei." She says sleepily. "What are you—"

Her words are cut off on glorious moans as I sink my tongue deep inside of her, catching every last drop on my tongue as I devour her whole.

My hands grips her hips as I pull her closer to me, wanting to drown in the taste of her. The way she now squirms against me, moaning my name as I feast on her.

I glide my tongue along her center again before sucking on her clit. I move one hand from her hips, descending a finger deep inside of her as I drink her completely.

Gods, she tastes like fucking life.

She begins grinding my face as I feel her tighten around my finger. I smirk as I lower my other hand from her hip, guiding my thumb down lower past her pussy. I press it up to her other hole.

"What are you—*oh*." She moans as I sink my thumb inside, wringing a gasp from her as she takes a staggering exhale out.

She quickly continues riding both my face and my fingers as I drink every sweet drop that drips from her pussy. Until I feel her clamp up around me as release spills out of her.

She screams my name as she cums on my lips and my fingers, leaving no drop unattended as I greedily take everything that she gives me.

As her orgasm dwindles I lower my fingers from her, rising up her body and pressing kisses along her skin until I hover above her.

She wraps her legs around me as I kiss her, sinking my cock deep inside of her as I fill her once again.

I grind my hips against her, feeling myself sink down her soft walls. Gods, I'm going to bust just from the feeling of being deep inside of her. Her cum gliding along my dick as she moans beneath me.

"Hmm? I didn't catch that." I purr as I lower my head down to her neck. I press a soft kiss there as I feel her pulse skitter beneath my lips. I lift my lips above her neck until just my breath glides along her skin.

She takes another ragged inhale in. "Fuck me harder."

I chuckle against her, watching as my breath causes her skin to jump. I keep my same pace as I say, "But you feel even better when you're needy for me." I lower my lips as I trail my tongue along her skin. Causing her to exhale sharply as she squirms beneath me.

I lower my hand to her clit, slowly circling it as she cries out for me. I lower my head down her chest as I hover my lips above a nipple. Softly blowing air on the hardened peak as I continue thrusting in and out of her. "I love seeing you so worked up for me." I say, grinning against her.

"Rei—" She moans out, my name the sweetest reward on her lips as she begins to come undone beneath me. I watch as her eyes begin to roll to the back of her head as she cums on my dick.

I lift myself up as I quickly haul her up, unsheathing myself for only a moment as I twirl her around. I lift her ass up as I grip her hips, sinking myself deep inside again as I ram myself into her rear.

Her ass recoils with each thrust into her and it sends me into a heated daze.

I lower a hand from her waist and gather her hair into my fist, tugging upwards until her head is slightly raised off the bed. "Your moans, your pussy. Mine. All of you belongs to *me*." I groan out roughly as my own orgasm builds rampantly within me. "Now take this dick just like I know you can."

Melinoë cries beneath me as her pussy drenches my cock, sending me straight over the edge as I spill myself inside of her. Whimpering as my body trembles with my own release.

Fuck I can't stop cumming. She's so fucking *good*—

"Fuck." I groan out as I continue ramming into her, my skin buzzing with my release as my ears begin to ring. I finally slow down when my release begins to finally trickle down. Sweat beading at my brow and at the tips of my hair.

I pull out and lay myself down beside her, both of us catching our breaths for several long moments before she's the first one to speak.

"I fear at the rate we're going," She begins as she finally turns herself over onto her back, wiping the slick strands of hair away from her face. "If we don't stop to eat and hydrate ourselves, we'll keel over from lack of."

I chuckle as I bring her closer to me, kissing her forehead. "I fear you are right. I guess that's a good thing I took the necessary precautions beforehand."

She looks up at me, tilting her head as her brows knit together.

I look over to the door, having heard Aven drop off a plate of food a half hour ago while Melinoë was sleeping. Him having suggested he bring up breakfast in bed today as he assumed we'd maybe not be so keen on leaving the bedroom.

And well, he was right.

I sit up from the bed, walking over to the door and opening it. I lower down to pick up a large tray and stand up straight again, turning around to show Melinoë. "Breakfast is served, My Lady." I wink.

She laughs as she seats herself up, her gaze roaming over everything on the tray.

A carafe of hot coffee, two mugs, and a large saran wrapped dish of scrambled eggs, bagels, cream cheese, sausage, toast, and an assortment of fruit.

I bring it over to the bed and lay it on top, grabbing the carafe and pouring some coffee into a mug before handing it to her.

"This is perfect." She says, a satisfied exhale escaping her. She takes a sip of the coffee before setting it on the nightstand. A faint grin of mine forming when I notice the slight tremble in her hand.

We both begin digging into the food Aven prepared for us, both of us clearing the tray completely aside from a half eaten bagel and a few grapes.

Melinoë curls up to me as sleep ensues in her tired gaze. Vowing to myself this time that if she were to fall asleep again, that I'll actually let her sleep instead of waking her for my own selfish need to pleasure her.

"We both probably need a shower as well."

I laugh against her, gliding my hand along her shoulder as she places hers on my chest. "Nonsense. We just smell like…" I lower my head, sniffing her. "Like we've been having sex for days."

She giggles against me, and it's a sound that I could live off of forever. "Exactly what I mean. But actually," She begins as she leans herself up onto her elbows, hovering over me. "You know what would even sound better?"

"Hmm?" I ask, gazing at her as I trail my hand down her back.

"A nice, hot bubble bath with a bottle of wine." She makes a low humming noise of appreciation. "Now that sounds wonderful."

I chuckle. "That can be arranged, Mrs. Kallias."

She beams at the use of my last name, a glow emanating off of her so fiercely, so beautifully. "Say it again." She says softly as she presses a kiss to my nose, then to my lips.

She raises herself on top of me as I grow hard beneath her again. I groan in pleasure as I say, "Mrs. Kallias."

She smirks deeply at me as she grinds against me. Rubbing her wet pussy along my shaft as my hands lower to her hips, guiding her along me.

"Does my husband want to see what his wife can do for him?" She asks, sparking a wild hot need deep inside of me.

My *husband*.

Gods, we are never going to leave this bed.

She raises herself up so her breasts hover in front of my face as she grinds against me. Teasing me. "Yes, he would."

She slips my cock inside of her, her grin smoothing out as she gasps at my fullness stretching her. Her hands rest on my chest as she leans forward, and rides me slowly and passionately into euphoric oblivion.

My back leans up against the cast iron tub, Melinoë's damp back leaned up against my chest. After having finally agreed to get some much needed rest, we awoke several hours later to wanting to utilize the clawfoot tub. So I drew up a bath for both of us, and rounded up a bottle of wine from the cellar in the basement.

She leans her head up against the crook of my neck, our pulses sharing the same slow, steady rhythm as we bask in nothing but the stillness of one another.

She brings her wine glass up to her lips before setting it back down onto the cart. Leaning herself up from my chest, she reaches for the lavender and vanilla scented soap. "So everything has been taken down already?" She angles her body to look at me while she scrubs the soap on her shoulders, then her armpits.

I nod. "I stepped out onto the balcony not long before you awoke and saw everything had been cleared already."

She raises her eyebrows. "Wow, Nora really was on top of it all. From every detail." She chuckles as she lowers the soap down her chest.

A faint grin curves up my lips as a soft chuckle escapes them. "I imagine she had some help from Dimitri and Aven." I smirk at her. "Possibly also your mother. I can't imagine they knew what to do with all of those chairs and tables."

She laughs, my gaze trailing down to her jet black strands gathered behind her. "My mother told me the chairs and tables would *disappear* once tomorrow—today, came. She said she willed them to do as such, so I can imagine how much of a help that was alone."

I lift myself up and grab the soap from Melinoë's hands before she guides it lower down her body.

She smirks as she turns herself towards me, pushing herself to lean back on the opposite end of the tub as she lifts a leg out from beneath the water.

I grab her foot, lathering the bar of soap there before massaging it into her skin. She lets out a long exhale, closing her eyes as she leans her head back. "There's something that I saw in Apollo's memories that I remembered the other day."

I keep my gaze on her sated face as I dip her foot below the water, rinsing the soap off before lifting it again. I lather the soap up her calf, massaging her skin as I do. "What was it?"

She shakes her head vaguely. "It was a memory of him talking to the Pythia. He was telling her that Zeus was requesting to be told his fate, and know the prophecy. But when she looked up at him, she asked him which one. Insinuating that there were more than one."

"What do you think the other prophecy is in regards to?" I ask.

She slowly opens her eyes, locking restful eyes with me. "I know this sounds crazy, but…I think it's about me."

I tilt my head as I rinse the soap off before moving higher up her leg. "How come?"

"Because when she asked him, Apollo said to only speak of the one involving Zeus and his children. That the other one doesn't belong to him, so they'd keep it that way—"

I watch as her expression smooths out, her eyes widening slightly as her gaze trails away. I lower her leg underneath the water as I watch shock ripple across her face. I set the soap down as I move closer to her. "What is it?"

She slowly locks eyes with me as she says, "I know it's about me." She pauses for a moment as she lifts her hair back over her chest. "She asked about the girl—meaning me. And he said I had to be the one to request it…" A look of realization flashes across her eyes. "But only after he reclaimed his power back from the land."

I still for a moment, blinking once before I say, "Referring to me."

She nods her head, scooting herself closer to me as she wraps her arms around my neck. "What we learned so far about twin souls…we know The Fates always have a divine orchestration for their union. What if the reason why I had to wait is because this other prophecy involves you?"

I knit my brows together, trying to piece together parts of my life to try and understand why me reclaiming my essence would have anything to do with a prophecy I'd have no knowledge about. I know, and remember, everything that is to understand about my lineage and the land from which I originate from.

But what Melinoë is saying is true. Twin souls always have a bigger purpose larger than either of them. What if there is something bigger than us? To what our paths entail?

I look at her as I brush a damp strand away from her cheek. "Am I even allowed in Apollo's Temple?"

Melinoë giggles briefly below me, easing the tension that began to grow in her face. "I don't see why not. The Temple is open to the public."

I exhale as I shrug my shoulders. "Well what does it take to request hearing about a prophecy then?"

"I…don't know." She knits her brows, shaking her head. "When I went with him and Zeus last time, there was nothing special we had to do. We just went through a door down to the bottom of the Temple. But when I saw Apollo in Elzwin, he said if I ever needed to request—"

She stills against me as her eyes widen slightly. "He told me all I needed to do to request his presence was to ask for him from the Pythia. He's been trying to tell me this whole time to ask about this other prophecy."

"Well…" I say as I pull her closer to me, lifting my hands to caressing my thumbs against her cheeks. "What would you like to do, wife?"

A glimmer of a smirk curves up her lips. "I want to see what this other prophecy is about. And—" Her nostrils flare as she takes a whiff, grimacing. "Oh, you do smell."

I chuckle as I lower my nose to my pits, taking a whiff and—yeah, I maybe smell like sweat.

But hey, we've been at it since last night so what did she expect?

"Really?" I say, lifting my arm up higher. "I think I smell fabulous." I lift my shoulder closer to her as she tries to back up when I bring my arms around her. Keeping her close to me.

She laughs in my embrace as she tries to push away from me, opting to splash water at me.

"Oh, so we're fighting dirty now are we?" I ask playfully. I scoop some of the bubbles up into the palm of my hand and smoosh them onto her nose. Laughing as they fly everywhere when she exhales briskly out of her nose.

She scoops some bubbles up, forming them along my jaw. My focus wholly fixed on the wide, glorious smile on her face. "There, now you have a beard."

I grin as I feel the bubbles lightly popping along my skin. "Do you want me to have a beard?" I ask, turning my head to the side and smirking. One of my eyebrows raised.

She ponders for a moment before saying, "I prefer you just the way you are." She lowers her lips to mine, pressing a soft kiss.

When she pulls away she laughs at the bubbles now gathered on her cheeks.

I bring my hands up to her cheeks, wiping the bubbles away as I gaze at her. At the simple happiness lighting up her face. "I love you."

Her smile grows brighter and bigger. "I love you." She says as she wraps her arms around me again, pulling me in for another kiss.

She straddles me and—soon enough, the bath we prepared for bathing purposes *only* becomes wholly more erotic.

CHAPTER 81

Melinoë

I step out onto the ashen soil as smoldering warmth suffocates itself against my skin.

Not warmth. Fire.

I lift the back of my hand and press it beneath my nose as I try to drown out the potent stench of metallic. I take another step forward as my booted foot meets the crimson spilled on the pavement. My gaze follows the trail of blood in front of me, lifting my gaze—

My breath hitches as I see Apollo standing before me as an inferno of bright orange billows high behind him. "It's starting, Melinoë."

I knit my brows together as I take another step forward, stepping further into the puddle of blood. "Where are we? What's starting?"

His golden gaze locks onto mine as I hear a piercing scream surface from somewhere far behind him. "When you awake, it will already be too late."

I search his tanned face, my gaze lifting to behind his back. My eyes widen both in utter disarray, and understanding.

Fire billows out of building windows and doorways as the structures begin to collapse. Smoke rises high above the village as I feel my chest squeeze at the utter destruction before me. I lower my gaze to the blood beneath my feet, lifting my gaze again to follow it. To find where it's coming—

I jolt up right in bed, conscious once more.

"Rei." I bark out as I jump out of bed, rushing over to the closet. I push the door open and find the first pair of leggings and tunic I can, throwing them on.

I hear Reimus rustle from the bed, his voice groggy with sleep. "What is it?" He says as he meets me by the closet.

When I look up at him, the sleep from his eyes vanishes as he sees the concern and sternness on my face. Without question, he rushes in to throw some clothes on as well. "What did you see?"

"Fire. A lot of it." I smooth the shirt over myself as I hurry out of the closet and throw some boots on. When I look down at them, I freeze for a moment as I see the striking resemblance. "I saw Apollo, too. It was a warning. I know it was." I slip them on as Reimus meets me by my side. Clothed and ready to go in less than a minute.

We look over at each other for a short moment, the unspoken words of what we both need not to say hanging between us.

I will a portal open as both of us step through it, immediately overwhelmed from the heat of the smoldering fires ahead of us. I mentally prepare myself to rush to the aid of whoever is badly hurt. That there will most likely be no salvaging left of whatever is left.

But as we both step into Elzwin, it's even worse than what I'd expected.

The portal closes behind us as I can see nothing other than what is right in front of me. Not the overwhelming heat of the buildings being lit on fire, or the smoke that wafts all around us.

All I can fixate on are those who chose to remain in Elzwin. Their limbs hanging loosely from their bodies as they hang from pikes, making a line formation in front of the shops of Elzwin.

I take a shuddering breath in as I look upon their faces, stepping closer to them as I feel my boot squish against the blood that runs from their wounds.

Blood that runs from their heads hanging limply off their necks.

I halt as my fists coil together tightly, anger and disgust both fighting to dominate their presence under my skin.

"Melinoë." Reimus says softly.

I already know what he's going to say. That there's nothing that can be done now, that the shops are already dismantled and burnt down. That there is no salvaging anything of Elzwin at this point.

That all it is now is a wasteland.

I find myself unable to look away from the bodies, from the way their mouths gape open as pain was the last thing they felt before he killed them.

A punishment meant for me to witness.

My power quickly rushes to the surface as shadows coil themselves around me. I feel their familiar touch as a newer one emerges itself with them.

Their tiny sparks become tangible tethers of eather as they dance along my skin, joining with the darkness brewing around me.

At the shuffling of feet to my right, I look over to see soldiers in gold-plated armor rushing towards me. Their swords drawn and at the ready.

I smile at them as cold, brutal anger flows through me. I tilt my head to the side as I turn towards them, my voice calm against the storm raging within and around us. "Either you are eager to die, or you're just that stupid."

I lift my hands and as they rush closer to me, I will the tendrils of shadows and lightning to latch onto each of them. Watching as their bodies convulse violently before disintegrating into a fine dust.

Their bones all that remain as they plop to the ground.

I stand there for a moment, listening and searching for any other soldiers who are courageous enough to advance towards us. When I see and hear nothing stir through the plumes of smoke, I retract my power back into myself.

I step towards the ten bodies piked before me. My chest tightening as I gaze upon each of their faces. People who made the choice not to leave Elzwin, but who were innocent nonetheless.

I feel Reimus approach my side, his silence stretching between us before he finally breaks it. "That I have never seen before."

I let his words pass through me, my gaze wholly on the people before me. Staring blankly at them.

I feel his hand brush up against mine, the weight of his energy pulling me back just enough. "We could bury them. They deserve that much." His voice ending on a harsh note.

I watch as silhouettes begin to form around each of their bodies. The energy then separates itself entirely until their souls stand next to the vessel they just came from. Some of them immediately look at me, confusion rippling along their faces as they yearn for answers.

The rest look at the state of what their physical bodies are in. Mortified and deeply unwell by their final moments as a living mortal.

I shake my head slowly. "Not in this kind of state." I turn towards Reimus, meeting his gaze. "I can feel their unrest. They won't crossover to The Underworld with their bodies still—" I work on a swallow, pausing. "I fear it is a disservice if we leave their bodies as is."

Rei watches me silently before giving me a nod. He turns his gaze to the bodies as he steps towards them.

"Why—" One soul cries out. Her face scrunched in horror. *"W—we just wanted to stay where we had always called home."*

"Why did he do this to us?" Another soul cries out. His pained voice nearly debilitating.

Her lips quiver as she says, *"I wasn't ready yet."* She shakes her head. *"It wasn't my time yet."*

My heart lurches in my chest as I feel the pain seeping out of each of them. I walk towards them as they crowd around me. "I'm so sorry." I say to none of them in particular, feeling the sentiment still stands for each of them.

My throat works on a swallow as I steady my voice. "None of you deserved this."

I look over at Reimus, giving him a nod. I watch as fire pools in his palms before he gently shoots it outward onto their bodies.

They look over at Reimus, at what he's doing before turning their gazes back to me. I watch as understanding at the reality of what they are now settling in, as the finality that they are indeed dead blankets over them.

"What happens now?" One soul asks.

"You will be guided to The Underworld, where you will drink from The Lethe before being ushered into The Asphodel Meadows. Where your soul will rest."

I watch their faces as they process my words, watching one of the souls vanish before me as Reimus burns his body to ash.

One of the souls looks at me in alarm.

"Don't worry." I say, cutting off whatever she was going to say. "You cannot be harmed now. I promise."

And as one by one, I watch each of them disappear in front of me as their mortal flesh disintegrates into ash. Feeling the emptiness of their energy slip away from me like a cloak slipping off of my shoulders.

Reimus gently tugs on my hands, guiding my gaze away from where they just stood. "We should warn the others."

I exhale a long breath as I nod my head.

"Do you need a moment first?" Reimus' stern face lowers into a frown as he watches me.

"No." I will a portal open for us as I approach it, Reimus at my side.

And before we step through it, I look over my shoulder at the place that was once my home. The library that I once spent most of my time in, the market I frequented. All of it now burned to a desolated village of ruin by Zeus.

—

"What we need to start doing is gathering allies."

I stare at the flames calmly roaring within the fireplace, unable to truly listen to what everyone else is saying at this moment.

As soon as Reimus and I got home we gathered everyone in our living room. My mother, Hades, Makaria, Hecate, Dimitri, Nora, and Dionysus. And ever since I took my stand in front of the fireplace, I've been unable to peel my gaze away from it.

The image of those people cementing itself in my mind. The cruelty Zeus inflicted upon them for no reason other than to spite me.

"Even if Artemis and Apollo aren't truly on Zeus' side, that doesn't guarantee that they'd actually stand with us when it comes to war."

"It is no longer an if." Dionysus says. "War has already begun. And knowing Zeus, he already has every step mapped out in front of him."

"Well what about the people here?" I hear Nora's voice ring out. "Yes, we're protected behind the shield but…" Her voice trails off. "What if he found a way around it?"

"He won't." Hades says assuredly. "I intentionally created the shield eons ago so it can only be tampered with likeness in power. Which means it can only be willed by myself—"

"Or Melinoë." Reimus finishes for him. The feel of his body next to mine miniscule against the calm rage brewing beneath me.

"Does anyone know that?" Dimitri asks.

"No one other than myself and Persephone."

I blink once as images resurface in my mind, words playing themselves like a record as I finally pull my gaze away from the flames. "Reimus is right."

Everyone goes silent as I turn away from the fireplace. "We need to start gathering allies. Apollo and Artemis may not be the only ones who actually stand against Zeus. And if there are more gods that aren't as loyal to him as he believes, then we can persuade them to ally with us."

"Possibly." Hades gently chides in as he takes a step forward. "There are some gods and goddesses who have strong ties with Zeus who will not be so willing to budge."

Hades pauses for a moment. "Who may see kidnapping you, and giving you over to him as a way to win more of Zeus' favor with them. Giving *them* an advantage."

I nod slowly. "That is a risk I'm willing to take."

Makaria stands up from the couch, concern flashing in her gaze. "Melinoë, using yourself as bait is not the answer."

"I'm not using myself as bait. But if it will allow us to see where the gods and goddesses in his council truly stand, and if they would stand with us when the time comes, then that's a risk I'm willing to take. Because when the time comes, we will need all the help we can get to distract those fighting by his side. Long enough to get him alone so I can move in."

"What are you saying?" My sister asks.

I look over at Hades, then my mother. A finality in my tone that won't be persuaded otherwise. "If I am Zeus' greatest threat, then I will fulfill that part of the prophecy to the fullest extent."

My mother watches me with a mixture of fear and pride in her gaze.

"That I will be the one to kill him."

My sister watches me—everyone seems to just watch me for a small moment as silence stretches between us.

"But for right now, we must go see Apollo. There's something he's been trying to tell me. I must go see what it is."

"We?" Dimitri asks.

I nod my head, looking over to my husband. "Reimus and I."

Reimus lowers his hand to mine, squeezing it gently as he nods his head. That silent exchange between us without me needing to even say it.

That this is something that cannot wait. That we must go now.

I will a portal open beside me as Dionysus steps back from it. I look at everyone. "We will return soon."

Reimus and I waste no time stepping through the portal, leaving everything else behind us back in our living room.

As we step out onto the lush, grassy terrain of Delphi.

Arriving at Apollo's Temple.

CHAPTER 82

The bright sunlight above warms my skin and the top of my head as my boots sink into the grass. I look up at the tall doric columns ahead, the evergreen vines coiling along the steps leading up into Apollo's Temple.

I look over at Reimus. "I don't know if I'm right or not on this, but whatever we find if I am…"

He cups the sides of my jaw, the soft weight of his skin calming me. "We will handle it together. No matter what."

I smile faintly against his hands as he pulls me in for a soft kiss.

I bring my hands up to his, lowering them down and leaving one clasped to his as we turn towards the Temple. Beginning our short trek to the main steps.

I watch as a woman descends the steps with an empty basket, her hair pulled up into a tight bun as curls hang against her cheeks. She looks over at me as Reimus and I descend the first step, turning her gaze away quickly after she forces a close-lipped smile.

I expect my heart to begin racing, my skin to clam up as I anxiously wonder if Zeus will be here. About what would happen if he saw us, and how Reimus would get home if Zeus were able to kidnap me again.

Except none of those thoughts and feelings come up. Instead, my mind remains clear and free of worry as a calm, quiet rage ensues instead. My back and my head straight as I climb each step, without the sharp paranoia to cause me to look over my shoulder every second to see if he's around.

Because the next time I'm in his vicinity, it will not be meekness he is greeted with. It will be as a harbinger of nightmares, of death incarnate.

We reach the top of the steps as I guide us both to the far back of the Temple, towards the familiar door that leads down to the bottom level.

I pull the door open, Reimus closing it behind us as we descend the winding steps. All the way down until we reach the bottom with nothing but a flicker of light at the end of the hallway to let us know that we're not alone.

As I had expected.

We walk down the hallway until we get to the opening, the cauldron situated before us as tiny tendrils of smoke waft out of it.

"I had wondered when I'd see you." The Pythia says from her seated position behind the cauldron.

I step around the cauldron, Reimus close to my side. "I would like to request Apollo's presence."

The Pythia lifts her head up, the hood of her robe slipping just an inch as her gaze locks onto mine.

"I would like to be told the prophecy. My prophecy."

A smirk lifts up her lips as she nods slowly. "Very well, then."

She begins softly chanting to herself, soft humming interrupting her words every now and then. After several long moments, she stops when I feel the air charge around us.

I look over to the portal willed in the room as Apollo steps through it. He looks over to me immediately. "Hello, Melinoë." He looks over beside me. "Reimus."

"Apollo." I say, nodding my head slightly.

"I imagine you went to see Elzwin yourself. After I warned you." He says as he steps closer to the Pythia.

"I did." I say calmly. Too calmly.

"I am sorry I could not have warned you earlier. It is as I said, Zeus is confiding in no one at this time what his plans are."

"How were you able to tell her?" Reimus asks from beside me.

Apollo taps the side of his forehead. "With the gift of prophecy also comes the gift to bestow such premonitions onto others. It is not a gift I bestow carelessly as it always comes with a price."

So that would explain it then.

"I'm afraid we do not have much time, as I cannot risk much time spent away from Zeus' palace. He will become curious if I'm gone for too long." Apollo's golden gaze locks onto mine. "But I will ask you once, Melinoë. Are you certain you want to hear the prophecy—*your* prophecy? As once you hear it you cannot forget it."

I exhale a steady breath as I nod. "Yes. I understand."

He nods his head. "Good." He lifts a hand and waves both me and Reimus to step closer to him.

We approach him as the Pythia turns to Apollo, lifting her hand up to his forehead and going into a trance once again.

She mumbles to herself before stepping back, opening her eyes. "She who will be his greatest downfall and restore balance and harmony to the lands both North and South. A Guardian of Souls, Goddess of Nightmares. As The King of Gods damns the girl's fate to be born to another, The Fates will damn him in return for his interference with what they conspired for her future. That she will hold not one, but two great powers wielded by two great Kings."

I blink as I watch the Pythia step closer to me. Her gaze alighted on mine.

"The King, in an effort to prevent his same father's fate, will take the desperate measures to conspire the children as his own. With the misguided judgment that all three children will wield his, and only his powers. Only to be damned by the second born who will wield powers both his, and who her father was meant to be. The King of The Underworld, and The King of Gods, both of their essences to then flow in her veins. Making her the only goddess ever to wield not one, but *two* great divinities. It is with her great power that she will bring dissolution to the structure that once was, and rebuild it into what will be. A new world, a new order."

My eyes widen as my hand falls from Reimus', blinking back the words that have just come out of her mouth. Knowledge that I had already heard and knew, that I have now seen with my own hands. That I can wield both shadows and lightning, something that Zeus didn't think were possible. Or just was too arrogant to think could happen.

The Pythia tilts her head at me as she asks, "You still don't get it, do you?"

I knit my brows together as I shake my head. "I do. I have Hades' shadows, and Zeus' lightning. I know that—"

The Pythia laughs, stifling my words. "You silly girl, you do not just wield those powers, you *are* those powers. You are Zeus' daughter biologically, but The Fates still gave you Hades' essence not just to spite Zeus but because it was always meant to belong to you." She pauses for a moment. "Zeus had no idea his actions would've created not only the greatest threat to himself, but to every god and goddess around. Because you sharing his divinity not only makes you powerful, but makes you an heir to Olympia."

I stand there still and silent.

"But you also share Hades' same powers, his essence. Because The Fates orchestrated yours and your siblings' paths to be shared with him. As you three were meant to be *his* children, not Zeus'. But you are the only one who shares both of their powers, making you different from your siblings entirely."

I get that, I share both Hades' and Zeus' powers. But why does she keep repeating that? Why does that matter—

I feel everything freeze over inside of me as understanding overwhelms me. My skin chills at what I had not ever expected, what I never put together until now.

Apollo steps forward as he proves what I'm thinking is in fact true. "It means that you are an heir to not one, but *two* realms, Melinoë. You are the first goddess in history to have that kind of power, that kind of title. Making you the most powerful goddess in all of the realms."

I feel Reimus look over at me, but I can do nothing but stare at Apollo.

Apollo narrows his chin as he says, "That if Zeus can only be successfully overthrown by who shares his same blood and gifts, then you—by the laws of The Fates, would take his place as the rightful heir to Olympia."

AUTHOR'S NOTE

This book was by far the best, and most challenging to finish. I mean, never in my whole life did I think I would write a SEVEN HUNDRED page book. Fuck, that's a shit ton. But I think aside from that, I found this book hard to finish because during the end of editing this book, I was finding myself pretty burnt out and exhausted. This is the fourth book I've written in a year (technically 13 months but, whatever) and my mind was beggggggging for a break. And though I am eternally grateful for writing this series, and proud of myself for building this incredible world and story through my characters, I was exhausted to say the least. But man, the end result of this book? It was infinitely worth it. As is every work of literature I write because nothing compares to the process of a book from start to finish.

I think I am sharing this to also shed light on the bittersweet feeling that lingers because as some of you may have wondered—or suspected, this series is coming close to its end, and I find myself wanting to cry even just typing that right now but—with everything in life, all good things must come to an end, right?

It feels like just yesterday I was brainstorming everything that would occur in this series. And as I wrote this book, there was no way I could condense it because it would've left out SO many important goodies that y'all need to have in order to see everything come full circle.

So with all of that being said, thank you. If you've stuck with the series this long then I send you my utmost gratitude. I am grateful to be here and be doing what I love each and every day. Xoxo

ABOUT THE AUTHOR

Michelle Rossa is the author of the Shadows and Fire series, and her work centers around Adult Romance and Fantasy. From writing poetry, to daydreaming fantasy worlds inside her head, Michelle has had a vast imagination since she was a child.

When she's not writing, she's most likely spending her time out in nature, snuggling with her cat Diva, or re-watching The Vampire Diaries for the millionth time. Outside of her passion for writing, she practices as a psychic medium and tarot reader. She is greatly passionate about all things astrology, the left hand path, occult studies, Greek mythology, non-conformity to societal/gender standards, and advocating for women.